PENGUIN

# The Truth About Her

# The Truth About Her

ANNIE TAYLOR

PENGUIN BOOKS

PENGUIN BOOKS

UK | USA | Canada | Ireland | Australia
India | New Zealand | South Africa

Penguin Books is part of the Penguin Random House group of companies
whose addresses can be found at global.penguinrandomhouse.com.

First published 2023

001

Copyright © Annie Taylor, 2023

The moral right of the author has been asserted

Set in 12.5/14.75pt Garamond MT Std
Typeset by Jouve (UK), Milton Keynes
Printed and bound in Great Britain by Clays Ltd, Elcograf S.p.A.

The authorized representative in the EEA is Penguin Random House Ireland,
Morrison Chambers, 32 Nassau Street, Dublin D02 YH68

A CIP catalogue record for this book is available from the British Library

ISBN: 978-1-405-95458-7

www.greenpenguin.co.uk

*For Ruthie*

# Prologue

It's such a horrible shock. A gut-wrenching surprise.

And yet it's not.

That family.

That mother.

Those good looks, that house, three beautiful children. All that money.

If it was going to happen to anyone, it was going to happen to the Lowes, wasn't it? You can't be that golden for that long without a little of the shine starting to come off.

Poor Matthew, though, they all say. Poor little Matthew. Such a bright, beautiful boy. Even those who never met him have seen the photos – whether in the papers, on the TV, or on his mother's very popular Instagram page it doesn't matter – they all know who he is now.

Who he was.

A boy of three, kidnapped from his home, spirited away in the night to God knows where.

The back door was open, they whisper. In December. Left unlocked. The house sits directly on the beach – beautiful views, of course, but it means it's easily accessible.

Who would forget to lock their back door in the middle of winter?

No sign of forced entry, no footsteps in the sand to follow.

Disappeared, taken, who knows? He's gone.

Matthew Lowe is missing.

# I

I pull the car to a stop and stare out at the view in front of me. All the way from Gatwick the sky has been grey and low, a compressing monolithic sheath that has put the world on mute. But as I look out at the cabin in front of me, and the view beyond, I see the sea. It smashes and grabs at the shoreline, all that movement and unbridled freedom, showing off under the heavy, leaden sky.

The cabin is small, but boxy and contemporary, a kind of modern-day beach hut. I can see straight through its huge windows, hiding nothing. On Airbnb the owners had called it *Whitstable's Best Kept Secret: The Getaway From It All Cabin*, and that's exactly what I want.

To get away from it all.

The photos on Airbnb had looked professionally done. They had been taken on a light-filled summer's day, the sky through the window a burning blue, everything perfect and just so, from the small but glossy kitchen to the black pot-belly of the wood-burning stove in the living room, and the queen-sized bed in the sleeping mezzanine.

A cabin built just for one.

Online, it had looked perfect, idyllic. Now, though, it looks almost austere in its modernity. It's all angles and edges, and too-big windows that are too easy to peer through. It sits at the end of a long line of much older tumbledown huts. In summer I imagine the beach busy, swarming with visitors, but now all is silent, empty. The particular loneliness of the seaside in winter. With the engine of my rented car turned off, all I can hear is the far-off roar of the implacable sea. I think back to the din of the city, the sounds and memories – the reality – I was trying to escape and it barely seems real.

Getting out of the car, I grab my bags and pull out my phone for the lockbox code the owner sent me late last night. 'Four five four three,' I say to myself. It can't be more than a couple of hours since I left the airport, brief words exchanged at the car-rental kiosk, but it honestly feels like for ever since I said anything out loud. The flight from LA is weighing on me, and I try to work out how long I've been awake, what time my body thinks it is, before wearying of even that minor thought process.

The lockbox opens instantly and easily, as does the heavy door once I've slid the key into the lock and turned it. As if someone else were with me, I pick up my bags from the small porch, and say, 'Here we are,' as the door swings wide, ushering me inside.

The silence continues as I walk in. I drop my bags to the floor and hurry to shut the door. It's not the cold so much as the emptiness, the space, the shadows in the corner that have me shivering. With the door now closed I stand in the middle of the room. It's just like the photos, only colder, lonelier and less well-lit. Turning towards the kitchen, I spot a welcome basket and a postcard on the kitchen island:

*Welcome, Callie!*

*We're so glad you've chosen to spend your time here, at the Getaway From It All Cabin. Help yourself to cookies from the tin, wine from the fridge, and all the goodies we've left for you in your welcome basket. If you need anything at all, please don't hesitate to get in touch with either one of us.*

*And don't forget to come visit me, Vanessa, at my store in town!*

*All best,*
*Vanessa, Justin, JJ, Emma, and Matthew Lowe*
*X*

I turn the card over and, yes, it's a beautifully shot, carefully branded marketing postcard for Vanessa's shop, The Lowe Down.

The name snags at me, rings a bell, but my brain is fuzzy and my body is heavy, ready for bed.

Putting the card back on the island, I inspect the contents of the welcome basket – there's a tin of what look like homemade cookies (chocolate and hazelnut, according to the perfectly scripted, handwritten label), a large bag of sea salt and cider-vinegar crisps, a bottle of red wine, a smaller one of local cider, a loaf of sourdough bread, tea bags from a bespoke tea company in Margate, and some jars of jam. In the fridge I find more of the promised wine, this one a New Zealand Sauvignon, the green glass frosted with cold, as well as butter, eggs and a few other groceries.

I ease the Sauvignon from the fridge, spend a few minutes crashing through drawers locating the corkscrew, and pour myself a glass.

3

Probably I should make myself a cup of tea instead, but as soon as the wine hits the back of my throat, I stare out through the panoramic windows at the thrashing sea and make peace with my decision.

My phone begins to vibrate in the back pocket of my jeans, and I know who it will be even before I pull it out. *Mum*, the screen glimmers.

'Hi, Mum,' I say, having let the phone ring for a little too long.

'Did you arrive okay?' she asks, without even a 'hello'.

'Yes, I'm here. I was about to WhatsApp you.'

'Was the journey all right? Is the place nice?' she asks breathlessly.

'Are you walking somewhere?' I ask.

'Just got out of the tube. I'm late, actually. Meeting your aunt and uncle at the RA.'

'That's nice,' I say, hearing how dull the words sound.

'Yes, I'll be sure to send them your love. Now, tell me. Is it as gorgeous as the photos?'

'It's lovely.' Too lovely, I think. So lonely.

'Okay,' she says, still breathless, still running late as always. 'Well, send me pictures, okay? Maybe wait till morning, though. I want to see it in all its glory. And call whenever you want. Text, email, Zoom, WhatsApp, carrier pigeon. We're all here at the other end of a phone call.'

'I know,' I say, and there's the unmistakable crack in my voice, the wrench that makes my mother suck in her breath and stop walking.

'Callie. You're going to be okay. You'll get through this. And if you don't, well, that's okay too. You just drive home the moment you want to, or send me a text and I'll be there as soon as humanly possible.'

'I know,' I say again. 'I know.'

'I don't quite understand why you want to do this, why you feel you need to, but you're there now.'

'Yes,' I say.

'Just as long as you're home for Christmas,' she says, and I roll my shoulders at the familiar demand.

'I know, Mum. We've discussed it. I'm checking out of here on the twenty-third.'

'Good. That's good.' There's a pause in which neither of us says anything, and I can hear the familiar sounds of London all around her. I close my eyes and picture it: the blue-white angels flying over Piccadilly, the golden-lit windows glowing in the winter dark, pavements packed with shoppers and tourists, commuters and loiterers, all sweating beneath their layers of winter clothing.

And then Mum cuts in, 'I just –'

'I know, Mum. I know you don't understand. I just . . . I can't deal with all that right now. I can't deal with anything right now. I just want to be surrounded by – by nothing.'

'Oh, Callie,' Mum breathes. I can picture her face as well as I can picture the scene surrounding her. Broken and collapsed, a moment of searing pain and grief before she takes a deep breath, straightens and is back to herself again: a planner and a perfectionist, an unruffled doer, who even in a time of crisis will have a bullet-point checklist to tick off. 'Would it be too much to ask you to text every hour, on the hour, just to let me know you're okay?'

This brings a tiny smile to my face. 'Maybe,' I say. 'I'm almost thirty-four after all.'

There's another pause and I hear Mum sigh before she says, 'Okay, darling. Well, I've reached my destination. Call if you need anything, okay?'

'I will,' I say.

'Love you,' she says, and there's yet another little pause before I repeat the words back to her and we say goodbye.

I find myself in a pool of otherworldly silence. Outside, what little light there was is now draining from the sky and I realize I haven't turned on any lights yet. The windows are floor-to-ceiling. On any other day, they would flood the cabin's lower level with light, but now they serve only to make the open-plan living room and kitchen feel colder. Shivering again, I take the sturdy but nevertheless non-child-friendly floating staircase up to the mezzanine.

Up here, there are more windows, the low bed framed by a triangular window that looks out onto nothing but the shingle-studded beach and the far-off sea. On the other side of the bed there is the free-standing bathtub. Trying not to think, I turn on the hot-water tap, pouring in the complimentary bath salts and oils that sit to the side. Then, exhausted, I sink to the floor, back resting against the side of the tub as it fills, wishing I'd remembered to bring the bottle of wine with me, instead of just my glass.

## 2

Morning. The low, flat light of a winter's day fills the room. I roll over onto my stomach and stare through the window. The view is a sight to behold: the tide is out and the beach goes on for ever, the sea lining the edge of the horizon.

But it's months since I've been awed by anything, and even this view, which once would have filled me with intense sea-salt-encrusted joy does nothing. I want to want to jump out of bed, to walk along the beach, chase the horizon, maybe even run into the freezing waves of the North Sea. But instead all I want is nothing.

I roll back onto my side, into a foetal position, wincing at the word 'foetal' even as it echoes in my brain. The empty wine bottle judges me from the bedside table. I squint at it, daring it to make me feel any worse, but then I can't stand it any longer. Throwing off the bedclothes, I grab the bottle and the glass sitting next to it. As I walk towards the staircase I pass the bath – there's still water in it. I forgot to drain it last night. The water is cold now, of course, and preternaturally still. It makes me shiver, the sight of it, the knowledge that even this simple task is beyond me. Or it was last night. How did I ever make it up here in one piece? I plunge my hand into the cold water and pull out the plug. It makes a deep *thwup*, reverberating around the cabin.

Downstairs I throw the wine bottle into the recycling bin and put the glass into the sink. I open the fridge and stand there in its light, reminding myself of what people do in the mornings.

Coffee.

Eggs.

Toast.

## 3

Evening.

I pour myself my first glass of wine the moment the light starts to leave the sky, and not a second sooner. The sky is so big here, and the sunsets last for ever. Even on a dull grey day like today, I'm still treated to a streaky mackerel sky.

I have managed to build and keep a fire going in the wood-burning stove. I have spoken to my mother again, fielded WhatsApp messages from my sister, Thea, and told them to send my love to my father.

I haven't opened my laptop yet. I haven't even taken it out of its bag. I have put away the food I brought with me, even though the sight of it sends exhaustion rocking through my bones. I haven't eaten anything since my scrambled eggs on toast this morning; the dirty dishes and pans are still with my wine glass from last night, soaking in the sink.

I don't want to cook anything. When I try to imagine what I might make for myself tonight from the ingredients sitting in the fridge my mind falls into the black hole where my imagination used to live. I should have piled my trolley high with microwave meals, three-minute tortellini, baked beans, Heinz tomato soup, anything that provides my body with enough nutrition to keep going for an afternoon, an evening, a night longer.

I open the freezer, praying that my hosts, Vanessa and Justin, might have left something edible in it, although I doubt it. They don't seem the type to shop in the freezer aisle. But – hallelujah – there's frozen pizza, pepperoni, sitting among the ice trays and a bottle of vodka rolling around in the bottom drawer. I squeeze my eyes shut in relief, then free the pizza from its icy coffin, eyeing the vodka for later.

I eat the pizza on the sofa, where I have been all day, watching whatever my Netflix algorithm sees fit to put in front of me. The bottle is open, my glass now full of red wine. Orange flames lick at the door of the stove. Outside I hear the crash and moan of the waves: the tide has come in. The flames of the fire flicker in unison with the swell of the sea, and if I hold myself still enough, I feel as though I am borne upon it. I let myself feel I could be sucked down into it, just for a second, and then I press play on the remote and the TV drowns it all out.

# 4

Afternoon.

I sleep until past noon, make eggs again, coffee.

I'll have to leave the cabin. There's enough eggs and bread to last me until the next morning, but nothing else in the freezer now except ice and vodka. More importantly, I'm out of wine.

I shower in the little downstairs bathroom, spending too long standing in the steam of the powerful rain shower. I like how it clouds and crowds me, surrounds me, until suddenly it's claustrophobic. I flick it off and force myself to get dressed.

I have brought with me a strange assortment of clothing, but fashion something suitable for the weather and public consumption. It'll mostly be hidden by the comforting shield of my winter coat. I sit on the sofa in my coat and stare outside for what feels like the thousandth time. I can do this. I made it all the way here. I got to an airport, and on a plane, and arrived in another country all on my own. I can cope with a small town, and a supermarket, and wordlessly passing my credit card to a stranger. I think about making a list: it'll make the shop easier to bear, but even writing feels too much.

As I'm leaving, I spot the postcard for the cabin owner's boutique on the kitchen island and snatch it up. The Lowe Down. It appears to sell homewares, expensive candles and bath products, as well as takeaway coffee. I stuff it into my pocket, thinking I should probably stop by to say hi.

I get through my shopping as quickly as possible, although when I check the time on my phone, I've been gone from the cabin longer than I'd thought. Time is sticky now. Slow. Hours and days appear never to end. Then I blink and a whole week's gone by. It's been six months of this. Ever since June. The summer went by in a black hole of a flash, days lost to bed, tears and depression, but now I'm aware of every minute, every second ticking by, until, bam, it's almost Christmas. In the shop, I use one of the checkout machines, but as I pass the only cashier on duty I can feel her eyes on me. It's as if she's been watching me the whole time, wondering at my sightless stare as I wandered the aisles of this seaside Sainsbury's Local.

After throwing everything into the car, I wonder if I can stand to swing by The Lowe Down. I'll have to talk to someone, hear my voice. Hear someone else's voice. But it's been days since I saw anyone, so I stamp my feet to get some warmth back into them and walk down the high street.

It doesn't take long to find. The Lowe Down has a prime position, just a short walk from the famous pink façade of Wheelers Oyster Bar.

Walking into the store, I'm rocked by recognition. The walls are painted the kind of pink that looks like fresh plaster, and there's a large concrete block in the middle of the shop: a kind of plinth, upon which candles, mugs, plant pots and artisan-crafted wooden spoons jostle for position. Is it just everyday *déjà vu*, or have I been here before?

Just then a door opens and closes at the back, and the woman walking through it calls a friendly 'Hi! Welcome!'

Her waterfall of auburn hair tips me off almost immediately. As soon as she turns, I remember where I know her and her store from. The name should have been enough: this is Vanessa Lowe or @thelowedown, an Instagram influencer with close to a million followers. I watched her renovate, decorate and launch this business on Instagram Stories and in her feed.

'Vanessa?' I say.

'Hi!' she says again, just as cheerily.

'I'm Callie,' I say, walking towards her. 'I'm renting your beach cabin.'

Her face falls into a wide-open smile. 'Callie! I'm so glad you stopped by to say hello. How are you doing? Oh, God, is everything okay for you out there?' she says, pressing her hand over her heart.

'Everything's great. I wanted to thank you for the welcome basket. It was very generous. Much more than I was expecting.'

'We like to go the extra mile, and a welcome basket is the least we can do.'

'Are you . . . Sorry, this is so weird, but I think I recognize you from Instagram,' I stutter.

Two pink spots appear high on Vanessa's prominent cheekbones. We're standing by the till now. I've followed her over, wanting a closer look, making sure it really is her.

'Yes,' she says, holding a hand up to her heart again and

widening her eyes at me, 'God, it's so weird that this happens to me now, you know?'

'I . . . Well, no, I don't,' I say, 'but I can imagine. This is the first time I've ever recognised someone from Instagram.' I take a deep breath – this is the longest I've spoken to anyone other than my mother on the phone for days, and I can feel a headache brewing by my right temple.

Vanessa is smiling still and says, as if we're both in on a secret, 'Well, don't worry. I find it strange too.' She's beaming as she says, 'How are you finding the Getaway? It's not too lonely out there for you at this time of year, is it? Or is someone staying with you?'

'No. It's just me.'

'A private retreat?' Vanessa asks, genuine interest lighting her eyes.

'Kind of. My mum booked it for me as a Christmas present before I head back to London in two weeks. Well, just under two weeks now.'

'Oh! How lovely. So, if you're Callie, the Antonia Thorne who made the booking, is that your mum?' she asks, a little hesitantly.

'Yes.'

'She's not . . . She's not the architect Antonia Thorne, is she?'

It's my turn to widen my eyes at her. 'Um, yeah. She is. You know of her?'

Vanessa nods frantically. 'Yes – oh, my God, this is amazing. My husband owes me five pounds! I just knew that was her in her Airbnb profile picture. We're huge fans of hers. Huge.'

'You're huge fans?' I ask, slow to catch on. 'Of my mother?'

'Yes! God, that sounds ridiculous. I should explain. Justin, my husband, is an architect, and Antonia's work has been a massive inspiration to him. Her 'A Mirror on the World' house is just our ultimate building, like, our absolute favourite. We would *die* to stay there one day.' Her eyes are glistening now, and the sweet red spots that appeared when I admitted to recognizing her have spread across her face.

I smile at her. I feel the strain of it and hope she doesn't notice. In her excitement, I imagine she won't. I know that my mother's work produces this kind of fervour among design fanatics, but I've never experienced it first-hand without her there to mitigate. So, I say what I know Vanessa wants to hear.

'It was the design of your cabin that made her book it for me, actually. She said all those windows made it a kind of mini Mirror House.'

'Oh, my God. Justin is going to die when he hears that! It's his design. His baby . . . Well, our three children are his actual babies, but you know what architects are like,' she says.

'I do,' I say.

'Oh, wow. Okay. We're going to have to have you round for dinner. I'm sorry, but it's non-negotiable. Justin would kill me if he knew you were staying in the Getaway and I didn't invite you over. How would tomorrow night be?'

I think of the empty relief of the cabin, the nothingness of the sea that edges it. The reason I'm here. Then

I think of the energy and life, the verve and love inside Vanessa's home: I've seen snippets of it in her Stories and all over her grid. I don't know which I'm more afraid of: the isolation or the company.

But Vanessa is staring at me, eyes wide and hopeful, those red splotches of excitement still decorating her face, and I realize I don't want to disappoint her. I met her only a minute ago, but I feel I've known her much longer: the power of the Instagram feed. Or maybe I just don't want her to know why I'm here. Why I'm so determined to be alone right now.

I came to be wiped clean, and maybe tomorrow night I can spend the evening with people who don't know me, who don't pity or want to fix me. With whom I can be someone new.

I smile, and hear myself say, 'Yes, that would be lovely.'

As I'm leaving the store, Vanessa calls to me: 'Hey, what's your handle?' She means my Instagram handle. 'I'll follow back.'

I turn back to face her. 'Oh, um. It's Calistagram, but there's nothing much there, really. I haven't posted anything in a while.'

But Vanessa just waves a hand at me, her eyes already on her phone, scrolling, scrolling. 'Calistagram?' she says.

'Yeah, it's a portmanteau. My full name is Calista. Although no one calls me that.'

'It's good,' she says. 'Cute. Funny.' And then, in a singsong, 'Here we go. Calistagram. Callie Thorne. Writer and . . . PhD student at UCLA. Ooh, LA. Fancy. I love LA.' She makes a face at me to let me know she's teasing. 'How long have you been out there?'

'Almost five years. I went for my Master's in cinema and media studies and stayed for the PhD.'

'Oh, wow. Well, I guess LA is the best place to be doing that, right? What do you write?'

'I haven't in a while, but mostly reviews and stuff for Maven. You know the website?'

Vanessa's face scrunches into a facsimile of thought. Then she clicks her fingers, face smooth again. 'Kind of like Jezebel, right?'

'Exactly.'

'I know it,' she says, and when she grins at me I see the stretch. Maven published an article earlier in the year – not by me – that was fairly critical of the kind of Instagram influencer Vanessa is. It was particularly venomous about the way these Instagram mothers – or momstagrammers as they phrased it – use their children to sell or further their brand. Vanessa, or @thelowedown, was cited in the article. I wonder if she's about to rescind my invitation to dinner, but she says no more so I give her my most genuine smile – the best I can muster. Instead she reiterates the request to have me over, taking one of her branded postcards and writing her home address on the back.

'Seven thirty,' she says, and even though I haven't made plans in months, I promise I'll see her then.

## Sixteen Months Ago

Vanessa Lowe has been living in Whitstable for three years and eight months and has amassed close to a quarter of a million Instagram followers, moved house once, and scrapped plans for several kitchens when she first meets Rachel Donovan.

It's the hesitancy of the tap on her shoulder that annoys her most, causing her to shrug it away, assuming it to be a fly or a wasp or some other pest. Vanessa appears absent-minded about a lot of things – she has cultivated an ease and an elegance that many would describe as effortless, but can only be achieved through great effort and force of will. But Rachel doesn't know this yet, and she doesn't know that hesitation, second-guessing, dithering are all some of Vanessa's many pet hates. The human foibles that hold back decision-making, hold up the day, suck time away from Vanessa's carefully coordinated life.

Rachel taps again, a little less hesitantly, this time with an awkward clearing of her throat, and Vanessa turns. They are standing outside Little Dolphins Montessori Nursery, both women waiting in the hot sun of an August afternoon for their children to be released from a few hours of someone else's care. Rachel can feel the insistent scratch of the sun at her bare scalp – she recently shaved

18

her head, but this heatwave has made her second-guess the decision – and thinks she can see pink forming on the shoulders of the woman whose attention she has managed to gain, a fuchsia glow joining up the amber constellations of Vanessa's freckles.

'Vanessa?' Rachel says, as much hesitation in her voice as there was in her tap-tap. 'Vanessa Lowe?'

'Yes?' Vanessa says, angling herself towards the other woman, who is shorter and smaller than her, dark brown skin glowing in the sunshine. Vanessa breathes any annoyance out of her as she speaks, making sure she sounds friendly, welcoming. That's what people expect around here. That's what people expect from her.

Rachel smiles, relieved. She's not wrong – she hasn't just mis-recognized someone, hasn't assigned a stranger a familiar face through sheer loneliness. 'I thought so,' she says, still smiling. 'I follow you on Instagram.'

'Oh,' Vanessa says, delight opening her face, eyes huge, smile wide, a tinkling laugh of self-deprecation. 'Oh, my God, that's so cool. Do you live round here too?'

'Just moved in a few days ago. This is my daughter Sadie's first day at nursery so I'm a little worried.'

'Oh, she'll love it, they all do. I have to practically drag Matthew away whenever I come to pick him up,' Vanessa says, her grin full of sharp, white teeth.

'Matthew, that's it,' Rachel says, with a click of her fingers. 'I was trying to remember the name of your youngest. Sorry, it must be a bit weird for you that I know more about you than you do about me.'

Vanessa smiles, always smiling, and shakes her impressive

auburn hair. 'Well, we'll have to rectify that. How about we start with a name?'

Rachel laughs. 'God, sorry. Such shit manners these days. Rachel Donovan,' she says, sticking out her hand for Vanessa to shake.

'Toddlers make toddlers of us all, don't worry about it,' Vanessa says, taking Rachel's hand, then turning sharply as the nursery doors open and she hears the rising chatter of tiny humans swarming the playground.

Rachel can see Sadie in the thick of it, surrounded by new friends, the sound of all their voices a loud engine of collective joy. *How has she made friends so quickly?* Rachel wonders at the rubber-ball resilience of small children. With age is meant to come wisdom, but as far as Rachel can tell, all it brings is an increased sense of fear and ever-growing anxiety, both of which are a hindrance when it comes to making friends. She is more relieved than she'd care to admit to have recognized Vanessa's face in the scrum of mums – and other carers, she reminds herself – in front of the nursery. In London she would never have introduced herself to someone she recognized from Instagram of all places, but here it felt almost rude not to.

As Rachel watches her daughter approach, Sadie doesn't make the beeline for her that she was half expecting, half craving – a clingy return to Mummy after these few hours away – but Sadie is a people person, an extrovert, a playtime hunter, a fearless pint-sized friend-making warrior. Instead, Sadie bumbles over to her mother, new friends peeling off to their own mums and minders, even the occasional father. Over the top of Sadie's head, her brown curls spreading exuberantly towards the sky, Rachel recognizes Vanessa's little boy coming out of the nursery hand-in-hand with one of the carers whose name Rachel can't remember.

Matthew is staring adoringly into the young woman's eyes, and she is looking down at him, talking quietly. She has white-blonde hair, a glittering halo in the too-hot sun. She looks up at something Matthew says, and squints across the playground towards where Rachel and Vanessa are standing. Vanessa raises her arm, and Matthew tugs at the carer's hand. Squinting, Rachel is alarmed to see that Matthew looks as though he is about to cry. But Sadie is saying something to her now, and all Rachel can do is swiftly glance in Vanessa's direction before squatting to hear about her daughter's day.

Vanessa's head is cocked, watching her son and the carer having a discussion, as serious as if they were in a business meeting. Vanessa clicks her tongue, raises her arm again, this time a little impatiently, and sighs. She is keeping a careful eye on her son and the nursery worker, as well as on Rachel and her daughter. She doesn't want to make a scene, but there's something about the people who work here that fuels her frustration. She sends Matthew here because she needs some time to herself, and because this is widely considered to be the best nursery in the area. But everyone is just so *interested*, and *nice*, and passive-aggressively chronically nosy.

And now there's this new mum to deal with. Vanessa casts a glance at her, sizing her up. Rachel is the only Black woman in the small crowd of people waiting for their children, and she is very clearly, very recently down from London. She's wearing Birkenstocks and an oversized bright yellow linen shift dress. Her bag is a canvas tote proclaiming allegiance to a south London farmer's market at which she's presumably no longer a customer.

Parents have begun to lead their children home, the little crowd dispersing into the summer afternoon, but Matthew is still hovering at the entrance with his favourite nursery worker. Vanessa can see his little lip tremble, and she pulls herself up to her full height, ready to go over. Rachel has stood up, is turning away from the nursery building with her little girl, a smile and a wave as goodbye to Vanessa. Is she wondering why Matthew doesn't want to leave nursery? Is she sizing Vanessa up, asking herself why her son doesn't want to go home with her?

Suddenly Vanessa says, 'Wait, Rachel. Do you want to get a coffee? We could treat the kids to an ice cream.' She glances down at Sadie as she says this, and the little girl almost vibrates with enthusiasm, glancing between the stranger and her mother with anticipation.

'Sure,' Rachel says. 'Why not?'

Just then, Matthew careers across the playground towards them, stumbling as he tumbles into his mother, who crouches to give him a squeeze. 'There you are,' she says. 'I've been waiting for you.'

Matthew buries his face in Vanessa's neck as Rachel and Sadie watch. Vanessa looks up at Rachel with a smile that, for a second, seems like a gloat, scheming and self-satisfied. But then Vanessa stands up, her hand resting on her son's head of auburn curls, her smile different – or did Rachel just imagine it? – and says, 'Come on, Matthew. We're going to get an ice cream with our new friends Rachel and Sadie.'

And Rachel smiles back, relieved and pleased to have someone to go somewhere with, as they steer their children out of the playground and towards the sea.

A little later they stroll along the seafront, each with an ice cream in hand – Vanessa and Rachel having decided together that they, too, deserved one on such a hot afternoon. The children have made friends quickly, and they walk slightly ahead, legs a little unsteady, cones wobbling in sticky hands.

Vanessa hates to eat ice cream from a cone – too messy – so dips elegantly at her small pot with a tiny biodegradable spoon while Rachel tries to eat hers before it completely melts in the sun, chasing ice-cream trails down her hand and arm with her tongue. Ice cream always makes her feel like a child. Not the fun of it, the treat, but the mess. The inevitable spots between her fingers where it has lodged, sticky and stuck. It is interesting to her that Vanessa clearly feels the same, but has decided the cone isn't worth the fuss, the fun. Rachel keeps glancing at her, expecting her to whip out her phone and start taking photos. She posts every day – twice a day – and is often on Stories, but Rachel hasn't seen her take a photo yet, not even of Matthew, who features prominently on his mother's page. The children are calling to one another, whoops of joy. Vanessa smiles indulgently at them and turns to Rachel, catches her watching. 'Don't they make everything look such fun?' she says. 'Toddlers.'

Rachel smiles back. 'It's hard to imagine everything being so brand new, the way it is for them.'

'Right. Sometimes I think I'm jealous of it. Of my children. Is that terrible?'

Rachel laughs. 'I don't think so. It's pretty normal.'

'Oh, phew,' Vanessa says, with a raised eyebrow and an arch in her voice. 'Is Sadie your first?'

'No, she has an older brother, Marcus. He's five.'

'Oh, that's the same as Emma, although she's almost six. Where is he today?'

'He's with my mum. She came down to help us unpack and settle in at the new house.'

Vanessa nods, and Rachel watches as her auburn hair catches the light, turning copper, burnished and bright. If it wasn't for Matthew and his matching curls Rachel would wonder if Vanessa got hers out of a box. She's not sure she's ever seen someone with that shade before – not in real life. 'And is it just the three of you?' Vanessa is asking, giving Rachel a sidelong glance. 'You and the kids?'

'What?' Rachel says. 'No, my husband's with us. He's working.'

Vanessa nods again, her eyes on the children ahead, and serenely dips her spoon into her ice cream, taking a slow, methodical lick. She went for a small salted caramel, while Rachel, who couldn't choose, did a scoop of coffee and another of Nutella.

'And do you work?' Vanessa asks, stopping suddenly and grimacing. 'Sorry. Tell me to shut up if I'm being too nosy.'

'You're not being nosy, you're making conversation. And, yes, I do work. At least, I think I do. It's complicated.'

Vanessa laughs. 'It sounds it.'

'I left my job to move down here, but I'm hoping to set myself up as a freelancer. Self-employed. For now I'm just concentrating on getting everyone settled, and moving in.'

'Oh, what do you do?'

'I was in social media and marketing for RITA. They're an ethical clothing brand.'

'Of course, I know RITA. Wow, that's cool. Are you missing it?'

'I am, actually. It's only been a week, but I took a whole year off for maternity with Sadie, so I hadn't been back long when I left. Ideally, I would've carried on working for them, but they weren't keen on having me working from home full time.' Rachel sighs and looks towards the sea. The tide is out, and the water is a long walk away from them. If it wasn't for the number of people on the beach, the shimmer and haze of the heat paired with the wide stretch of sand and shingle would look almost alien, otherworldly. But the shouts of children and the chatter of families make it familiar, known. Everything is bright, burning: the sun, the sky, the primary colours of summer clothing. This is why they moved here, Rachel thinks, for the salt of the sea, and the walk along the beach after nursery, school, work. For long summer evenings spent watching the tide inch in or away from them, winter walks on misty days. She swallows a sense of loss she hadn't expected to experience, reminds herself she wanted this as much as Tom did – it wasn't just about convenience, about the kids. This is the life she's made for herself, the path she's taken.

She turns and Vanessa is looking at her closely. The kids have stopped running on ahead, and have settled on the seawall, legs swinging. Vanessa smiles at her, a small, knowing smile, and reaches out to pat her shoulder. 'I felt a bit lost when we first moved here too, don't worry,' she says quietly, like she's letting Rachel in on a secret. 'I know it feels like you should just be grateful and excited to be living somewhere so bloody picturesque, but it doesn't mean it's home yet.'

Rachel blinks away tears. 'Yeah, it's not home yet. That's all it is.'

'You'll get there. Where are you living?'

'Just there,' Rachel says, turning to point back the way they've come. 'It's right on the front. An old fisherman's cottage. We're renting at the moment – my husband's determined to find the perfect place to renovate and make our own – but we ended up having to move before the school year began so we could get Marcus settled, and we hadn't found anywhere.'

'It's not the best time to buy at the moment. The secret's definitely out about Whitstable – it feels like so many more people have moved here since we did. Is your husband a builder?'

'He's a lecturer at Canterbury University. An academic. Why?'

'Oh,' Vanessa says, as surprise rises across her face before she steers it away. 'Mine's an architect,' she continues quickly, as if in explanation. 'I guess I just assumed when you mentioned renovating that yours was in the business too.'

*So, why didn't you assume my husband was an architect?* Rachel thinks. She could say it out loud if she wanted, could ask – demand. She has every right to. But she doesn't. Instead she watches a white gull rise upwards, screeching loudly as it rockets into the bright blue of the sky. She could screech and rise, but she's tired. Exhausted. And she wants to make a friend, to find her own mooring in this new town, this new home. So she takes another lick from her cone and says nothing.

**thelowedown**

**2,375** posts **57K** followers **1,001** following

**Vanessa Lowe**

Wife * Mother * Lover

Liked by **theotherraydonovan** and **9,721 others**

**thelowedown** Cobbled streets, choppy seas, can't lose . . . that's the saying, right?? 😊 😜 😊 Well, as you can see . . . WE DID IT. We took the plunge, dived right in, hoisted up the mainsail, and dropped anchor in a new town (how many sea puns can I fit in a sentence???) AND I COULDN'T BE HAPPIER. I always knew it was the sea for me. I spent much of my childhood in Cornwall, and even though I loved my time in London, I am so glad to be back where the waves meet the shore. It might not be my beloved home county, but *this* home county is only an hour on the train from London, so that makes it even better, right? RIGHT? Just kidding, no competition here, just happy days from here on in. We're currently settling into our new home and, trust me, I can't wait to show it off . . . just not yet, 'cause it's an absolute state, OK? You know me – everything in its place, and a place for everything (or should that be PLAICE??). 🐟 But for now . . . fish and chips on the beach are calling 🐟 🍟

View all 127 comments

**WildWildWe** Whitstable! The bloody best. Can't believe you took the plunge, mama! Big love to the whole fam, and enjoy your new digs (bet they're gorgeous)

**Sheandtheshebang** What's your fish n chips order? You gotta go for mushy peas every time haha

**Katrinaandthebabes** Big moves, lady! So proud ⊘

3 years ago

27

# 5

It's just dinner.

It's just dinner.

It's just dinner.

It's just dinner. I say over and over and over to myself on the drive to Vanessa's.

But when I pull up in front of the Lowes' house I wonder if this is a good idea.

Like the cabin, their house is right on the water, but unlike the cabin, it's on its own private road, and where the cabin is modern and smooth, the Lowes' home is rustic and worn but in the most moneyed way possible, with exciting modern additions in all the right places.

I crunch up to the front door, but before I've got there, Vanessa has opened it and is standing in its inviting glow, with a smile, to welcome me in.

From inside I can hear the shouts of children over a stereo system that's currently spiralling out Leon Bridges.

She gives the same cheery 'Hi' as she did at the store, except this time it's matched with a hug.

She smells faintly of moss, but very expensive moss.

'Callie, come in, come in! Are you okay with no shoes? Sorry, it's a rule for the kids and we like to do a good-enough-for-the-kids-good-enough-for-adults kind of thing.'

I start taking off my coat and shoes, handing over one of the bottles of wine I picked up yesterday.

'Oh, you shouldn't have. That's so sweet.'

'I would've brought you one of the bottles you left at the cabin, if I hadn't already drunk it,' I say, with a dry chuckle.

There's a second – less than a second – when Vanessa says and does nothing. Her eyelids flutter infinitesimally, but then she laughs, following my lead. 'Well, that would've been fine. We leave those for guests because we love them too,' she says, giving me a conspiratorial nudge with her elbow.

She leads me down the hallway and then we're in an open-plan dining room and kitchen. Here I can see what is kept hidden from the driveway, which is that the entire back of the nineteenth-century building has been given over to a wall of stylish, devastatingly on-trend Crittall windows. Off to the side, through original stained-glass doors, is the living room, full of squishy sofas, low coffee tables, a huge bookcase, and a vast abstract painting that seems to suck all the oxygen from the room.

The table is already laid for dinner, and I see there are four, not three, place settings.

Oh.

I haven't planned for another guest. All I was thinking of was meeting Vanessa, her husband and possibly the kids.

'Justin's upstairs putting Matthew to bed, and making sure Emma and JJ are okay,' Vanessa says, as if reading my mind. 'He'll be down in a second. He's so excited to meet you – I pointed out that your mum won't be here, but he wasn't deterred.' She's standing in the kitchen now: marble and brass, and sleek forest-green cupboards.

'So, the question is, open the wine, or start with something a little more exciting? I'm getting really good at a French 75.'

'That sounds literally perfect,' I say.

Vanessa bats her eyelashes and does a little twirl as she opens the fridge. I spy three bottles of Veuve Clicquot, one of which she retrieves, before the door is slammed shut. 'Well, you can't exactly go wrong with champagne, can you?' she says, twisting out the cork with practised ease.

'Or gin,' I offer.

She raises the now-open bottle of champagne at me and takes a quick swig. 'Exactly.'

We're sipping our cocktails when Justin enters. 'French 75s, eh?' he says, with a raised eyebrow at his wife. 'You're going to drink us out of house and home.'

He kisses her delicately on the cheek before turning to me and proffering his hand. 'It's a pleasure to have you in our home, Callie. I'm Justin.'

'Nice to meet you,' I say, suddenly awkward, but just about managing to remember to stick out my own hand and shake his.

Justin is shorter than I imagined but, like his wife, almost supernaturally good-looking, faces that belong on billboards and movie screens, the covers of magazines. He has a shock of dark, dark hair that doesn't quite sit properly, green eyes, a very well-defined jawline and a soft burr of an accent. Scottish.

'I know this is probably the worst thing I could possibly say to you,' Justin says, gazing hard into my eyes as, next to him, Vanessa makes him a cocktail, 'but you're going to have to tell me absolutely everything about your mother.'

I laugh, and it comes out higher-pitched than I would've liked. 'There's not much to tell, really. She's a pretty normal person, just a very talented, highly successful one.'

Justin's eyes widen. 'A wonderful epitaph. I hope they write that on my tombstone one day,' he says, and I can't tell if he's joking or not. Then he winks. 'In all seriousness, though, have you been to the Mirror House?'

'I went to the opening, yeah. The whole family did.'

A Mirror on the World, or the Mirror House as it's more colloquially known, is probably my mother's most famous privately owned project. She designed it for a Scandinavian telecoms billionaire, and it sits on a private island in Norway, its mirrored sides jutting out over the craggy archipelago, reflecting the natural beauty that surrounds it. 'God, that must've been amazing,' Justin says breathlessly, and I nod.

'It was, yeah. I was thirteen, though, so couldn't really appreciate it as much as I would now.'

'You mean for its architectural achievement?' Justin asks earnestly.

'I was thinking more for the alcoholic entertainment, but yours sounds better,' I say.

Justin laughs as the doorbell rings, and Vanessa places a hand on his arm. 'Don't interrogate her too much, love. We've got a whole dinner to get through your questions,' she says, and heads off to answer the door.

Justin smiles an apology at me, and I swallow hard. The fourth guest is here, and although I'm managing to make an okay impression so far, one more person feels like one too many.

'So, do you mostly stick to residential architecture?' I ask, waving my arm to indicate the building we're standing in.

'Actually, no. I designed the Getaway mostly as a pet project, and then drew up the designs for renovating this place, but the firm I work for is largely corporate.'

'This house is stunning,' I say, meaning it, 'and the Getaway is great. Vanessa mentioned you used the Mirror House as inspiration, and you can totally tell.'

'Thank you!' Justin says, smiling as widely as his wife, and placing both his hands over his heart. Standing like that, he looks like an imitation of Vanessa in her shop yesterday, and I wonder who picked up the move from whom. 'We've had a few complaints that the Getaway goes against the historic architecture of the region, blah, blah, blah, but who really cares, eh?'

'My mum always says there's no other way but forward,' I say.

'Yes,' Justin says, eyes alight. 'I love historic buildings, don't get me wrong, but that's just what they are: history. We have to make our own present, our own future. Otherwise those who come after us won't know what our reality looked like, how we lived, what we loved, the things we paid attention to, what was important to us –'

'Oh, God,' comes a male voice from the hallway, 'are you giving your designing-the-future speech again, Justin?'

Justin gives me and the latest guest a sheepish grin, just as the stranger claps an arm around his shoulders. He's taller than Justin by quite some margin, and where Justin is dark-haired and porcelain-skinned, this man is fair-haired, with light brown, almost-blond stubble stippling his oval face.

'Callie,' Vanessa says, following the man into the kitchen, 'this is my brother Adam. Well, my ex-stepbrother Adam, but there's no need to get into that without a few more drinks in us, right?'

'Hey, Callie. Nice to meet you,' Adam says to me. His voice is low, smooth, and yet somehow hard, honey pouring over concrete in the sunshine.

'You too,' I say, jaw clenched.

I was raised going to parties and functions, opening ceremonies and award shows that I was far too young to attend. Mum liked to bring the whole family along to everything she did, a kind of passive-aggressive fuck-you to anyone who thought she couldn't have children and a notable architectural career at the same time. She had help, of course – au pairs and nannies, babysitters and willing grandparents – but she liked to show us off whenever she could. I got good at smiles and small-talk, shyly nodding along to stories about my academic achievements, taking surreptitious sips of champagne whenever I could. And all the while just waiting until we could go home.

It was all good practice, though, for moments and evenings like this, when I want to run, as fast as I can, back to safety, back to comfort, back to isolation. I can still manage to talk and smile, to laugh and joke, to drink and eat, even appearing as if I want to be there.

I remind myself that I do want to be here, that I can be whoever I want with these new people.

But then, in a pocket of quiet, when Justin and Adam

start to discuss something between themselves, Vanessa touches my arm lightly, feather-soft, and says what I was hoping beyond hope she wouldn't say. 'Callie, I saw your posts. On Instagram.' Her warm brown eyes are reaching for mine, and I force myself to meet her gaze. 'I'm so sorry for your loss.'

# 6

'Callie?' Vanessa says, leaning forward to place a hand on my knee. 'Are you okay? I'm so sorry. Maybe I shouldn't have said anything. I felt I had to after seeing your posts.'

We're in the living room, sitting on one of the linen-covered sofas. I can just about remember Vanessa ushering me in here after seeing my stricken face.

I can still barely hear her, but I nod, swallow.

Nod.

Swallow.

'I'm so sorry, you look so shocked. Here,' she says, standing up. 'I'll get you some water.'

'No,' I say, reaching up to pull her back onto the sofa. 'No, it's fine. I'm fine.'

She sits. Her eyes are peering into mine again. They're watery and red – she looks as if she's trying not to cry. 'We don't have to talk about it if you don't want to,' she says, in a hush.

'I don't want to talk about it,' I say. 'I came here specifically not to talk about it.'

Vanessa blanches. 'I'm so sorry,' she says again, on a breath that trembles with almost-tears.

'It's okay. Thank you . . . for . . . I appreciate . . . but I was actually looking forward to an evening where no one knew about it,' I say.

'But the posts . . . You gave me your handle . . .' Vanessa

says, her voice stronger and her face now confused, rather than apologetic.

'I know,' I say, on a long sigh. 'I keep meaning to delete them, but I just don't have the energy.'

'You lost your baby,' she says. 'That's completely understandable.'

I close my eyes.

'What was her name?' she asks quietly.

'Ada,' I say. Three letters gasped out into the air between us, here and then gone. I haven't spoken her name in months.

'I'm so sorry, Callie. It must be – well, I can't even imagine. And your . . . husband? Partner?'

'Boyfriend,' I say. 'Partner . . . Whatever. Russell. He's not . . . We're not . . . He couldn't . . . Well, I guess there are some people for whom a relationship is a kind of checklist. Things you sign up for and things you don't. This wasn't one of them.'

'That's awful, Callie. How callous.'

I sigh. 'I'm not doing him much justice, or being very fair. It was too much for both of us. I couldn't think of anything beyond myself, and he needed someone who could. It's better this way, I think.'

'Still. That's so hard. You've been through so much . . . I really didn't mean to make you even more upset. I just wanted to let you know how sorry I am. I can barely imagine . . . If anything happened to any of my children, I don't know what I'd do.'

I'm unable to respond. This is why I've stayed away from people: the burden of having to hear, accept and carry their sympathy is simply too much. Exhaustion pours through me like a drowning wave, its undertow strong and impossible to resist, and I wonder how I'm supposed to get through the rest of tonight. I've been holding myself rigid with anticipation and anxiety, but then Vanessa's arms are around me, her warm body pressing into mine.

Tears lodge in my throat, burn at my eyes.

Vanessa whispers into my ear, 'If you ever want to talk, you can. But when you're ready, we'll sit down for dinner and pretend this never happened. You're just having a nice evening with new friends.' Her words sound so strong, so sure. It's exactly what I want, what I need to hear.

I nod against her shoulder and, after another second or two, I pull away.

There are two circle-shaped tear stains on the shoulder of her ice-blue satin blouse, and I point at them while blowing my nose on the tissue she's passed me. 'Sorry,' I say. 'I've ruined your gorgeous shirt,'

Vanessa rolls her eyes at me, laughs. 'It's hardly ruined. I love your jumper, by the way,' she says, reaching out to finger the soft wool of my dark green sleeve, which is shot through with gold thread. 'I was just thinking how well you match my kitchen.' She gives me a wicked little grin, and I smile back.

We sit down to eat a few minutes later, Justin standing to uncork a bottle of wine while Vanessa dishes up her Asian short-rib beef stew. Adam complains about the choice of side dishes.

'Cauliflower rice, Ness?' he says, with a groan. 'Why do you hate me so much?'

Vanessa pinks a little, throws him a look, which he accepts with a grin, while she says, 'It's healthier!'

'Yeah, okay. Keep telling yourself that as you ladle out spoonfuls of red meat. Because it's white rice that's the leading cause of heart disease, after all.'

I laugh and Adam glances at me, smiling. His eyes are hazel, half green, half brown. As if Justin's green eyes, and Vanessa's brown ones have met in the middle. Except he's not related to either of them.

'So, ex-stepbrother, right? Is it time to explain that further, or do we need more wine?' I say.

Justin barks out a shot of laughter and says, 'Oh, we definitely need more wine, Callie. Always.'

Adam rolls his eyes at Justin as he takes his bowl from Vanessa. 'It's really not that crazy a story. Our parents were married for – what? Almost ten years, Ness?'

'A little over,' she says.

'Right. From when I was about eleven, and Ness was ten. So, we were step-siblings for pretty formative years. And we're still close.'

'Do you have any other siblings?' I ask. 'Either of you?'

'I have a brother – well, we both have a brother – who's four years older than me. But Joe and Ness have never been as close.'

'We weren't at school together, and he went off to uni when I was only thirteen, so we never really lived together. We don't know each other as well. Anyway, he lives in Australia now,' Vanessa says, by way of explanation. Then, throwing a frown at Adam, 'I love Joe, though, you know that.'

'Yeah, but not as much as you love me,' Adam says, with a flashing grin.

Across the table Justin smiles at me and says, 'If you

thought families were complicated, wait till you meet the Lowe-Fuller-Talbot-Novaks.'

'That's a lot of surnames,' I say.

Adam laughs and holds up his hand, pushing down a finger at a time as he says, 'Ness's married name, my surname, Ness's maiden name, Ness's mum's new name.'

'So, your mum remarried?' I ask Vanessa.

'Yeah, years ago. She's back in London now.'

'What about your dad?' I ask Adam.

'Well, he never remarried,' he says, taking a swig of red wine before placing the glass back on the table a little too firmly, 'and he passed away a few years ago.'

'Oh,' I say. 'I'm so sorry.'

Adam takes a deep breath and says, 'It's okay. It was a long time ago.' It's Vanessa he's looking at while he speaks. Vanessa's gaze glides to mine, and I wonder what she's thinking.

Lines of worry crease her face and she bites her bottom lip, but then she says, 'Harry was a wonderful, complex man. We all miss him every day.'

'Wonderful, Ness, really?' Adam says, on a splutter of disbelieving laughter. 'He was an impossible, difficult dick who ended up dead because he was too fucking proud to admit he needed help.'

'Wow,' I say, staring at Adam.

'What?' he says, turning to me.

'Okay. Adam, d'you want a breather? The heaters are on outside if you need a smoke,' Justin says.

Adam stands, walks through the kitchen and opens one of the glass doors, letting in a blast of cold air that I can feel even from across the room. I watch as he lights a cigarette and proceeds to hug himself, staring out at the never-ending darkness of the sea that lies just beyond Vanessa and Justin's garden wall.

'Sorry about that, Callie,' Justin says. 'We probably should've steered clear of family talk, after all.'

Vanessa stretches a hand across the table to me, not quite reaching my arm, but trying nevertheless. 'He's not always this bad when his dad comes up. Harry's a bit of a minefield. I probably should've warned you, sorry.'

'It's fine, Vanessa, really. Look how I reacted when – Well, never mind. How long since he died?'

Vanessa turns to Justin, a question mark in her eyes. 'Five years in February, I think?' Justin nods, and Vanessa nods back. A team.

'Harry was an artist,' Justin explains, resting his elbows on the table and leaning forwards. 'Pretty successful for a while, but he was also . . . Well, he was volatile. Adam and Ness didn't have the easiest time of it growing up. Harry and Ness's mum, it was like a ticking time bomb.'

'I don't know about that,' Vanessa says, and swallows some wine. She's looking at her husband and there is a single clear line between her eyebrows. It's the first time I've seen them disagree on something. '"Ticking time bomb" is probably a bit much.'

'Well, you'd know better than me, obviously, but your childhood memories aren't exactly good, Ness.'

Vanessa blinks at her husband, takes another sip of wine. It's quite clear to me that she's trying to communicate something to Justin. That this isn't the time or the place.

I clear my throat, help her out. 'You said Adam's dad was an artist. Is that . . .' I turn to take in the abstract painting hanging over the fireplace in their living room '. . . is that by him?'

The painting is hundreds of different blues, greens, greys and black. When I walked into the living room earlier and first saw it, my immediate thought was of the Cornish coast in winter. An angry tyrant of a sea thrashing incessantly against indifferent rocks.

'Dad left it to me in his will, but there's nowhere suitable for it where I live, so I gave it to Ness and Justin to look after,' Adam says, from nowhere. I didn't hear the door open or close behind him, or feel the blast of frozen air, while I was staring at the painting.

He appears calmer now, joins us again at the table, smiling bashfully at Vanessa, just the merest whiff of tobacco smoke encircling him.

'Well,' I say, dragging my eyes from the painting, 'he may have been a dick but at least he was a talented one.'

## Fifteen Months Ago

Vanessa and Matthew are sitting on the sea wall just in front of Rachel's house, waiting for her and Sadie to emerge so they can all walk to nursery together. Rachel hasn't been to Vanessa's house, so she doesn't yet know how far out of her way the other woman has to come to pick her and Sadie up, but Rachel is grateful. Knowing Vanessa, making friends with her over the past few weeks, has eased the transition to life in this seaside town by a huge amount. She has been introduced to other parents, she has been assured that Marcus's new school is a good one, she has been led around the various shops, cafés and restaurants that Vanessa deems worthy of her patronage.

Rachel waves as she and Sadie leave the house, closing the door to lock it and shouting at Sadie to wait for her before crossing the road to their new friends. Vanessa and Matthew are sitting with their backs to the sea, watching as the world trundles by, and Rachel wonders at this. She can barely take her eyes away from the sea, these days. She has finally begun to stop missing Crystal Palace, and to let the magic of her new home sink into her bones. She cannot believe she wakes up to this every day. She is astounded every time she leaves the house, early, before the kids have woken and, with a towel wrapped around her, walks down to the sea and goes for a swim. She can't believe this is now her life, not a holiday, a break from reality.

But Vanessa has lived here longer. Maybe the everyday magic of the sea and their surroundings has worn off. She doesn't need to stare into the distance at the sea to remind herself it's there. Vanessa grins at her, shouts a cheery 'Good morning' that, beside her, Matthew mimics. Rachel laughs and greets them, watching as Matthew slips from the sea wall with his mother's help, and Sadie bowls into him for a hug. They are firm friends now – best friends, as they proclaim to their mothers, loudly and often. They are similar in some ways, both precocious and winning, albeit in different ways. Matthew is soft and cuddly, goes in for a hug immediately, charms strangers' socks off with his wide eyes and that bouncing halo of curls. Sadie is louder, smarter. She is just as charming but in a different way, Rachel thinks, although she is sure she has seen Vanessa flinch or wince when Sadie has raised her voice or let out a particularly piercing screech of joy. Rachel has been known to wince too, but it feels rude coming from another mother.

She shrugs away the thought, as Vanessa reaches behind her and pulls out an iced coffee for each of them.

'Are you a mind-reader?' Rachel gasps.

Vanessa laughs. 'Wouldn't that be something?'

They're walking along the front now, the children pushing themselves on tiny matching scooters. Sadie's was a gift from Vanessa and family – a hand-me-down from her eldest son, JJ, but it looks so new and shiny that Rachel has to wonder.

'I have a question for you,' Vanessa says, ducking her

head over the straw of her iced coffee. She drinks some, then proceeds. 'How do you and your lot feel about barbecues?'

'I don't know how we *feel* about them, but we *think* they have the potential to be fantastic,' Rachel answers, smiling at her friend.

Vanessa smiles back. 'Well, I think it's high time we brought our families together, so I'm proposing a barbecue at mine. Sunday okay?'

Rachel is gazing at Sadie as Vanessa says this, and suddenly – looking at her tiny daughter, hearing her new friend's offer – she feels a lightness in her chest, a ballooning of feeling that could lift her feet off the floor and send her floating into the sky. Tears prick at her eyes, but she blinks them away.

And then she turns to Vanessa. 'Yes! Sunday's perfect. That sounds brilliant.'

# 7

Adam drives me home. I've had too much to drink while he's had just one glass of wine.

'I don't drink much,' he says simply, answering a question I didn't ask while turning on the engine of his van. 'Something about having an addict for a father put me off.'

'I'm sorry about earlier,' I say. 'I didn't mean for the conversation to get so personal. I was actually trying to avoid it, to be honest.'

We're crawling through the quiet cobbled streets of Whitstable. My cabin is at the other end of town from Vanessa and Justin's home, out along the main road, by the famous pub with the Michelin star.

Adam nods once, a shadow of a movement in the light of the dashboard, and I wonder how much he knows. What Vanessa has told him from scrolling through my Instagram feed. I haven't updated it in months, but the last few posts are from the worst days, weeks, moments of my life and I can hardly bear to look at them, let alone think about somebody else doing so. I should delete them ... I *could* delete them, but they're also a kind of memorial. A digital memorial. To the pain and the loss, yes, but also to the fact that for a week, for five days, I was a mother: I had a daughter, she was here, existed.

'Are you an artist too?' I ask, my voice scratchy with

45

feeling, my mind desperate for distraction. 'Like your dad?'

Adam seems to scowl a bit. 'What makes you say that?'

Although not immediately obvious, his jeans have a few paint splatters on them, and there's paint hiding along his cuticles. I gesture towards them, and his scowl deepens. 'Those are from house painting.'

'Oh.'

There's a beat of silence, as the headlights of the van sweep over the cute cottages and quaint shop fronts of the town, and I wonder if Adam is ever going to talk again. 'I am an artist, though,' he concedes. 'I think. I don't know. Haven't painted anything in a while. I've been helping Ness out for the past few months, renovating one of their properties.'

'One of them?' I ask, and Adam nods. 'How many others do they own?'

'Oh, a few. They're all beach houses, converted cottages, holiday homes, that kind of thing. They're mostly empty at this time of year, but they'll fill up over the next couple of weeks as we get closer to Christmas and New Year,' he says.

'A property empire,' I say.

'Oh, yeah,' Adam says. 'It's getting pretty feudal out here.' He laughs, but I'm not sure how sincere it sounds.

A few more minutes tick by in silence, and then we're stopping in the car park by the Michelin-starred pub. We get out of the van. Then Adam coughs, clears his throat and points. 'That's me. If you ever need anything.'

He's indicating one of the more run-down beach houses that share the same spit of land as the Getaway.

'You're my neighbour,' I say.

'Yeah, it's another of Ness and Justin's places. It's not as nice as the Getaway but it does me fine.'

The Getaway is at the other end of the row, the last before what feels like the end of the world, but he's still mere minutes from my front door. I thought I was on my own out here, but it turns out he's been here all along.

# 8

I wake to a loud bang. The sound, reverberating around the cubic cabin, rushing through my consciousness, pierces me awake.

My body stiffens, readying itself for the worst.

But then a now-familiar voice calls my name in what sounds like alarm, and I shoot out of bed. 'Vanessa?' I say, walking down the staircase.

Vanessa has let herself into the cabin. A small boy is standing a little away from her, auburn curls, green eyes, happy smile as he stares up at me, and I self-consciously tie the cord of my dressing gown a little tighter.

'Callie? Thank God, I thought something terrible had happened,' she says, looking from my face to the rest of the cabin.

I haven't tidied or put anything away since I got here. The sink overflows with dishes I have yet to wash up. Balancing next to it is the baking tray I found to cook the pizza on the first night, traces of tomato sauce and days-old cheese stuck to it. Cushions that were once carefully scattered over the vintage leather sofa lie on the floor, and blankets abandoned where I've left them.

'Sorry,' I say, following her gaze. 'I wasn't expecting company. Is everything okay?'

Vanessa takes a deep breath, reaches out a hand, and finds the comforting curls of her younger son's head.

'Everything's fine. I should be the one saying sorry. I don't want you thinking we make random spot checks on our paying guests,'

'It's your cabin,' I point out. Then I gesture towards the kitchen. 'I need coffee. Would you like one?'

'Sure. Thank you. I was . . . I was just at Adam's and thought I'd drop by and see if you wanted a lift back to your car.'

'Oh, thanks. I was planning on walking back to it later, but it's probably not the best weather for it,' I say, putting the kettle on.

'Definitely not,' Vanessa says, turning to the window. Beyond it is a wall of impenetrable white, the sea obscured by a thick fog. 'Matthew, come and meet my new friend, Callie,' she calls to her son, who's still in the entryway between the living room and the kitchen.

'Hi, Matthew,' I say, turning back from preparing the coffee, and trying to mimic Vanessa's bright tone. 'It's lovely to meet you.'

He holds out his hand to me, reminding me forcefully of his father the night before. I glance at Vanessa, who's laughing a little, as I take Matthew's hand and shake.

'Nice to meet you too,' he says, slurring 'nice' so that it comes out as 'nyshe'.

My chest constricts, squeezing like an accordion, as I stare down into his clear green eyes. He tugs away his hand, reminding me I'm still holding it, just as the kettle whistles.

I catch Vanessa giving me a strange look as I turn away from the child and fill the cafetière with hot water.

'Honey,' Vanessa says, talking to her son, 'why don't

you have Mummy's iPad and get comfy on the sofa? I'll be with you in a minute.'

I take a few minutes, collecting myself, as I rustle around the kitchen, finding clean mugs and pouring the coffee. When I pass Vanessa hers, she places one of her hands on mine, and says, 'Sorry, he only goes to nursery three days a week, and he's with me the rest of the time.'

'Why are you apologizing?' I say, but it comes out thick, heavy, so I take a deep breath and try again. 'It's fine, Vanessa. I'm fine.'

'Really?' Vanessa asks, peering into my face. 'Because I wouldn't be. Not after what you've been through. If I'm honest, Callie, I came to check up on you as much as anything else. I had a lovely time with you last night, but I meant what I said. You can talk to me anytime.' She peers at me, taking in my pale face, my dense morning breath, my unbrushed hair, and I can see her mentally adding up the amount I had to drink last night, the fact I had to be driven home. 'Seriously,' she says, leaning towards me, taking my hands in hers. 'I know we just met, but you can talk to me.'

'I already have a therapist,' I say, the words as brittle, broken as I feel.

Vanessa jerks back, as if frightened. But that's wiped away as she smiles grimly. 'You're right. Of course you are. It's not my place. None of my business. I'm sorry.'

'No. I'm sorry. Thanks for . . . Thanks for coming over. He's gorgeous,' I add, tilting my head towards Matthew in the living room. 'He looks exactly like you and Justin.'

'He does, doesn't he? It's almost freaky. You haven't met them yet, but Emma is much more like me, and JJ . . .

Well, JJ's at that awkward stage where he's turning from this cute little kid into an actual person. No one warned me how weird that would be.'

'How old is he?' I ask.

'JJ? He turned thirteen last month. Matthew's three, and Emma's nine.'

'That sounds like a handful,' I say.

'Roughly twenty handfuls, if I'm honest.'

'It can't be easy,' I say. 'Three kids, the shop, plus Adam mentioned you guys own other property in the area.'

'It is hard. Definitely. But I do have help so there's that.'

'In the shop?'

'Yeah, but I have an assistant, too, Carmen. She's amazing, always there for me when I need her. She helps with the Instagram stuff, the shop, of course, and the rental company.'

'Is it all through Airbnb?' I ask.

'And a few other more niche sites.'

'I had no idea from the Airbnb listing that you were the host or owner. I'm surprised you don't promote them more through your Instagram. You'd get loads of guests that way, wouldn't you?'

'Yeah, we would. But Justin wants to keep the rental stuff as separate as possible from the Instagram and the shop. He wasn't even sure about me leaving those postcards in the welcome basket, but I managed to persuade him.'

'Why?' I ask. You'd think any business owner would be pleased with the kind of free advertising a platform like Vanessa's Instagram profile would provide.

'Oh, he's convinced one of my followers is going to

come round and kill me one of these days,' she says, with a wave of her hand and a laugh in her voice.

I laugh, because she does, but then I ask, more seriously, 'Really? Why?'

Vanessa is quiet for a second or two, as she gazes at Matthew, who is happily tucked up on the sofa, staring at the screen of his mother's iPad. 'My former assistant, before Carmen,' she says slowly, not taking her eyes off her son. A shiver rolls through her, and she shakes herself out of her reverie as I take a sip of coffee. 'She ended up being a bit of a nightmare.'

'What happened?' I ask.

'She was new to the area. A young son, and a little girl close to Matthew's age. She introduced herself to me – she'd been following me for years and recognized me. We got on really well, had so much in common, and she was looking for work. This was right when I was starting to focus on the shop. We had such similar taste, seemed to agree on everything, and that's so much a part of building a brand, a vision, you know? So, I asked her if she wanted to work for me, and she jumped at the opportunity. She was in marketing before having her kids and moving here, and I just thought it was all too good to be true. And it was. It totally was.' Vanessa shifts on her stool, drinks from her mug, and I think she's done. That's it. But she's just settling in. 'She started this other account. Anonymous. And she'd leave me these messages, these hateful, judgemental, self-righteous messages, and meanwhile, in real life, she was . . . getting more and more like me. We'd always had similar taste, but suddenly she'd be wearing the exact same outfit I'd worn the week before, or reading the same book I was reading. It was like she wanted to be me . . . I was always aware that this kind of thing might happen with Instagram. She was a follower before she was a friend, and eventually it felt like all she really wanted was to be me. Or at least to have my life. She was certainly a little too interested in Justin. I think she fell in love with him a bit, or maybe it was because she wasn't very happy with her husband. I even thought . . . Well, anyway, then she started sending things to the house.'

'What kind of things?' I frown.

'Well, at first it was nice things. Flowers. Cupcakes. Presents for the kids. This was when she was trying to get back into my good books. Or so she said. But it turned nasty . . . She realized I'd figured out her angle and, well, I won't go into the details, but shit was involved. Literal shit. And then she set the house on fire.'

I've just taken a sip of a coffee, and I swallow it too quickly, the liquid burning the back of my throat. 'What?' I splutter.

'We were lucky because we caught it quickly, and it didn't do too much damage, but we had to redo the kitchen almost entirely. That's all beside the point, though. It was terrifying, an actual nightmare, and I knew it was her, but we had no way of proving it so we couldn't press charges.'

'What happened then? She must've left you alone at some point.'

'I'd already fired her, of course. She'd been working at the shop a bit, and then on our rentals, but I took out a restraining order. She and her family ended up moving away. It was sad, really. I don't think she was a terrible person or anything. I just think some people don't know how to cope with jealousy.'

As Vanessa's been talking, I realize I have a dim recollection of all this. I hadn't had much time for social media during the summer, but I remember Maven reporting on the Instagram influencer who alleged she'd had her home burned down by a frenzied follower.

'That's a pretty extreme form of jealousy,' I say. 'It must've been so scary. For all of you. Especially the kids.' My eyes are drawn to Matthew, still on the sofa, and Vanessa sighs.

'Well, Matthew's too young, of course. He didn't have any idea what was going on. But JJ and Emma, that's a different story. JJ dealt with it worst. It's interesting. He's come to understand what I do over the past few years, and he really doesn't like it. Obviously, my fiery little follower didn't help much.'

'He doesn't appear as much on your Instagram as the other two, I noticed. Is that his choice?'

'Partly. I guess it's hard to say which came first, but I noticed when he turned eleven or twelve that my posts featuring him were getting fewer likes and comments. I guess it's just that kids aren't as cute as babies, right, but it bothered me, and . . . Well, it's totally my fault, but I'd talk about it with Justin and friends, and I didn't realize it at the time but JJ must've overheard a few times.'

'That can't have been easy for him,' I say.

'No, and I absolutely hate myself for even talking about it now – for caring. I mean, really, who cares how many likes any of my posts get, let alone the ones about my children? All that matters is that they're healthy and happy and . . . Oh, I don't know. It made me realize a few things about myself, that's for sure,' Vanessa says, scrunching up her face in dismay.

'Did you ever think about leaving Instagram? Or not posting photos of your children?'

'I did, yes, but they're such a huge part of my life it didn't seem like an option. So, I let JJ approve any photos I post of him now, although I have a feeling that as he gets older he won't be approving any at all,' she finishes, a little sadly.

'Well, some people are just camera-shy. I hate having my picture taken.'

Vanessa nods, but I can tell she doesn't really understand. I imagine she's loved having her photo taken all her life. We've both finished our coffee, so I tell Vanessa I'll get dressed and she can drive me back to my car. I don't want to take up any more of her time than necessary.

But, more than that, I'm starting to feel the walls of the cabin close in on me, with the fog pressing in from outside. It's so still and otherworldly, and every so often there's a pool of quiet when neither of us speaks, and all I can hear are the low murmurings of Matthew on the sofa. They're a warm drone, a slow buzzing, that to anyone else would sound like comfort, contentment.

But I can feel myself holding my breath, waiting for the moment those delicate sounds stop. If I do it for much longer, I'll stop breathing altogether.

## thelowedown

**2,459** posts **250K f**ollowers **1,022** following

**Vanessa Lowe**

Wife * Mother * Lover

Liked by **theotherraydonovan** and **11,459 others**

**thelowedown** Hey there, cutie pie! Let me introduce you to my new Girl Friday, the wonderful and charismatic Mrs Rachel Donovan . . . Rachel moved to Whitstable a mere three months ago, and we've since become firm friends. Our children go to nursery together, and we're two down-from-London gals with a yearning to feel more deeply connected to our local community. So, when I mentioned to her that I was setting up a new business (ssh, more on that later 😊), it seemed only natural that we put our two heads together and created something beautiful. So, Rachel will be my right-hand woman as I move forward with The Lowe Down Ltd (lol), and hopefully put out into the world what I've been dreaming of inside my head for years 💜

View all 258 comments

**theotherraydonovan** Aw, shucks! You shouldn't have! Love how a nursery bump-in and online follow has turned into a real-life friendship – don't know what I'd have done here without you this summer!

**Charliewarlie54321** where's your dress from

**Singwhenyourwinning** Can't wait to see what you do next! Everything you do is gold

16 months ago

## Fifteen Months Ago

The day of the barbecue is brilliant. It's as hot as if it were still the middle of summer, when in fact the kids are back at school and the year is starting to turn, the days waning. When you look up into the sky, Rachel thinks, you can tell: there's something different about the heat at this time of year. It might feel as though it could be July, but a September sky is delicate and hazy, soft focus. It feels better, almost, this trick of the year, one final day before the leaves are changing colour and jumpers taken out of cupboards and drawers.

Rachel has decided that they should walk to Vanessa's. It's too beautiful not to, and it's just along the coast, an easy walk with the sea up alongside them the whole way. Tom is slouched at the bistro table in their tiny courtyard garden, twiddling his thumbs over the screen of his phone. He hasn't met Vanessa yet, and Rachel thinks he's a bit nervous. She has shown him Vanessa's Instagram profile, the number of followers, the unattainable perfection of all her posts. 'She has three kids?' he says now, perplexed. 'How is everything so . . . so clean?'

Sadie is sitting on Rachel's knee, sweating into her mother's bare thighs in the morning heat. Rachel would like to put her down, but every time she has tried to this morning there have been tears, and she doesn't need any more tears. She wants to eat her croissant in relative peace. She leans around her small daughter, tearing off a piece of the flaky pastry and daring to dip it into her cup of coffee. Leaning even further forwards to avoid spilling any over herself or Sadie, she shoves it into her mouth. Speaking around it, she says, 'They probably have a cleaner.'

'Oh,' Tom says, giving her a look, 'they're those types.'

From behind Sadie's back, Rachel rolls her eyes so that Tom can't see. 'I wouldn't mind being those types. Who likes cleaning?'

'You're not working at the moment, though,' Tom says. He says this lazily, an off-hand comment that comes just before he sips his coffee. There is no bite to his words; he doesn't think he's being judgemental or offensive, or starting something. But Rachel is suddenly sitting ramrod straight, jostling Sadie as she does so. There is a sharp, vicious buzz in her blood and it thrums at her throat as she stares at her husband.

'I'm trying to set myself up as a freelancer,' she says. Her mouth feels dry, as though her words should get stuck there, trip over themselves. But, luckily, the sentence comes out smoothly, doesn't betray her. 'And, besides, what do you call looking after your children all day?'

Tom gives her a look that she immediately hates. 'Yeah, but Marcus is back at school now, Sadie's in nursery most of the day, and you're not actually *working* yet . . . You don't have any clients.'

'Finding clients is work, Tom.' It's Tom's turn to roll his eyes, except he doesn't try to hide it behind a toddler's back. 'It is,' Rachel says, feeling more herself now, getting into her stride. 'It's a bit like how you spent the whole summer working, even though there wasn't any teaching happening.'

Tom stops his endless scrolling but doesn't look up immediately. And when he does, it's to mumble, 'It looks a bit far to walk today, Rach. Their house is bloody miles up the coast by the look of Google Maps.'

But Rachel shakes her head. They're walking.

Tom is right, of course, and Vanessa's house is too far away on a hot day, with two young children. Not that she would ever admit that to him.

So they arrive hot, frustrated and annoyed. Rachel has pushed Sadie in her buggy most of the way, and Sadie is in tears over how hot she is. She has wriggled and fussed, trying to get out. They have had to stop and start, stop and start, then bend down and reason with her. But there is no reasoning.

And now, somehow, they are lost. Tom has got the measure of the map wrong, and they can't find the bloody front door to the house. They are standing on the concrete promenade, red-faced, Rachel and Tom bending their heads over his phone. Tom puffs air out of his cheeks, looks up and around them. 'I don't get it. It should be here.'

'Oh,' Rachel says, pointing at the screen. 'It's that road there we need. We can't access it from the beach – we should've turned off back there and walked through town.'

'Walked through town? I thought the whole bloody point of this exercise was to walk along the beach.'

'Well, yeah, but we needed to turn off. I can't magic up a road where there isn't one, Tom.'

Tom sighs, the sound grating in the hot, humid air. Rachel wipes her hand over her sweating neck. She can feel it starting to burn, the tell-tale prick.

And then, like magic – the same non-existent magic Rachel was just talking about – a woman in a white column dress appears on the prom, a hand shielding her eyes from the worst of the sun, her thick auburn hair pulled into a long ponytail that swishes with health and vitality.

'Vanessa?' Rachel says, and the woman swivels towards them, eyes widening in delight.

'Rachel! You're here – you're all here! Welcome, welcome.' She beckons them towards her. 'I was just coming out to scoop up JJ, but I can't see him anywhere.' Rachel looks out over the beach and realizes they are right by The Street, Whitstable's famous disappearing sandbar. It is visible for now, stretching out and away from them, as if it might go on for ever, but she feels a shiver, despite the heat, run down her back as she thinks of either of her own children out there alone. 'I told him to be back by now to welcome you, but JJ's not exactly one for time-keeping,' Vanessa continues. 'Anyway, let's get you up to the house. You must be starving. And gasping for something to drink, I'd imagine. You didn't just walk here, did you?'

Rachel tells her they did and introduces Tom, who has been strangely mute, almost rapt, throughout the whole interaction.

'Tom! God, how good to meet you,' Vanessa says, as they shake hands. She starts to walk towards the house and it takes Rachel a second to realize that Vanessa is still holding her husband's hand, leading the way. She stares at them, wondering who is holding onto whom, and suddenly they separate. Vanessa is pushing through a gate, hidden and overgrown, in the wall and they are in her garden.

Rachel should've known, of course, should've expected something like this. She has seen the photos on Instagram, skipped through Vanessa's Stories enough times to recognize certain parts of it vaguely. But seeing it in person isn't the same thing. It's something else entirely. The house is above them, the path turning into steps, the garden terraced and sloping in different areas, all of it reaching up to the house, which is either Victorian or Edwardian, Rachel can't tell. It is wide and low with Gothic peaks and its original stained glass.

Vanessa comes and stands next to her, gazes up at the same things Rachel is staring at, and says, 'God, I know. So much work to do. But we'll get there.'

Rachel turns to her. 'You're renovating?'

'Yup. The whole thing. It's gorgeous, but it needs so much modernizing, and Justin is obsessed with old and new, so it's perfect for him. A pet project.'

'How long have you been here?' Rachel asks, as she follows Vanessa up the terraced garden towards the patio that adjoins the house. She thinks she knows the answer – she has been following Vanessa for a while, of course, but she is programmed to ask questions, to make small talk, to create a feeling of ease with other people by asking them about themselves.

'Oh, a little over two years now,' Vanessa says, glancing over her shoulder at Rachel. 'We wanted to start the work as soon as we moved in, but it wasn't the right time, with Matthew being so small and two other children.'

They've reached the patio now. It's bathed in September sunlight, and, once Rachel turns back the way they've come, she can see it has the most incredible view of the beach. Vanessa turns with her and says, arm outstretched, finger pointing, 'Oh, there he is. That's JJ.'

Rachel peers into the distance, the wavy, hazy horizon, where the sea and the sky and the sunshine blend, but Vanessa is right: just where she is pointing, a small figure, a shady cut-out against the sunlight, is growing larger. Vanessa shakes her head as she regards her elder son's slow approach to the house. 'He absolutely loves it out there.'

'Aren't you terrified he'll get swept away? The Street disappears so quickly.'

'Oh, he's a strong swimmer. And he knows the tides, these days.'

'How old is he?' Rachel asks, because the figure looks so small, even though it's getting closer, and, though she'd never admit it to her new friend, she is uncomfortable with what she considers to be Vanessa's laissez-faire attitude towards a child and the unpredictability of open water.

'He'll be twelve in November,' Vanessa says.

'So, he's eleven,' Rachel says, the words slipping out, gilded with judgement. She can feel Vanessa turning her gaze on her, the slide of her eyes over Rachel's face, which now begins to blush and burn. She can also tell the moment Vanessa decides not to pull her up on it, to let it go.

The other woman ruffles herself up, then claps her hands and turns away. 'Right! Lunchtime! You lot must be absolutely starving. I know my team is. And speaking of my team, Rachel, come and meet Justin, my husband.'

And so the rest of the afternoon goes, slipping away as easily as a glass of the excellent rosé Vanessa provides. Rachel is introduced to Justin, who presides over his gas barbecue, tongs in hand, a whole chicken rotating on the spit of an integrated rotisserie. He is already chatting happily to Tom, both with a beer in hand, bonding over meat and heat, talking a little more loudly than is strictly necessary – although the children are shouting nearby. But his eyes widen with delight as Vanessa makes the introductions, motioning to Rachel.

Rachel expects him to wave an arm, hands full of tongs and beer, and beg off any contact, but he puts down his toys, takes off his oven glove and brings Rachel in for a hug.

'So, you're the woman who's stolen my wife's heart,' he says. He has a soft Scottish accent, and is shorter than Rachel was expecting – much shorter than Tom, who is six foot three.

Rachel glances at Vanessa, who smiles indulgently, and Rachel laughs. 'I suppose so! Although I think it was a mutual theft, so we're probably even, aren't we?'

'I'm sure you are,' Justin says. 'And you're going to help out with Vanessa's shop too?'

Rachel glances back at Vanessa, but she's busy tidying a pile of linen napkins that doesn't need tidying. Helping with the shop has been mooted twice before, and then only idly over coffees in the sun. Rachel is desperate to get back to work, to find something else to do with her days, to start bringing in some money, and Vanessa mentioned the lifestyle shop she was planning to open last week. She hadn't known those two casual conversations had morphed into an actual plan. Rachel feels as though she has signed a contract when all she was looking for was a napkin to doodle on. Does she really want to start mixing business with pleasure? Is working with friends ever a good idea? But Vanessa is so successful already: she has a quarter of a million followers on Instagram so any shop she opens is bound to do well. This would be an opportunity wasted if Rachel says no.

When Rachel takes too long to answer, and the silence has gone on just a beat too long, Vanessa grins at them all. 'Oh, Rachel was a big shot in social-media marketing in London, Justin. She's not interested in my small-town project.'

'No, no, no, of course I am,' Rachel says. The ice-cold surface of her wine glass is beginning to slide in her hand, and she summons a smile as big as Vanessa's. 'God, I'd absolutely love to be involved, Vanessa, of course I would. Actually, you know what? I was thinking last night that RITA would be a great brand for you to stock. I could help set that up. They usually only sell online but I left on very good terms.'

And the smile Vanessa turns on her feels like a spotlight, full-bright. Rachel is taken aback by its power. She'd thought she already had a handle on Vanessa's myriad grins, but she realizes now that her new friend was only ever at half-wattage before.

'Oh, that would be wonderful, Rachel,' Vanessa says, reaching out to grab Rachel's arm. 'Do you really think they'd be interested?'

'Of course,' Rachel answers, and the two women drift to the beautifully set table, away from their husbands and towards the pod of playing children. Just as they're sitting down, Vanessa leaning forward to pull the wine bottle out of its ice bucket, the garden gate slams.

The figure Rachel presumes to be JJ makes his way up the garden path, but when he seemed earlier to be sauntering slowly up the sand, Rachel sees now that he is taking the steps as quickly as possible, rushing through the garden, his hands deep in his pockets, his body rigid with barely contained annoyance.

'Stop and say hello, JJ,' Vanessa says coolly, not looking up from the glass of wine she is pouring.

'Hello,' JJ says, as if on command, passing the table without even a glance at her.

'JJ. Please.'

The boy stops abruptly, sliding a little on the gravel in a way that Rachel finds almost theatrically comical. He turns, in a similarly robotic manner, and stares at his mother. 'This is my friend Rachel,' she says, and JJ switches his attention to Rachel, not quite meeting her eye.

'Hello. Nice to meet you, Rachel.'

'Lovely to meet you too, JJ. Have you been in the water?'

The boy's hand automatically reaches up to his head, where his hair lies damp against his skull, and nods.

'I went earlier this morning, and I'll probably go again when we get home. It's just so refreshing, isn't it?' Rachel says.

'You like to swim?' he says.

'Love it,' Rachel says.

'JJ's on the school and county teams for swimming,' Vanessa says.

'And athletics and cricket,' JJ says. He has reverted to his robot-like mannerisms, and with any other child, Rachel might think they were boasting, but that's not the case with JJ. It's like he's filling in blanks his mother left, ticking off the list as he goes.

Rachel smiles at him, trying to win him over, and says, 'Well done, you. That's brilliant. There's nothing like swimming in the sea, though, is there?'

And JJ finally meets her gaze, as he says, 'No. It's brilliant.'

'Don't do that, JJ,' Vanessa says, leaning back in her chair and taking a sip of her wine.

'What?' JJ says, startled.

'Copying Rachel's word. It's lazy. You can come up with a better one, can't you? Let's be a little more imaginative here.'

Rachel regards Vanessa, squinting at her in the glare of the sun.

'I'm not at school, Mum. I can use whatever word I want.'

'No, you can't. You have to learn to be articulate and original. You can't just parrot what other people are saying.'

'Vanessa,' a low voice says, from behind them. Justin has joined them, leaving Tom in charge of the endlessly rotating chicken. 'Everything doesn't have to be a pop quiz, you know. Especially on a Sunday. You have a good swim, JJ?'

'Yeah, pretty good,' JJ mumbles, his eyes downcast.

Rachel is watching carefully, her gaze grazing from JJ to Justin to Vanessa.

'I thought it was "brilliant"?' Vanessa says, smirking at her son.

'Ness,' Justin says, squeezing his wife's shoulder. 'JJ, why don't you go and get changed? We'll save you some chicken.'

JJ nods at his dad and slopes silently into the house. When Rachel reaches for her glass, she sees her hand is shaking a little, but then Vanessa is smiling, yet again, and says, 'Still a year to go, but he's already behaving like a teenager. I constantly feel like I'm punishing him when all he wants to do is swim or play football or be on the computer.'

'Poor guy,' Justin says, leaning over his wife to grab a carrot baton and swirl it in some homemade hummus.

Rachel is somewhat mollified, although she can't forget the look on JJ's face when his mother spoke to him. Is that just the look on all boys' faces when their mothers force them to do better in company? Is this what Rachel has to look forward to with Marcus? She takes another sip of wine, and this time she can taste something chemical, almost petrol-like, but then she swallows it, and it goes down just as easily, and Justin says something that makes Vanessa laugh, and Sadie and Matthew, Emma and Marcus come running up to the table, and the food is ready, and she forgets all about it.

# 9

Two days go past.

Morning. Afternoon. Evening.

Morning. Afternoon. Evening.

I haven't heard from Vanessa since she took me back to her house to pick up my car, but then suddenly, at around four in the afternoon, she messages me: *Would you like to come round this evening? Nothing fancy – just pizza and a film or two with the kids, if you're up to it.*

It's such a delicate, yet sturdy branch. Nothing could be more appealing than pizza and movies, but I may have used up all my energy socializing three nights ago, so I waver, my thumb hovering over the screen of my phone, before answering. *Sounds lovely*, I end up writing, after much deliberation. *What time do you want me?*

Vanessa's response comes almost immediately: *Any-time! We're just home, hanging out* 😊

Vanessa's arms are heavily laden when she opens the door to me, a basket of washing balanced on one hip, while in the other hand she carries a box of brightly coloured plastic toys.

'Okay, so currently playing is *Paddington 2*. Emma wants the new *Mary Poppins* next, Matthew's demanding *Dumbo*, and JJ's trying to convince me he's old enough to watch *It*, because he's almost the same age as some of the child actors in it,' she says, with an eye-roll.

'I remember trying to use that kind of logic at his age,' I say, removing my coat and shoes in the hallway.

Vanessa laughs lightly. 'Well, I told him there's no way, but I doubt he'll shut up about it all night.'

The screening room is snug and dark, with one wall taken up entirely by a larger-than-life screen. Three children lie in a variety of different shapes over the huge U-shaped sofa that takes up most of the room, and Vanessa makes the introductions.

'Matthew you've already met,' Vanessa says, ruffling the hair on her youngest son's head as she stands over the couch, 'but this is JJ, and here's Emma. Guys, this is my and Daddy's new friend, Callie.'

Emma pops up immediately from her prone position, while JJ stays seated, eyes glued mutinously to the enormous screen in front of him.

'Hi!' Emma cries. She's standing up on the couch so that we're practically the same height and she can peer straight into my eyes. Vanessa wasn't lying when she said Emma took most after her: she has the same auburn hair as her mother and younger brother, with Vanessa's big brown eyes, and lightly freckled nose and cheeks. She smiles as widely as her mother too, ecstatic to meet me, excited to have someone new to charm.

'Hi, Emma,' I say, 'nice to meet you. I hear you're proposing we watch *Mary Poppins Returns* next. The original was my favourite when I was growing up. I used to watch it whenever I was sick and home from school.'

'Oh, my gosh, me too!' Emma rushes at me. 'Right, Mummy? Don't I always watch *Mary Poppins* when I don't feel well?'

69

Vanessa nods. 'You do, yes, sweetheart, but you watch the new one.'

'Which is exactly why we shouldn't watch it tonight,' JJ mutters from his corner of the couch. 'She's seen it like a thousand times.'

'That's true,' Vanessa says, looking at her daughter with equanimity. 'Maybe we should watch something other than *Mary Poppins Returns* as you've seen it so often.'

'*Dumbo!*' Matthew cries, crawling up the back of the couch, so that he's hugging his mother's side, like a koala.

'*Nooo*,' JJ groans. 'We watched that at the weekend. Mum, please. Can we watch something else?'

'We're not watching *It*, JJ,' Vanessa says shortly, and then, much more brightly, 'Why don't we let our guest decide?'

'Oh, God,' I say, a deer unable to make a decision, caught in the headlights. 'How about *The Lego Movie*?' It's the first thing that comes to mind that could possibly keep a three-year-old, a nine-year-old, and a moody thirteen-year-old all entertained.

Vanessa nods her head in approval, and no one launches a complaint, so we all settle in to watch it together. Towards the end of the film, Justin returns from work with a pile of pizza boxes in hand, picked up in town as he walked home from the station. If he is surprised to find me there, cosily ensconced with his family, he doesn't show it. He is as bright, cheerful and welcoming as his wife, his daughter and his younger son. Only JJ seems to have an off switch in this family.

Over the course of the evening, Matthew migrates to my side, snug and warm against me. The silkiness of his soft curls astounds me, the warm weight of him adding to the pressure in my chest that is always there now. At one point I think I feel Vanessa's eyes on me, and glancing over at her, I see her smile softly in my direction before mouthing, 'Are you okay?'

I nod, unable to speak, and return my attention to the film.

But I can still feel her watching.

Later, Matthew is taken to bed. He's fallen asleep in the crook of my armpit, and Justin lifts him easily into the air, barely disturbing him. Matthew mutters and murmurs something, Justin chuckling softly at his son's sleeping gibberish. I stay with Emma and JJ as Vanessa follows him upstairs to tuck her youngest child into bed.

A few minutes later, I get up to go to the loo. Leaving the cocoon of the screening room, the rest of the house feels cold and strangely silent. Its airy hallways make me shiver as I go in search of the closest bathroom, and there's something almost sepulchral about the building as I go from room to room. The air is closed, cold, all light and life left in the screening room. I can't hear anything from upstairs where presumably Justin, Vanessa and Matthew are.

The rush of hot water as I wash my hands warms me, as does the cosiness of the downstairs bathroom, but just as I'm leaving, closing the door quietly behind me, I hear the staccato beats of a strained conversation coming from above. The bathroom is tucked away at the bottom of the staircase, and I look up, seeing two pairs of feet at the top of the stairs above me.

Neither Justin nor Vanessa appears to have noticed me exiting the bathroom, and those short, sharp words continue uninterrupted.

But I can't hear them.

Not quite.

They are standing very close, almost soldered together. I shuffle up to the bottom of the staircase, trying to hear better, but if anything, it makes it harder, so I move away. Then, as I'm walking down the hallway, it's as if the sound's turned up, because suddenly I hear Justin, clear as day, as he says, 'What were you thinking?'

His voice isn't raised: I've wandered into an echo chamber, found the exact spot where the sound from the top of the stairs travels straight down to the hallway. I wonder if either of them knows this spot exists.

'It's fine, Justin,' I hear Vanessa say. 'Everything's under control.'

'No, it's not. I'm not going through all this again. I'm not putting up with it, Vanessa.'

I wonder what Justin is putting up with. It's hard to imagine what strife might be causing this argument. Until now, I'd been pretty sure Vanessa and Justin were preternaturally happy together, their family as perfect as perfect gets.

Then I remember Vanessa telling me about her fiery former assistant.

They're arguing about me.

He's worried I'm going to get too attached to his wife, his family. Maybe even burn his house down.

I'm putting my shoes back on in the hallway when Vanessa finds me.

'You're leaving?' she asks, genuine surprise filling her voice.

'Yeah, sorry. Suddenly feeling exhausted,' I say.

'Oh, okay. You and Matthew both, I guess.'

'Right. Turns out I have the same bedtime as a three-year-old.'

'Well, we did let him stay up a little later than usual, to be fair,' Vanessa offers, with a wry smile.

'That makes me feel much better.'

Vanessa pulls me into a hug before I leave, whispering, 'Let me know if there's anything you need,' then letting me go.

I tell her I will. But all I can think about are Justin's whispered words, travelling down the stairs and into the hallway without their knowing.

I hurry out of the door, shutting it with a louder bang than I intended. Only when I'm in the car and out on the road do I unclench my jaw, release my muscles, relax my breathing.

# I O

I wake to banging on the front door, my name like a jack-hammer against the concrete grey morning.

Stumbling downstairs, still not yet awake, my feet almost miss a few steps when I see who's standing outside. The door is mostly reinforced glass, surrounded by a wood frame, and within that frame is Adam, beyond him nothing but the shingle beach and, in the far-off distance, the sea.

'Hello?' I say, finally opening the door to him.

'Callie,' he says. 'Sorry to bother you so early. It's a bit of an emergency.'

He looks frantic, wild, his voice jagged and rough in the cold morning air. I tell him to come inside, and he follows me, but it's almost as if he's not listening to me or paying any attention. He's looking around the cabin as if he's searching for something.

'Matthew is missing. You haven't seen him, have you?'

'What?' I ask, after a pause in which I try to piece together whatever is going on. 'Matthew's missing? Vanessa's little boy?'

'Yes. They woke up this morning and he wasn't in his bed. They've called the police, but Ness asked me to come round and check he wasn't here.'

'Why would he be?'

Adam is lifting up cushions now, looking under blankets,

searching through the non-existent nooks and crannies of this sleek space, as if Matthew is a scampish puppy, hiding from his owner.

'Adam,' I say, trailing him around the cabin, 'he couldn't have got inside without me knowing it. There's only one way in and out, and the door's been locked since I got back last night.'

But Adam isn't listening, and I have to say his name again and again before he halts his fruitless search. 'Adam, can you please just explain to me what's going on? How can Matthew be missing?'

He takes a deep breath. 'Ness and Justin woke up this morning, and Matthew wasn't in his bed. They searched the house, up and down. It's not like he's never been up before them before – but then they realized the back door was open.'

'They think he went outside and wandered off?' I ask.

Adam gives the most desperate shrug I've ever seen. 'I don't know. I don't think they know.'

'But why would he go outside on his own at night? The cold, the sea . . .' I trail off, thinking of Matthew's small body stumbling down the beach in front of his parents' house, of the way that stretch of land is famous for disappearing and reappearing as the sea takes it prisoner, then gives it back. I can almost feel the small warmth of him as he leaned against me and fell asleep last night.

How long would a small child last outside in mid-December? What was he doing? Where was he going?

And how long did his family have to find him?

## Fourteen Months Ago

It's almost Halloween when Rachel comes home to find Vanessa in her kitchen.

'Oh, my God,' Vanessa says, turning towards her as Rachel enters the room. 'It's you! You scared the shit out of me!'

'I scared *you*? Vanessa you're in *my house*. What are you doing here? How did you even get in?' Rachel drops her bag to the floor by the kitchen table. She feels as though she should be more shocked than she is, seeing her friend there without her knowledge, but perhaps she is too tired to feel shocked.

'Your back door was open – I just assumed you were upstairs so I came in.'

'You didn't try ringing the front doorbell? Like a normal person?'

Vanessa laughs. 'I did, but there was no answer – which I know now is because you weren't home – but I thought I could hear voices from the garden, so I came round the side and saw that the back door was open.'

'The back door was open?' Rachel says. She had been about to sit down, but now she strides over to the back door, pulling it to and fro, as if that could tell her anything. The keys are in the lock, their I ♥ New York key ring knocking jauntily against the yellow paint of the door. 'I swear I locked this earlier. I only had it open to empty the compost bin.'

'You must've forgotten,' Vanessa says soothingly. 'Easy enough to do. And no harm done, just me strolling round, being a nosy neighbour.'

'Thank God it was only you, though,' Rachel says, feeling a little panicked now, glancing around the kitchen to see if anything's amiss. 'Maybe I should check upstairs, in case anything's been taken.'

Vanessa nods. 'I don't think you'll find anything – everything seems perfectly normal to me, but better to check.' Rachel is halfway to the stairs when Vanessa calls, 'Wait! What if someone's up there?' She follows Rachel, lowering her voice to a whisper as she gets closer. 'Want me to come with you?'

Rachel looks at her, then up the stairs, to where everything appears to be lying still and silent, devoid of human activity. But Vanessa grabs her arm, squeezing gently as she says, 'We'll check it out together. We're a team, right?'

It's not until after dinner, when the kids are in bed, everything has been cleared away, and Rachel and Tom are sitting on the sofa together, watching television and drinking large glasses of red wine, that Rachel says, 'I think she has a key.'

'Who?'

'Vanessa. I think she has a key to our house. I would never leave the back door unlocked. I've never left a door unlocked in my life. I'd add more locks to doors if I could.'

Tom reaches out and shakes her shin, which is hidden under a blanket. It's a chilly night, the first real autumnal evening they've had since moving here. Earlier, Rachel watched the sea mist gather over the water and creep up towards their cottage. She had shivered in happy anticipation of all the cosy, wintry nights to come in their new house. But now the candles she lit and the fire Tom laid seem weak and futile. Someone was in their home earlier, someone who wasn't meant to be. What good are candles and a fireplace against that?

'It's easy enough to do, Rach,' Tom is saying now. 'I know you're a security freak, but you've probably let your guard down a bit since moving here, don't you think? We left the door unlocked loads in the summer.'

'Yeah, but that's because we were always coming and going from the beach. One of us was always in sight of the house. I just wouldn't leave the back door unlocked, I know it. I can feel the key in my hand as I turned it this morning. I put it back behind the bread bin.'

'If you put it back behind the bread bin, how did it end up in the door?' Tom asks.

'She put it there.'

Tom shifts on the sofa, turning to look at Rachel, 'Vanessa did?'

'Yeah.'

'But why would she have a key to our house, anyway? And what would she have been doing here? Other than coming to see you?'

'I don't know.'

'Where's all this suspicion coming from, Rach?'

'I don't know,' Rachel says again, and that's the truth of it. She just doesn't know. She has been friends with Vanessa for months now, and they've become close. Or, at least, sometimes it feels as though they've become very close, then something will happen, or Vanessa will do something that makes Rachel question how much and how well she really knows her. Because Vanessa, for all her Instagram Stories and sharing, is something of an enigma. Rachel feels as though they became close very quickly, but perhaps the speed at which the friendship moved kept things at a surface, slightly superficial level. She had assumed that making friends with someone like Vanessa would mean entry into a wider social circle. In fact the opposite is true: more often than not, their coffee dates and play dates are for two. Rachel doesn't have a problem with that *per se* – in fact, she was flattered, at first, to discover that she was one of the very few to be drawn into Vanessa's sacred inner circle. But now, a few months on, she wonders.

'She has a perfectly beautiful house of her own,' Tom points out now.

'I know,' Rachel says, turning her attention back to the television, taking a big sip of wine. Tom shakes her shin again, a comfort and an annoyance that doesn't go away, until she says, 'I'm just being silly.'

'You're just being stubborn, more like. You can't admit that you might've left the back door unlocked.'

Rachel takes a breath, is about to retort, but then she looks at her husband, who is entranced by the TV again, and sighs. 'Yeah, you're right. It's just so unlike me.'

'Maybe you're a whole new you down here?'

'Maybe.' But Rachel doesn't want to be a whole new Rachel. She wants to be herself. She wants to trust her gut.

I go over to the Lowes' with Adam, and when we get there, a police car is parked on the private road. The front door is wide open and I can hear raised voices coming from inside.

Walking in with Adam, I can't help but feel I'm intruding. I want to help them find Matthew, of course, but I barely know these people. Should I be here in this moment of crisis, of emergency, of potential grief?

'Callie,' Vanessa calls, as soon as she sees me. Her eyes are wide, her whole face strained. 'Callie, was he at yours?'

'No,' I say, taking her hand because she's reached out for me, almost involuntarily it seems, and leading her back towards the kitchen. I help her sit on one of the uncomfortable but beautiful brass bar stools, her back to the implacable seascape, and she slumps over, defeated and deflated. 'Vanessa, what's happened? Where's Matthew?'

'I don't know,' she cries. 'I don't know! We can't find him.'

Through the glass doors I can see Justin and two police officers pacing the grounds, looking concerned. As I watch, they walk through the gate to the promenade that passes behind the house, then to the beach beyond. They spread out, scattering across the shingle, as if Matthew had anywhere to hide on that wide, flat beach. JJ is standing at the doors, as if keeping watch, as he, too, stares at his father and the police officers, his face pale, stricken. I'm about to say something to him, when Vanessa looks up, eyes watery, face blotchy. 'Close that, will you?' she says, her voice short. I think she's talking to me, but it's JJ she means, even as he continues his silent vigil. 'JJ, please. Close the door. It's freezing.'

'I'll do it,' I say, getting up from my stool.

'No, he has to learn,' Vanessa almost mumbles. 'He never listens to me.'

But JJ moves to the door, closes it and turns back towards his mother.

'Thank you,' she says, with a sigh. He is about to say something, but Vanessa continues to speak: 'Go upstairs and sit with Emma, please, JJ.'

'I don't –'

'JJ, go upstairs. Please. I can't deal with you right now.'

I watch as the boy swallows, and his eyes swim with tears. He must be so confused. But he obliges his mum, heading out of the kitchen as silent as a wraith as Vanessa stares at her hands, twisting the rings on her fingers.

'Is there anywhere in the house he likes to hide? Somewhere he goes when you're playing hide and seek, maybe?' I finally ask, desperate to help somehow. As if all Matthew needs is some out-of-the-box thinking.

But Vanessa's jaw is set differently. 'The boathouse,' she croaks.

'You haven't checked there yet?' I ask.

She is peering out through the window to the beach where her husband has disappeared from view. 'I don't know. Justin might've done.' She runs the sleeve of her jumper under her nose, leaving a trail on the oatmeal-coloured material.

'Well, let's go and check, just in case,' I say.

The boathouse is a dark, damp space. Inside, there are a few boats, all in a state of disrepair, but also old pieces of furniture, big boxes full of discarded but still wanted items, plenty of places to hide.

'Matthew?' Vanessa calls, a little tremulously, heading straight to the furthest corner and a medium-sized antique wardrobe with a broken door jutting piratically off its hinges. 'Matthew, honey, are you here?' she says, pulling the not-broken door of the wardrobe open, and peering inside.

But there's nothing. Just a pile of blankets and bed-linen.

She crumples to the floor, squatting in front of the wardrobe, which she'd opened, expecting a small boy looking for Narnia-like magic, and instead finding the worst thing possible. Nothing. 'He's not here,' she moans. 'Where is he? How can this be happening?'

'What did the police say when they arrived?' I ask.

Vanessa is still crouched by the wardrobe, head in hands. 'They just asked us questions about when we last saw him, what he was wearing, who he'd been in contact with, whether he'd ever been a sleepwalker.'

'Has he ever sleepwalked out of the house?' I ask quickly, because this is possibly the most benign reason behind Matthew's disappearance. Although with the sea right outside their door, and a chilly December night, it could still potentially lead to tragedy.

'No,' Vanessa says. She stands, turning back to me and her face is a picture of distress, an edge of hope sliding across her eyes. 'But maybe? He's so young . . . Just because he hasn't done it before doesn't mean he couldn't have started, right? I think I remember JJ doing it once or twice when he was younger . . . Maybe it runs in families.'

'Yeah. There's nothing to say he couldn't have started sleepwalking.'

Vanessa's eyes turn glassy, filling with tears again, and I watch as she bites down on her bottom lip, and says, through the stutter of sobs, 'The only thing is he's too little to open the back door on his own . . . He's not tall enough to reach the lock and he's not strong enough to open it. We always have to do it for him.'

There's a deep pocket of silence in the dank air of the boathouse as we stare at each other, letting what Vanessa has just said sink in.

'So . . .' I say, not trusting my own voice.

'So someone must've taken him,' Vanessa says, her voice a hollow cave filled with fear.

The first news report comes through over the radio as I'm driving from the cabin into town a little after four thirty in the afternoon.

I spent the morning searching the beach and the area around Vanessa and Justin's house, later going back to my cabin and continuing the search around there. I wandered up and down the beach in front of the Getaway, got the manager of the pub to help search there, and walked as much of the Saxon Shore Way footpath as I could before the light began to leach from the sky. My sense of how wrong this was grew with every step I took, every flutter of something that drew my attention out of the corner of my eye. I couldn't stop thinking about Matthew leaning up against me, small, tired, warm, sleepy and safe in the comfort of the Lowes' screening room last night. How could that be less than twenty-four hours ago? And there, at the edge of everything, skimming the unreachable edge of every horizon, was the sea. Because it's the sea that's the most tragic prospect, of course: the idea that he might, somehow, have wandered into those waves, tiny and alone, in the middle of winter.

Now I'm heading into Whitstable where the family and the police will coordinate a search of the entire town, shops, businesses, houses, and anywhere else he might be hidden. The coastguard is out scanning the sea and the shoreline, but here in town every inch will be scanned and searched for Matthew Lowe, every member of the community given a printout with his face on it, auburn curls, like a burnished halo, surrounding his small, round face. His sweet, still-babyish face will be instantly recognizable to so many already, of course: a frequent fixture on Vanessa's Instagram page, there must be thousands of women around the country who'd know his face anywhere. So, where could he possibly be hiding?

A crowd has already gathered outside the police station when I get there, and it takes me a minute to spot Vanessa's crown of auburn hair – so similar to her missing son's – near the top of the steps. She is huddled with Justin, grasping the lapels of his navy-blue pea coat, while Emma in turn clutches the edges of her mother's black winter coat. But I can't spot JJ anywhere. Though that's understandable. Seeing him at the house earlier, it was clear he was taking the disappearance of his little brother particularly badly.

There are way too many people in the crowd to count. I stand at the edge of the gathering, shuffling a little, uncomfortable, an outsider, an interloper. But I was searching with the family earlier in the day, was one of the last people to see Matthew: it would feel wrong to be anywhere but here. Besides, if anyone knows the world-tipping fear and pain of a lost child, it's me. If there's any way, however small, however insignificant, that I can help find Matthew and bring him home, I'll do it.

The search is a coordinated effort between the police and the fire brigade. We are told to divide into pairs: each pair will be given a section of the town and surrounding area to search methodically. I'm about to approach a stranger, offer to buddy up, when Adam appears. 'The police want to talk to you before you join the search, Callie,' he says. His voice is tight, his face drawn and pale, and in the dark light of a winter's evening, he looks like he's aged ten years since I first met him at the Lowes'.

'Why?' I ask, something sharp digging deep inside my chest.

'Just routine stuff, I think. Ness mentioned to them that you were at the house last night. They're going to interview me too, so we can search together afterwards, if there's time.'

I nod, but my neck feels stiff, twisted, as if I've pulled it, an elastic band stretching too far, about to break. The crowd is organizing itself into pairs, forming a line in front of several local firefighters and police officers who are assigning areas to search. I follow Adam through the crowd and up the steps, where Vanessa and Justin greet me, wan, washed-out, distress written on every line of their faces.

'Callie, thanks so much for agreeing to talk to the police,' Vanessa says. 'I completely forgot to mention to them this morning that you'd been at the house last night.'

'It's fine,' I say. 'I'm happy to help.'

Emma is still clasped to Vanessa's side, and I look around, searching for JJ, but before I can ask where he is, Vanessa jumps in: 'JJ's not good with crowds, so he's back at the house. My mum arrived an hour or so ago, so she stayed with him, just in case . . . just in case Matthew shows up there.'

I'm holding on to Vanessa's thin string of hope, but I

don't think, after all these hours, that Matthew is some-how going to toddle back into his home, as if nothing has happened.

In the police station I'm ushered into an interview room, offered tea and water, both of which I accept – I feel desperately thirsty and desperately tired.

'So, Miss Thorne,' the officer who is taking my state-ment says, sitting down in the chair opposite me, 'you're a visitor to Whitstable, is that right?'

The officer, Detective Constable Joseph Whitman, is young, too young to command authority. He has a thick, sandy moustache hovering over his top lip and no other facial hair. Light grey eyes peer across the table at me, and I can feel his nerves. He swallows deeply and nods, as if he's giving me the go-ahead to speak.

'Yes. I'm staying at Vanessa and Justin Lowe's rental cabin just outside town,' I say, and supply the exact address.

Whitman is taking assiduous notes, head bent, scrib-bling. 'And are you a friend of the Lowes? How do you know them?'

'I didn't before I got here. Like I said, I'm renting their cabin for two weeks through Airbnb. I met Vanessa at her shop a couple of days later, and she invited me round for dinner.'

'So, that's what you were doing there last night? You were there for dinner?'

'Yes, but that was actually my second visit. I went over for dinner for the first time on Tuesday night.'

'Okay, good. Thanks. And did you meet Matthew on any of these occasions?' Whitman asks.

'Yes. I saw him last night along with his brother and

sister, but I met him for the first time a few days ago . . . That would've been on Wednesday, I think, on the twelfth. Vanessa came round the morning after we'd had dinner, and Matthew was with her.'

'And that's it? Those are the only occasions you've been in contact with Matthew Lowe?'

'Yes.'

'And how did he seem last night, Miss Thorne?'

'Fine,' I say. 'Happy, well-behaved, sweet . . . He fell asleep while we were watching *The Lego Movie*, and his dad took him to bed. That was the last time . . . the last time . . .'

'The last time you saw him?'

'Yes.'

'And were you ever alone with him?'

'No, never.'

'And what about Matthew's parents, Vanessa and Justin? What did they seem like last night?' Whitman asks.

Before I can answer, the door pops open and a woman walks in. She doesn't introduce herself to me, just nods at Whitman, who seems even more nervous now than he already was, as she leans back against the wall facing me, and says, 'Carry on, DC Whitman. Don't mind me.'

'Um, right, yes . . .' He's scanning the pages of his notebook, totally lost. 'Oh, um, so, yes, Miss Thorne, can you tell me how Vanessa and Justin Lowe were behaving last night?'

'They seemed normal to me, but I've only met them a handful of times.'

Whitman nods, but then the unknown woman cuts in, 'Could you just walk us through the evening from your perspective, Miss Thorne?'

She isn't in uniform. Instead, she's wearing a charcoal grey trouser suit, almost black, with an oyster-grey fine-knit jumper under the jacket. There's one gold chain around her neck, the small pendant lying just below her collar over the fabric of the sweater, and she has thick, black-rimmed glasses that match the sweep of her black hair, but almost swamp the fine-boned features of her face. She smiles at me, but through the lenses of her glasses, I can't tell if the smile reaches her eyes. 'I'm Detective Chief Inspector Varma,' she says.

Whitman isn't surprised by this – clearly he's already been briefed – and I try not to let my surprise show as I say, 'Sure. Well. I got there just before five, I think. Vanessa opened the door to me, and I went with her into their screening room where the children were already watching a film. We all hung out there for a while, and then a bit later Justin arrived with pizzas. It was probably about seven thirty when he took Matthew up to bed.'

'Can you remember what time it was when Justin arrived home from work?' DCI Varma asks.

'Six, six thirty maybe? I can't remember exactly, sorry.'

'Did you spend the entire time in the . . . ah, screening room? You didn't move into the kitchen or dining room to eat the pizza?'

'No. We stayed where we were.'

'The whole time?' Varma presses.

'I went to the bathroom once.'

'And was that upstairs where the bedrooms are?' Varma asks. She's still leaning against the wall, Whitman relegated to observer. A blush has crept over his face and neck since Varma's arrival, but it's impossible to tell whether it's because he's embarrassed by being usurped or hoping to impress a senior colleague.

'There's a bathroom on the ground floor, right by the stairs. I haven't ever been upstairs,' I clarify, and Varma nods.

'I understand you were back at the Lowes' house this morning, Miss Thorne. Did you go upstairs then, at all? Into Matthew's room?'

'No. I haven't been in Matthew's room. This morning I helped Vanessa search the boathouse, then the garden and the beach. I didn't go upstairs.'

'And I understand you checked your own cabin, and the area surrounding it there for Matthew too?' Varma says.

'Yes. Adam – Vanessa's stepbrother – was with me. He's the one who told me Matthew was missing, and came over to check Matthew wasn't at the cabin, hiding somewhere.'

'That's Adam Fuller you're referring to?'

'Um, I can't remember his last name, to be honest, but that sounds right.'

'Why would he or Vanessa think Matthew was at your cabin, Miss Thorne?'

'I don't know. I asked him the same thing, but I think they were just being thorough. Trying not to panic too soon, you know?'

'Thank you, Miss Thorne, I just have one more question, and then we'll let you go and get your fingerprints taken.'

'Fingerprints?'

'Yes. Just for elimination purposes. We'll be doing a complete forensic examination of the Lowes' home.'

'Right. Of course,' I say.

Varma leans forward from her perch against the wall, her eyes fixed on me through her glasses. 'Were you aware of Vanessa Lowe before you came to stay at her cabin?'

'Yes,' I say, and I can't help it: I start to shift in my chair.

'So, you follow her on Instagram?'

'Yes, but I didn't know she owned the cabin . . . and, besides, it was my mother who made the booking, not me. It was only when I went over to her shop that I recognized her and made the connection.'

'So, you didn't specifically choose to come here and stay in the cabin because you're one of Vanessa Lowe's social-media followers?' Varma asks.

My heart knocks, just once, extra loudly at my chest and I stare into DCI Varma's brown eyes. 'No,' I say, and even I can hear the startled gasp at the core of the word.

And it's all I can do to hope that Varma and Whitman translate my surprise as innocent, rather than suspicious.

'Okay. Thank you, Miss Thorne. DC Whitman will see to your fingerprinting now,' Varma says, staying in the interview room as I follow Whitman out of the door. I stick close behind him, like a lost puppy, but my mind is still in the interview room with Varma, wondering about that last question. Did she really think I came here just to stay in the house of an Instagram influencer I follow? And, if so, where did she get that idea from? Vanessa? Or Justin, perhaps. More importantly: what has that to do with Matthew's disappearance? Something trills at the back of my mind, an ice-cold thought that sends shivers down my spine: surely, they don't think I had anything to do with this?

## Thirteen Months Ago

It's the middle of November and a very rare date night for Rachel and Tom. A *double* date night.

It was Vanessa's idea, launched on Rachel and Tom ten days ago when they were last at the Lowes' house for Sunday lunch. To Rachel's surprise, Tom jumped at the prospect just as jubilantly as Vanessa had suggested it, and now here they are, having dinner in one of Whitstable's tiny restaurants, the glow of which fills Rachel with warmth as she nears it.

Pushing open the door to the restaurant, her glasses steam up almost immediately. She has only recently started wearing them with any regularity – in London she was a dedicated daily lens wearer, but here, in Whitstable, she has decided she doesn't mind how she looks when she leaves the house with her chunky spectacles on. She actually thinks she looks pretty cool.

She hasn't got used to the steaming up, though, and now she pulls them off, annoyed and a bit embarrassed at how easily annoyed and embarrassed she is by this simple phenomenon – it makes her feel like a cartoon nerd, Velma from *Scooby-Doo* or some other sidekick. It doesn't help that, once she puts her glasses on, and follows the incredibly young waitress to the table, she sees Tom and

Vanessa are already there, sitting side by side on the snug banquette, looking surreptitious and caught out as she pulls out a chair and sits down.

'I thought you were working late,' she says to Tom. This had been the line for getting out of coming home first and helping her put the kids to bed before a neighbourhood babysitter arrived.

'I was. Faculty meeting,' he explains to Vanessa. 'So, I decided to come straight here.'

'He *was* actually a little late,' Vanessa says to Rachel, leaning across the table towards her and conspiratorially pouring a glass of wine. 'If not as late as my husband.'

'Well, he's coming all the way from London. I only had to get here from Canterbury. Are the kids all right? They go down okay?' Tom asks Rachel.

Rachel, taking a gulp of wine, swipes a hand over her forehead and squints at him over the rim of her glass. 'Fine, yes. Marcus is in bed but wanted another story, so I left that to Becky.'

'Becky Beals?' Vanessa asks.

'Yeah. Lisa at the nursery recommended her.'

Vanessa smiles a little tightly. 'We've used her. Now I know why she couldn't babysit for us!'

'Oh, shit, sorry, Ness,' Rachel says. She has only recently started calling Vanessa 'Ness', and it still feels strange and slightly forced in her mouth, but she knew she had to as soon as Vanessa started shortening her own name to 'Rach'. So, now they are 'Ness' and 'Rach', even though neither woman enjoys the diminution of her name.

'Oh, it's fine, don't worry about it. We should've thought ahead and joined forces! Had her look after them all at ours.'

93

'Next time,' Rachel says.

Tom's eyes widen as the door to the restaurant opens and Justin walks in. 'Sounds like a lot of work for poor Becky.'

'We'd pay her extra.' Vanessa pouts. 'Loads extra.'

'We'd pay who loads extra?' Justin says, joining them at the table while unwinding his scarf and smiling down at them. Rachel is sure she sees something approximating mild alarm in his usually bright, welcoming eyes.

'Becky Beals,' Vanessa says smoothly.

Justin smiles but it's clear he doesn't recognize the name of the woman who has regularly taken care of his children. Sitting down, he sighs heavily and reaches for the wine bottle. 'God, the train was a nightmare tonight. I had to stand half the way here. I'm fucking exhausted.'

He knocks back three-quarters of his glass in one, and Rachel looks at Vanessa, who meets her eye, imperceptibly shaking her head.

'Well,' Vanessa says then, punctuating the word with a short, sharp clap of her hands, 'we're not just here to commiserate over long commutes and unavailable babysitters. We're celebrating.'

'We are?' Tom says.

'We signed on the lease for The Lowe Down yesterday. We're officially in business!'

'We?' Rachel asks.

'Justin and I! Isn't this exciting? I can't wait to start planning everything with you, Rach. There's just so much to do, and I know you're going to be the biggest help.'

Rachel swallows, and stares at her friend. Turning to Tom, she sees her husband reaching for the champagne that the waitress has miraculously brought over. Popping the cork, he grins at Rachel, and then at their two new friends.

'Well! Congratulations to the mighty Lowes! A force to be reckoned with.'

He pours Vanessa and Justin's glasses first, letting them clink in celebration before pouring for himself and his wife. Rachel takes the glass from him and smiles at the faces around the table. She feels desperately hungry and also as though she might cry. The tears are there, at the back of her eyes, scratching and insistent, but they're not tears of happiness or celebration. She can't figure out why. But then she looks into the shining eyes of her new friend, who seems delighted to be working with her, and she pushes them away, clinking her glass with Vanessa's, taking a sip of the dry, heady drink. 'To The Lowe Down!' she says, then sips again and listens to Vanessa and Tom chat about the new venture. Tom is asking considered, interested questions, as he always does in social situations, and Vanessa is answering animatedly, as she always does in any situation.

At one point, Tom says something that makes her laugh and she reaches for his upper arm as she throws back her head, that mane of auburn hair billowing as though a strong wind had just blown through the restaurant.

Looking at her menu, which she has ignored until now, Rachel realizes that Justin, who is also examining the menu, hasn't said a word since Vanessa's announcement. Not even 'Congratulations' or 'Thank you'.

She catches his eye as he smiles indulgently at her. 'I'm going for the sea bass, I think. What about you?'

Rachel has still barely looked at the menu, but she smiles back, which makes her feel as though they're in cahoots. 'Oh, I love sea bass.'

'It comes with samphire and caper butter,' Justin says, with a raised eyebrow, as though he's testing her.

'Even better.'

Justin laughs, leaning back in his chair, finally a little relaxed as he and Rachel take in their spouses on the other side of the table in a shared moment of understanding.

## 13

I open the door to the cabin and shut it gratefully behind me, relishing the comfortable warmth. All I want to do is run myself a bath and crawl into bed. It feels like a month, rather than merely a day, since Adam woke me this morning. But then I think about Matthew and any comfort feels wrong.

Instead I collapse onto the sofa, turning on the TV in time to catch the BBC local news. As I sit there, my eyes grow heavy, and a dull, persistent ache starts up at the back of my head. I'm practically asleep when Vanessa's face fills the screen.

Her makeup is perfectly done, her eyes watery. I can't help marvelling at how good her hair looks, and how well the colour of her emerald-green jumper sets it off. She is talking straight to camera, sitting behind a table with Justin next to her.

'Matthew is a fun-loving, sweet-natured, beautifully behaved little boy who has never once given us any reason to be anything but extremely proud of him. My husband, our other children, JJ and Emma, and I all love Matthew deeply and cannot wait to welcome him home. Matthew, if you're listening to this, we can't wait to watch *Dumbo* with you again, sweetheart . . . Even JJ says you can watch it however many times you want once you're home.' Tears track down Vanessa's face, and she sniffs, reaching for a tissue Justin has proffered and blowing her nose. 'Sorry,' she whispers, voice trembling. She takes a deep breath, continues: 'We don't know yet what has happened to our beautiful boy, but we're asking everyone to look out for him. He is three years old, with curly auburn hair, green eyes and a very small scar on his forehead, right by the hairline, that he got by tripping over on our gravel driveway last summer. We believe he may have been taken from our home last night, and when we last saw him, he was wearing green-and-blue-striped footsie pyjamas. There's no other clothing missing from his room, and we're very worried about how cold he must be without any shoes or a coat. Please, if anyone has taken him, please, please, bring him back to us. Just let him go. We cannot imagine life without our dear little boy, and I cannot imagine anything worse than never seeing him again.'

After Vanessa finishes, the camera switches attention to another woman sitting on the other side of Justin. It's DCI Varma.

'We believe Matthew Lowe went missing from his home between the hours of midnight, when his parents went to sleep last night, and seven thirty this morning, when Vanessa Lowe first realized her son wasn't in his bed. There was no sign of forced entry at the house, but the back door was unlocked and partially opened, indicating that Matthew may have exited via this point. Because he didn't make a sound in the night, we are assuming he left the house alone, or that he was led from his home by someone who may be known to him in some way.'

I turn the TV off once Varma finishes her debrief.

*Led from his home.*

The words ring in my ears. I can't help thinking of Varma's final question before I was taken to be fingerprinted. Has Matthew really been kidnapped? And could it be possible that Varma thinks it was me? The idea shudders through me, setting off alarm bells, pinging fear through my body.

But Vanessa's plea is still in my mind, which makes me think of her Instagram Stories. I pick up my phone and open Instagram for the first time in weeks. I head straight to Vanessa's profile, ignoring all the notifications waiting for me.

The multicoloured ring encircling Vanessa's profile picture indicates that she's been on Instagram Stories in the last twenty-four hours, and there, in the top left of her grid, is a photo of Matthew. I click on it, feeling nervous for some reason. It makes sense for Vanessa to use the power of her online platform to find her son, of course, but I'm also filled with a powerful sense of unease. Would I be able to stop and update my Instagram if my son was missing?

Matthew fills my phone screen. The photo seems to have been taken a month or two ago, when it was still autumn. He's standing in a pile of fallen leaves, reds, browns and golds covering the sunshine yellow of his wellies. He's grinning at the camera, well used to his mother taking photos of him, his happiness spooling out of him, practically palpable even through a phone screen.

I scroll through Vanessa's photos, trying to work out how many there are of Matthew, but eventually I lose count. Staring into his photogenic face, a shiver runs through me as I think of all the followers Vanessa has, and how many people there are in the world who know exactly who Matthew is, what he looks like and where he lives. Looking back to her older posts, it's clear how much her following has grown. Before she moved out of London, Vanessa's follower count was significant, but not notable. One of many influencers trying to distinguish themselves in a sea of similarly styled women. But ever since the move to Whitstable, her likes and followers had increased until she was one of the most popular influencers in the UK. I can't help but notice that this increase in activity also coincides with Matthew's visibility on his mum's page. First as a baby, then as the toddler he is today. Prior to the move and Matthew's birth, Vanessa was much more focused on lifestyle images, and styling tips. Even though JJ and Emma would've been around, Vanessa didn't feature them nearly as much in their younger years as she has done with Matthew.

I stop scrolling at a photo of him, wide smiles against a blurry background of one of the local beaches. Looking at the caption, I see it's an ad for a kid-friendly sunscreen. It's far from the only photo of Matthew in Whitstable. Vanessa's address isn't publicly available, but it wouldn't be hard to figure out which town she and her family live in – all her photos of the store are geotagged, and Whitstable is pretty recognizable, as British seaside towns go.

Anyone following Vanessa could be doing so for much more nefarious reasons than interior-design inspiration and parenting insights. Going back to the latest photo of Matthew, in which Vanessa calls on her followers to help find him, I discover I'm not the only one of her followers to have this thought.

*Did anyone else immediately think of that psycho who burned down her house when they saw this?* reads one comment.

In reply to it, another says: *Definitely. This has Rachel Donovan written all over it. Is she still on Instagram? I think she blocked me.*

Another comment says: *Wow, Vanessa really attracts the creeps, doesn't she? So sorry this has happened to you, Ness! Stay strong and hang in there . . . The whole country will be out looking for Matthew.*

Rachel Donovan. The arsonist assistant Vanessa told me about when she was here a few days ago. She isn't tagged in the comment, so I search for her name, knowing full well how unlikely it is that I'll be able to find the right Rachel Donovan in the glut of Instagram search results. There are too many results to count, but nothing much to tell one from another, so instead I head back to Vanessa's profile and scroll down to around the time she said Rachel Donovan had been harassing and following her. I know I'm on the right track when I spot a photo of a smoke-filled, fire-destroyed kitchen. It's from August and it's a much more real candid shot than she usually posts. The comment below the photo reads:

thelowedown
**992K f**ollowers

**Vanessa Lowe**

Wife * Mother * Lover

Liked by **singwhenyourwinning** and **others**

**thelowedown** No pretty flowers, gorgeous kids, or perfectly styled flatlay today folks. I took this photo with my hand shaking, tears in my eyes. All my hard work, hours poring over kitchen designs, picking out the perfect handles, choosing the most photogenic colourway, all for nothing. But we're all right and we have insurance so, really, where's the hurt, you're probably asking? Well, here's the hurt: I'm pretty sure this was done on purpose. Those of you who've been following for a while and actually bother to read my long (some might say too-long) captions, and watch all my Insta stories will know that I've been battling a very particular demon recently: the green-eyed monster. And, no, not my jealousy, but the unfortunate jealousy of another woman, who is clearly not only worryingly interested and invested in my life, but also mentally unstable and in need of help (I say this with as much love and understanding as I can muster because, hey, we all need help, right, but also . . . MY FUCKING KITCHEN BURNED DOWN). I'm not naming names here, because this is a public platform and I don't want to be sued for libel on top of everything, but just know this: I know who you are, I know what you've done, I know where you live and, believe me, the proper authorities have already been contacted. Hold your littles and your loves close today, dear friends. If walking into my kitchen this afternoon has taught me anything, it's that everything can be taken from you in one hot minute.

4 months ago

There are thousands upon thousands of comments below the caption. Far too many to attempt to read them. So, instead I head backwards in time even further, looking through all those posts and photos, captions and comments from when Rachel Donovan was Vanessa's assistant – from when, in fact, they were friends. Eventually I find a photo with someone called @theotherraydonovan tagged in it and, assuming this is her, follow through to her profile.

And there I find photo after photo of the two of them together, smiling at the camera, Vanessa sleek and unruffled, smile warm and welcoming, and Rachel's face pressed up against hers, smile just as wide, if not wider. Under the first of them together Rachel has written:

*Guess who I met at the nursery gates today?? Only @thelowedown! Turns out our kids are in the same class . . . I've followed Vanessa for years now, and it was such a strange thrill to recognize her when I went to pick Sadie up today. I immediately introduced myself and she couldn't have been friendlier . . . Moving here from London – where I've lived my whole life – it's so nice to know that I've already got links here in a new town! We all know how hard it can be to make friends as an adult, but the mum bond is a strong one, and it turns out Instagram followers can sometimes even turn into IRL friends!*

Looking at Rachel's feed, I realize she's something of an influencer herself. She doesn't have as many followers as Vanessa, but even before Rachel moved here and met Vanessa, she was getting hundreds of likes on most of her posts. She's a social-media marketer, so I guess that shouldn't come as too much of a surprise: she knows how to market herself online. Although, if I'm honest, her presence has more of an authentic air than Vanessa's: fewer flatlays and more in-the-moment shots. I pore over each post, trying to find the obsession behind each one, trying to find the stalker, the harasser, the woman who set fire to another woman's kitchen renovation. I can't see it, but we're all so good at hiding our real selves online now that I'm not surprised. She must be there somewhere, though, the green-eyed monster lurking behind the Instagram filter.

But did she take Matthew? That's the real question, the reason I'm here, scrolling through her feed.

She stopped posting anything around the same time as Vanessa's kitchen fire. Then there's a huge gap. The most recent one is a classic Instagram shot: a red coffee cup, intricate latte art, stripped-back wooden tabletop, and the corner of a paperback just in shot. And then the caption:

*And breathe. It's been months since I last posted anything, and if I'm honest it's been good to look at life without looking through a lens for a while. But I'm back! Instagram is my favourite social-media platform by far, and instead of the constant comparison game I used to play, I'm going to reclaim myself as the Independent Woman I know I am, take charge of my own life, steer my own ship, grab the bull by the horns, carpe diem and just about every other cliché you can imagine, and go right ahead and enjoy myself. But first, coffee.*

I read the caption over and over again. It should be so innocuous. Especially underneath that photo – a version of which I've seen every day since I first started using Instagram. But something about it snags and pulls at me, tells me to watch out, be careful. And then I click through to the page of the coffee shop the photo is geotagged in. It's just half an hour away in Margate.

And then I look at the date when it was posted: just two days before Matthew was taken.

# 14

There's a knock on the door less than an hour later and I look through the windows, half expecting to see a police officer. But it's Adam again.

'Hi,' I say, ushering him inside out of the heavy rain that has been falling since I arrived back at the cabin.

'Hi, sorry to just drop by again. I was going to call but then I realized I don't have your number. Ness wanted me to check up on you. Make sure you're okay.'

'Vanessa asked you to check up on *me*?' I say, sitting down on the sofa with a heavy thump. 'Shouldn't it be the other way round? She must be going through hell right now, and she's still thinking about me?'

'Vanessa thinks of everything,' Adam says, and something makes me glance at him. But his voice is light, his face clear, albeit exceptionally tired. I offer him wine and, despite his claim when I first met him that he wasn't much of a drinker, he nods mutely. He's joined me on the sofa, sinking into it, leaning back his head and closing his eyes as I wander into the kitchen and pour us both a glass.

'It's absolute pandemonium over there at the moment,' he says, when I hand him a glass, answering a question I hadn't yet asked but was on the tip of my tongue.

'They really reckon someone took him?' I'm thinking of DCI Varma's words on the TV earlier.

Adam nods. 'I think so. It's . . . To be honest, it's what I was scared of. Matthew just isn't the type of kid to wander off on his own. He's a mama's boy, through and through.'

'He's three,' I point out. 'Aren't they all mama's boys at that age?'

Adam shrugs. 'Yeah, you're probably right, but that's even more of a point. Kids who run away, they're normally like eleven at least, right? It's teenagers who do the run-away thing. When did you last hear of a toddler running away from its parents? Going missing in a supermarket, sure, getting left behind on a bus, maybe. But getting out of its own bed and disappearing from home? It's like something in a Stephen King novel, not real life.'

'What does Vanessa think?' I ask.

There's a pocket of silence, the only sound the hiss and pop of the wood-burner. 'She's . . . she's a bit fixated on this woman, Rachel . . .'

'Rachel Donovan?'

'Yeah. What was she? An Instagram follower?'

'They were friends first, I think. They worked together.' I pick up my phone and show Adam the photo on Rachel's Instagram that I was just looking at.

He stares down at it, saying nothing until the screen goes dark. Then he lets out a loud, disgruntled sigh. 'I don't get it. Any of this. Instagram . . . followers, influencers. The whole thing. What is it you think we're looking at here?'

'I don't know,' I say, taking back the phone. 'It could be nothing. It's just a photo of a coffee, after all. But this is also a woman who apparently harassed your step-sister to the point where she burned her kitchen down.'

Adam says nothing. He's staring straight into the fire, the flames licking at the smoky window, orange and red, the occasional flicker of blue.

'I can't imagine what Vanessa's going through right now,' I say, into the silence. 'Just getting through that press conference . . .'

'Yeah. She's good at putting a mask on for the world,' Adam says. 'She's been doing it for most of her life.' I don't reply, and eventually Adam turns his head to me. 'I just realized that could sound pretty bad. I'm not saying Ness isn't genuine, just that she's always worked to be viewed in a certain way. It boils down to her relationship with her mum, which – if you ask me – is totally fucked.'

'How?'

There's a pause while Adam sips his wine, staring into the fire still, and I can tell that he's trying to figure out where – how – to begin. 'It's hard for me to give a fair representation of Janet. I spent a lot of my childhood watching her terrorize Vanessa.'

'Terrorize?' I say, sitting up a little straighter. Adam hasn't moved from his slouched position on the sofa, but this is a big word, a heavy accusation.

'Yeah,' he says softly. 'They've moved on from it somehow but . . . it's not something I can forget.'

'What do you mean by "terrorize", Adam?'

He leans his head to the side, still staring into the jumping flames of the wood-burner. But then he snaps to attention, his eyes on me. 'Ness never talks about this stuff. Never. I'm not sure I should either.'

'Okay,' I say slowly, but I'm disappointed.

'Janet was volatile . . . Actually, that's not fair. Both our parents were. You know some people just bring out the worst in one another and confuse it for passion? That was them. But Janet. She's brittle. Hard work. She takes a lot of management, like you're constantly walking on eggshells, or trying to make sure you don't accidentally hit some kind of nuclear-reactor button. That was Ness and me growing up. Constantly trying to make sure we didn't say or do the wrong thing.'

'But isn't she looking after JJ and Emma at the moment?' I ask.

Adam nods. 'Ness claims she's changed, but I don't know. I still get this feeling when I'm around her . . . I don't know how to describe it.'

'Must have made for some awkward Christmases.'

Adam lets out a half-hearted laugh. 'How did your interview with the police go earlier?'

'Fine,' I say slowly. I don't know whether to mention Varma's final question, that it's had me worrying, wandering in circles this evening.

'She's good, I think. Varma, I mean,' Adam says.

'Yes,' I say.

'Sharp. She's a specialist, apparently, in missing-children cases. So, if anyone's going to find Matthew, it's her,' he says, adding, a little belatedly, 'hopefully.'

## Twelve Months Ago

It's December before Vanessa invites Rachel to see The Lowe Down. She had expected an invitation sooner – it's two weeks since Vanessa told her and Tom that she'd signed the lease for the shop.

But Vanessa has been curiously enigmatic over the past couple of weeks, still sending profuse and prolific WhatsApp messages every day, and still updating her Instagram in a kind of promotional fervour, but Rachel has seen her face to face only outside the nursery and school gates. She has grown used to their coffee dates and shared meals, has grown used to their friendship, in fact, so this pause has felt noticeable. She's missed her. Without Vanessa, Rachel doesn't have much of a social circle, or a social life. She's met some other wild swimmers, has shared warming teas with them on particularly cold mornings, like today's, but so far, she hasn't met anyone else who feels like a friend, rather than an acquaintance or a neighbour.

Rachel is carrying two coffees now, holding them tightly in her gloved hands as she taps at the glass of the front door. Vanessa whips around at the sound, uncharacteristically frowning, before the frown is wiped away with relief and she unlocks the door to let Rachel in.

'Oh, thank God. Coffee. You're a star, Rachel. A whole constellation of them.'

Rachel laughs. 'It's a flat white, Ness, not a winning lottery ticket.'

Vanessa turns to her with wide, panicked eyes. 'It's flooded, Rach. The entire back half of the building is just letting in water.'

'Oh, fuck. How the hell did that happen? Didn't you have a building inspection before signing the lease?'

'Of course we did,' Vanessa snaps, then puts out her hand to pat Rachel's arm. 'Sorry. It's just been a tough couple of weeks.'

'What's been going on?' Rachel asks, as mildly as possible, looking around the empty shop, searching for something to sit on to no avail.

Vanessa takes a deep breath and, looking up at the ceiling as if searching for answers there, says, 'It's JJ. We were called into his school because he apparently got into a fight with another boy, and JJ . . . I mean, I can barely believe it, but he left this scratch down the other boy's face. If you saw it, you'd think a wildcat had done it.'

Vanessa squeezes her eyes shut as if she's trying to hold back tears, and finally looks directly at her friend. Her face is wan, washed-out, except for the redness around her eyes that makes Rachel think she might have been crying before she arrived. 'Oh, Ness,' she says, holding out her arms to hug her friend, who collapses gratefully into them.

'And you wouldn't believe how unsupportive Justin is being . . . I've barely seen him since we got called into the headmaster's office, and he's been no help whatsoever with the shop. I know he loves his work, and his commute is horrendous, but I feel . . . so alone, Rach.'

Vanessa says all this with her face buried in her much shorter friend's shoulder, her voice muffled and quiet, almost childlike. Rachel holds her tightly, letting her relax against her, and says, 'You're not alone, Ness, you know that. You've got so many people who would be happy to help you out. Take me, for example. What can I do? We're in this together, remember? So, put me to work! Give me a spreadsheet, a to-do list, and I'm in my happy place.'

Vanessa extricates herself from Rachel's arms and wipes her face with a tissue she has drawn from her coat pocket. She swallows, gaining control of herself, trying to find her usual voice, her usual strength. 'You're right. I know you're right. It's just so hard for me to ask for help. Oh, God, I sound like such a cliché. I hate being a cliché!'

Rachel laughs, glad her friend is looking and sounding more herself. 'Shall we get out of here?' Vanessa continues. 'I know it's not even lunchtime yet, but can we go and get a drink or something?'

'Of course we bloody can,' Rachel says. 'We can get drunk and make plans, and put the world to rights, all before nursery pick-up.'

They go to the Mermaid Inn, which has been beautifully renovated by friends of Vanessa, although neither of the proprietors appear as they sit with their midday drinks and Vanessa tells Rachel about JJ's fight at school.

'I can't get a word out of him about why he did it. That's the most disturbing thing. He's never been violent . . . Difficult and, I suppose, taciturn is the right word, but never anything like this. Although he does play all those awful video games. Do you think it could be that? Am I a bad mother for letting him play them at such a young age?'

'You're a normal mother, Ness. Most twelve-year-olds spend most of their time online, these days.'

'But what about those games? How can we be sure we're not raising an army of bloodthirsty teenage boys?' Vanessa says.

Rachel laughs, short and staccato in the warm, enveloping fug of the pub.

'You think I'm being stupid and high-strung,' Vanessa says, reaching for her drink. Both she and Rachel had ordered French 75s – Rachel's favourite cocktail, which is far too decadent for a weekday afternoon, in Rachel's view, but which Vanessa cooed over when they arrived.

'No, of course I don't. I guess we just don't know how growing up with all this stuff is going to affect children of this generation. We just have to be accepting of it, and steer them away from harm wherever possible.'

'That's very philosophical.'

'Maybe. Ever since the fifties there's been some new thing that's got parents worked up about their children, and how they're going to turn out, and for the most part, they've all been fine.'

Vanessa sighs and leans back in her seat, fiddling with the stem of her cocktail glass. 'I suppose you're right. I just wonder how many of them left a scratch the length of a ruler along another boy's cheek.'

Later, Rachel is lying in bed scrolling through Instagram. Vanessa had taken great pains to get the perfect shot of her French 75 earlier, raving about how much her followers would love to discover her new favourite cocktail, but it hasn't made an appearance on her grid or in her Stories yet. Instead, she has posted a video of Matthew running down the beach towards her with the caption *Love winter beach days with my beautiful boy.*

Rachel watches the video several times. She doesn't know why – she was there, after all, just out of shot. But watching it over and over again, she feels a pit of nausea open somewhere in her abdomen. She glances at Tom, who has already fallen asleep, his face serene against the pillow, and turns back to her phone, watching the video again. Matthew's hair waves in the wind, the angry December sea crashes in the background. The child's jubilant cries are barely audible over the crash of waves. Why does it bother her that this video was shot two weeks ago? Why does she care that Vanessa makes no mention of how rough her day was in the caption? Rachel knows as well as anyone that what we put online is only about five per cent of the real picture.

So why does she feel like she's watching a lie being told in real time?

# 15

Panic lines the streets as I walk through town the next day. I woke up with a pounding headache just a few hours after having fallen asleep, words like 'missing', 'abducted' and 'kidnapped' beating at my subconscious and shouting me awake.

They fill my brain as I walk along the street now.

Missing.

Abducted.

Kidnapped.

These words, the fact that I'm on my way to help search for a missing little boy, walking along the streets of a panicked town, are completely at odds with the season. It's Christmas, or nearly Christmas, and everywhere I look are reminders of the festive feeling that normally defines this time of year. The lamp-posts are decorated with fir trees and snowflakes that light up at night; the store fronts glitter with snow scenes and nativities; round wreaths hide the door knockers of quaint cottages. My heart squeezes in my chest as I think of Matthew lost in all this, of the Christmas morning Vanessa, and Justin, and Emma, and JJ will soon wake up to.

We're going to do another search, but this time, instead of looking for Matthew, we're looking for something – *anything* – that might lead us to him. A sock, a shoe, a piece of torn fabric.

Vanessa and Justin's house has been dusted for prints, searched for DNA, but apparently they're not confident of finding anything. These days, everyone knows to wear gloves. So, we'll be on the lookout for dropped gloves too.

We're meeting in front of Vanessa's shop, and while I stand there in the drip, drip, drip of the persistent rain, I can't help thinking about security. Cameras. Surveillance. Floodlights that come on the moment any movement is detected. Vanessa and Justin's house is a recently renovated ode to twenty-first-century modernity: it's hard to believe that they didn't put in private security cameras when they installed the at-home cinema and remote-controlled window blinds.

As I'm thinking this, I feel someone sidle up next to me. Adam looks as tired as I do. He smiles as I catch his eye, but I can't smile back.

Just then someone steps out of the shop to address the gathered crowd. It takes me a second to realize it's Vanessa. Her hair is covered with a pale pink woolly hat, and she's bundled up in a silver Moncler coat. It's not really cold enough for such an Arctic style: despite the rain, the air is strangely warm for December, and I can't help thinking that the silver of the jacket feels out of place, anachronistic. Maybe she just wanted to be visible for the gathered crowd, a metallic beacon for her lost little boy.

'Thank you so much for coming out, everyone, even in this weather.' She takes a deep breath, the sound of it shivering and echoing down the microphone. When she starts speaking again there's a tremble, a quiver, as if she's holding back tears. 'Matthew actually loves the rain. He loves wearing his wellies, and his beautiful bright yellow raincoat, so this feels appropriate in some ways. Please remember to be on the lookout for any scrap of material that might be from the clothes he was wearing on the night he was taken. Blue-and-green-striped pyjamas . . .' she takes a deep breath '. . . and we now believe he was also wearing his navy-blue wool duffel coat . . .' Vanessa's words fail her, and her face crumples, tears dripping from her eyes, as Justin comes forward to put his arm around his wife's shoulders and draw her backwards.

Taking over, a man I've not seen before steps in, nodding at Vanessa and Justin. He coughs once, stares out at the crowd and begins to speak in one run-on sentence. 'I'm Mark Simmons, a specialist in leading searches for missing children. I'm glad to see you haven't been put off by the weather today. We're at a crucial juncture in our search for Matthew, and your help could make all the difference . . .'

Mark continues to talk, explaining exactly how the search will be undertaken, and what we should do if we find anything, but before he can wrap up his speech, there's a yelp from Vanessa. Pulling herself free of Justin's hold, she takes two tentative steps towards the gathered crowd and lets out a bloodcurdling scream. She's pointing to the edge of the group, her gaze laser sharp, her voice loud, clear, and as cutting as razor wire. 'It's her! It's her! She's here!' She turns towards Mark Simmons and the other police officers. 'What are you waiting for? Go and get her!' She rushes into Justin's arms, beating at his chest and shouting back into the crowd, 'It's her! She took my baby!'

## Twelve Months Ago

It is a freezing Saturday when Rachel, Tom and the kids next visit the Lowes for a late lunch to celebrate an early Christmas together. The fog is thick and freezing, the sea invisible beyond the impenetrable wall of weather.

Vanessa has decorated the house beautifully, of course: a hand-embroidered tablecloth from Italy on the table fascinates Sadie with its snowflakes, rocking horses and tiny houses. Candles are placed everywhere: tall and proud in vintage brass candleholders, low and stocky in cute glass tea-light holders. Tom mutters something about fire safety as they walk in, catching Rachel's eye in a way that makes them share a laugh for the first time in ages.

'Ness, it looks like you're ready for a magazine feature in here,' Tom says, as they sit down. He has started calling her Ness too. Rachel tries to remember the first time she noticed it and can't. She hasn't figured out what Tom makes of Vanessa at all, really. When they're with the Lowes, she can tell he has a crush: the effusive comments, the teasing, the unnecessary – but chaste – touches.

But when it's just the two of them – Rachel and Tom – his comments and remarks about Vanessa are teasing to the point of disparagement. Rachel is disappointed that her husband can have a crush on someone, find them attractive, yet have little or no respect for them. Somehow, it all rolls together to make Rachel feel sorry for Vanessa, of all people. Because she can see that Vanessa encourages Tom's crush, that she enjoys the position this puts her in, over Tom, over Rachel, over Justin even. That she likes this power play and is probably very used to playing with it.

But she doesn't hear Tom when he's making fun of her, and that makes Rachel sad. She sighs now, unfolding her beautiful gingham napkin, and feels Justin turn to her.

'Wine, Rach?'

'Please.'

Justin pours a comically large amount into the elegant red wine glass, filling it almost to the top, whispering, 'Just say when,' and making her laugh.

She reaches for his arm. 'Stop! Stop – that's way too much!'

'Oh, you know you're going to drink it all,' Justin demurs, winking at her as he pours himself the same amount. Rachel laughs again, leaning back in her chair, finally able to relax. One of the best things about lunches, dinners and drinks at the Lowes' is that she never has to worry about the kids. They all get on so well together, and the Lowes' house is designed to hide and entertain children so that the parents can pretend it's just the four of them. There is laughter and chat, sometimes cries and screams from the children, of course, but it feels enveloped and cosseted in this house. Their childish energy is absorbed perfectly into its walls, and even when one or two career into the dining room or living room or wherever the adults are sitting, it's an amusing distraction, rather than an annoyance. Even now, Rachel can see them all playing in the living room, JJ enlisting Emma's help to build the younger children a cushion fort. Matthew is screaming in delight as his older brother tackles and tickles him.

Watching this, how playful yet gentle JJ is with his younger brother, Rachel can't imagine him hurting anyone, let alone getting into a fight. 'How's JJ getting on?' Rachel asks Justin now, as she reaches carefully for her very full wine glass.

'JJ?' Justin says, looking at the children playing beyond the glass doors of the living room. 'He's fine, I think.'

'So, he's got over the fight?'

'The fight?' Justin says mildly.

'Didn't you get called into the school a couple of weeks ago because he'd got into a fight with someone?'

'Oh, yes. God. Sorry, my brain's been all over the place recently. That bloody fight.'

'Do you know how it started yet? What made him do it? He just doesn't seem the type to me. Look how carefully he's playing with the younger ones now.'

Justin tips his head to the side, watching their children. 'It was out of character, you're right, but JJ is . . . a little more complicated than you might at first think. He's so gentle and loving with Emma and especially Matthew, but he can be moody and even angry at times.'

'Of course. But you're not worried about it?'

'I am worried about it, of course I am. I don't want my son growing up thinking that violence is a solution for . . . anything. But he's explained what happened, he's been given a month of detention and he's grounded until further notice. So. What else can we do?'

'Oh, so he did explain what happened?' Rachel says, reaching now for a chicory leaf and dipping it into some of Vanessa's homemade beetroot hummus. 'Ness said he wouldn't say a word about it.'

Justin blinks at her, then glances at his wife, who is deep in conversation with Tom. 'No, he said the other boy had said something ... crude about her. About Vanessa. About her Instagram et cetera. It was that one about shaving her legs. Do you remember?'

'Oh,' Rachel says, as she reflexively looks at Vanessa, reassessing, wondering. 'She didn't tell me that.'

'No,' Justin says quietly. 'Maybe she was embarrassed.'

It's impossible for Rachel to imagine Vanessa embarrassed by anything. She's too in control, too smooth and unruffled. But she can easily imagine Vanessa cropping and framing something to make it more palatable. Buffing blemishes and rounding harsh edges, shoving unsightly flaws into her shadowy corners. Making it all a little more manageable and presentable. That, she can easily imagine.

## 16

It's Rachel Donovan.

The crowd gathers around her, closing ranks.

I can't catch full sight of her through them but I think I recognize her. She's shocked to find herself the centre of attention, and I have to wonder why: surely she must have known the danger of coming here. How it would look.

Adam shakes his head. 'I can't believe she fucking showed up here. She must be insane.'

'You really think she'd come if she took him?' I ask.

'They say that's what they do, don't they?' Adam says.

'Who?'

'Murderers, kidnappers . . . They insert themselves into the investigation, get close to the family, join search parties.' His gaze moves from Rachel Donovan to me. 'You must've heard about that before?'

'I guess so,' I say.

'Ness is convinced it's her. I was over there this morning and she wouldn't talk about anything else.'

'Did Rachel pay particular attention to Matthew when she was living here?' I ask.

'Don't know. Like I said, I wasn't here when all the Rachel stuff went down.'

She's shorter than I expected – she can't be much more than five foot five. She's also one of the only black people here, and I can't help feeling uncomfortable at the way the largely white crowd has mobbed her at Vanessa's behest. I watch as she cringes away from an older man who is reaching towards her and wriggles her way out of the crowd. Once free, she sprints down the street, without a backward glance.

She doesn't look like a kidnapper. A stalker. But, according to Vanessa, that's exactly what she is. I think back to her last Instagram photo, the one that could be a post of just about anything yet seemed to signal a change, a shift, in her attitude. She was going to 'carpe diem', as she said. Grab the bull by the horns. But could she really have been referring to kidnap? The idea seems absurd. Preposterous. But I never could have guessed when I arrived at the Getaway that a week later I'd be taking part in the search for a small child. I would have told you the idea was absurd. And the fact is: someone has to have taken him. He didn't wander off on his own.

And if someone took him, who's to say it wasn't Rachel Donovan?

'Come on,' Adam says, bringing me out of my reverie. 'Ness looks like she could do with a little help.'

I follow Adam to where Vanessa and Justin are still huddled together, held back from following Rachel by DCI Varma.

'We've already interviewed her, Mrs Lowe, and she has an alibi,' I hear Varma say, as we approach.

'Yeah, her husband,' Vanessa spits, from within the arms of her own husband. 'You really think he wouldn't lie for her?'

Varma takes a step towards Vanessa, placing a hand on

her arm. 'Isn't there a chance Rachel was just here to lend a hand, show support, like everybody else?'

'I've told you what she did to me,' Vanessa says slowly, every word a bullet cracking through the air.

'Allegedly,' Varma says, and I watch Vanessa's face take on a life of its own: consternation, horror and, finally, indignation flitting across it. She doesn't say anything to Varma, disgust apparently stopping her. Instead, she seems to notice that Adam and I have appeared, and Adam steps forward, whispering something inaudible in her ear. She narrows her eyes and flicks her gaze to me, then says something to Adam I can't hear.

Before I know it, he's turning me away, a hand on my back, ushering me through the crowd.

'What was that about?' I ask him.

'Don't worry about it right now,' he says. 'Let's just join the search. It's the best way for us to help. For now.'

We're divided into groups, assigned an official investigator to follow, and the search begins. The rain continues to fall, turning cold as the day wanes. The search lasts hours, yields nothing. Matthew seems to have disappeared so completely it's as if he never existed. The only thing to indicate that he did is the posters of his face that have been pasted to telegraph poles and streetlamps, joining all those Christmas decorations. They've been stuck on noticeboards, and put up in the window of every shop, restaurant, café and pub that lines the town's high street. It is a stark contrast: the cheerful red, green and gold of the season next to the photo of a missing child. He should be here, staring into the windows of beautifully decorated shops, tugging at his mum's arm, planning his list for

Father Christmas, trying his first mince pie. Instead, we search in the rain, looking for any scrap that might lead us to him.

And then there are the camera crews, reporters, photographers, filling the Christmas-bedecked cafés, restaurants and pubs. Their bulky vans can be seen every few metres, spiky aerials and TV dishes adorning their roofs. I slow down as I drive past them on the way out of town. As I was leaving I saw Vanessa talking to one of the many female TV reporters. The cameras weren't rolling but I doubt it'll be long before they are. There's something about all this that feels familiar. As if I've read it in a book somewhere, seen it on film, watched it all in real time on the BBC news. It's made for TV, for the movies, for tabloid splashes, and Reddit threads: a beautiful mother with an army of adoring followers and fans, her equally handsome husband, and their endearing child suddenly gone.

But as I'm thinking this, a woman rushes into the middle of the road, chased by another woman holding a microphone, and several men carrying cameras. I screech my car to a stop, braking so suddenly my stomach clenches against the pull of my seatbelt. It's Rachel. Still being pursued.

# 17

An hour or so later Adam knocks on the door of the cabin. I've just showered, washing away the rain with the power of scalding water.

'Sorry to drop by unannounced again,' Adam says, as he shuts the door behind him. 'Ness asked me to come and talk to you. She has kind of a . . . proposition for you.'

I frown at him. 'A proposition?'

'Yeah. Can we sit down?'

'Sure,' I say, and offer him a glass of red wine. He accepts, and by the time I've retrieved us both a glass, he's settled on the couch, looking like he lives there.

'Ness wants you to befriend Rachel Donovan. Only if you're comfortable with it, though. She was very adamant about that,' Adam says.

The silence in the cabin is heavy, calming. Complete. I'm not used to this kind of quiet: I've only ever lived in cities. First London, then Edinburgh, now LA. It was what I was looking for when I came out here: a silence so complete it could cut out all the noise. But now I want to hear something. Sirens, street sounds, cars, the shouts of kids, the rolling thunder of heavy trucks. The silence is hard to read. Not just hard – impossible. And so is Adam.

He's staring into the flickering flames in the wood-burning stove. Shadows graze his face, giving him a darkness that wasn't there before. 'Callie?' he says, turning to me, catching me watching him. He smiles a little rue-fully. 'I know it's a weird thing to ask. A big thing. You barely know Ness. Or me. Or Matthew. But she's so sure Rachel has something to do with this, and the police don't seem to be taking it seriously.'

'Why?'

'Why what?'

'Why aren't they taking it seriously? I'm no detective, but I think I would be.'

Adam shrugs. 'I imagine it's because she has an alibi for the night in question.'

'The whole night?' I ask. 'Matthew could've been taken at any time that night while Vanessa and Justin were asleep. How can they be so sure she didn't just leave the house while her husband was asleep and get home before he woke up?'

Adam's eyes flash. He grins for a split second, maybe less. 'That's exactly Ness's line of thinking. But there's nothing she can do about it. She's being watched every minute by reporters, police. Even Justin.'

'Justin?'

'He can be a little overprotective,' Adam says shortly. 'But, anyway, Ness was thinking that you could kind of befriend Rachel, try to figure out what she knows, whether she's involved. Sorry, it's a pretty out-there plan.'

I don't say anything for a while. It is an out-there plan. And it's a lot to ask of someone you've only recently met. It makes me wonder just how desperate Vanessa has become that she's stooped to hatching plans and carrying out amateur sleuthing. Or asking near-strangers to carry it out for her. But why shouldn't she be desperate? Her son is missing, and the person she thinks took him isn't being investigated by the police.

When you lose someone, your whole world becomes one of desperation. Small and desperate. When Ada died, mine was whittled down to the size of a pinprick. My life had been about to get exponentially bigger and suddenly there was just me. And I felt even smaller than I had been before, diminished by my loss. It was a selfish kind of grief. There was no room in it for Russell. I had carried her, birthed her, and now she wasn't here so only I could grieve for her. There is no sense in a loss like that, though. At least, that's what I tell myself. I could only react and behave in the way I did. I could only do what I could to get through the days.

And Vanessa is doing what she can.

She is holding on to hope, garnering attention, turning everyone's eyes towards Matthew when he needs it most.

So, really, who am I to judge?

'Callie?' Adam says again, pulling me back to the room.

'Okay,' I say.

'Okay? You'll do it?'

'I'm still not a hundred per cent clear on what "it" is but, yeah, if it helps find Matthew, I'll do it.'

Adam takes a deep breath, lets it out slowly. 'Ness said you'd understand. I don't know what made her so sure, but she seemed to think you'd get it.'

'It's a long story,' I say. I'm holding back the tears, hoping he doesn't ask me to expand.

'We've all got one or two of those,' is all he says.

## Twelve Months Ago

The Lowes throw a huge party for New Year's Eve. They do it every year apparently.

When Rachel and Tom pull up to the house, the street and driveway are already crowded with minicabs and cars, guests being dropped off, tripping on the high-heeled shoes they never normally wear, pulling up the zips of coats against the harsh winter night.

'I feel like we're arriving at a premiere or something. This is ridiculous. Do you think there'll be a red carpet?' Tom says, laughter and disbelief mingling in his voice.

Rachel and Tom have ignored New Year's Eve for the past few years. Young children and late-night parties are known not to mix well. Last year, the last they spent in London, they ended up ordering Domino's, too tired to make anything themselves. Thinking of it now, Rachel regrets it. They had known it would probably be their last New Year in London – they had already started planning the move – but they hadn't made the most of it.

In the years before children, and even when Marcus was very young, they had always been to or thrown parties. Nothing as grand and luminous as a Lowe party, but small dinner parties at which they hadn't sat down for the main course by the time they were popping the cork for midnight, and dessert was served close to two a.m. Nights that ended, inexplicably, at five or six in the morning when you checked, bleary-eyed and drunk, the time on your phone and exclaimed in shock.

And before that, before Tom, before true adulthood or, at least, pretending to be an adult, Rachel could remember long nights out in London, neon and golden, cigarette butts and sticky beer under her feet, a heady beat in the ears, cheesy chips and a crowded night bus home. Those nights, like all the others just like them, feel a million years ago. Rachel looks at the people filing into the Lowes' exquisite home and agrees with Tom: it does look like a premiere, or as close to that as either of them will ever get. It looks exactly as she knows Vanessa will have wanted it to look: elegant, elevated. Elite.

They are met with coupes of champagne served by hired waiters, Tom and Rachel sharing a look as they take their first sips. They weave through the crowd, searching for their hosts. Rachel, who has been there what seems hundreds of times by now and is almost as at home there as she is in their own house, feels out of place and adrift. She recognizes barely anyone. She's not used to feeling uncomfortable here, and she looks back at Tom, who is clearly feeling the same.

'Do you ever just think, *who are these people*?' he whispers to her, as they slink through the living room. Somehow, Rachel knows he is referring to Vanessa and Justin, not the crowd of strangers surging around them.

Threading her fingers through his as she feels someone knock against her, Rachel nods. 'Most of the time they seem so normal, and then they go and do something that reminds me they're like –'

'Super-super rich?' Tom finishes for her, with a laugh. Spotting Vanessa's crown of auburn hair, Tom squeezes his wife's fingers and gestures towards her. 'There's our host. In all her glory.'

Rachel looks up into Tom's face then, but his eyes are glued to Vanessa, who is wearing a bronze silk dress that perfectly complements her famous hair. Rachel knocks back the rest of her champagne, the alcohol shooting straight to her head. She wants to be drunk, but she doesn't want to have to deal with the ramifications of drunkenness, and is suddenly very aware of how many people are present at the party.

Tom has taken the lead, and is pulling her towards Vanessa, who is delighted to see them. She hugs first Rachel, then Tom, noticing that Rachel's glass is already empty and waving down a passing waiter to pour her more. Shepherding them away from the crowd, Vanessa leads them towards the kitchen's French windows, which are open to help with air flow.

'God, I'm so glad to see you two. Sorry this crowd is such a bore. It's mostly work people for Justin, although God knows where he is right now.'

'You looked like you were having fun,' Tom says, referring to the small knot of people Vanessa had been entertaining, and was being entertained by, when they walked up to her.

'Oh, I always *look* like I'm having fun, Thomas,' Vanessa says, raising an eyebrow and laughing. 'Although, actually, that lot *are* quite fun.'

'Well, this is a step up from our celebrations last year,' Tom says, and explains about the Domino's delivery. Vanessa smiles indulgently, but Rachel is 99 per cent certain her friend has never had a Domino's in her life.

'There's food in the dining room, if you're hungry. Oh, and I had this amazing idea – that little fish and chip van, you know the one? Well, they're going to be outside from one o'clock so people can get something when they're going home or just if they're hungry. Isn't that a cute idea?'

'Incredible,' Tom says, just as Rachel says, 'Oh, my God.'

'I know.' Vanessa is clearly delighted with herself. 'Actually, Rach, I'm so glad you're here now. Can you help me with some photos? I want to post some videos and photos to Instagram Stories.'

Rachel nods. Her head already feels heavy with champagne, as though it might pop.

'Great, thank you so much. I tried to persuade Justin to get some shots of me earlier, but he wasn't having any of it,' she says. 'Were the kids all right when you left?'

Rachel smiles. 'Yeah, they were great. So excited for their sleepover. It's Becky I feel bad for.'

'Becky will feel better when she gets her bonus tomorrow morning,' Vanessa says, sipping her champagne.

'Where's JJ, though? I thought you said he might come too. Did he go to a friend's or something?'

'No, he's upstairs. He refused to leave. Nothing against you and your house, of course. I told him you said he could bring his PlayStation, but he refused to leave his lair.'

'Well, it must get a bit boring for him, always hanging out with the younger kids,' Tom offers.

'Oh, he's just being difficult. We appear to have marched right into the thick of the teenage moodiness stage,' Vanessa says, looking around the room at her guests. 'Although I'm starting to wonder if my husband is planning to spend the entire evening in *his* lair. Maybe it just runs in the family.'

Rachel follows Vanessa's gaze, but Justin isn't there. Vanessa hasn't confided in her, but Rachel thinks she's worried about her husband. About his working, his drinking, his commuting, the long hours he spends away from his family and from her. Vanessa has painted a picture for the world, but Justin is refusing to be drawn into it. Rachel wonders what this golden couple was like three years, five years, ten years ago. It is hard to imagine them without the gilding, the trappings of wealth and status, the three beautiful children and the house on the sea. Did they ever live in a one-bedroom flat together? Somewhere with bad water pressure and shared hallways no one ever cleaned? Had they ever been late paying their bills, their rent? Had they once treated themselves with a three-course meal for fifteen pounds from M&S and called it a date night?

Rachel looks at Vanessa now and tries to imagine her sitting on the top deck of a London bus. Tries to imagine her managing the scrum of a commuter train. Tries to imagine her laughing, hot, sweaty and tired, in a sunny beer garden after work on a warm day. She can't see it.

Rachel cannot imagine intersecting with Vanessa and Justin at any point in her life before she'd come to Whitstable. She hasn't thought about it for a while, but that was presumably what had made her follow Vanessa on Instagram. She was aspirational. She is an aspiration. Tom is right: who are these people?

The thought causes her to gulp more champagne, more than she intended, and she ends up spluttering, making Vanessa and Tom laugh.

'Sorry,' she gasps. 'Went down the wrong way,'

Vanessa, still laughing, passes her a napkin. Taking it gratefully, Rachel wipes the side of her mouth and takes a deep breath. She is already feeling too drunk. It's annoying, really: she's had only two glasses, but that's enough, these days, apparently. 'Actually, I think I might just get a bit of fresh air,' she says to Vanessa and Tom, who frowns at her.

'You'll freeze,' he says, looking pointedly at her dress and bare arms.

'Oh, don't worry, there're blankets on the patio,' Vanessa says.

'See?' Rachel says, handing her husband her empty glass. 'She's thought of everything.'

But Rachel doesn't stay on the patio. After grabbing one of the aforementioned blankets, she wraps it around herself and heads down the garden path, towards the beach.

She is not expecting to find Justin there.

'Ssh,' he says, appearing out of the darkness and making her jump and yelp.

'Justin! Shit! I had no idea you were down here. I thought you were inside somewhere.' Squinting at him through the darkness, Rachel realizes he's holding something in his fingers. 'Oh, my God, you're vaping. You *vape*?'

''Fraid so. Please don't tell Ness.'

'She doesn't know?' She wonders why Justin would need to keep it a secret from Vanessa.

'She thinks it's tacky,' he explains.

Of course she does. 'Your secret's safe with me.'

'I thought as much. You have the face of a good secret-keeper. Enigmatic.'

'You think I'm enigmatic?' Rachel laughs. 'I think I'm an open book.'

'Well, maybe I'm reading the wrong page,' Justin says, in such a way that, against every single one of Rachel's better judgements, something rockets through her, a flare going off in the dark.

She is flustered, and what follows is a rich, potent silence, during which she wishes she had brought her drink with her, just for something to do.

'How's it going in there?' Justin says, with an awkward cough.

'Good. Great, I mean. You guys really know how to throw a party.'

'Vanessa does. I've never really considered myself a party person. Never truly happy when there's more than, ooh, seven people in a room.'

Rachel laughs, even though she knows he isn't joking. 'Well, you could've fooled me.'

'I'm pretty good at that, yeah. Isn't that mostly what getting older is? Fooling everyone that you know what you're doing. Fooling everyone that you've got it all together. Fooling everyone you're having a good time.'

'You're not having a good time?'

There is another silence while Justin sucks on his vape

and contemplates the seemingly endless blackness of the beach in front of them and, beyond that, the sea.

'No, no, I don't mean tonight. It's just been a tough few weeks.'

'At work?' Rachel asks, knowing he has been spending more time working recently, according to Vanessa. She is watching him carefully as he turns to her and she waits for his reply.

'At work, yes. That's what I meant.'

'And how's JJ doing?'

Justin sighs heavily, and the sound seems very close to Rachel's ear. She hadn't noticed, but he has moved closer to her, and now they are standing side by side, the rough wool of his coat brushing up against the luxurious mohair of the blanket she picked up off the patio. She can smell the vaguely sickly smell of his vape pen, even though he has stopped smoking it, slipped it into a hidden pocket somewhere.

'JJ is . . . JJ,' Justin says with a dramatic, overly large shrug. 'It's almost like he's two people sometimes,' he says, after another short pause.

'He's a kid,' Rachel says, wishing she could offer up something more profound, more helpful. 'He's always seemed very polite and thoughtful to me.'

'Really?' Justin says, turning to her in the dark.

'Yeah. He seems lovely. It's so hard to believe he'd attack another boy and leave a scratch like that.'

Rachel feels, rather than sees, Justin nod next to her. 'I know. But it's not as if the other boy didn't get a few goes in. We went swimming a couple of days later, and there were these bruises on JJ's arms, as if he'd been grabbed really, really hard. There were practically fingerprints. When I think that that other kid didn't even get punished . . .'

'Vanessa didn't mention that,' Rachel says.

'Vanessa didn't mention what?' says a voice from behind them.

They turn, as if caught, and find Vanessa staring down at them from just beyond the garden gate. She is backlit by the gaudy lights of the partying house, a shadowy figure haloed in bronze.

'We were just talking about JJ, babe,' Justin says, with a sigh.

'I don't want to talk about him right now. We're throwing a party, Justin, in case you'd forgotten. People are asking for you.'

'Sorry, sorry, I know I abandoned you to it.'

'And, Rach, you must be frozen half to death by now,' Vanessa says, her voice cold.

Rachel pushes through the garden gate, smiling at Vanessa, but even through the dark, she can tell that the smile Vanessa returns doesn't quite reach her eyes.

## thelowedown
**750K** followers

**Vanessa Lowe**

Wife * Mother * Lover

Liked by **theotherraydonovan** and **others**

**thelowedown** Who else loves a new year? Me. I love turning over the page of a new diary and seeing all the possibilities a brand-new year brings, but I also love paying my respects and offering thanks for everything the past year has brought me. Because I'm nothing if not grateful, and this past year has been beautiful. And, most importantly, it brought new friends and fresh opportunities into my life. So, thank you to my team – Justin, JJ, Emma and Matthew – for being the best team ever, and thank you to @theotherraydonovan for coming to Whitstable to shake things up! We've got such an exciting year ahead, and I can't wait to share it all with you, my lovely followers 🕯️⊘ 🤎

11 months ago

# 18

The next day, I take my laptop and a book and drive to Margate, setting myself up at the same coffee shop Rachel last tagged herself in on Instagram. It's a nice place, old-fashioned gold lettering on the storefront windows: *Coffee* and *Bakery*. I order a flat white, and a homemade cinnamon roll, warm from the oven, and take a seat. Sitting here, waiting for a woman – a stranger – who may or may not appear, I'm filled with a bubbling anxiety. If there wasn't a child missing, it might feel exciting. I keep thinking of it as a 'sting' or a 'honeytrap', but with the ever-present knowledge that Matthew is still gone, I also feel a heavy burden of responsibility. What if I mess this up, and don't get anything useful from Rachel? What if she doesn't show up?

But, luckily, it isn't too long before Rachel appears – she arrives a few minutes after school drop-off, just as I'd thought she might. She's with another woman, another mother I presume, and they proceed to sit down at the table in front of mine. Rachel's back is to the window, facing the room, so I have a clear view of her. I listen to their conversation, trying not to make it too obvious that that's what I'm doing.

But when I hear them mention Vanessa's name for the second time, I lean forward and say, *sotto voce*, 'Sorry, but are you talking about Vanessa Lowe? I follow her on Instagram. Isn't it just terrible what's happened to her son?'

My eyes are on Rachel's face, and for a second I'm terrified I've made the wrong move. Her face is still, completely immobile, her eyes narrowed, and I'm pretty sure she's stopped breathing. It feels like the whole room has been put on pause as she stares at me, but then her companion turns in her chair to face me.

'Oh, my God, yes, it's insane, right? I can't believe anything like that could happen to someone I know. Well, kind of know . . . Rachel actually does know her.'

'Really?' I say. 'Have you spoken to her? I feel awful for what she's going through right now.'

'It's awful,' Rachel says, through her teeth.

'I can't even imagine,' I say. 'I'm Callie, by the way.'

'Penny,' Rachel's companion says, pointing to herself, then introducing Rachel.

'Are you new to the area, Callie?' Rachel asks.

'Sort of,' I say. 'I'm here for a couple of weeks on a kind of retreat. A writer's retreat.'

'Oh, wow,' Penny says. 'A writer in our midst. How exciting. This must be an absolute gold mine for you, all this stuff about Vanessa and her poor little boy.'

'Well,' I say, shifting in my uncomfortable chair, 'I don't really write crime or thrillers. And isn't this the kind of thing we'd all rather be reading about than witnessing? It's horrifying.'

I shift my gaze back to Rachel and she's still staring at me, sizing me up. Other than her clear distrust of me, she's impossible to read. An inscrutable mask securely in place. It takes me by surprise, this wall: in her Instagram posts from before she was accused of stalking Vanessa, Rachel came across as chatty, forthcoming, friendly. Not circumspect and suspicious. 'Have you met her?' she asks me. 'Vanessa, I mean.'

'Yes. I'm staying in a cabin she and her husband own and rent. I met her when I arrived. That's the only time, though I saw her at the search party yesterday, but that hardly counts.'

Rachel nods. 'I was there too. At the search party. You might have noticed the commotion.'

'You were?' I ask, just as Penny swivels sharply in her chair, asking the same question.

Rachel nods again. 'I just felt I had to do something. I imagine that's why you went too,' she says to me.

'Yes. Although I bet half the people there just wanted to see Vanessa and her family, witness the car crash as it happens. Rubberneckers.'

'Oh, yeah,' Penny says sadly. 'It'll certainly draw that kind of a crowd.'

I'm watching Rachel, but my comment doesn't appear to get her back up. She just nods mildly in agreement, then lets herself become distracted by her coffee, her croissant, her phone.

I leave the coffee shop when they do, but take my time getting back to my car. And just as I'd hoped she might, Rachel approaches me as I'm unlocking it.

'You should be careful around her –Vanessa, I mean,' she says.

'Sorry?' I say, and it's genuine surprise that fills my voice. This is the last thing I expected Rachel to say.

'She has a way of . . . twisting things.'

'Vanessa does?' I say. 'Vanessa Lowe?'

'Yes. Vanessa Lowe.'

'What a strange thing to say about a woman whose child is missing,' I say.

Rachel takes a deep breath, lets her eyes leave mine for a second, then looks back at me. 'It probably does sound strange, but that doesn't make it any less true.' She walks away from me.

'Rachel!' I jog to catch up with her. I needed a way in, she's just given me one and I've foolishly shut the door too soon.

She doesn't stop walking once I'm by her side, so I talk and walk. 'I know who you are, by the way. You're the woman Vanessa accused of stalking her and burning her kitchen down.'

'Yes,' Rachel says, the cold word filling the cold air. 'I'm the one she accused of *arson*. And now she thinks I've kidnapped her child.'

I don't know what to say. I don't want to make a false move, but I also can't figure out what the right move is. But then she makes the move for me.

'You're a writer,' she says. It's a statement, rather than a question.

'Yes. But I'm not a journalist. I promise I'm not here to get a story out of you,' I say.

There's a pause in which I realize it's started to rain again. It feels like years since I saw even a patch of blue sky, since wintry sunshine cut through my day. Instead the world is a grey-and-white blanket. It comforts even while it suffocates.

'Maybe you should,' Rachel says, and it takes me saying 'What?' and her repeating herself, for me to really hear what she's saying.

# 19

She takes me back to her house. There's the offer of more tea or coffee. Then Rachel looks out of the window at the grey day that fills it, and up to the clock that adorns her kitchen wall.

'Fuck it, do you want something stronger?'

It's not even midday, and I'm not sure I do, but I don't want to say no. I want to make her feel comfortable. And I certainly don't want to make her feel as though I'm judging her, just by refusing. So I agree.

She's biting her lip, though, questioning herself, judging herself.

'How about a hot chocolate with a hit of something extra? Or an Irish coffee or something?' I suggest.

And her face clears. Relief. 'What a great idea. Perfect.'

We sit there with hot chocolate and Cointreau as she walks me through her relationship with Vanessa Lowe.

'I was so happy to recognise her at first. To meet her. Not because she's famous – or Instagram-famous anyway – but because . . . Well, it was like turning up at a party where you don't think you'll know anyone and suddenly you see someone familiar. It was a relief. I thought I'd immediately have someone to talk to, someone to introduce me to people, a way in with the other mothers. Someone to share a coffee with, grab a drink.'

'But she wasn't?' I ask. 'Was she stand-offish?'

'Not at all. That's the thing. She was so welcoming at first. And we really hit it off. I mean *really* – we were inseparable for a while. I was working for her, our kids were mates, constantly round each other's houses.' Rachel takes a sip of her hot chocolate, and I lean towards her.

'So, what happened? Where did it all go wrong between the two of you?' I ask.

'You mean, how did we get to her accusing me of arson, and now kidnap?' she asks, with a mirthless bark of laughter. 'I honestly don't know. I mean, I do know. She thought Justin and I were having an affair . . . Or, at least, that I was trying to sleep with him. We were working together by then, you see. Me and Justin. I actually helped him design and set up the cabin you're staying in. The Getaway.'

'Really?' I'm taken aback because Vanessa has never mentioned this.

'Yeah, we were close. But we definitely weren't having an affair. I tried to reassure Vanessa but she became distant with me and weird. Honestly, it was like being ghosted, but by your friend and boss, rather than a date. Then, the online harassment started. At first, she didn't tag me in any posts, but I knew she was talking about me, and so did her entire following. And they were tagging me in the comments like there was no tomorrow. I ended up deleting Instagram from my phone. I had to for my mental health, for my physical safety. And, of course, then the rest of the town followed suit. A few people weren't affected by it, but most of the mums at school and nursery followed her, and seemed to believe her. I'd never been particularly close with any of them, but now I was being iced out. And it was all over a pack of lies. Everything she was accusing me of doing was a barefaced lie.'

I'm watching Rachel carefully for anything that appears disingenuous, for a sign that she's not who she says she is, or that there's another side to her – one that could hurt and harm a child. But I can't see it. It doesn't feel like she's hiding anything, or telling a story. If anything, she appears to be getting a great weight off her shoulders.

'I keep trying to work out if she knew exactly what she was doing, setting her followers against me like that. It's hard to believe she wouldn't understand how much worse it would be for me . . . I mean, it's hard enough being a woman on the internet, let alone a Black woman. But then again, part of me thinks she's so unaware of anything outside her own bubble that maybe she wouldn't realize.'

'She's not aware of her own privilege, you mean?'

Rachel chuckles. 'To put it lightly. She's not exactly woke,' she says, raising her eyebrows. 'Mum told me I shouldn't do it – move to Kent, that is. Said it was madness to move somewhere so small.'

'Where did you move from?' I ask.

'Crystal Palace. You know it?'

'I'm from Blackheath,' I say, by way of explanation – they're not exactly next door but south London is south London.

Rachel raises her eyebrows again, this time in genuine disbelief and asks, 'You didn't go to the girls' school, did you?'

'Yeah,' I say, wondering if it's possible Rachel and I are old classmates without realizing it. There's no way we could've been in the same year – the school is so small, I would have been bound to know her, but there's a chance we could have been a few years apart. 'Did you?'

'No, I went to Virgo Fidelis. But my mum taught there for years. You might have been there at the same time as her. Augustina Brown?'

'Mrs Brown?' I say. 'She was my chemistry teacher. And head of sixth form.'

'That's her,' Rachel says, with a genuine grin. 'Wow, how weird. It's such a small world sometimes.'

I feel a bit dizzy from this revelation. 'And has it been bad? Living down here?' I ask.

'Not too bad. I definitely notice the looks and micro-aggressions more now than when I lived in London. Not that it doesn't happen everywhere. But it's a bit better now we're in Margate. Whitstable was maybe too small.' She glances at me. 'A bit too white. I felt horrible about Marcus and Sadie being practically the only brown kids in their school. It's definitely more diverse here.'

'Do you think you might have moved from Whitstable anyway, even without everything that happened with Vanessa?'

'Yeah. I know she'd love to think she ran us out of town, but we were only ever renting in Whitstable, getting a feel for the place. It was definitely the push we needed, though, don't get me wrong.'

'And you're saying Vanessa just made it all up? The arson, the online harassment, all of it?'

'Not just made it up, I think sometimes she was doing it to herself . . . Sending herself stuff and all that.'

'And you think she set the fire too?'

'I'm not sure about that one. Maybe it was just an

accident – an electrical fault or something, and she tried to make it look like it was me. Or maybe by that point she believed all her own lies. Maybe she really thought I did it. I don't know.'

'But why? Why on earth would she do that? Why would anyone do that?' I ask.

'I honestly don't know, but I did notice . . . Do you have any idea how much her follower count went up throughout that whole thing? When all this was going on?'

'No,' I say.

'Well, it was in the thousands. People were following like it was a storyline on a soap. They couldn't get enough.'

'There's nothing the internet likes more than a feud,' I concede.

'Especially when it's an entirely concocted feud. What does it matter that I was bullied off Instagram? That I got home one evening to find the police on my doorstep, accusing me of arson?'

'You really believe she did all that just to gain followers?' I ask.

'To get attention. To make people love her, make them sympathize with her, make them wonder why no one was as obsessed with them as I allegedly was with Vanessa, and to make them think there must be something really special, something exceptional about Vanessa Lowe,' she says, gasping for air when she stops speaking.

'Wow, you've really thought about this,' is all I say.

'It's all I *have* thought about. You see, the real irony is that Vanessa accusing me of being obsessed with her really has made me obsess over her. Just not for the reasons she thinks.'

'And that's why you were at the search party yesterday? Because you're actually obsessed with her now?' I ask.

Rachel sighs. I take a sip of my hot chocolate and it's sweet, so sweet. It's too much for me, really, but Rachel has finished hers and is now scooping out the thick dregs at the bottom of the mug with a teaspoon. 'I went because I wanted to see her in person. Wanted to make sure what she was saying was true.'

## Ten Months Ago

The problem with the roof slows down the renovation of The Lowe Down, and it's mid-February before Rachel and Vanessa sit down to talk about the shop again.

They are sitting in their favourite café on a surprisingly beautiful day. Just over a week ago, there had been flurries of snow that refused to settle, but now crocuses and snowdrops pepper the earth in the parks, and the air feels soft, the sun has some warmth, and the sky is a promising pale blue.

'God, what a day,' Rachel says to Vanessa, as they take their seats by the window. 'Makes you glad to be alive.'

Vanessa smirks at her. 'You're such a dad sometimes, Rach.'

Rachel laughs. 'You're telling me. You know I spent three hours unblocking our toilet the other day? Tom was nowhere to be seen, and wouldn't have known what to do even if he had been.'

Vanessa sips her flat white, eyeing her friend over the rim of her cup. 'Can I ask you somewhat of a personal question?'

'Sure,' Rachel says, a small line forming between her eyebrows, 'as long as it's not about what was blocking the toilet.'

Vanessa gives her a serene smile. 'You complain about Tom quite a lot. You do like him, don't you?'

Rachel laughs at the question. It's all she can do. But Vanessa is still squinting at her, head cocked to the side in curiosity. 'Of course I like him,' Rachel says. 'I love him.'

'Does he know that?' Vanessa asks so quietly it's almost a murmur.

'Of course, he does, Ness. Come on. Why? Has he said something to you?' Rachel panics, thinking of all those times she has seen Tom and Vanessa deep in flirtatious conversation, remembering the look of rapture on Tom's face when he spotted Vanessa at the New Year's Eve party.

'No,' Vanessa says slowly. 'He hasn't mentioned anything. You just have a tendency to . . . nit-pick.'

'Nit-pick?' Rachel says.

Vanessa turns her palms towards the ceiling, as if laying it all out there. 'You just know how you like things done.'

'And you don't?' Rachel bristles. She can't move. She feels as though she's been pinned down, like a butterfly, yet she also can't believe the sheer hypocrisy of this woman, who doesn't allow her children to leave a single personal item anywhere in the house other than in their own bedroom lest it ruin a shot.

Vanessa sighs, turning her coffee cup on its saucer, demurely staring into the frothy milk. 'Let's not do this. I'm sorry I brought it up.'

Rachel takes a deep breath. Her teeth are clenched, her jaw tight. She thinks of the sea, calm and glassy, of pushing through it with strong arms, feeling the water lap over her, salty and all-encompassing, rendering her weightless, held.

Reaching for her coffee, she looks at Vanessa. 'Sorry, Ness. You just managed to hit on the exact complaint Tom has been making for years. The problem is, he expects everything to be done for him, and when he does something – anything – he expects some sort of reward. It's exhausting.'

'You think I don't understand that?' Vanessa says, eyes free of judgement, her mouth unsmiling. It is the most guileless Rachel has ever seen her, and suddenly she realizes that this woman is an enigma who shares everything and nothing when all she herself wants is a real friend.

# 20

'She thinks Vanessa's lying? About her son being missing? Like some weird Munchausen by proxy thing?' Adam is astounded. 'She really said that?'

We're in my cabin. It's late afternoon and a low winter gloom is filtering through the vast windows. I lit the wood-burning stove as soon as I came in, and I've got a few lights on, but there's still something essentially lowering about this light, this time of day. I shiver sitting on the sofa, even though it's warm in here.

'Did she give you the creeps?' he asks, meaning Rachel.

I think back to Rachel, to her comfortable, well-designed kitchen, her clear, direct voice, the jut of her chin as she told me her story about Vanessa. I can still taste the chocolate-orange sweetness, even though I didn't finish it. 'She was maybe a little intense, but she seemed pretty normal, if I'm honest.' I refrain from adding that I liked her.

Adam shakes his head vigorously, his eyes narrowing. 'She's accused Vanessa of making up the disappearance of her child, Callie. There's nothing normal about that.'

'She didn't exactly accuse Vanessa of that,' I say. 'Although I suppose it was implied.'

But Adam isn't paying any attention to me. 'And she thinks this is all about Ness wanting more Instagram followers?' he asks, running a hand through his hair. He's not really talking to me now. 'How can anyone even think that? It's – it's insane. As if social media matters that much to anyone.'

I don't say anything. After a few seconds Adam turns to me. 'Callie? It's insane, right? How could anyone think that?'

I shrug, taking a few extra seconds to answer. 'She seemed pretty messed up by everything that happened between her and Vanessa. She's upset and angry. Maybe she's just not thinking straight.'

'I'll say.'

'What really happened with the kitchen fire? Was it ever proved that Rachel had had anything to do with it?'

'There wasn't any physical evidence, so they couldn't prove anything,' Adam says.

'So, why did Vanessa think it was her?' I ask.

'It was just too much of a coincidence, I guess.'

'It's pretty extreme,' I say.

'Rachel just accused Ness of lying about the abduction of her son. What makes you think she *isn't* extreme?'

I don't bother to correct Adam, but it wasn't Rachel I was referring to as extreme: it was Vanessa's accusation.

## 21

Two days go by and there's nothing. No news is good news, except when it comes to the search for a missing little boy in the middle of winter.

I spend my days watching rolling news, checking the BBC app for updates and scrolling through Instagram. I don't hear from Vanessa, Adam or Rachel, but I don't really expect to.

Vanessa is everywhere, though. As absent as her son is, she is present.

I watch every Story she uploads, her face pale and grave, eyes puffy from crying, which she sometimes does on screen. Every post she makes to her grid has thousands upon thousands of comments from followers and well-wishers. She, or Matthew I suppose, becomes a Twitter moment, and the next morning she's being interviewed on one of the nation's favourite morning shows.

The interview is set up in their living room. I recognize the sofas and the soft furnishings, the square of angry greys, blues and greens of Adam's father's painting that is just visible in the corner of the screen.

Vanessa is composed, self-possessed. She cries silently whenever you would expect her to, reaching for Justin's hand in her moment of increased pain. The interviewer laps it up, rolls around in the perfection of it, the viral potential of it.

The interviewer asks Vanessa if she blames Instagram for Matthew's disappearance, and later that day the headlines are all about the deadly dangers of sharing our lives online, of allowing people to follow every moment. Vanessa shakes her head wordlessly in response, sniffs, wipes tears from the corners of her eyes, takes a deep breath, and says, 'No. No, I don't blame Instagram. I blame whoever took him. Whether they did so out of jealousy, revenge, hatred, obsession – I don't know. But I blame them.'

And in those words I hear her, once again, lay the blame at Rachel's door. The jealousy, revenge, hatred, obsession.

'And do you have any theories about who that is?' the interviewer asks.

'I do, yes,' Vanessa responds firmly. She stares directly into the camera, so used to having one on her. 'I absolutely know who did this. And they know who they are.'

It's Justin who reaches out to her now, making soothing noises, trying to pull her back. He's thinking of lawsuits, perhaps, of slander and libel, how much they can cost. 'We don't know anything for certain,' he says, and his voice cracks even in its softness. He doesn't look directly at the camera like his wife. He doesn't seem able to. He can barely look at the interviewer, and all this surprises me. The few times I've met him, Justin has seemed like the consummate showman, someone who can get though anything in public, who always has something to say whatever the situation, someone who glides through life with a grin intact. I wouldn't have expected him to smile through this, of course, but when he speaks his every word is leaden, weighted, freighted. He has lost all sense of self, his essence ripped from the centre of him, his character replaced by a dead weight that is slowly suffocating him.

It is pure grief, yet when viewers start to analyse the performance of both parents, it's Justin they are critical of, suspicious of, even. He can't look anyone in the eye: he must be guilty. When I turn off the TV and finally go to bed, it's the faces of Justin and Vanessa that greet me when I close my eyes. I stare back into theirs, trying to see something in them, my half-asleep brain snagging on something and every part of me feeling so heavy.

Throughout all of this, the only person I talk to is my mother, who is so concerned by what's going on that she tries to convince me to come home early. It almost works.

But then, one chilly grey morning, the sea and the sky meeting as one in the far-off horizon, five full days after Matthew's disappearance, he is found.

And I am the one who finds him.

## Ten Months Ago

'Hi!' Vanessa calls, as she sees Rachel approaching in the street, throwing her arms straight up into the air so she resembles a human starfish. 'You wore it! I can't believe you wore it!'

Rachel laughs as her friend throws her arms around her neck and sways them from side to side in celebration. 'Of course I wore it,' Rachel says, still laughing as she extricates herself, and does a little curtsy to show off the rose-pink boiler suit she's wearing, perfectly matching Vanessa's own rose-pink boiler suit.

'Well, if we're going to do all the hard work ourselves, we may as well look absolutely glorious while doing it, right?' Vanessa says, as she unlocks the front door of the shop and pushes it open.

It's the end of February – finally – and the shop's roof has been repaired at last. The truly hard work has, of course, all been done for them, not just the roof, but the electricals, the plumbing, the replastering, and even the sugar wash. The coats of paint they are set to apply over the next few weeks are merely ceremonial, the boiler suits a costume for this play.

It's a fun game, though, and Rachel isn't complaining. After feeling shut out of the proceedings since before

Christmas, she feels part of the team again. The shop hasn't opened yet, but Rachel is already on the payroll. It's not a lot, compared to what she was earning with RITA, or even compared to what she imagined she might charge when she went freelance, but it's something. Moving here, living on one salary and her savings, has cost Rachel a lot, not just financially. But she feels as though she has found her footing in her new life, her place in Whitstable. She is making a living for herself and has something to talk to Tom about over dinner, other than their two children and his work. She has been in touch with her old colleagues at RITA, and they've agreed to supply the new spring range in an exclusive deal. It's normally only stocked in a choice few boutiques in major cities and online, and Vanessa was delighted by the news.

Now they're going to paint the walls of the shop plaster pink and wait for the carpenter to arrive to install the bespoke pale birch shelves and display cabinets.

'Did you see my post last night?' Vanessa asks, as they unravel the plastic sheeting to protect the floor.

Concentrating on her task, Rachel shakes her head. 'I'm trying not to look at social media between ten p.m. and ten a.m. at the moment. I was falling asleep with my phone in my hand. It didn't feel healthy.'

Vanessa doesn't say anything for a few seconds and Rachel is worried she's offended her: Vanessa is a woman whose entire life is refracted through her phone. But when she looks at her, she is merely crouched in a corner, trying to get the weightless plastic to settle. 'Good for you,' she says, once she has manoeuvred a paint tin to stop the sheeting rising up. 'You're a stronger woman than me.'

'Doubtful.'

'Did you swim in the sea this morning?'

'Yes.'

'I rest my case,' Vanessa says, with a smile. 'Well, anyway . . . It was my first post with Le Creuset. For their range of new colours.'

'Oh, shit, Ness, I completely forgot. Sorry.'

'It's fine, don't worry about it. It's done really well so far.'

But Rachel already has her phone out of her pocket and is opening Instagram, heading straight to Vanessa's page to like her post. 'Looks gorgeous,' she says, looking up to see Vanessa watching her.

'Yeah, not bad, right?'

There is a pause during which both women get back to the task in hand. Vanessa is pushing her paint roller up and down the wall, as she says, 'You've got a lot more followers recently.'

Her tone is mild, almost casual, but Rachel thinks she can detect Vanessa's moods pretty well by now, and she glances at the other woman, who is studiously applying more paint to her roller, eyes averted. 'Yeah, I guess all your reposts and tags have had an effect.'

'But you had quite a few even before we met,' Vanessa points out.

'Well, I did work in marketing,' Rachel says. She is still watching Vanessa, pale pink paint dripping from her roller onto the plastic they've just laid out.

Vanessa smiles at her. 'So, it's in your blood?'

'Something like that. I've never done a campaign like this before, though. You must be so excited.'

Vanessa is still smiling as she flicks her roller to get rid of the excess. Paint arches across the floor, coming to land on the white leather of Rachel's chunky Chelsea boots. 'Shit! Sorry, Rach. Oh, God, we'd better get that off right now.'

Rachel stares down at the shoes, perplexed, then up at her friend. Vanessa's face is a picture of apology, her cheeks almost as pink as the paint in her embarrassment.

'It's fine,' Rachel says. 'It's my fault for wearing white shoes to a paint party.'

Vanessa smiles again, but Rachel knows she doesn't mean it, just like she knows that the little flick of the paint roller wasn't an accident.

## thelowedown

**790K** followers

**Vanessa Lowe**

Wife * Mother * Lover

Liked by **WildWildWe** and **others**

**thelowedown** It's here! The day has finally arrived and this is really happening. The Lowe Down has gone IRL, baby!! I can't even begin to tell you how much work has gone into making this dream of mine a reality, but here she is, in all her glory, MY SHOP. I'm so honoured to be stocking so many brands and makers I've worked with in the past, or have long admired, and so excited to share all this with the community and with you guys. So, now, when anyone asks me where I got my dress, or earrings, or notebook I can say: MY SHOP 🌀. As the kids have got older it's also been so important to me to create something a little more . . . tangible for them. They know Mummy works, of course, but you know what's hard to explain to a child? Being an influencer (who are we kidding? It's also hard to explain to parents, and accountants, and friends with 'real jobs', and the woman who serves you tea at the beach, etc. etc. etc.). So, creating this shop feels like I have something to show for myself – something to show my kids, and everyone else, and be able to say: here, this is who I am. This is what I do. Okay, I'll stop going on and on now, but this really is a momentous day and an occasion to celebrate and I can't wait until I see some of you in store 🌀 💜 🥂

9 months ago

## 22

For the first time since I arrived at the cabin, I decide to go for a walk. I need to remind myself of the outside world, its smell and its shape. Its noise and touch. The cabin has become womb-like, a wood-clad chrysalis forcing me towards a transformation I'm still not quite ready to accept.

But the beach is right outside, the tide out, and from here I can walk all the way to the heart of Whitstable if I want. I wrap up warm – it's not particularly cold, but the wind can come screaming down the flattened beach like a whip. I walk on shaky foal legs. Legs that were once strong and used to running and hiking, and now feel like liquid. The salty tang of the sea air breathes new life into my lungs, onto my skin. Taking deep, full breaths, I stand in some milky sunlight, closing my eyes against it, then trudge onward, one foot in front of the other, crunching across the shingle.

I've probably been walking for about half an hour when I spot it.

An inch of blue and green, as bright as summer in the monochrome of the beach's pebbles and shingle.

It's some way off, caught on some rocks that mark high tide. I run up to it, slipping and falling in the uneven shingle, heart pounding in my chest the whole way there, my limbs more liquid the closer I get.

I can't bear to bring myself to articulate what I think I'll find when I reach that tiny square of blue and green. I want to get there and be proven wrong. A trick of the light. A midwinter mirage.

But I see the whole thing before I'm ready, and there's a strangled yell, a dead, echoing sound that reaches my ears long after I've made the sound, just a few seconds before I realize it came from me.

I pitch forward into the shingle, damp soaking the knees of my leggings as I reach out a hand to the soft auburn curls that are spread over the pebbles like blood.

# 23

My hands are stiff, freezing, unwieldy as I unlock my phone and dial 999.

The police arrive before I'm ready. Before I can even form full sentences.

I know before they get there that he is gone.

His lips are blue, his skin ice, his small body already a little bloated and disfigured.

I don't even need to press my two forefingers to his neck to know I'll find no tremor of a heartbeat there.

I'm still sitting beside him when they arrive. Someone puts their hands on my shoulders, pulls me up.

'Callie.' It's DCI Varma's voice, low and warm. It doesn't belong here. It's completely at odds with this moment of horror and tragedy.

'She's freezing,' I hear her say to somebody, then someone else is pulling me away from the scene and towards the road. There's an ambulance, with a police car, and a dark car I imagine is Varma's unmarked vehicle. The paramedic draws me to the ambulance, its back doors open to the winter air, and we climb in through this gaping mouth, where there's a gurney for me to sit on, and a silver hypothermia blanket to be placed around my shoulders.

I sit there for what feels like hours before Varma turns up, and I am transferred from the ambulance to the back of her car.

I am in an underwater world now. Swimming through frozen, uncharted territory, and every time Varma speaks to me, it's all I can do to squint and frown at her. It's impossible to hear what she's saying, but I see her mouth make the shape of the word 'shock'.

It doesn't cover it, though. It's too short a word, too few syllables. It doesn't stay long enough in the mouth, doesn't stick long enough in the air.

The world doesn't come roaring back to me until we get to the police station.

## Nine Months Ago

It's a frozen Sunday in March and Rachel, Tom, Marcus and Sadie are at the Lowes' for lunch again. Rachel has made and brought the pudding, a pineapple upside-down cake that is as delicious as it is kitsch. Vanessa gave her tinny, false laugh when Rachel told her what she had made when they arrived, and she knew she'd taken a wrong step.

She's trying to work out what she should've made instead while she's standing in the kitchen, looking for a cake knife, when Justin walks in with some dirty plates.

'Third drawer down,' he tells her.

'Thanks,' Rachel says. 'I've now searched every inch of this kitchen, by the way.'

'Ah, so you know all our secrets.'

'Well, I know you have an impressively large elastic-band ball building in that top drawer.'

'Oh, that's all me.' Justin chuckles. 'Physically incapable of throwing anything away that might prove useful at some point in the future.'

'What was it Morris said about beauty and usefulness?'

'Oh, a William Morris fan, are we?'

'No need to sound so surprised,' Rachel says with her head down, concentrating on cutting the cake into even slices. 'I did do design at uni.'

'Now, why didn't I know that about you?' Justin asks, pouring himself a glass of wine from the bottle he's just opened.

Rachel glances up. 'Probably because we all went to uni about a million years ago. I've barely thought about my degree since.'

'Whereas I'm forced to think about mine every day,' Justin says.

'You love it though, don't you, architecture?'

'I suppose so. You have to, to begin with. But I haven't thought about whether I enjoy my job or not in a very long time. I suppose buildings still interest me, but it's a very long time since I got my hands dirty. It's all just management now.'

'Sounds like you need a passion project. Like Ness's shop.'

'You could be right. We actually bought this old shack – actually a couple of them – right on the beach. They're just sitting there at the moment, but there's tons of potential.'

Rachel doesn't say anything as she plates the cake, arranging the slices on Vanessa's beautiful earthenware, dolloping rounded scoops of thick Greek yoghurt next to them. She wonders what it must be like to have so much money that you forget you bought 'a couple of shacks' right on the beach. She knows that Justin comes from money, and that his architectural firm is very successful. But she's never asked Vanessa about how much she might be earning through Instagram. She feels a burn of jealousy, momentarily furious at how easy everything seems to be for this family, physically sick at the thought they never seem to have to worry about money – about anything at all. And then she swallows it.

Justin has poured her a glass of wine, and she has a large swig, then indicates that he should help her carry the plates of cake through to the dining room.

'Are you okay?' he asks. His head cocks to the side, just as Vanessa's does when she looks concerned, and his eyes narrow a little.

'I'm fine,' Rachel says, feeling a little unsteady as she balances two plates in one hand, a plate and her glass in the other.

He is staring right down at her. He is not a particularly tall man, but Rachel is short and she is suddenly very aware of his presence. 'Are you sure?' he asks again. 'You look a bit sick . . . It wasn't the chicken, was it?'

'No. No, it wasn't. The chicken was delicious. I just felt . . . I don't know how I felt. Woozy.'

'We could join forces, you know,' Justin says, as if he hasn't been listening to her.

'What?'

'Well, if I go ahead with this "passion project", as you termed it, it would be good to get some help with the design.'

'Wouldn't you want Vanessa to do that?' Rachel asks, although what she really means is, *Wouldn't Vanessa want to do that?*

'She's so busy with the shop and the kids, I don't want to add anything to her plate.'

Justin heads back towards the dining room. As Rachel follows him to where their families are sitting and chatting, laughing and making a mess, she wonders how she has managed to become the go-to Girl Friday for both Vanessa and Justin. About why this shiny, successful couple keep drawing her into their side hustles. Before sitting down, she glances at Tom, managing to catch his eye for once. He grins, quirking his eyebrows to mean *Everything okay?* But she doesn't know if it is. Everything looks okay, more than okay. It looks good – perfect even. But perfection has never been Rachel's aim. She's too smart to go after something as unachievable as perfection. So why – and how – has she found herself here, surrounded by the trappings of perfection, reaping none of the rewards?

## 24

They bring me tea. And water. Varma even offers me her coat because I can't stop shivering.

I accept the tea and the water, decline the coat. Despite my shivering the room we're in is stuffy, the warmth lying over my burned-in chill, like a thick layer of sweat.

'Talk me through your morning, Callie,' Varma says, when she returns with my drinks, and takes the seat opposite me. She has tea too, takes a sip, leans back.

My heart hasn't stopped hammering since I saw that incongruous flash of blue and green on the winter-grey beach, and it's not about to stop now. I drink some of the tea, taking a moment, but my heart pounds even heavier in my chest. An angry fist knocking down the door of my ribs.

'Callie?' Varma says again, something flashing though her eyes, making her sit up straighter.

I clear my throat, meet her gaze, and talk her through every moment of my morning leading up to finding Matthew.

'And you were on your way into Whitstable?' she clarifies.

I shake my head. 'I was just going for a walk. But I was headed in that direction, yes.'

She scribbles something in her notepad, which she's been doing throughout the interview, even though it's being filmed. I have to presume that several other officers are sitting in another room somewhere, watching the recording.

'And when was the last time you saw Matthew? Alive?' Varma asks.

There's a beat, a brief pause, before I say, 'We've already gone over this. During my first interview.'

'Just remind me.'

'It was at Vanessa and Justin's house. Last . . . Friday I guess it was. Sorry, I can't remember the date.'

'Friday the fourteenth,' Varma says.

'Really?' The days have run together since then. 'Okay. So, Friday the fourteenth. I got there about four thirty, five-ish, I think, and Matthew was taken up to bed about seven thirty.'

'And that was the last time you saw him? Being taken up to bed?'

'Yes.'

'So, just to clarify, on the night before Matthew was discovered missing, you saw him last at seven thirty p.m.?'

'Yes,' I say emphatically, staring into Varma's eyes. She nods professionally, and makes yet another note.

'And how much longer after Matthew went to bed did you stay at the Lowes'?'

'Oh, um, not long. I stayed downstairs in the cinema room with Emma and JJ for a bit, while Justin and Vanessa were putting Matthew to bed, and then I went to the bathroom and . . . Well, I overheard them arguing and thought it best for me to head home.'

'Very discreet of you. Did you mention this argument in your interview last week?'

'I can't remember. It wasn't so much an argument, as raised voices. If I'm being totally honest, I thought Justin was referring to me, so I decided it would be better if I wasn't there.'

'So, you heard one of your hosts talking about you behind your back, and you decided to leave without a word? You didn't confront him about it?'

'No, of course not. And, besides, it wasn't without a word. I said goodbye to Vanessa when she came downstairs. And it's not like I thought Justin was badmouthing me or anything – it just seemed like maybe he was concerned I would be another Rachel. Vanessa had told me he was wary of her Instagram followers because of what had happened with Rachel, so I figured maybe he thought I might be like that too. I don't know.'

'You're referring to Rachel Donovan here?'

'Yes.'

'Have you ever met Mrs Donovan?' Varma asks. She's wearing her black, square-framed glasses and the overhead strip lighting occasionally catches on the lenses, hiding her piercing eyes. It does so now, and it's like a warning: tread carefully.

'Yes,' I say.

Varma coughs, leans back in her chair, looks at me appraisingly. 'You have? In what context?'

'I met her by accident a few days ago. I drove over to Margate, just to explore and maybe get some writing done in a café, and it turns out that's where she lives now, and she happened to be in the same café.' I shift in my chair as I speak, nervous at this bending and stretching of the truth. I wonder if Varma can tell how uncomfortable I am. But of course she can – this is her job.

'And she just happened to introduce herself to you?' Varma asks.

'No,' I say slowly. 'I overheard her, and the friend she was with, talking about Vanessa.'

'So you just . . . joined in?' Varma asks, scepticism lining the arch of her eyebrows and the lift in her voice.

'They were sitting right by me,' I say, as if it was the most obvious and normal thing in the world to interrupt a stranger's conversation, when actually it was anything but. 'It felt weird not to say anything . . .'

Varma squints, tilts her head, takes a few breaths, leans back in her chair yet again and caps her pen. For a brilliant second I think the questioning is over, but then she crosses both arms against her chest, and says, 'You're a confusing proposition, Callie, you know that, right?'

'I am?' I croak.

'Oh, yes. A visiting writer on a solo retreat, right before Christmas. A follower of Vanessa on Instagram who just happened to book herself into the Lowes' holiday home without realizing it. Someone who, for much of her time here, has kept herself to herself, yet went out of her way to make friends with Vanessa and Justin, has taken part in every search for Matthew, and happily introduced herself to a stranger – a former friend of Vanessa, in fact – in a coffee shop. So, what is it? Did you come here to be alone, or to make friends? Are you a reclusive hermit or a social butterfly? These are the questions I'm asking myself about you, because I can't quite figure out your place in all this. Your role. Why are you here?'

I start to form an answer, my throat constricting and contracting, but Varma raises a hand for me to stop, and quickly checks the time on the watch she wears on her right wrist. 'It was a rhetorical question, Callie. I have to go and talk to Vanessa and Justin Lowe now. Although I am going to have to ask you to stick around.'

'Oh, you mean at the station?' I ask, assuming she'll be back to ask more questions in due course.

'No, in town.'

'That's fine. I'm here until the twenty-third, and then I'm going back to London. For Christmas.'

She stands up, straightens her jacket. 'No, you're not. You're staying here until I say you can go.'

I stare up at her, momentarily dumbfounded. Does she really suspect me? She's about to leave when I find my voice again. 'Can I ask a question?'

She stands perfectly still for a second, not saying anything, then nods. 'He . . . hadn't been dead long, had he?' I ask. I haven't been able to stop thinking about him, stop seeing that small body lying on the beach. In the moment I saw him I couldn't help thinking of seeing Ada. Matthew was older than she'd ever got to be, but that pull on my stomach, the feeling of my heart burning through my chest was the same as when we'd turned off the machines that were keeping her alive, and we watched her last breath.

Varma must be able to see the pleading, the pain on my face because she deflates, her shoulders drooping for a millisecond, before she straightens herself. 'No, I don't think he had. We'll know more after the autopsy, but I think it's fairly safe to say he was probably kept somewhere.'

I can't bring myself to say anything. I'm completely mute, a rock lodged in my throat, so I nod, and Varma nods back, and then that's it. She's gone.

## 25

I walk back along the beach. An officer offered to drive me back to the cabin, but after being in that interview room, I craved space, air, room to breathe. I know as soon as I see the blue-and-white tape fluttering in the December wind that I've made a mistake. The area is a hive of activity, police officers, forensics experts, a medical examiner all coming and going around the white tent that has been put up over where he was found. Where I found him.

And there, at the edge of the scene already, photographers, reporters, locals. I feel sick just looking at it, a weight so heavy in my chest I can't breathe, despite all the space, all the air, the salt of the sea.

I hurry past, head down. I'm probably more conspicuous than if I'd stopped to gawp as everyone else is doing, but not long ago I was kneeling beside that tiny body and I can still feel the cold coming off his skin, see the spread of his curls against the indifferent shingle beneath him.

My long strides don't stop until the Getaway is in sight. But before I can get there I'm stopped in my tracks by the sight of Adam outside his own small cabin.

'Callie,' he says, as I approach. His face is clear, content almost.

He doesn't know.

'Adam,' I say, taking a step towards him. His face changes as soon as I speak, from open to wary, casual to closed. As if something in my face, my step, my stance warns him of what's to come. How do I tell him? How can I? Who am I to tell him his nephew has been found dead?

'What's going on, Callie?' he says. It's strange, but his voice is already familiar to me. When I got here, it had been so long since I'd spent any real time with anyone. And I've spent more time with Adam – a near stranger – than anyone else over the past few weeks. The past few months even. But I can't confuse that for closeness. I'm not sure we're even friends. We're acquaintances who found themselves together in a crisis, and now that crisis has changed, and I'm not sure I can be the one to tell him in what way.

'Callie,' he says again, this time harshly, and I finally reply.

'Have you checked your phone recently?'

'Yes,' he says.

'Oh.'

'Why?'

'Adam, they found – I mean, I found Matthew this morning.' I say it as clearly as possible, but every word feels heavy in my mouth. I can't believe I've managed to push them out, but I have done.

'Matthew?' he says, his voice cracking. His face has gone blank, as though he can't quite take in what I've said. Or he doesn't want to.

'I'm so sorry, Adam.'

'What? They found him . . . They found him! That's . . .'

'No,' I say, trying to make him understand.

'No? No. Oh, God, you mean . . .'

Adam takes a step back, stumbling over himself. His entire face has shut down, no emotion showing. When he finally looks at me, his eyes are dark, too dark, so dark I take a step backwards almost falling off the wooden decking in front of his cabin. He reaches out to grab my arm, to stop me falling backward. His eyes swerve to meet mine as he catches me and they're back to normal now, the green in his hazel catching what little light there is on this low winter day.

'I – I need to ring Ness,' he says. His voice is dull now. It's lost its raw, confused edge.

I watch as he places call after call to Vanessa, to no avail. I offer that she must be at the police station by now, and he nods sharply, trying Justin too, getting nothing. Eventually, frustrated, exhausted, he tells me he's going to drive to Vanessa and Justin's, try the police station if they're not there. I nod, mute, and watch as he gets into his van. Before leaving he winds down his window and leans out. 'Where was it?' he shouts. 'Where was he?'

I tell him, looking back the way I came, to that wide stretch of beach, the tide on its way back in.

Finding Matthew so close to home, so close to safety, feels like another twist of tragedy: the fact that he was so near yet so far from home at the same time.

But it also makes me wonder where he was for almost a week, wonder where whoever took him was holding him, wonder where he broke free from, where he was running to, and who he was running from.

## Nine Months Ago

It's a steel-grey day again when Rachel meets Justin on the beach. They're right by the Sportsman pub, and Rachel looked wistfully in at the customers tucked up in the warmth, enjoying their seafood lunches as she got out of her Ford Fiesta. Justin was nowhere to be seen, so she wandered down to the shore, trying to get her bearings. Although she's been living in Whitstable since last August, she hasn't been down this way since they moved in. The last time she was here it was years ago, when she and Tom were still day-trippers and they took a day off work to go to the Sportsman for his birthday lunch. That was before Marcus and Sadie, before Tom had got his job at the University of Canterbury, before they'd ever thought about leaving London.

The beach is different out here. It's part of a coastal path, windblown and almost desolate on this March day. The small houses – buildings, really – that line it are ramshackle and charming in their own way, but definitely don't scream Justin and Vanessa Lowe to her. She's surprised they would buy anything out here, and wonders if they have more money than sense sometimes. She is peering into one of the buildings, trying to work out if anyone's at home when she hears Justin call her name.

178

He's waving at her, struggling over the pebble beach in his inappropriate shoes. She can't help laughing as he approaches, and he joins in her laughter as he gets closer.

'Well, don't I look like quite the dick?' he says, by way of hello.

'You do know you live by the sea, right? Not in the middle of Manhattan?' Rachel says.

Justin smiles, sheepish, as he says, 'I have to go into town afterwards. Big meeting.'

'We could've rearranged,' Rachel says.

'No, no. I've been looking forward to this.' He says this with absolutely no inflection, no deeper meaning in evidence, and starts trudging up the beach, away from the car park. 'This is it,' he calls, outside the last building in the short row of houses. He has charged ahead of Rachel, more sure of his step than she would've guessed he'd be in those shoes, and his voice almost gets lost in the wind.

The building is a wreck, but it's a good size, and Rachel is caught by the views on almost every side. It's like the end of the world out here. 'Wow, it's a looker,' she says wryly, as she reaches Justin.

'Isn't she? No, we're going to pull it down obviously. And then the world's our oyster. I'm thinking something super-modern, big windows, nothing huge or fancy, but cool and cosy, you know?'

Rachel turns her back on the wrecked building. 'Just imagine waking up to this.'

'I know.'

'You have to have a giant window by the bed.'

'Uh-huh. That's what I'm thinking.'

Rachel sighs, still staring at the view, and shoves her

hands into her coat pockets. The air is biting – it feels like they've gone back in time, the promise of spring in February ripped away and replaced with another winter. She still can't work out why Justin invited her out here. It's nice to be asked – it's nice he thinks of her as someone to ask advice from but, really, why? He's surrounded by people, at work, at home, who are more qualified for this kind of thing than she is.

'Will you rent it out?' Rachel asks Justin, pulling herself out of her reverie.

'Yeah, I suppose. Airbnb, that kind of thing. We have several other properties we want to do the same with.'

'You said you had another place down here?'

'Yeah,' Justin says, pointing back the way they'd come, in the direction of the car park. 'Just a few houses down.'

'And you'll do the same thing there too?' Rachel says. How will the people who live or stay in the houses in between feel about being sandwiched between two contemporary and cosy wooden boxes?

'Not yet. But maybe eventually.'

Rachel studies him as he contemplates the row of run-down beachside huts and buildings, and knows what he's seeing: a long line of contemporary wooden huts, and money, money, money. 'When did you buy these places?' she asks.

Justin tips back his head, looking up at the grey sky. 'Oh, where are we now? March? It must have been last summer. God, I don't know where the time's gone. It was meant to be a big project for Ness to spearhead, but then she got a bee in her bonnet about the shop and lost interest in this. I suppose building and renovating are more my area anyway, but I decided someone needed to take the reins.'

'Ness doesn't want to be involved at all any more?' Rachel asks.

'She does, but she's got her hands full.'

'So do you by the sounds of things.'

'That's why I brought you out here. I meant what I said at lunch, Rach. I was hoping you'd be interested in project-managing this for us. I think you'd be really good at it.'

Rachel squints at him, disbelieving, then huffs a puff of frigid air out of her mouth. It's so cold it leaves a mist hanging in the air as a reminder that spring hasn't yet arrived. 'Really?' she says, moving so she can look at Justin face on. 'Me?'

'Yeah, why not? You seem surprised.'

'I have absolutely no experience in this, Justin. Not to mention that I already work with your wife, have two kids, and . . .'

'And what?'

'Well, I thought I was your friend. Yours and Vanessa's. Do you offer all your friends jobs? This is just . . . weird.'

'Oh,' Justin says. He has been staring intently at Rachel but now turns his gaze towards the beach shack, clearly confused and maybe even embarrassed. 'Sorry. I really didn't intend to be . . . weird.'

'I can get my own job, is what I'm saying,' Rachel says, looking at his profile. She has managed to forget exactly how handsome he is after spending so much time in his and Vanessa's presence. Almost as if she has become inoculated against their beauty. But every now and again she'll be struck anew by how attractive he is. She doesn't fancy him, not really, but here, on this very windy beach, in the freezing cold, it seems more obvious than ever.

'I know. God, I know that. Sorry, I – I didn't mean any of this to come across as condescending or . . . charitable. You're the most capable person I've come across in a long time, Rachel. I trust you. I just know you'd do a good job.'

'Really,' Rachel says, her scepticism so pronounced that it doesn't even come out as a question.

Justin lets out a bark of laughter. 'Yes, really. Really, really, really.'

'And Vanessa knows about this? You've run it past her? I don't want to be stepping on any toes, and I don't want her to think I'm abandoning her and the shop, just when it's getting going.'

Justin sighs and sits down abruptly on the cold, damp shingle of the beach. Looking down at him, Rachel spots the strands of grey in his dark hair that are normally hidden from her view and is surprised to find herself dropping down to join him there, shuffling her bum into a more comfortable position, glad that she wore her longest, most waterproof coat.

'I haven't yet, but I will, I promise. I don't want to put you in an awkward position.' He has picked up a smooth, well-worn pebble, is turning it over and over in his right hand.

There is a long stretch of silence before Rachel says, 'Everything okay?' as lightly as possible. She has rarely seen Justin so pensive.

He's rolling the pebble in his hand in time to his nods. 'Ness seems okay to you, right?' he asks, dropping the rock back on the beach and locking Rachel into his gaze.

'She seems fine,' Rachel says, taken aback. 'She seems how she normally seems.'

'Which is?'

'Very much Vanessa,' Rachel says, with a light laugh.

Justin doesn't seem satisfied by this answer. Maybe he is thinking what Rachel is currently thinking, which is that she doesn't know Vanessa all that well. Or, at least, she hasn't known her very long. To Rachel, Vanessa is manicured and mercurial. She is beginning to suspect that she will never really know her, and that even in becoming friends with her, she is still only being given a peek around the curtain that frames the picture of the life Vanessa has painted for herself and her followers. Even on the damp, uncomfortable pebbles, sitting next to Vanessa's husband, Rachel is still constantly wondering if making and being friends with her was the best idea. Still trying to work out if she is indeed friends with the woman, or being tugged along in Vanessa's wake. There are times when she thinks she sees Vanessa fully, or almost fully, and that all Vanessa needs is a true friend to tell her she doesn't need to try so hard. And there are times when she believes herself a fool for having taken on the role.

Because Rachel is too old, and has had too many friends, to be truly fooled by a friendship. She's not seventeen, or twenty-seven any more: she's had women come and go, but for the most part others have stayed. She is not a woman without friendships – she's always needed them, always wanted them, always taken care to maintain and retain them. This was one of the things that made moving to Whitstable so hard at first. The move from London was a wrench, when not being walking distance, or a bus ride, or a tube journey from her friends felt like a loss so large she actively grieved it. Tom didn't understand. He had his family with him, and his friends at the other end of a WhatsApp group chat, and that was enough for him. But it wasn't for Rachel.

Enter Vanessa.

But the more she spends time with Vanessa, the more Rachel has to admit how uneasy this relationship feels to her. She looks at Justin, who is gazing out at the water: not only do he and his wife constitute her entire social circle outside her family here but they are also responsible for her salary. The thought is not a good one. It does not make her want to hitch her wagon to them even tighter by taking Justin up on his offer. When he turns back to her, smiling so compellingly, she is not sure what she'll say when he eventually, inevitably, asks if she'll take on the job.

# 26

It's impossible for me to stay inside. The cabin has turned from a comforting womb to a cage, the world outside banging at the door, pressing itself in on me.

There's nothing for me to do, though, no way for me to help, so I go for another walk, battling against the wind that has picked up, lashing at my face, sending salt spray into my eyes. It feels good to fight the weather like this, to push back against the world, even just a little. It's the first time I've felt like this in months, the first time I've felt there's any fight left in me.

I should have turned away from the crime scene. Hadn't Adam said the other day that perpetrators always returned to the scenes of their crimes? And now here I am, clearly in Varma's sights as her number one-suspect. I could easily have walked in the other direction, but my feet play a trick on me, lead me back to where I found Matthew. But before I can get there, something stops me. Something I didn't notice this morning before I found him, and something I missed in my hurry to get home earlier. A door to one of the winter-abandoned beach huts stands open, cracking against the hut's side in the wind. The sound is rhythmic, as tension-building as any soundtrack to a horror movie as I stand, frozen, staring at it.

It might be nothing, of course.

Many of these beach huts won't have been visited for

months. Full to bursting with life and beach toys in summer, they stand empty now, colourful reminders of bluer skies, warmer winds, children's laughter ringing in the air.

I take a few tentative steps towards it and stop. I can't help where my mind takes me: that this could be where Matthew has been for the past five days. And if that's so, I can't go any closer, can't touch it, can't inspect it. If he was in there, I can't be the first to know.

So, for the second time today, I draw my phone from the pocket of my coat with trembling hands, and call the police.

## 27

DC Whitman sits with me in the Getaway while Varma oversees the forensic search of the beach hut. I have no idea what they've found – if they've found anything at all – but Whitman seems nervous.

'Do you know the Lowes at all?' I ask.

He's jiggling his right knee up and down, up and down, up and down, but he stops the moment I speak to him. He nods slowly, then says, just as slowly, 'I kind of know the Lowes. Everyone kind of knows them.'

'They're town celebrities,' I offer.

He shrugs. 'I guess. It's a bit more complicated than that, though.'

'How come?' I ask.

'There've been some, ah, local disagreements around how many houses they've been buying and renting,' he says, shifting uncomfortably in his chair, as if acutely aware that he's sitting in one of the Lowes' buildings. 'Town meetings have been a little strained recently,' he says.

'Town meetings?' I say, rolling the idea around in my mind. The concept is so quaint to me that it feels almost exotic.

'Yup,' Whitman says, with a rising of his eyebrows.

'So, not everyone here is a fan of the Lowes?' I ask.

'I don't know if I'd say that,' he says, rubbing a hand

across his chin and jawline. 'Do they have "fans"?' he asks, sounding worried, confused, as if he should've been a fan of theirs all this time.

'It's just an expression,' I say, although I can understand his confusion – Vanessa does have fans of a sort. What are her followers, if not a kind of fan?

'Right, right. Yeah. I mean, no, yeah, there're definitely some in the town here who are bigger fans of theirs than others,' he says, in a rush.

'And which part of the town do you belong to?' I ask. 'The fan part or the not-a-fan part?'

Whitman shifts again, his gaze jumping around the room, from tasteful vase to 42-inch television, to cashmere rug, to perfectly distressed leather armchair, to gourmet kitchen, brass fixtures and poured-concrete countertops. 'I've lived here my whole life,' he says finally, shortly.

'So . . . not-a-fan?' I say.

'I've got nothing against them personally,' he says quickly, adding, 'and they certainly don't deserve any of this. But they bought all these houses, did them up, and suddenly they're worth hundreds of thousands more, and either they've sold them on to people like them, or they rent them out to people –'

'Like me?' I interrupt.

He stiffens, sits up straight, buttons himself up, and I wish I hadn't said anything.

'People can't afford to live here any more,' he says stiffly. 'The people who actually live here, who're from here, I mean. Who work here. And with her Instagram and that . . . My sister follows her, and it's just like – How're we ever supposed to compete? I know it's not a competition, but look at her photos and her life and it's just, like, fuck, man.' His shoulders slump as he relaxes into his seat. 'None of that's the point, though, is it? Their kid is dead, and no one deserves that.'

## Nine Months Ago

'So, don't do it,' Tom says simply, later that evening. They're in the kitchen, the kids in bed, dinner eaten. Tom is doing the washing-up while Rachel sits at the table, her feet up on his empty chair, a cup of redbush tea in hand. 'You're already working at the shop with Vanessa, and you said when we moved here that you wanted to be able to spend more time with Sadie and Marcus after nursery and school. You work on this project with Justin, and you know it's going to take up all your spare time.'

Tom hadn't been surprised when Rachel relayed her meeting with Justin and his offer to him earlier in the evening. He didn't find it strange or disconcerting that their friends kept offering her jobs. He just took it at face value that people would want to hire his wife. She was smart and capable, hardworking and fun to be around. Who wouldn't want to work with her? In some ways, this was nice – Rachel knew that. Tom had such faith in her. But sometimes he also had too much faith in the world and other people. He wasn't sceptical or cynical in the ways she was – he didn't have to be. He had no need to question things that fell into his lap: he assumed they always would because they always had and that they were always meant to do so.

Rachel didn't have that luxury.

'What do you make of them? Vanessa and Justin?' Rachel asks his back.

'What do you mean? I like them, you know I do. I thought you did too,' he says, his eyes flickering to the window where his reflection meets her gaze. 'We spend enough time with them.' He looks quizzical now, suddenly realizing that something is up. 'I mean, fuck, Rach, they're basically our only friends here.'

'I know, and I do like them, of course I do,' Rachel says slowly, trying to figure out exactly what she wants to say – exactly how she feels. 'But something about them makes me feel uneasy.'

Tom gives a little shrug, turning his attention back to the large saucepan that only just fits in their washing-up bowl. 'Because they're so rich?' he asks.

'I guess that's part of it. But it's not just that. I can't really describe it. I feel like . . . I'm being used somehow, but I don't know how.'

Tom looks over his shoulder. His hands are wrist deep in the water still, but his focus is off the saucepan. 'You feel like they're using you? Rach, that's crazy! What would they be using you for?'

'Well, thanks.'

'I don't mean it like that,' Tom says, and attempts a laugh. 'I just mean – they have everything. I think they just like your – *our* – company. What's so hard to believe about that?'

'Nothing, nothing . . .'

'We're incredibly charming, Rach,' Tom says now, with half a grin.

'Ha-ha, sure we are. But don't you think it's odd that they've both basically handed me a job?'

Tom is quiet, finishing the saucepan, placing it just so on the drying rack, taking off his apron – his apron! – washing and drying his hands. Sometimes, after so long together, Rachel has to remind herself that she really does love him. Other times, like right now, it hits her full in the chest and spreads through her, like warm, burning embers. He joins her at the table, pulling out one of the other chairs so she doesn't have to relinquish her footrest.

'Maybe it is a bit odd,' he says at last, thoughtfully. 'But maybe that's more about them ... We haven't met many other friends of theirs, have we? I have a feeling that maybe neither of them really knows how to have a relationship that's just based on ... shared enjoyment,'

'Rather than what? Money? Some kind of transaction?'

Tom shrugs. 'Yeah,'

'So, you think they keep trying to pay me to spend time with them because they don't know how else to keep people around?'

'Maybe.'

'Well, isn't that a bit weird?'

'Yes, definitely, no doubt about it, but that doesn't make it disingenuous. I think essentially they're good people and just want to be friends with you, Rach.' Tom grins at her again, this time wolfish and charming. 'Who can blame them, eh?'

Rachel smiles. She isn't quite convinced, but she wants to stop wondering and worrying about it. Tom moves back onto the chair he'd occupied at dinner, moving her feet and bundling her into a hug.

'You deserve good things, Rach,' he says, murmuring into her ear. She squeezes him, feeling herself relax against him. He has missed the point. She knows she deserves good things. The problem is in trying to determine if this is a good thing or not.

But he's trying, and she feels comforted. For now, at least.

# 28

It's dark by the time DCI Varma returns. The knock at the door breaks a prolonged silence between me and Whitman, and we jump. We have all the lights on inside, so out of the windows there is only an inky, impenetrable blackness from which Varma has suddenly appeared.

I open the door, and she steps into the cabin, looking harried. She pulls her hat from her head, leaving a mess of thick dark waves, and shoves her glasses up into them. Before she says anything, she wipes a hand across her face, subtly obscuring a yawn. Putting her glasses back on, she finally says, 'DC Whitman, can you escort Ms Thorne back down to the police station? We need to ask her a few more questions.'

'We can't do that here?' I ask. I'm bone tired, and my eyes flick involuntarily towards the mezzanine where my bed is.

'I'm afraid not, Ms Thorne,' Varma says, her voice as heavy as my body feels. Her eyes meet mine and I flinch. There's too much despair. Desperation. Disgust. Fear.

I suddenly remember she's been in that abandoned beach hut all afternoon. And beneath the fear, disgust and desperation, there's something even more human in Varma's eyes: exhaustion. I heave out a sigh through my own exhausted body and nod my assent. It's the least I can do, after all.

We can hear the other police officers, still along the beach, as we troop out of the cabin, and I follow Whitman to his patrol car. It's the distant sound of professional shouts, of busyness, the rhythm of people doing what they're supposed to be doing. It's an alien sound here, and it seems so out of place that it's as though the whole area has changed. Has lost some essential part of its character. And that's when I realize it has, that nothing here will ever be the same, that there will always be a Before Matthew, and an After Matthew. A wound, wide and raw, has been torn through this community, and somehow I have found myself at the centre of it.

## 29

'Explain to me why you didn't tell me – or anyone – about that beach hut this morning, Callie,' Varma says, throwing a file onto the table between us, then taking a seat.

Her eyes are back to normal. She's had a coffee – or two – and she's neatened up her hair, freshened her face and her makeup, and her thick-rimmed glasses are back in place, forming a transparent shield between us.

'I didn't see it,' I say. I haven't been offered coffee or tea, and I haven't been offered water, and I would like one or more of them. My head feels as though my brain has been replaced with bricks, and my throat feels like it's now lined with barbed wire.

'You didn't see it?' she asks, exasperation in every word.

'No.'

'Didn't you walk that exact same route this morning? You must've walked right past it,' she says.

'I must've done, yeah, but I didn't notice it. Maybe the door hadn't blown open this morning. That's why I noticed it this afternoon, the door banging in the wind.'

Varma doesn't look as though this really answers her question. 'Have you walked that way much since you've been here?'

'No. This morning was the first time I'd felt up to it.'

Varma arches her eyebrows a little at this. 'So you hadn't

seen those beach huts before? Noticed anything about them?'

I take a second to think. 'I'm not sure. I remember helping to search the beach just after Matthew went missing. I remember thinking the beach huts needed to be searched, but there wasn't anything in particular about them that made me take notice.'

'Until this morning.'

'Until this morning,' I repeat. 'Those beach huts must've been searched by the police, though, right? When Matthew first went missing?'

Varma shifts in her seat, but never takes her eyes off me. 'That's what we're trying to ascertain. How we could possibly have missed him, if that's where he was being held.'

'If?' I ask.

Varma doesn't say anything for a long time, and I begin to feel uncomfortable beneath her gaze, desperate not to show it.

'There was a bed in there,' she says thoughtfully, breaking the silence. 'Clean sheets, books, toys, several changes of clothes. An iPad, even. Nowhere to charge it, of course, but it seemed to be fully charged, so we think whoever took him would take away the iPad, charge it, bring it back for Matthew. He was being taken care of. It was . . . maternal, almost.'

'Maternal?' I parrot, my voice scratching against the air between us.

Varma nods, staring at me. 'You don't have children, do you, Callie?'

The question takes my breath away. It's a grenade

thrown into this quiet, marooned room. I wait for a second for the grenade to go off, but when it doesn't, I take a deep breath, sucking in air that I've temporarily denied myself. This is still a question I don't know how to answer. I had a child, for five days, but now I don't. How do I even begin to explain that? Here, of all places? The thought of bringing Ada into this room by speaking her name sends revulsion coursing through me, so I answer in the simplest way possible, even though it couldn't possibly cover the whole story, the real truth.

'No,' I practically whisper, my heart breaking as I say it and I catch sight of Varma's face, my blood running cold at her impassive look.

## Six Months Ago

Rachel and Justin aren't ready to unveil the cabin until June. It's a Friday evening on one of those June days that could be April or October or even March – cool, blustery, grey skies. It's not what either of them imagined, each envisaging a long, summer evening, the sky ever-changing as the light leaked out, reflected back at the guests through the enormous picture windows that mark the downstairs living area, and the mezzanine bedroom above.

Still, they can't control the weather, as much as they have joked about wishing they could in WhatsApp messages during the past week. Rachel has hired her favourite waitress from her favourite local café to pass round canapés, and the island in the open-plan kitchen is set up as a bar, champagne coupes filled to the brim with a signature cocktail called the Getaway, just like the cabin. It's basically a French 75, her speciality, but with a sprig of rosemary, a rim of rock salt. It's made with a local gin that has a clean, savoury taste that Rachel and Justin agree is evocative of the beach, the sea, the view outside the vast window.

Rachel and Justin.

Rachel looks at him now and sips her cocktail. It's strong, and it's only her second or third sip. The alcohol shivers through her, going straight to her head, to her toes. Justin is talking to someone. Next to him, JJ is following the conversation, and Rachel watches as Justin draws his son into it, making him laugh, prompting the other man standing with them to ask JJ a question. Justin hadn't told Rachel he was bringing JJ tonight, but she's glad he's here. Every time she's seen him recently, he's appeared withdrawn, even a little aloof. But here, talking with his dad, being treated as an almost grown-up, he's come alive. When they arrived, he'd complimented Rachel on all her design additions. He'd particularly loved the big-screen TV, of course, and the smart speaker in the kitchen, but when he'd walked into the forest-green wet room on the ground floor he'd let out an appreciative 'Woah!' that had made her and Justin laugh. He'd even suggested they should get some dry robes to leave in the tiny cloakroom so guests could go for winter swims, an idea Rachel had made note of on her phone. It had been nice to see him excited, enthusiastic. Rachel could see where he took after his dad, and even, a little, where he took after Vanessa.

Suddenly, someone's arm is around her waist, a warm weight against her cotton dress, turning her towards them. For some reason, Rachel is expecting Vanessa, but it's Tom and she giggles.

'Oh, my God, Rach, are you drunk already?' Tom asks, teasing, but also a little disbelieving.

'No, it's this drink. Have you had any? It goes straight to your head, I tell you.'

'I'll stick with beer, then. Someone needs to be able to drive us home. This is a good turnout, eh? You guys must be pleased.'

Rachel drops her voice and leans into her husband. 'I'm still not quite sure why we're doing it, to be honest. Whoever heard of a launch party for a *holiday cottage*?'

Tom laughs fondly. 'Ah, it's nice to know you're still in there.'

'What's that supposed to mean?' Rachel asks, looking up into her husband's eyes. They're clear and penetrating – he's holding the neck of a beer bottle in one hand, but Rachel doesn't think he's had a drop yet. Those are the eyes of a very sober man.

'Just that you've been a bit . . .' he glances at Justin and says, *sotto voce* '. . . Lowe-ish, the past few weeks. It's nice to know you're not quite one of them yet.'

'I couldn't afford the price of admission, babe,' Rachel says, and this gets a big laugh from Tom, who pulls her closer, kissing her lightly on the mouth, then releasing her and taking a big gulp of beer.

'I'm proud of you, though, really,' Tom says now, a little more seriously. 'I can't believe you did all this.'

'Well,' Rachel says, wondering if that was really quite the compliment Tom seems to believe it was, 'Justin designed the building, of course.'

'Yeah, but you did everything else, right? Or did Ness get involved at some point too? Where is she by the way?'

Just then Justin sidles up to them, having dispatched his guest. 'There they are. The life and soul of the party,' he says, with a grin.

Tom grunts, his gaze grazing over the tops of the heads of the assembled crowd. 'Justin, where's your better half? Shouldn't she be here by now?'

'Stuck at home, I'm afraid,' Justin says.

'What?' Rachel asks, 'You didn't tell me. Why? What's going on?'

Justin shakes his head while sipping his drink. 'Nothing to worry about. Matthew's got a bit of a funny tummy and she didn't want to leave him.'

'Oh,' Rachel says. She hasn't seen Vanessa for several days, and has been worrying about her. She has become distant, and if Rachel is totally honest, maybe even a little passive-aggressive. Rachel had thought that working with Justin might strain things between her and Vanessa, but when she'd raised it right at the beginning – straight after Justin had suggested they work together – Vanessa had just done her wide-eyes-hand-on-heart-who-me thing and told her she was being ridiculous: she couldn't think of anyone better for the job than Rachel, and how great was it that they were all working and spending so much time together now?

But the thing was, they weren't spending much time together any more. The cosy double dates have dried up, the invitations for Sunday lunch are far less frequent, and Ness and Rachel's regular coffee dates far less regular. Instead, Rachel has spent much of her time recently either with Justin or in a virtual, digital conversation with him. If she's being completely honest with herself, she's felt as though she were in the throes of an affair. She just hasn't been able to work out if it's her husband or Vanessa she's been cheating on. She knows she's going to have to make the first move when it comes to Vanessa, though. This is their first . . . not fight, not really, but their first break, and Rachel is well aware that she is the grown-up in this situation. As much as she loves Vanessa – and she thinks she does – she's come to understand that there are many, many ways in which the other woman is somewhat immature. She won't come to Rachel with a problem, so Rachel will have to go to her, tease it out of her, force her to confront it, be a big girl. She has had to do this a lot in her life, and while she does not relish it, she is at least comfortable with it.

She takes another sip of the cocktail, letting it linger in her mouth, enjoying the sensation and then – once she swallows – the bubbles and the alcohol ricocheting through her bloodstream. She looks around for JJ, worried he might have got lost in this crowd of boring adults, but instead she spots him standing by the wood-burning stove, talking to someone she recognizes from the school gates – the father of one of his friends, perhaps? Tom and Justin are talking, but every now and again one of them will glance at her, including her in the conversation although she has long since lost the thread. What she has enjoyed most about designing the Getaway – and spending time with Justin – is how much it has helped her feel like a grown-up again. She'd thought she was getting it from her work with Ness earlier in the year, but this experience has shown her that it never felt like a partnership with Vanessa. Her friend may be emotionally immature, but when it comes to control, Vanessa is unable to relinquish it. Is that a sign of immaturity too? Rachel licks her lips after another sip of her drink. Or is it something else? Something Vanessa?

She sighs, thinking about her friend and the chat they'll have to have, then turning her attention back to Tom and Justin.

A local councillor has walked in. Justin wraps an arm around Rachel, enfolding her in his distinctive smell – something woodsy and clean with just the vaguest too-sweet hint of what Rachel knows to be his vape – and leads her across the room to the new arrival.

# 30

By the time I get back to the Getaway, exhaustion ruins my mind, runs riot through it, twisting and turning everything, churning the world into a twisted ball of anxiety that sleep, however much I want it, simply cannot penetrate. I try to distract myself – with books, with Netflix, with my phone, with lavender essential oil – but I'm still awake when dawn begins to break through the cover of low-hanging clouds, and the cabin begins incrementally to lighten. And I'm still awake when three loud bangs break through the dull silence and send my heartbeat skipping. I'm so tired it takes me a second to realize that it's just someone's idea of a knock at the door, rather than gunshots. I feel bloodshot and broken as I walk down the stairs, tying the cord of my dressing-gown as I go.

My heart shudders again when, through the glass panel of the front door, I see the silhouette of a man. Justin.

'Hi, Callie,' he says, when I open the door and let him in. 'Sorry for being here so early.'

'Justin. I'm so, so sorry. I can't even imagine –'

'Callie, please. I'm sorry, but I just can't,' Justin interrupts. His voice is hollow, his too-handsome face drawn and pale. His gaze doesn't meet mine, unlike every other time I've met him, when he has seemed almost too good at making eye contact. Instead, his eyes skip around the cabin. I tidied up overnight, wandering the rooms in a fugue state of sheer exhaustion, but determined to force the routines of tidying and cleaning to clear my mind and send me to sleep.

It didn't work.

But at least the cabin is presentable: one less thing for Justin and Vanessa to worry about at least.

'Callie, I'm sorry, but I'm afraid we're going to have to ask you to move out of the Getaway early,' Justin says.

'Oh?' I say, surprise in my voice, but then Justin turns, and coming up the short set of steps behind him is DCI Varma. My stomach drops as I remember her questions last night, and I realize Justin isn't making a courtesy call: I am a potential suspect in the investigation into the death of his youngest child, yet here I am, staying in his Airbnb.

'Hello, Callie,' she says. Ranged behind her is a platoon of scene-of-crime officers, and Varma stops at the doorway to put little blue plastic booties over her shoes before coming into the cabin. 'We're here to search the cabin,' she says, somewhat redundantly. 'And we're going to have to search your rental car too, I'm afraid.'

'Don't you need a warrant?' I ask.

'Neither the cabin nor the car is your property so, no, we don't,' she says cheerfully.

'That's why I'm here,' Justin says, still sounding exhausted. 'Vanessa's booked you a room at the Mermaid. I'll give you a lift over there.'

I know the Mermaid Inn. I've seen it on my walks through the town.

Varma tells me I have to leave everything as it is, that my property will be returned to me as and when. All she lets me take with me are my phone and wallet, so it's not long before I'm getting into Justin's BMW. I take a long look back at the Getaway before he pulls away. It's hard to imagine I'll ever come back, but despite everything that's happened, it's started to feel like home. Or, at least, a home. It's another cold, grey day and the steel sky is reflected in the cabin's endless windows. I can't see the cosy sofa, the wood-burning stove, the stylish kitchen, or the floating staircase up to the mezzanine. All I can see is a never-ending grey sky, reflected and reflected and reflected, over and over and over again.

## 31

Justin drops me outside the Mermaid Inn. 'You should think about getting in touch with a lawyer, Callie,' he says, as I'm reaching for the door handle. 'Just in case.'

His tone is thoughtful, gentle. This isn't a threat, yet something about it reeks of the ominous. I've never had to get a lawyer in my life.

'It's the right course of action, I think. Just precautionary, of course. I . . . don't think you had anything to do with any of this.' He looks almost embarrassed now, and follows it with 'Do you know anyone? I can give you a few names if you don't know where to start.'

I can only imagine how many lawyers someone like Justin Lowe must know. But I can't accept a recommendation from him. I may never have been in a situation like this one before, but I've watched enough movies, read enough books. I shake my head, thanking him, and he's driving off almost before I'm out of the car, let alone got the deep teal-green door of the inn open. It's an ancient building, snuggled up on the high street in Whitstable, an old pub that's been renovated and reinvigorated, made fashionable enough for picky Londoners. Inside, it's a blend of contemporary design, perfectly chosen antiques, and expertly clashing prints with more than a nod to the greens and blues of the sea. The woman behind the front desk is smooth, cool and discreet, with a straight-cut bob and starched white shirt tucked into blue mom jeans.

Her name is Martha, she says, and she owns the pub with her business partner, Clive. As she gives me a tour, she tells me she used to be a gallerist in London, but now she selects art and antiques, fabrics and paint samples for her beautifully appointed boutique hotel. I take this all in, deadened to her enthusiastic sales spiel. I simply follow her, mute, through the corridors of her inn. If she notices how blank and dazed, how jaded I am, she doesn't let on. But when she asks where I've arrived from and I tell her I've been staying at the Getaway, something clicks. She spins around on her heel, eyes wide as she stares at me.

'Oh, my God,' she says. Her voice is low and rich, humming with education and elegance. 'I can't believe it, I just can't. Matthew is just – *was* – God, see? He *was* just such an adorable little boy. And Vanessa and Justin . . . I can't imagine what they're going through.'

'It's terrible,' I say quietly, in agreement. 'Are you friends with them?'

Martha nods. 'Yes. We're not close or anything, but we're friends. We move in the same circles, have very similar interests. Do you follow Vanessa? On Instagram, I mean?' she asks. 'Her style is so . . .' But then she stops, shakes her head. 'Well, it hardly matters right now.' She takes a deep breath, steadying herself, slipping back into professional-host mode, and tells me about the cheese and wine hour at six, that food can be ordered anytime from the pub kitchen, and that the bar is open until midnight.

Her words wash over me, barely making an impact. I

can't stop seeing Varma walking up the steps to the Getaway, can't stop thinking about her and her team searching the cabin for any clues that I might have hurt – have killed – Matthew. Nausea lurches through me, and I tip forward, almost losing my balance. Martha grabs my arm, setting me upright. 'Let's get you to your room,' she murmurs, suddenly cottoning on that I am no ordinary guest. She settles me in, leaves me there, sitting on the edge of the bed as my eyes gaze around the unfamiliar room. When the door shuts, I take my phone out of my coat pocket, my hands shaking, unsteady, as I call my mother at home in London and wait to hear her voice.

## Six Months Ago

It takes Rachel three days to track down and catch up with Vanessa after the Getaway party. She's called and messaged multiple times, asking how Matthew's doing and expecting – hoping – that Vanessa would reach out to ask about the party and the cabin.

But nothing.

Instead it was Justin who ended up returning her messages to Vanessa:

*Things not good here, Rach – Ness now down with tummy bug and me desperate not to get it! Ness seems to think safer for her and Matthew to hole up together so I'm leaving bottles of water and Dioralyte outside his room to keep them hydrated. Feel like a prison warder.*

Rachel responded with sympathy and they exchanged messages for the rest of the evening – easy, fluid. But that just made her feel worse. She needed to sort things out with Vanessa, clear the air. There was a knot in her stomach she desperately wanted to untie. So, here she is on a bright sunny morning, two flat whites in hand, pushing open the door to The Lowe Down with her hip.

Vanessa is bent over the till, which is positioned on top of a poured-concrete plinth. When, months ago, Rachel had caught sight of how much that plinth had cost to

install while going through some of the shop's paper-
work, she had almost swallowed her tongue in shock. She
hadn't said anything to Vanessa, of course.

'Ness?' she says now, tentative.

The bell above the door had rung as she'd walked in,
but Vanessa had made no sign or move of acknowledge-
ment.

She flips her head up now, as if caught out, eyes wide
and shocked. Rachel looks to see what Vanessa was poring over when she walked in, wondering if, perhaps,
something there could have been the source of her shock,
but it's just her phone.

'Rachel,' Vanessa says. Rachel can see her controlling
her face – bringing it back into beautiful neutrality. She's
not smiling, but she no longer looks shocked or even
angry, which Rachel swore she had detected.

'Hi, I just wanted to come and see how you were doing.'

'I'm fine, Rachel. Why wouldn't I be?'

Rachel has wandered to the middle of the shop floor
and is standing there – like a lemon, she feels – still clutch-
ing the two coffees.

'You've been ill? You and Matthew? How's he feeling –
any better?'

Vanessa has stopped looking at her. She is busying herself with some papers on the concrete plinth as she says,
'Matthew's much better. There wasn't anything wrong
with me.'

'Oh,' Rachel says, finally depositing Vanessa's coffee in
front of her. She feels a mild thrill of victory when
Vanessa reaches out for it, almost mindlessly, and takes a
sip. 'Justin said you'd gone down with it too.'

Vanessa shakes her head. 'No. I was fine. Just busy looking after three sick kids.'

'Oh,' Rachel says again. 'He didn't mention Emma and JJ were ill too.' But Rachel wonders if this can be true – JJ had been fine at the event, and she could have sworn she saw him on the beach yesterday with a friend.

Vanessa sighs, looks Rachel in the eye. 'Of course he didn't.'

'I'm sorry, Ness. I don't understand. Why would Justin say you were ill if you weren't?'

'I don't know, Rachel. Why does he do a lot of things?'

But Rachel still feels as though she's missing something – something big. So, she takes a breath, letting the air out of her puffed cheeks in a theatrical manner, and says, 'Okay, Vanessa, we need to talk about this. I can tell you're angry with me, and with Justin, and I just want to clear the air. I'm confused about this whole tummy-bug thing, but that's really beside the point. You've been ignoring me and I know it's because of Justin, and I just . . . I have to say that there's no reason to worry. At all. If that's what you're worried about.'

Rachel half expects Vanessa to say something cutting – to ask her why she, Vanessa Lowe, should ever have to worry about her husband and another woman. But she doesn't. She places her coffee firmly on the counter and says something that Rachel would never have predicted.

'I know. I've been behaving irrationally. Appallingly, really.' Here she swallows, looks away from Rachel, taking in the empty shop, then at her hands. 'Can we go somewhere else? Can we go for a walk?'

'Of course,' Rachel says. They lock up the shop, Vanessa

turning the sign over to read 'CLOSED' to passers-by and they walk down to the beach together, neither of them talking until they reach it, when Vanessa finally launches into her story.

'Justin had an affair. A few years ago, before Matthew was born.'

'Oh, my God. Were you –'

'Yes, I was pregnant with him.'

'Oh, Jesus, Ness. I'm sorry. I honestly had no idea.'

'No. Well. It's not something I like to . . . There's this image of us. And I know what people think of me, that I've created that image, that idea – and I have. But that doesn't mean I haven't become a victim to it too.'

Rachel swallows. She has long since finished her coffee, and wishes they had picked up another, just to give her hands something to hold. It's not a particularly warm day and they're walking into a strong wind so she stuffs her hands into the pockets of her light cotton jacket.

'What do you mean by "victim"?' she asks eventually. The word has made her wary. The whole confession has confused her, of course – she can see that Justin is not particularly happy in his marriage, in his life, even. But she hadn't pegged him as a cheat. She has had to admit to herself recently that their easy connection has spilled over into flirtation at times, but she has also convinced herself that this is almost entirely innocent. At least on her part. She has enjoyed his attention, but it's Tom she goes home to at night, and that return has always been a relief. A joy even, more recently. So, yes. On her side, there has been nothing to it – two people enjoying one another's company.

Has there been more to it for Justin? Has he been looking for something else? An escape?

Vanessa is talking again.

'I mean that I've felt at times like I can't leave.'

'And have you wanted to?' Rachel asks.

'Yes and no. I've wanted to, but I don't want to deal with the fallout. If I could just pluck him from our lives, without anything else changing, I would. But I know it doesn't work like that. Everything would change. I've built this whole life around our marriage, our family – not just a life, a living. This is how I make my money. I can't just blow it all up. Everything else – everything – is in his name, apart from the money I make from Instagram.'

'Really?' Rachel asks, shocked.

Vanessa's hands are tucked into her coat pockets too, and even with her hair up in a ponytail, the wind is so strong it whips it around in the air, strands of auburn flicking all around her face. 'And all the money I make from Instagram comes from us being a family – the perfect family. So I can't leave. Or, at least, I feel like I can't leave.'

Rachel is silent, trying to take all this in. She has seen the cracks in their relationship, of course, although she never would have guessed at this level of foundational rot. She knows Vanessa hates how much time Justin spends away from home. His commute is long, and his job intense, and although she has never come right out to Rachel and complained about it, the little passive-aggressive jabs and eye-rolls have indicated that it's a sore point. Rachel sees now, with a belated pang of guilt, that building the Getaway cabin over the past few months would've meant even more time away for Justin from his family. More time spent with her. It's easy now for Rachel to understand why Vanessa might resent her and even the cabin: they are symbolic of Justin's desertion. And although, of course, nothing was going on between her and Justin, it can't have been easy for Vanessa to sit back and watch, or hard for her to make the leap to outright suspicion. Rachel had had no idea about Justin's affair, no idea Vanessa entertained such strong feelings about leaving.

'And the affair?' she asks quietly, the words almost lost in the wind. 'Do you know who it was?'

'Yes. Charlotte. She was new at his office. I suspected something for months. It went on for a while – not just a one-time thing.'

'Is that what he said it was? A one-time thing?'

When Vanessa doesn't answer her, Rachel says, 'Ness, you did talk to him about this, didn't you? Confront him?'

When Vanessa still doesn't answer Rachel stops walking, turning her friend towards her by pulling at her arm. 'Vanessa, tell me you spoke to him about this.'

It's a while coming, but eventually Vanessa shakes her head, her eyes distraught as she stares at Rachel. 'You think I'm an idiot,' she says, her voice thick and heavy.

'No, of course not,' Rachel says. 'I'm just trying to understand –'

'You can't possibly understand,' Vanessa interrupts.

'Well, I can try,' Rachel says, a little offended. She brushes it off, though – they're talking about difficult personal things, and if there's one thing Rachel has figured out about Vanessa it's that this level of sharing doesn't come easily or naturally to her. 'If you didn't ask him, how did you find out he was cheating on you?'

Vanessa is staring off into the distance, the flat grey sea filling her eyes. 'I'd suspected something for a while. It was when we'd first moved down here. He was never home, always at the office, always on the train, always on the phone when he was here. They had this big new client and they were preparing a massive presentation for them. They'd been working all hours on it. That's how Justin hid it. The perfect excuse . . . Well, I'm not proud of this, but I went up to London one day and I followed them.'

'Okay,' Rachel says. 'I don't want to sound like I'm making excuses here, but how do you know for sure that it wasn't just all for work? He does work a lot.'

'Oh, I know,' Vanessa says, with an edge to her voice, hard and brittle.

'It wasn't the first time,' Rachel says.

'No, it certainly wasn't. And do you want to hear the worst thing? That's how we met.'

'You mean you worked for him?' Rachel asks, suddenly confused. She realizes, though, that she has no idea how Vanessa and Justin met – she has always imagined them walking into this life fully formed, as a pair, perfect and shining. And that's when she understands what Vanessa means, about how trapped she is, about how she can't leave, because if Rachel thinks of them as being intrinsically, fundamentally connected, then Vanessa must do so even more.

'No, I didn't work for him. I mean, that that's how we met – an affair.'

'Oh,' Rachel says.

'So, now you see. I really should have known better.'

'I don't think that, Ness. I believe people can change.'

'You do?'

'Of course.'

'He didn't tell me, you know, about his wife. In case you were wondering. He was with me, I mean really with me – I was introducing him as my boyfriend, having dinners with him multiple times a week, the whole shebang – for six months, and that whole time he was married. Don't you think there's something sociopathic about that? That level of deception? The ability to disengage yourself from certain parts of yourself, your life, to compartmentalize like that. Isn't that just . . . psychotic?'

Vanessa turns to her, tears in her eyes. Her face is very pale, although there are two spots of pink in her cheeks – her emotions leaving physical evidence of her feelings.

'I had no idea,' Rachel says. 'No idea he was even married before you.'

'Julia. That was her name. Julia and Justin. Poor woman.' Rachel's eyes widen, and Vanessa holds out a hand, touching her forearm lightly. 'Oh, God, no, don't worry, she's fine. Living in Edinburgh now. But Justin really did a number on her. I should have known then that he'd end up doing the same to me. But you see, don't you? Why I've been so worried? I feel bad for suspecting you, but sometimes I think I wouldn't put anything past my husband.'

Later, Rachel is sitting up in bed trying to read. Knees up, book splayed in front of her, she has been staring at the same page for more than a minute, unable to take in the sentences. Next to her, Tom breathes softly as he turns the pages of his book, concentration intact, his tortoiseshell reading glasses making him look even more like himself than usual.

'Did you know Justin was married before Vanessa?' Rachel asks. Neither of them has spoken for a while and her voice cracks through the silence of their bedroom.

'Justin?' Tom says, barely looking up. 'No, this is the first I'm hearing of it. Are you sure?'

'Vanessa told me this morning. He was still with his wife when he and Vanessa met.'

'Huh,' Tom mumbles, shifting in the bed so his book falls from his hands as he turns to her. 'That sort of makes sense to me.'

'Really? Why?'

'All of Vanessa's insecurities, the way she tries to make them appear so perfect all the time. It's like she's trying to prove something, don't you think?'

'You think Vanessa's insecure?'

'Massively. Don't you?'

'I suppose so.'

'Don't get me wrong – her confidence is convincing, but it's all for show, isn't it? They're not really happy. They're certainly not perfect.'

'No, you're right.'

'Did she know about the wife?'

'She says not,' Rachel says. 'Not at first, at any rate.'

'But you don't believe her.'

Rachel sighs, thinking of Vanessa on the beach, telling her about Charlotte and Julia, the other women in Justin's life. After that they had gone for lunch together, sheltering in one of the pubs, cosy and warm after their blustery walk, their friendship once again settled and secure.

Vanessa had seemed lighter, a weight lifted, a confession made. They hadn't talked about Justin again, as though the matter was over and settled, as though they had decided that Rachel was Vanessa's friend, first and foremost, and Justin relegated to a side character. But walking home from nursery after picking up Sadie, Rachel's feeling of nausea had returned. The unsettled-stomach sensation that something wasn't quite right. It was the way she had often felt after spending time with Vanessa: vaguely seasick, like returning to land after a period on the water when you haven't quite got the ground beneath your feet.

'Do I have any reason not to believe her?' Rachel asks.

Tom raises an eyebrow. 'I think only you can answer that, babe.'

# 32

Varma calls me into the station the next morning. I've been trying to eat my breakfast, stomach a twisted knot of anxiety, when I get the call. She offers to send someone to collect me, but the police station is a short walk from the Mermaid, so I tell her I'll be there as soon as possible.

I'm grateful for the time spent outside, and the morning is cold and bright – the cloud finally lifted, the sun cracking its way through. It feels as though the world is opening up again, the hermetically sealed town returning to normal life, and my anxiety is soothed by this. But as soon as I walk through the doors of the station, the day suddenly dim again, I remember why I'm here.

Varma smiles thinly at me by way of greeting, and I follow her down the now familiar corridors, to her interview room of preference.

'I need you to explain a few things to me, Callie,' she says, when we're all set up, names, date and time all stated, and the camera recording somewhere, invisible, watching. 'The first is how Matthew Lowe's hair got inside your rental car.'

I blink at her. My breath stops short in my chest.

'What?' I manage to croak out.

'Strands of Matthew's hair have been found in your rental car. We did a forensic search of your cabin and car yesterday. We got the results back this morning, and they're a match.'

'I – I don't know,' I say, lost and scrambling. I swallow, wishing I had some water, panic pushing at my breast-bone, filling my lungs with cement. And then: 'Wait. I . . . The first time I went to the Lowes' house, I'd had too much to drink to drive home, so I left the car there. I didn't go and pick it up until the next afternoon. Maybe he got in then. Messing around or something.'

Varma's face creases. 'Without the keys?' she says.

'Oh,' I say, deflating immediately. 'Sorry, I didn't think of that. It's the only explanation I have for you.'

'It's not an explanation at all, Callie.'

I stare at her, shaking my head, mirroring the shaking in my voice, in my limbs and hands, as I say, 'You can't think . . . I didn't hurt Matthew. What reason could I possibly have to hurt him?'

'Maybe you didn't mean to hurt him,' Varma says, and her voice is gentler now. It makes me cringe, the delicacy of the proposition, and it's only then I notice the file sitting in front of her, because she flips it open and pulls papers out of it, turning them to face me, laying them out in chronological order. 'I'd like you to explain these to me, Callie. If you don't mind.'

And her voice is so gentle still, so full of pity it cracks me in two.

But I've already been cracked in two.

So, before she can say anything else, I look into her warm brown eyes – as full of gentle pity as her voice is – and say, 'I think I need a lawyer.'

## 33

Varma's sigh fills the sterile room, but she doesn't look surprised by my request. She must've known it was coming. She nods, her gaze still pinned to me. She reminds me that I haven't been arrested – yet – that I'm here of my own free will, that I can leave at any time, and then offers me a court-appointed lawyer, whom I refuse. I tell her I need to make a call, and as my phone hasn't yet been taken from me, she leaves me alone in the room to place it. The file is still open in front of me, the printouts arranged in chronological order. As I press the call button, I pull the furthest page towards me. She hasn't gone all the way back to the beginning, but she's seen enough.

I'm reading over the familiar but distant words when Mum finally picks up.

'Callie, thank God. What's going on?'

I give her a brief overview, ending, 'Mum, I need a lawyer.'

'Good. Yes. Luckily, I called my friend Bernadette last night, and she's said she'll come down to Kent with me. We can be with you in a few hours. Just sit tight.'

There's a pause where I try to say thank you, anything, but can't.

I place my phone on the table. I expect Varma to be back in the room almost immediately, assuming she's watching everything from another room somewhere, but she doesn't return, and instead it's just me and those print-outs, those photos, those lost words, staring back at me.

I pull them closer to me, force myself to look directly at them.

But I don't need to read them to know what they say.

After all, I took those photos, wrote those words, posted them.

## Six Months Ago

It's a bright but cool day in June and, sitting at the kitchen table with her laptop open, Rachel has her fingers wrapped around a mug of coffee having just spoken to her mum. They're trying to arrange a visit, a time for Augustina to come and stay with them, or a few days later in the summer when Rachel and the kids might head up to London to see their grandma.

For whatever reason, this conversation has got Rachel thinking about Justin's ex-wife. Maybe it's the London connection. Now that she feels more settled in Whitstable, London feels far off. Yet Justin heads there every day, making the commute, two hours each way – more really – and a daily life lived in a city that Vanessa has no real idea about. It's like having two lives, Rachel muses. It would be easy, maybe, to allow that double life to seep into your romantic and sex life. A life so divided, so compartmentalized already – and a two-hour train trip to shed one version of yourself and slip on another? It would be easy to start thinking an affair could come with the territory.

Before Rachel can stop herself she googles 'Julia Lowe', wanting to know more about Justin's first wife. There are plenty of hits, too many really, and she has no idea where to start. Vanessa didn't tell her anything about Julia, other than her first name, and chances are she's since changed her surname – or never took Justin's in the first place. Rachel clicks on a few links here and there, opening a new tab each time and navigating back to Google when she deems it unsuccessful. Taking a sip of her coffee she tells herself this is just idle curiosity, nothing more, but then she opens Facebook and heads to Justin's page. He doesn't have as many friends as she'd thought. Although, as Rachel acquaints herself with his virtual presence, she decides she isn't so surprised by this. In fact, despite his current wife's profession and follower-count on Instagram, Justin doesn't strike her as the type to have a Facebook account at all. It doesn't take her long to find Julia, though. Not now that she's got into her stride. Way back in the depths of his photos, Rachel finds some from his first wedding, and the woman in white standing next to him, beaming, is tagged as Julia Slater.

It was a small wedding apparently. They married in front of just twenty friends and family, the ceremony held at Edinburgh's City Chambers, the reception at Timberyard. Having already seen Justin and Vanessa's wedding photos, Rachel is brought up short by the differences between the two. Vanessa and Justin had got married in a stately home in Oxfordshire, the honeyed walls of the house forming the backdrop to all their staged photos, the sun picking up the bronzed halo of Vanessa's hair, all followed by a jaw-droppingly expensive honeymoon in Bora Bora. Justin looks like a different person entirely in these photos, or at least like a different version of himself. Looking at the dates of when they were posted, she quickly works out that Justin's first marriage happened at the relatively young age of twenty-five, and that by the time he turned thirty-four he was already bored of his first wife and moving on to the second. Clicking on Julia's name in the tagged photos, Rachel is taken to a private profile, which she is already unsurprised by. Just looking at the woman in the photos, Rachel can tell she is entirely different from Vanessa. So, she googles 'Julia Slater, Edinburgh' and soon finds her. She's a solicitor, a partner in her own firm, on the board of a charity that offers mentoring to children from lower-income families applying to university and their first jobs. She has bobbed brown hair, and sparkling grey eyes. In almost all of the photos Rachel can find of her now, she wears dark jackets, bright shirts, and tailored, wide-legged trousers. Aside from the private Facebook profile, Rachel cannot find a single other social-media account, or any information about her outside her work life. But there she is, a successful, accomplished, attractive forty-something, the former wife of Justin Lowe.

Rachel drums her fingers on the kitchen table, staring at these photos of a woman she's never met. What is she doing? What is this achieving? But then, before she can stop herself, she looks up Justin's architectural firm and scrolls through the website until she finds reference to anyone named Charlotte. In the photo she finds on the firm's blog about their summer party from the year Matthew was born, Charlotte is a fresh-out-of-university blonde, with the kind of straight, swishy hair that always looks glossy. A wide-eyed Becky-with-the-good-hair and access to her parents' credit card, judging by the Diane von Fürstenberg wrap dress she's wearing, and the

Mulberry handbag she's toting. Standing next to her in a summer suit, no tie, top two shirt buttons undone, his arm around her, is Justin. Rachel deflates just looking at the photo, as though it were confirmation of Justin's womanizing.

She thinks back to all their interactions and conversations, trying to track their friendship and scan it for signs of this man. Justin has always struck her as more down-to-earth than Vanessa. He clearly isn't as comfortable in front of the camera, doesn't court attention the way his (second) wife does. He is charming, yes. Very charming, really. But he has always struck her as genuine with it. Maybe it's simply in comparison to Vanessa's eternal glossiness. Or maybe it's because Justin always seems exhausted when she sees him. He's a man with a big, busy life, and it seems to be wearing him out. In comparison, Vanessa wouldn't dare let anyone see her tired. And, if Rachel is being honest with herself, it's these chinks in his armour – the heavy sighs, the weary yet handsome face – that have drawn her to him. As a pair, Vanessa and Justin project an air of invincibility, inevitability. But get Justin alone, and Rachel starts to question it.

But is he perhaps a chameleon, shaking off one identity and putting on another, according to who is around him? Just then her phone vibrates, gently shaking the table it sits on. Thinking it's her mother calling back to continue summer discussions, Rachel picks it up automatically, but it's not her mum, it's Justin – as if he's been called into being by her virtual investigations.

'Rachel? I don't know what to do. Can you meet me?'

Rachel sits up straighter in her uncomfortable wooden

chair, taking note of his voice. It sounds at once sharp and far away, and were he standing in front of her, Rachel is sure he would be pushing a hand through his dark hair, face taut in panic. 'What's going on?'

'It's Vanessa . . . She's . . . We had a huge fight last night. She's locked herself in our bedroom and she's refusing to come out.'

'Do you want me to come over?' Rachel asks. She doesn't want to, not really, but he is clearly calling for help and Rachel has always been someone who offers it.

'No, I'm not there. I had to get out, clear my head, but I honestly don't know what's going on.'

'Where are the children?' Rachel asks.

'They're fine. Emma and JJ are at school and Matthew's at nursery.'

'But today's not one of his days for nursery. I didn't see them this morning when I took Sadie.'

'I just dropped him off. I didn't want him in the house with her like that, and they were happy to have him,' Justin says. 'Look, Rach, I'm right by your house. Can I come in?'

'Yeah . . . Yeah, of course,' Rachel says, looking around herself at the kitchen and then back at her laptop where a photo of Justin and his supposed mistress smiles out at her. Jabbing at the trackpad, Rachel impatiently closes Chrome before slamming the laptop shut – as though Justin might be able to see it through the phone.

Moments later, Rachel is opening the front door and ushering Justin inside, urging him to sit down. She returns to the kitchen to make coffee, setting the stovetop Moka pot carefully on the gas hob. When she goes back into the living room, Justin is sitting in the corner of the sofa, staring blankly into space. He looks haunted almost, and she thinks of the faces of survivors after a natural disaster.

'Justin, you're scaring me. What the hell is going on?'

He snaps out of his reverie and turns to look at her. That's when she sees the mark on his forehead. An ugly red wound in the early stages of healing. Standing up, Rachel automatically moves towards him, holding her fingers towards the injury as Justin flinches away. 'What the fuck, Justin? What is this?'

Justin takes a deep breath, which sounds more like a strangled cry or groan. 'Ah, Vanessa broke a wine bottle over my head last night.'

Rachel's sharp gasp sounds like a record scratch against the dry, silent air of the cottage's living room.

'Luckily it wasn't full,' Justin adds, deadpan, although he doesn't bother to fake his own dry chuckle.

Rachel stands stock still in her living room, looking down at this man with a wound on his forehead, put there by one of her closest friends. 'Vanessa did this?'

'Yes . . . I believe you and she had a little chat about my, ah, infidelities yesterday?'

Rachel blinks at him, opens her mouth, closes it again, and then, in the silence of the room, hears the gurgle of the coffeepot next door. Relieved to have something to do, she rushes in to take it off the hob and leaves it to sit while she warms some milk.

'Rachel?' Justin prompts, having followed her through to the kitchen.

'Yeah, yeah. She mentioned she'd suspected you had an affair a few years ago. She told me she'd never confronted you about it, though,' Rachel says, her mouth and throat dry. 'She seemed . . . well, not fine exactly when I left her, but she didn't seem angry or – violent. It honestly seemed like talking about it with me had maybe helped a little. Released a valve, maybe.'

'Well, it released something.'

Rachel narrows her eyes at him, hands on her hips. 'Look, Justin, I didn't pull this out of her. She wanted to talk about it.'

'I know, I know,' Justin says, holding up his hands in a placatory fashion. 'I didn't mean to sound accusatory.' Rachel turns to pour their coffee and Justin pulls out a chair, sitting down at the table with an air of defeat. 'The thing is, Rach,' he says, reaching gratefully for the cup she holds out to him, 'she lied to you.'

'You mean you didn't have an affair?'

Swallowing coffee, Justin shakes his head. 'It's more complicated than that. She . . . The woman she thought I was having an affair with, she stalked her for months.'

'Charlotte?' Rachel says, noting the flicker of something that rides unbidden over Justin's face as he nods.

'She told you?'

'She told me her name. She didn't mention . . . stalking.'

'Well, I guess that's not surprising. It hardly paints her in a good light.'

'She really stalked her? Followed her?'

Justin wipes a hand over his exhausted face, stretching out his skin and jaw in a way that would be comical, were it not for the circumstances. After another gulp of coffee, he says, 'She even threatened her physically. She'd been following Charlotte for a few weeks by that point, not all the time, of course, but she found her on Instagram and started hounding her there too. Under a false account, not her own. And then she confronted the poor girl outside her flat in Battersea. She had a knife.'

'A knife?' Rachel repeats, almost robotically.

'She'd brought it from home. God, it was awful. Charlotte was very understanding about it, and I managed to convince her not to call the police or press charges. I tried to put it down to hormones as Ness was so pregnant by that point. She hated that, of course,' he says, 'accused me of gaslighting her when all I was doing was trying to protect her from being arrested at seven months pregnant. It was a mess, Rach. A fucking mess. It's taken us a long time to get back from that. To reach this equilibrium. I was terrified when Matthew was born, but he was a godsend, really. He was such a good baby, and he seemed to bring calm and equanimity back to her. Now I'm worried it's all happening again.'

'She thought we were having an affair,' Rachel says, almost immediately feeling like a schoolgirl reporting a friend's misbehaviour to a teacher.

'I know,' Justin says, with a sigh. 'She told me. Luckily, she seems to trust you – more than she does me because she's decided if I'm not sleeping with you I must be sleeping with Charlotte. Again.'

'But you weren't ever sleeping with Charlotte, were you?'

'No. Look, I don't want to paint Vanessa in too bad a light here. I was working far too much back then, especially considering the kids and Ness's pregnancy. I think she wanted to find a reason for me spending so much time away from home, but the fact is, my job requires long hours, and our move down here requires a long commute. I honestly didn't have time for an affair,' he says.

Rachel offers him a slightly wan smile, but she is full of a nervousness she can't quite pinpoint. Looking down at her coffee, she realizes it feels like the jitters of too much caffeine, but she knows it is something deeper than that. Once again, she feels caught up in this gilded couple whose problems are much, much larger than she imagined.

'The wine bottle,' she says, gesturing towards Justin's wounded forehead. 'Has anything like that happened before?'

The pause that follows her question is too long and too loaded for her to believe him when he says, 'No. Of course not.'

'But the knife she threatened Charlotte with?'

Justin shakes his head. 'I don't think she intended to use it, not really. She never actually did anything to Charlotte, just threatened and frightened her. I think she took it so that she could feel like a threat.'

'Justin, where is she now? Is she still at home?'

'As far as I know.'

'Do you want me to come back with you?'

'I'm not sure that would really help matters.'

'But she knows there's nothing going on between us, right?'

'Yes, but she won't be happy I've told you all this.' Justin checks his watch, closing his eyes in a pained way. 'I should be getting back . . . I need to check on her, make sure she's okay.'

'*She's* okay? Justin, your –'

'I know, I'm fine. We'll both be fine. But do you think you could pick Matthew up from nursery later? I'll call and let them know. And I'll be here later to get him. Just in case . . . Well, I don't know, but just in case.'

'Yeah, sure. Of course.'

Rachel gives Justin a hug at the door before he leaves. It lasts longer than it should, Justin reluctant to let go, to leave. Finally, Rachel gives him one last squeeze and unclasps herself. 'Let me know if you need anything,' she says, in an almost-whisper.

Justin, his face grim, merely nods and heads out of the door.

# 34

Varma is gone for hours, or at least it feels that way. She lets me sit there. Lets me simmer, lets me scan those pages, scour them. But the words and images are already scrubbed into my heart, scored into my brain, leaving scars upon scars. Tissue that has been changed for ever, reconfigured, but not repaired – never repaired. There are only three photos: the last I posted before I gave birth, a photo of me and Ada mere moments after she was born, and then the last photo I took of Ada, and the last I posted to Instagram. It was taken months ago, on a late June day. The photo is of her tiny pink fingers and barely-there fingernails, a miniature hand curled into a miniature fist. You can see the tiny hospital bracelet attached to her wrist, the Perspex of the glass shield she was surrounded by to protect her from a world she wasn't quite built for. By then she'd been in her see-through box for four days. She had stopped breathing just a few hours after she was born, had been raced to the NICU, where she was delivered to her box and they ran test after test after test after test. There was a hole in the box through which we could touch her, a window into her Sleeping Beauty world. If I'd been able to think of anything but her in those moments, I would have reminded myself that fairy tales originally existed as a warning, not a dream to be sold by Disney.

She died the next day. Two days after the solstice.

And I was plunged into a long summer of grief, when with every breath I took I felt as if I was drowning. I pull the photo nearer to me, daring myself to look at it properly. It's six months. Six whole months. A milestone no one would ever want to recognize. My fingers shake as they hover over the paper. I want to reach out and touch her, but I know there's nothing there, that a photo like this, when you've been through loss, can sometimes seem like little more than a mirage.

When Varma reappears, she is smiling at me as she closes the door behind her. The smile is as gentle as her movements. It's meant to soothe, to calm, to lull, but instead it fills me with anger, sets me right on edge. Because behind that gentleness there's not just pity but suspicion. She places a mug of tea in front of me, passes me a bottle of water, and takes her seat again.

'How are you doing, Callie? I hear your lawyer is on her way.' I look down into the murky brown tea as if it's there to harm me. But that's ridiculous, so I reach for it and take a sip. 'She called the station – Bernadette, I mean, your lawyer – and informed us that you mustn't be questioned without her present, but really, Callie, I just want a conversation for now.'

'About these,' I say, motioning towards the printed-out photos that lie between us.

'Yes. You can see why I'd be worried by them, can't you?'

'I should have deleted them,' I say, and I twist off the cap of the bottled water, take a long, deep pull. It's bracingly cold, sets my teeth on edge.

'I'm sure you've helped a lot of other women – a lot of

other parents – who have gone through the same thing. Or similar.'

I swallow. 'Maybe.'

'I'm not going to sit here and pretend I can even imagine what you went through. What you're still going through. To lose your baby at five days old, it's –'

'Unimaginable?' I say.

'Yes,' she says softly.

'Well, I don't have to imagine it,'

Varma flinches, but to give her credit, she doesn't look away. 'What was her name?'

'Ada.'

'It's lovely.'

'It was my grandmother's. She was from Whitstable, actually.'

Varma angles her head, interested. 'Is that why you came down here?'

'I suppose so. I grew up coming here, visiting her, staying for Easter and the summer holidays.'

'So, your mother grew up here, then?'

I nod.

'It must be nice for her, that you feel such a strong connection to the place.'

'I'm not sure she really understands why I'm here, to be honest. I'm not sure anyone does.'

'Help me understand, Callie. I want to understand. You really had no idea Vanessa and her family lived here?' She cocks her head, *faux*-concern, disbelieving.

I stare at her. I thought we'd covered this. 'I had nothing to do with Matthew's death,' I manage to say, after a few stalled seconds. 'And . . . and . . .' I lose my momentum, have to take a deep, wrenching breath, remind myself to breathe in, breathe out, that it's a process, an ongoing one, that I have to keep breathing. Finally, I gesture towards the printouts. 'And I had nothing to do with – with Ada. There was nothing anyone could do. She couldn't breathe on her own.'

'I know, Callie, I'm not accusing you of harming your own child,' Varma says. She's being gentle again, but she's firm. As if that accusation would be a step too far.

'But you are accusing me of harming Matthew Lowe.'

She spreads her hands, palms up towards the ceiling, as if the answer is obvious, when it's anything but.

I lean forward, body tense and rigid. 'I would never hurt a child. Never. And the longer we spend here, with you asking me these questions, the more likely it is that the real perpetrator is going to get away with it.'

'Why don't you let me worry about that?'

'I would love to let you worry about that, but you seem hell-bent on finding a link between . . .' I have to stop talking, take a breath '. . . between the death of my child and this tragedy.'

'I'm sorry this is upsetting for you, Callie, I really am. But grief and trauma can lead us to do extraordinary things,'

'Not this. Not me. You have no idea how hard this has all been for me. No idea. All I've done is try to help Vanessa and her family even when I felt . . . completely unequipped to do so. And now we're wasting time while whoever actually hurt him is still out there.'

'Callie, please,' Varma says. 'Think about my position for a second. Here I have a mother who's lost her baby, gone through something very few have and very few can even comprehend, and now another child is dead. What would you do, if you were me? Wouldn't you be asking all the same questions?'

We stare at one another for a long time and I wonder how I can possibly respond to that. What does she expect me to say? Finally, all I can think of is 'I don't think I should say anything else until my lawyer gets here.' The words leak out of me, the last gasps of air from a deflating balloon. I want to cry, to scream, to break something, to do anything, but she's waiting for me to snap, and I won't give her the satisfaction.

'Very well,' she says. 'We'll wait for Bernadette.'

And then she leaves the room, as gently as she'd entered it.

## 35

I really have been here for hours now. The door has remained resolutely closed, and it feels like a personal rebuke. As if Varma has given up on me completely, turned her back, shut the door and thrown away the key. It's easy to lose track of time here, to lose track of the world. In this hermetically sealed room, in this small seaside town, it's far too easy to forget about what lies beyond it. I can't remember what the weather was like when I woke up this morning. I can't imagine what the day outside looks like now. I can't remember what I had for breakfast, or what I ate for dinner last night. I try to imagine the world continuing, but it's as if it's become as stuck as I am. I can only imagine it as if it's been placed on pause. A snow globe, shaken up, and frozen in time.

But that's not true, of course, and now the door is opening, the spell broken, the snow globe shaken.

It's a woman I don't recognize. She's small, tiny in fact, with strawberry blonde hair, and a fierce expression. She's shaking her head as she enters, but then she turns to me, eyes catching mine, and the fierceness fades. 'Callie,' she says. Her voice is clear and smooth, the unbroken surface of a glassy lake.

'Bernadette?' I ask.

'That's me,' she says, with a dazzling smile. She leans across the table, hand outstretched, and I take it, shake it;

a lifeline. 'First things first. You're going to be absolutely fine. Okay? Say it with me now, "I'm going to be absolutely fine."'

I smile thinly back at her.

'Say it, Callie. I have to know you believe that.'

'I'm going to be absolutely fine?' I say, after a short pause, hesitation everywhere, the question evident.

She shakes her head again, but she's smiling. 'Okay, I guess that'll have to be good enough for now. It's my job to convince you you're going to be fine, after all.'

It's impossible to tell how old she is. There's an air about her of competence and maturity that makes me assume she must be older than me, but really she could be anywhere between thirty-five and fifty-five. Sitting here, I have never felt so young and so old at the same time.

'Have they been treating you okay?' she asks me, concern creasing her forehead.

'Yes. I suppose so,' I say, really not sure what she means by 'okay'. 'There haven't been any human-rights violations, as far as I can tell.'

Bernadette nods, and there are years of experience, of understanding, in that one movement. 'Well, at least you still have your sense of humour. Your mum told me to expect that, of course.'

I smile, strained, at her. I'm not really sure I was making a joke, and it's months since I had anything approaching a sense of humour, but it's easier to pretend I'm in on it with her. Even though neither of us actually laughed.

'Mum's here, by the way,' she says. 'She's checking us into the hotel.'

'Oh, right, thank you . . . Thanks . . . That's good to know.'

'She's booked us both rooms at the Mermaid, where you're staying.'

'She could just stay in my room,' I say. 'It doesn't look like I'll be going back to it any time soon.'

'Oh, you will,' Bernadette says. 'You'll be back there very soon, don't you worry. For one, you haven't been arrested yet. You could walk out of here any time you like, and there's nothing they could do about it. Although, if you ask me, you did the right thing. Showed you were willing to talk – albeit with a lawyer present.'

'So, what happens now?'

Bernadette's words have threaded a sense of relief through me, but I can't completely relax.

'It would be a good idea for us to have a little chat with DCI Varma, and then we can take you home and you can try to get some much-needed rest. Well, not home, but back to the hotel. How does that sound?'

## Six Months Ago

Approaching the nursery, Rachel is surprised – more than surprised – to spot that immediately identifiable auburn hair among the crowd of waiting parents.

'Vanessa?' Rachel says tentatively as she nears her, and is irresistibly reminded of the first time she saw her here.

Vanessa turns towards her. There is nothing on her face that speaks of a whole day spent in solitary anger or regret, nothing to give away the night before in which she broke a wine bottle over her husband's head. 'Oh, hi, Rach. I dropped Matthew late today as I had to go into the shop unexpectedly.'

'Ness,' Rachel says, lowering her voice so no one else can overhear, 'I know that's not true.'

Vanessa merely blinks at her, rapidly, and Rachel swears she can see her friend thinking, calculating. 'Ness, Justin came to see me today. So, please, just talk to me, okay? You can talk to me.'

'Can I?' Vanessa says sharply, turning away from her.

'Yes. Of course.'

Vanessa sighs, closes her eyes for a second and straightens herself, pulling up into her full height. 'Let's just get the kids and then we can go somewhere quieter.'

The 'somewhere quieter', Rachel is surprised to see, is

243

Vanessa's home. Rachel wasn't expecting to be brought here – she has already started to think of it as the scene of the crime. Contaminated. But Vanessa has always preferred her own turf to anyone else's, so they sit at the long dining table, the children in the playroom. Vanessa has shed her Burberry trench, is wearing impossibly chic tracksuit bottoms and a cream ribbed funnel-neck sweater. This is her version of casual and cosy, but just like everything else she does, it's a cut above anyone else's version. Rachel watches as Vanessa arranges herself at the table, pulling one of her legs up so that she can lean her chin on her knee. She's shivering, even though it's June and she has on her cosy outfit, so Rachel gets up, turns the kettle on in the kitchen to make them a cup of tea. She's glad of these few moments for herself – she is tense, anxious, her body taut and waiting as if for bad news. She is expecting more evasion, more lies when she returns with their steaming mugs, but Vanessa surprises her.

'I suppose he told you about the wine bottle,' she says. Her voice is low. Not exactly quiet, but a different register from normal, and she's staring at the table, one hand fumbling with the sleeves of her jumper.

'I saw the injury,' Rachel says. 'I had to ask.'

Vanessa's still staring down, avoiding Rachel's eyes. 'It's not what you think . . . Or, at least, I don't know what you think, but it was self-defence, I swear, Rach. I don't think . . . I don't think he was actually going to hurt me, but he was so, so angry and was coming towards me and I just didn't think. The bottle was there, I reached for it, and that was that. You should've seen his face after. I've never seen such shock.' She closes her eyes, and when she opens them again, she is finally able to meet Rachel's gaze. 'That's not how he told it to you, is it?'

Rachel takes a moment to answer, and in the silence Vanessa's look turns beseeching, 'He didn't really explain what happened. He said you had a row, that you were very upset, and that you hit him with the wine bottle.'

Vanessa nods, closing her eyes again for a moment. 'Of course. Of course I was the one who was very upset.'

'Weren't you, though? You *were* upset when we spoke yesterday . . . Did you finally talk to him about Charlotte?' Rachel asks, ignoring the fact that, according to Justin at least, this wasn't the first time Vanessa had confronted him about Charlotte.

'That's what we were fighting about, yes. Or, rather . . . we were fighting about you.'

'Me? Vanessa, we talked about this! There's nothing going –'

'I know, I know. And I do believe you, but I was trying to get Justin to see why I'd been acting so . . . Why I feel like I can't trust him. Why I always assume the worst. And look how he went running straight to you. I feel like I'm being replaced. By both of you.'

'Ness,' Rachel says, feeling the squirm of guilt, 'he was worried. I think he might even have been a bit frightened.'

'He has nothing to be frightened of!' Vanessa practically explodes, self-righteous anger lining her face.

'He told me you attacked Charlotte,' Rachel says quietly, holding her friend's gaze, forcing Vanessa to continue looking at her. 'That you followed her to her flat, and threatened her with a knife.'

Vanessa looks up towards the ceiling, as if trying to

ward off tears, then buries her face in her hands. 'It's true . . . Not all of it. Not the knife, but I did confront her like that. I didn't threaten her, though. I was seven months pregnant — how much of a threat could I possibly have been?'

'You told me you'd never spoken to Justin about any of this, Ness. But you must have done, surely, after all that?'

She looks up from her hands and shakes her head slowly. 'We both acted as if it had never happened.'

'What? How is that possible?'

'We're both very good at pretending, I suppose,' she says, twisting her hands together, twiddling at the stacked gold rings on her fingers. 'And Matthew was due so soon at that point, and we had so much on our plates with Emma and JJ and the move down here. And I was finally starting to take off on Instagram, getting partnerships and ad requests.' She shrugs, defeated. 'It was easy, really, to pretend nothing had happened, that we were okay. But he was so angry last night, Rach. He still claims they weren't having an affair when I know they were. They *were*.' Vanessa bangs the table with her fist for emphasis, her face contorted and red with frustration.

Rachel reaches across to still her friend's hand, to hold it. 'Ssh, okay. I know.'

'You do believe me, don't you? I bet he told you they weren't sleeping together, didn't he?'

Rachel nods, feeling the betrayal of Justin while also needing to confirm Vanessa's suspicions. 'But he also told me you were stalking her. Not just following her in London, but attacking her on social media.'

'That's not true . . . Well, I did track her down on

246

Instagram. Okay, so I suppose it is a bit true, but that makes it sound worse than it was. It makes me sound fucking crazy, but I swear to God, Rach, it's what anyone would've done in my position. I didn't attack her on social media, and I *did* follow her home, but only that one time, and it was from a *date* with my *husband*, so, really, who's the bad guy here?'

'They were on a date?' Rachel asks.

'Yes. And d'you want to know how I found out? Because that stupid idiot gave our home phone number as confirmation when he made the reservation for them. I was the one who picked up when they called here asking if my husband and I were going to make our reservation at fucking Hakkasan tonight.' Vanessa is shaking now, her hands trembling, her eyes red with the effort of not crying. She takes a deep breath. 'Look, I know I dealt with it poorly. I know I did all the wrong things . . . let things spiral, stayed with him when I should've left him, but that doesn't mean I deserved it.'

'No one's saying you did, Ness.'

Vanessa shakes her head, trying to regain control of herself, delicately wiping her eyes so as not to smudge her mascara. 'I just wish he'd own up to it, Rach,' she whispers, through unshed tears. 'He won't admit they were sleeping together, and I know they were, I *know*. I think they still are.'

Rachel is about to say something when the front door opens. JJ and Emma troop in from school. The house, formerly so still and quiet as Vanessa told her story, is filled with chatter and noise. The door slams behind them, making Vanessa wince as Emma shouts, 'Hello!' to her mum, and Matthew comes toddling out of the playroom, colliding with his big brother. JJ picks him up, walking him into the kitchen with Emma and Sadie following, stopping short when he notices Vanessa and Rachel sitting at the dining table.

'Oh,' JJ says, looking uncomfortable.

'Hi, JJ, hi, guys,' Rachel says, smiling. 'How was school?'

'Great!' Emma shouts.

Vanessa turns in her chair to smile at her daughter. 'Wonderful, sweetheart. Why don't you get yourself a snack? I think Matthew and Sadie might want one too.' Emma grins and runs straight to the well-stocked snacks drawer in the kitchen, as Vanessa switches her attention to her eldest child. 'JJ, put Matthew down, please. You have to get your homework done before your trumpet lesson.'

'I don't have much,' JJ says, still holding his brother.

'I find that hard to believe. You're always behind on your homework. Matthew, don't you think your big brother should be good and go and do his work?'

Matthew squirms in his brother's arms. '*Noooo*,' he says, burying his face in JJ's shoulder just as the doorbell goes.

Vanessa snaps, 'JJ, please. Just do as I say. I've got far too much on my plate right now to be worrying about you.'

Rachel catches JJ's eye as he puts Matthew down, and tries to smile at him, to let him know Vanessa is just stressed, worried, but the boy won't be drawn into it. He doesn't say anything, just gives his mother a slightly venomous look before turning from the room and going upstairs.

'God. Sometimes I wish they didn't grow up, you know?' Vanessa says to Rachel, before the doorbell goes again. 'Crap. That's going to be the kitchen designers. I completely forgot they were coming today.'

'Kitchen designers? You're getting a new kitchen?'

'Yes, I can't stand this one – it's so country. Old-fashioned.' She shudders. It's as if their entire conversation hasn't happened: Vanessa is on her phone, staring at the screen, flicking through photos, entirely herself again.

'Right,' Rachel says, standing up. 'I was just thinking I need to get Sadie home . . .'

But Vanessa is already gone, opening the front door and talking loudly to the designers in the hallway, laughing with them over her no-shoes policy, directing them towards the kitchen at the back of the house. Rachel slips out, getting Sadie's coat and shoes on as quickly as possible, giving Matthew a hug goodbye.

She is rigid with tension as she pushes Sadie's buggy towards the promenade. Looking out at the sea, with the tide low and the beach stretching for miles, she wants to feel relief, but all she sees is a grey, alien world offering nothing but uncertainty.

# 36

It feels different talking to Varma with Bernadette present. Not that I'm doing much talking.

Varma continues to fix me with her penetrating stare while she questions me, even though Bernadette is offering most of the answers. Almost all of which appear to be 'no comment'.

I'm finding it hard to concentrate, despite knowing it is absolutely imperative that I do so. If there was ever a time I needed to focus, it's right now, in this interview room. But as Varma's and Bernadette's words swim through my brain, the room slips out of focus. Even Varma's stare from behind her black-framed glasses can't reach me. Everything seems blurred at the edges, fuzzy and off-centre. I try to think my way back into the room, but I can't quite make it: I'm surfing a wave of exhaustion so vast, I'm afraid I might drown in it.

Suddenly, I feel a hand on my upper arm, warm and firm. It's Bernadette's, and as I turn to her, my brain finally tunes into the room again, tunes into reality. 'We need to get you home,' she's saying, throwing an apologetic glance Varma's way. The officer nods perfunctorily. 'We don't want you collapsing on us, now, do we?'

Varma passes me the bottle of water she brought me hours ago, and I swallow the last few mouthfuls, swimming back to the surface.

'Are you okay, Callie?' Varma asks.

'I'm fine,' I say.

'You're exhausted,' Bernadette says. 'Unsurprisingly. You've been here almost ten hours.'

'What?' I say. Surely that can't be true. It has felt as long as that – longer even – but I was so sure I'd get out of here and discover it had been only a few hours. That the interminability had all been in my mind.

'Come on,' Bernadette says, standing up, her hand on my back as I get to my feet.

Varma stands too. She is taller than Bernadette, not quite as tall as me. 'We'll be in touch, Callie,' she says, as Bernadette guides me out of the room. There is nothing threatening in her voice, but it still feels so. I swallow and nod, catch her eye just before I leave the room, catch her smile. I can't bring myself to smile back.

She's not a bad person, I know that. She's not my enemy. But she's the person who forced my recent past into the screaming present. Who printed out those posts – online grave markers of the worst moments in my life – and forced me to look directly at them for the first time since I posted them. I came here, not to forget exactly, but to get away from the reflection of myself in the dirty mirror of my life in LA, and instead it's been thrown right back at me, the glass in the mirror shattering around me, causing something so much worse than seven years' bad luck.

## 37

Bernadette gets me back to the Mermaid Inn somehow, but I'm still in a daze. A fog surrounds me, even though, for the first time in ages, it's a clear, cold night, stars blinking as we walk the frozen streets to the hotel, the full moon punching a perfect silver-white hole in the sky. Bernadette tells me to head straight upstairs, to take a hot shower, then meet her and my mum back in the pub downstairs for dinner. At the word 'dinner', my stomach lets out a hollow groan, and I remember I haven't eaten anything since breakfast.

Wearily, I head up to my room, but before I reach it, the door next to mine pops open, and a voice I haven't heard in person for months calls my name.

'Mum?'

'Hello, darling,' she says, opening the door wider, opening her arms. Her face blurs before I reach her and she draws me close. She's clearly tired, worn, but she still looks like herself, blonde hair dye covering her natural grey, grey-blue eyes sharp and observant, her long neck elegant and strong. She is tall and sturdy, wide shoulders that can carry a load and comfortably rest a head.

I cry silently into her shoulder and she holds me there, hand rubbing up and down my back as she makes comforting noises. 'It's okay, Cal, it's all okay. We're going to be fine,' she says, and I breathe deeply.

I am thirty-three years old. I have lived in a country other than my own for the last three years, and away from my parents' home for more than a decade. I have two degrees – and I am well on my way to my third. I have been pregnant. Given birth. Lost a baby. Experienced loss and grief, gone through trauma. But there's something about the glaring, blazing, halogen-bright lighting of the criminal-justice system staring you in the face that thrusts you into a kind of grown-up world you only ever read about, hear about, see on TV and the cinema screen. That turns you into a child. I feel too young for this. The whole time, I have wanted someone to take me by the hand and lead me out of this too-bright labyrinthine world to safety and straight roads, to signposts pointing the way towards . . . towards what? In short, I have wanted my mother.

And, thank God, she is here.

Mum draws me into her room, shutting the door behind us, and I shiver. Looking over to the window, I see it's open a crack: Mum would have her bedroom window open even in the Arctic. Ushering me towards one of the armchairs by the fireplace, she crouches in front of me, hands resting on my knees, and stares straight up into my face. 'Callie,' she says, her voice mild and low, sure, steady, yet stern. 'Callie, tell me everything. Tell me how we got here.'

So I do.

It takes a long time, and when I'm finally done, I feel hollow, burnt out. I think I know what she's going to say, but instead she stares into the distance, biting her lower lip, watching the dark world outside the window.

Then she stands, her eyes still not meeting mine, and says, 'This is all my fault.'

'What? How? Mum, come on. Of course, it's not.'

But she's still staring out of the window, still not looking at me. 'No, it is. I should've taken you home with me after we'd scattered Ada's ashes. I knew it was wrong to leave you there all alone, but I told myself – everyone told me – that you were an adult, that this wasn't something I could carry for you, but I knew they were wrong. That maybe I couldn't carry it for you, but that I could at least carry you.'

'Mum –'

'And if I'd done that, we wouldn't be here, and none of this would have happened.' She whips back to look at me, and her eyes are bright with anger – at herself, I know, but I can't help reeling back from it.

'It would have happened anyway, though, wouldn't it?' I say. 'Matthew would still have gone missing, and he'd still be dead.'

Mum lets out a breath, long and heavy, and slumps into the armchair across from me. 'But at least you'd have had nothing to do with it.'

It's a selfish thought and she knows it. The selfishness of self-protection, of motherhood, of the four walls of family: as long as we're safe, nothing else matters. Let the wolf blow down the doors of someone else's home, as long as we're safe and warm inside our own.

## Six Months Ago

Rachel has already been up for almost an hour when Tom finds her sitting in the kitchen. The back door is open, a lightweight breeze flowing in, and she has one of her giant mugs of tea – she invariably starts the day with one.

She's also on her laptop, scrolling, her eyes fixed to the screen.

'What are you doing up so early?' Tom says, with a yawn, as he refills the kettle. 'It's Saturday.'

'Couldn't sleep,' Rachel says, glancing at him briefly before turning back to her screen. His fair hair is standing straight up from his head and she smiles, appreciating his presence.

'What are you looking at?' Tom says.

Rachel swivels the laptop towards him. His eyebrows rise as he says, 'Rightmove. Ah. Back on the house hunt.'

'I just think it's time. We've been here a while now, and I love this house, but we can't rent for ever.'

Tom joins her at the table and squints at the screen. Without his glasses, he has to pull it closer to him, brows furrowing. 'Margate? I thought you wanted to buy here.'

'Just thinking about all our options. Keeping them open.'

'This doesn't have anything to do with all the Vanessa and Justin drama, does it?'

Rachel shrugs. She'd told Tom the story last night, but she hadn't been able to convey how she felt about it. He had received it like gossip – Tom was, in fact, more of a gossip than she was. Something to do with the departmental politics that academia seemed to breed. He had gasped, laughed, and lifted a wry eyebrow, exclaiming that they'd always known something had to be wrong with such a perfect-seeming couple, hadn't they? It had annoyed Rachel, that she hadn't been able to make him see this was serious. That she was conflicted. That she felt as though she'd been cast in a play without her consent and was being forced to act it all out onstage.

She feels more serene now, with the salt air moving in off the sea and wafting through her kitchen, the sun cracking through the clouds and streaming in through their windows. With a sleepy, benign Tom sipping his tea, and with her new resolve to make a change, to move on.

'I think we should go there today.'

'Where? Margate?'

'Yeah, take the kids, make a day of it. We can go to Dreamland, have some oysters, watch the sunset.'

'Okay. Why the sudden love for Margate? You said it was too London-ified.'

'No, you said that. I love London.'

Tom chuckles. 'Oh, yeah, right. You really think we should move there, though? I thought you were loving it here.'

'I am, I suppose. I just think maybe it's a bit too small.'

'For you and Vanessa you mean?'

'No, for us. Margate's still just half an hour on the train from Canterbury, so the commute won't be much longer for you than it is now, if that's what you're worried about.'

'I know, Rach,' Tom says, with a sigh. 'I'm not worried about anything, just trying to figure out where all this is coming from.'

'We always said the plan was to buy somewhere. We should view this as a trial run. It's been lovely, but I don't think it's the place for us. Not in the long term.'

'I had no idea you were feeling like this. What about Sadie's nursery? Marcus's school? We're going to make them start somewhere new again?'

'Marcus can stay where he is. I don't mind doing the school run. And Sadie will barely notice if we switch nurseries.'

'You mean without her best friend Matthew?'

Rachel looks at her husband. She knows he's raising fair points and that she's being somewhat irrational. Before this morning, she hadn't had a single thought of moving to Margate or anywhere else. But she woke up with such clarity of realization that the first thing she did was go online and look at houses for sale in the nearby town. They cannot stay here. She knows that. At first, she thought maybe she could slowly extricate herself from her friendships with Vanessa and Justin, but it needs to be a clean break. If they stay living in Whitstable, in such a small space, they will continue to see one another everywhere, and she will continue to be drawn into their lives, their world, their relationship.

She turned off her phone last night. It was the first time she'd done that in . . . well, ever. Justin had tried calling her twice, Vanessa had messaged her incessantly, and every time she'd reached for her phone and gone to open Instagram, she'd seen that Vanessa had uploaded to Stories again. It was all about her new kitchen now. She was sharing designs, and 'inspo', and at no point would any of her followers have any idea that she had had an emotional breakdown earlier in the day, and physically assaulted her husband the night before. Rachel remembers leaving Vanessa's house yesterday, the way the other woman had been able to switch so easily, so seamlessly from her tearful confession to Rachel to her smooth, warm welcome to the kitchen designers. Vanessa has a lot of switches, Rachel thinks, a lot of ways she can tick over from one version of herself to another, many masks she can don, pulling the wool over another's eyes in an instant.

Taking a deep breath, Rachel looks at Tom, who is gazing at her quizzically, still waiting for an answer. 'She'll adapt,' she says. 'Sadie will adapt. She's flexible. She'll get a new best friend.'

Tom sips his tea. 'Okay,' he says. 'Let's take a day trip to Margate then.'

## 38

Back in my room after dinner, I open Instagram on my phone. There's a fire crackling in the grate – it's been made up while I was eating, and the hiss, the pop, the comforting roar are all that accompany me as I enter Vanessa's name into the search bar, and her feed comes up.

The first thing I notice is that her following has now passed a million, and even though there is no new post from her, she has been on Stories, the pinky-orange circle almost pulsating before my eyes. I click on it, and lean forward over the phone, every muscle in my body tense and waiting.

Heavy breathing. The visceral sound of a nose dripping with un-mopped-up snot. A deep breath. A word started, then taken back. A sob. A hiccup.

There's nothing on screen, not really. A swirl of unidentifiable images – the phone held too far from her face, or maybe too close and out of focus.

Then nothing.

And then –

A close-up of Vanessa. Her face is red, white and blotchy, eyes rimmed red and wide, wide open. Her pupils are tiny. Her lips seem even bigger than usual, plumped and raw from crying. The shaky camera has gone. Maybe she's leaning her phone up against something or is in the grip of some steady-hand resolve. She takes a deep breath.

'I just had to identify the body of my younger son. For anyone who doesn't know yet, Matthew was found dead this morning by someone staying in the area.'

Me.

'They still haven't determined the cause of his death –' She takes a deep breath again, eyes staring longingly into the camera. Her lip wobbles a little before she continues. 'They think he might have escaped from wherever he was being – being held captive, and drowned, but there's a chance he was dead already, and the killer dumped his – his sweet little body in the sea somewhere near here in Whitstable.'

A long-drawn-out sob. A wail, really. The discordant, terrifying call of a mother who has lost her young.

I have never seen someone's else grief, someone else's pain, this close before. I've witnessed my own, of course, and we're all used to seeing it on television, at the movies, on stage. But to see it in person like this, through a screen, yet still so hideously real, there's something uncanny about it, something deeply unsettling. And yet didn't I do the same thing in committing those photos to Instagram in my worst moment, so that someone – anyone – could be witness to what I was going through, and somehow share the burden?

Is that what Vanessa is doing here?

I watch the rest of the video, tense and mute. She doesn't mention me, apart from that first oblique reference, but I notice she hasn't updated Stories since I went into the police station this morning. These are all from yesterday, almost twenty-four hours old, and about to be wiped from existence for ever.

I don't know what to do. Part of me wants to know exactly what she's thinking, wants to reach out, and I'm annoyed she hasn't updated her posts recently, meaning there's nothing solid for me to go on. To try to decipher whether or not she suspects me.

I remember her talking to me about Rachel Donovan in the Getaway cabin's kitchen. It feels like years ago. She had been wound up about it, but she hadn't been scared, not really. There was vitriol, and maybe even a little enjoyment.

Then I remember talking to Rachel in her own warm kitchen, and she had seemed indignant. Indignant and maybe a little self-righteous. I know Vanessa thinks Rachel did all this, but is it possible? That warm, bright woman in her warm, bright kitchen, could she really have taken Matthew, hidden him and left him to die?

My brain scrambles to make connections, to forge links, to figure out what's going on. What connects these two women, who's telling the truth, and whom I should believe. And where and how I fit into it.

It's late now. The time on my phone confirms it, even as my body feels it, right the way down in my bones. I'm exhausted, but the blue light of my social-media search has done its work, and I know, even if I closed my eyes right now, I wouldn't sleep. I think about calling my sister, but instead I find myself calling Adam.

'Callie,' he says, picking up almost straight away, his voice strident, calm, just a little surprised.

'Adam, good, I was worried you wouldn't pick up.'

There's a pause when I think I can hear someone else talking to him, but then he says, 'Of course I'd pick up.'

261

It hits a false note, and I know now, am suddenly sure, that he's sitting somewhere with Vanessa. That she's listening in. How long had they been waiting for my call?

'I just . . . I wanted to reach out to Vanessa, but I didn't want to intrude. She must be going through so much right now,' I say, 'but I know you'll get to her any message I have for her, right?'

'Of course,' Adam says.

'You must know I spent the day at the police station,' I say.

'Yes . . . Yes, we're aware.'

'I don't know how Matthew's hair got in the car, Adam. And I didn't do anything to hurt him.'

There's another pause, and I wonder if Vanessa writes something for him to say, whether she's directing this entire conversation. 'We heard you asked for a lawyer.' His voice has changed now, hardened.

'Yes. I did. But you have to know I would never have hurt Matthew. You have to believe that.'

'I don't have to do anything, Callie. Not for you.'

'You're right. I suppose what I should've said is that I want you to believe that. Because it's the truth. Honestly. I wouldn't hurt him – I couldn't hurt him. I didn't hurt him.' My voice is desperate, jagged, rasping. Shards of glass scraping down my throat. The exhaustion and the grief, the memories and the fear have finally caught up with me, and I can feel myself unravelling. All the threads I had spent so long pulling and holding together, just to get me to this point, all of them let go in the course of one day. How could anyone suspect me of this? How could anyone think I could bear to put another person through this? I want to say all this to Adam – or, really, to Vanessa – but my voice is stuck somewhere in my throat and I know, I just know, if I utter any more words they will be said through deep, racking sobs. There is silence at the other end. Or, rather, not silence, but heavy breathing. I take a deep breath, building myself up to speak again, but Adam stops me having to.

'Okay, Callie, I hear you. But I think it would best if you didn't contact me again. Me or any of my family. I think you've done enough.'

I let out a gasp, once again about to say something, but that's it. Adam hangs up and he's gone.

# 39

I've just woken, brain moving sluggishly into gear, light creeping at the edges of my room's heavy curtains, when the hotel phone on the bedside table rings. Martha at the front desk tells me someone's waiting for me in the library.

When I get there, I'm not sure how I feel about the person standing, shivering slightly, over the open fire, her hands outstretched towards the flame.

'Vanessa,' I say sharply, and she turns to me at once. She looks as wan and as red-eyed as she did in her Instagram Story. Her skin is stretched taut over her face, her eyes sunken, cheeks hollowed from days without rest. I feel something in me reach for her – I know that look, I've seen that face. But her being here strikes a new, different chord, one that sets nerves jangling through me.

'What are you doing here? I don't think I should be talking to you,' I say, turning back to the library's door, as if Bernadette might have been summoned by Vanessa's mere presence.

Vanessa wrings her hands. 'I don't either, but I had to come. I've been lying awake all night thinking about you. Thank you . . . Thank you for calling Adam last night. You didn't have to do that.'

I stare at her in disbelief. 'Vanessa . . .' but I don't know what more to say and my voice trails off into the chilly air of the room. Vanessa is still standing in front of the fire, blocking its warmth, and the normally cosy library feels cold. I look outside, but the day is foggy, a winter sea mist not yet lifted.

'I don't think you killed Matthew,' she says stoutly, staring straight at me still. 'I just don't. I don't think you . . . you would inflict on somebody else the same pain you've felt.'

My body is about to go rigid, stiffen in self-defence, but instead it seems to melt, fold in on itself, and I have to grab the back of one of the library's armchairs to stop myself falling to the floor. 'Thank you,' I manage. 'I wouldn't. I didn't.' I am on the edge of tears, on the edge of everything, really. The last few days have brought it all back. The panic, the fear, the desperate feeling of helplessness. The exhaustion of grief. All I want now is the impossible: to see Ada. And all Vanessa wants right now is the impossible: to see Matthew.

'I know,' she says, and I can see in her eyes that she does.

I swallow, take a deep breath. 'Adam didn't seem to know. When I spoke to him last night.'

'Adam is very protective of me. We talked for a long time after that, and I think he realized that he didn't believe you could have hurt Matthew either.'

I nod stiffly, relieved, but still wondering why on earth Vanessa is here. But then she says, 'I wanted to talk to you about Rachel.'

'Rachel Donovan?' I ask unnecessarily, as I feel my stomach slipping, a dip and surge as I anticipate exactly what Vanessa's going to say next.

'Yes. I think she killed my son.'

## Five Months Ago

It's almost a full two weeks later when Rachel bumps into Justin again. She's seen Vanessa at the school gates and nursery drop-off and pick-up, of course, but she's begged off any socializing with the excuse of too much work – she is finally picking up some freelance projects, which are, to her great relief, unrelated to either Vanessa or Justin – and later, her mum's visit. The weather has changed, all of a sudden, the way British weather does, and the damp June has turned into a scorching early July. All week it has felt so hot that Rachel swears she could hear the tarmac melting.

It's been days of too-hot tantrums, no-sleep nights, and an ice cream every afternoon. She's woken early every morning to get her swim in, and if it wasn't for that, she's sure she would've lost her mind. It is, everyone in town agrees, entirely too hot for England. It wasn't built to withstand this heat. But it's Friday, it's been a long week, and they have no wine in the house, so she rushed out just as Tom got home to grab them the last bottles of rosé in Sainsbury's. They aren't even cold – she'd been imagining them dripping with condensation, the ice-cold drink of her dreams – but she'll have to shove them in the freezer when she gets home to ensure maximum enjoyment. This is what she's thinking about, debit card already in hand, when she feels a tap on her shoulder just as someone says, 'Hello, stranger.'

'Justin, hi!' she says, surprised to find that she is, in fact, happy to see him,

'Long time, no see. I've been suffering withdrawals.'

Rachel laughs, and just as ever with Justin, she cringes at the schoolgirl sound she makes. Why does she always, always do that with him? 'Don't be ridiculous. It hasn't been that long, has it?'

'Just a measly fourteen days,' Justin says, with a white-toothed grin. 'Not that I've been counting.'

'Justin . . .' Rachel says, but it's her turn at the till and she has to turn away from him. She goes through the motions of paying for her wine, both bottles still clutched to her chest, before shoving them into her tote bag to take home.

She waits for him once she's done – it would be rude not to – and watches as he pays for a tube of toothpaste. It crosses her mind that he doesn't even need the tooth-paste, that it was simply a ruse to follow her into the shop, but she pushes the thought away again. What would be the point of that?

He's smiling again as he turns, sees her waiting, and they exit the shop. They stand in silence, absorbing the evening sun, until Justin says, 'I couldn't tempt you to a drink, could I?'

Opposite, on the other side of the street, the pavement is full of after-work drinkers enjoying their moment in the sun outside the pub. Justin tilts his head towards them, still smiling, and the thought, Rachel has to admit, is tempting. But then she adjusts the strap of her bag slightly, making it more comfortable on her shoulder, and the two bottles of rosé clink together.

'I think I'd better get these back to Tom, actually. He was desperate for a drink and about to be on bath duty when I left the house.'

'Fair enough,' Justin says, and Rachel wonders if he's expecting an invitation, wonders if he's trying to delay his return home. They have exchanged brief WhatsApp messages since he was at her house two weeks ago, but neither has broached the topic of Vanessa and it seems strange, false even, to be standing chatting while not mentioning the circumstances in which they last saw each other.

'How's Vanessa?' Rachel says finally. She can tell immediately that Justin would rather she hadn't mentioned his wife. His face changes, flinches, as if he's reminded of something he's been trying to ignore.

'She's fine,' he says slowly. 'We all are.'

'Really?'

'Well, I know she misses you.'

'Really.'

'But I know you've been very busy.'

'Yeah. We've had my mum staying. It's been lovely, but full on.' Justin nods in his usual encouraging manner, as if urging her to go on, the smile still in place, eyes squinting against the sun. Rachel continues: 'And we've been house-hunting.'

'House-hunting,' Justin exclaims. 'I had no idea you were looking to move at this point. I thought you loved the cottage?'

'I do . . . We do. We just think it's time to buy.'

'Ah, of course. Well, I can understand that. I was going to say I wish you'd told us if you were having problems with the house.'

A trick of the setting sun means that as he says this, Rachel is sure that, for a tenth of a second, the sun is pouring directly into Justin's eyes, distorting his face, making it impossible for her to meet his gaze. 'Why?' she asks. 'It's not as if you could've done anything about it.'

'Well, as the landlords, I'd say we probably could.'

'What?'

'What?'

'You're – you and Vanessa own our house?'

'Yes. You know that. Don't you?'

'No. We rented it through an estate agent in town.'

'They manage the property for us. Are you really telling me Ness never mentioned this to you?'

'No. Never.'

'You're kidding. Maybe she thought it would make things awkward once you guys became friends.'

'Maybe,' Rachel says distantly, but she's thinking of the time last year when she got home to find Vanessa standing in their kitchen. She had claimed the back door was unlocked, but clearly, Rachel sees now, she had just let herself in with her own key. How many other times has Vanessa been in their house without her knowing about it? What was she even looking for? Or was it simply that she could? There has always been something distinctly territorial about Vanessa. As sleek and preening as she is, there's also something feral, something visceral. She keeps her claws retracted most of the time, but Rachel knows they are there just below the surface, waiting for the least provocation to take a swipe.

Looking at Justin now, his face is free from guile, but she doesn't understand how he can be so calm, so *not confused* about this. Why hasn't he mentioned the fact that he and his wife are Rachel's landlords before? How could it not have come up at some point in the preceding year or so that they have all been friends? It feels like deceit to Rachel. Like a cover-up. But what would be the point of that?

'Rach,' Justin says, reaching out to graze the bare skin of her arm, 'you okay?'

'Yeah,' she says, clearing her throat which is suddenly very dry. 'I really should be getting home, though. Say hi to Ness and the kids, okay?'

She leaves Justin standing there without a backward glance – she doesn't hear his goodbye, doesn't register his confusion at her abrupt departure. By the time she gets home, she is shaking with something verging on rage but that also feels like fear. Tom is still busy with the kids, so she shoves both bottles of wine into the freezer and pours herself a finger or two of whisky, downing it like a shot. It's forever since she downed any kind of alcohol like that, and a long time since she had any whisky, but she can't bring herself to do a shot of gin, so she tries to relish the burn that so many people seem to love but leaves her wanting water. She's standing over the sink drinking a glass when Tom joins her. Even with her back to him, he seems to sense that something has happened.

'Rach? Everything okay?'

She turns to him, eyes wide over the rim of the glass. 'What's happened?' he asks, perplexed. And then, 'Did you get the wine?'

'Yes, I got the bloody wine.' Rachel gasps, as she finishes her second glass of water in as many minutes. 'It's in the freezer.'

Tom is still looking at her quizzically as he opens the freezer door and pulls a bottle out by the neck. As he pours them both a glass, adding ice cubes when he discovers how warm it still is, she tells him about Justin's revelation.

'That's deeply weird,' he says. 'How has it never once come up before? I don't understand.'

Rachel sips her wine. 'I don't either. You'd think it would have been the first thing Vanessa said to me when she came to the house, or I mentioned where we lived – "Oh, hey, I actually own that house." I mean, what the fuck?'

'It's very fucked up. I think we can agree on that. Although . . .'

'What?' Rachel demands.

'If anyone's not going to mention a house they secretly own, it's the Lowes. They're so laissez-faire about money. Don't forget they basically "forgot" they owned the Getaway cabin before you guys did it up.'

'This is different. This is our house. This means *our* house has always been *their* house. This whole time we've basically just been playing house in their actual house. It's creepy.'

'It could just be what Justin said to you – they didn't want it to be weird between us, so they decided not to mention it.'

'Well done, guys, way to make it not weird,' Rachel says, with a shudder. Tom sends her a look of sympathy and is about to say something when Rachel continues: 'Have you heard back from the estate agent about the Margate house?'

Tom shakes his head sadly. 'Nothing from the vendors about our offer yet. There's been a bunch of offers, though, the estate agent told me.'

'So, it's not looking good. Shit.'

'You didn't absolutely love that house, though, Rach. I know you didn't.'

'I know, but we clearly need to get out of here as soon as possible.'

Tom is silent for a while as he considers his wife. 'Is it really that big a deal? We've already decided to move, we're looking at houses. We don't want to rush into anything just because we're a bit creeped out. I mean, we've been living here for a year now. If they've been watching us secretly, they've seen it all by now.'

'You don't really think they have, do you?'

'No, of course not. I was joking. They're weird rich people, not voyeurs.'

'The two are hardly mutually exclusive, Tom.'

'You know what I mean. This is a weird situation to be in, but I don't think they're, like, *spying* on us.'

Rachel nods, as if in agreement, trying to feel comforted. Does she really think Vanessa and Justin have been spying on them? No. Does that make her feel any better? Any safer? Any less freaked out? No. Because she's just realized that, for a whole year now, her whole life has revolved around the Lowes. Every inch of it has been infected by them. Not only has her entire social life revolved around them, but they've also been the source of her income and the owners of the roof over her head.

It's too much, Rachel thinks, staring out at the court-yard garden with unseeing eyes. It's too fucking much. Something has to be done.

## 40

'I can't do that,' I say, shaking my head more than a little wildly.

Vanessa has just asked me to help her lay some kind of trap for Rachel Donovan.

She takes a step towards me, her intense stare turning even more so. 'But this could help you, Callie. Help direct police attention away from you, and get the person who actually hurt Matthew. Don't you want that?'

'Of course I do. But that's also exactly why I can't do it. I can't do anything that might look as if I'm interfering with the investigation, Vanessa.'

Vanessa's expression changes, disgust and frustration flitting across her beautiful face. They disappear as quickly as they arrived, and then she is staring at me with her imploring eyes, her clear, unyielding gaze. 'Because it might hurt you. Because helping me – helping Matthew – might hurt you?' she clarifies.

'Yes,' I say, the word swallowed in my shame.

She looks tired, mired in grief, the desperation that clings to it like a cancer in the beginning stages. But her hair is still an auburn waterfall, spilling perfectly in waves around and over her shoulders. It seems to quiver along-side her, as disgusted by me as she is. 'I'm sorry, Vanessa, I really am. I can't jeopardize myself even further. It all already looks so . . . well, guilty.'

'They haven't arrested you yet, though, have they?' she asks. 'You were only being questioned, right?'

'Right, but –'

She shakes her head, angry, righteous. 'I don't understand what they're doing. I've already told them how Matthew's hair might've got into your car, but they're stuck on it. They just won't listen to me about Rachel.'

'Wait, what?'

'Well, he got into your car to hug you goodbye, remember? When I drove you back to pick it up?'

I stare at her. Of course. Vanessa had driven me back to her house, and she'd been holding Matthew as I got into the rental car. He'd been waving goodbye to me, and I'd waved back, smiling, even though I could feel myself about to cry, and I remember seeing the moment Vanessa realized it, and whispered in her son's ear. His smile broadened, and he shouted, 'Hug!' through the closed window at me.

I had laughed, despite myself, despite my almost-tears, and Vanessa had smiled as cheerily, as genuinely, as she always did, and I'd opened my door, and Matthew had asked, do you want a hug? And I'd said, yes, I'd very much like a hug, and Vanessa had handed him over to me, never fully letting go, as they both bent down towards me, and we'd all been there, frozen in time, for a hug, and one or two or however many strands of Matthew's hair had somehow ended up in my rental car.

'You told them about that?' I ask.

'Of course. As soon as they mentioned it. It was the only time I could remember Matthew being in your car.' She gives me a slanted look. 'You didn't tell them?'

It takes me a second to answer. 'No . . . I didn't even think of it. They asked me if he'd ever been *in* the car but . . . I guess I forgot about that.'

She nods, and I can see in every line of her face how difficult it is to talk about her son like this. To talk about Matthew as if he's a riddle to be solved, not a person to be mourned. 'I'm sorry, Vanessa. You shouldn't have to be talking about all this with me. It's not your responsibility.'

She looks deflated now. Her energy has changed, as if she'd left the room, and she nods vacantly at me. 'And I shouldn't have asked you about Rachel. You're right. It's too dangerous for you. It wasn't fair.'

I tell her what she needs to hear – that this is the least unfair thing at the moment. That words like 'fair' and 'unfair' barely cover the cavern of unfairness that has opened in her world, and that she has every right to demand unfair things from the people in her life at the moment. She nods again, and I know she's listening, but I also know there's nothing I can say to make her hear me. And as I look at her, at the fear and guilt, defeat and worry that line her face, I see my mother last night in her draughty guest room upstairs, the wind shaking her open window. She had the same look on her face as Vanessa does right now.

All she's doing is asking me to help her, reaching out a hand that I'm refusing to grab. I can't pull her free of this – maybe nothing and no one ever will, not from something like this – but I can grab that hand, and let her know I'm right there with her.

# 41

It's not an elaborate plan, and for now at least it requires very little of me. All Vanessa asks me to do is to send a DM to Rachel Donovan, reaching out for a chat.

> Hi, Rachel, as you probably know by now, I've been questioned recently about the death of Matthew Lowe and it's got me thinking about what you said to me last week when we met. Do you really think Vanessa was trying to frame you for burning down her kitchen? Because some of the questions I was asked yesterday have got me feeling very uncomfortable. Sorry for reaching out like this, but honestly I feel like you're pretty much the only person I could turn to with a question like this.

Leaving my number, I sign off asking her to get in contact ASAP, and she does exactly that. Less than fifteen minutes later, my phone is ringing with an unknown number.

'Hello?' I say, on picking up.

'Callie Thorne?' a voice asks a little nervously. 'This is Rachel Donovan.'

I breathe out a sigh. 'Rachel, thank God. I was hoping it would be you, but I was worried it might be a reporter or something.'

'You've had reporters calling?'

'One or two. I had to have room service for breakfast

as apparently the pub is suddenly very popular with news teams.'

'I guess I shouldn't be too surprised to hear that. It feels as though everyone in the country is talking about Vanessa Lowe.'

'Has anyone contacted you at all?' I ask.

'Just the one. It was from someone who'd clearly been doing some digging and had come across all the stuff online about the fire, and our so-called feud.'

'What did you tell them?' I ask.

'Nothing. I'm not about to get into a mud-slinging match with Vanessa Lowe, days after her son has died.'

'Right. Of course,' I say, then dive in. 'Rachel, the last time we spoke, you implied that Vanessa might have staged Matthew's disappearance to gain sympathy and followers.'

There's silence at the other end, echoing the silence in my room. I am hidden up here, cloistered, protected. It was Bernadette's idea: she rang me before I had a chance to head down to breakfast this morning after seeing Vanessa. She was already in the dining room, hearing the voices, listening to the whispers. It was better I didn't come down to stir it all up. In a matter of days, I had gone from seeking refuge, searching for an impossible form of protection, to being forced into a seclusion that now chafed and chained me.

'I . . . I'm not sure I said that exactly,' Rachel says finally, weighing her words carefully. 'Besides, that was before Matthew was found. There's part of me that thinks, maybe, Vanessa could have hidden her son away for the publicity, but I definitely don't think she could hurt him in any way.'

'Are you sure?' I ask.

'Aren't you?' Rachel says, her voice travelling higher in surprise.

'I'm just not sure about anything any more, Rachel. What if it was an accident? Matthew's death? What if Vanessa *was* hiding him, like you thought, and he died accidentally?' These words come unbidden – from nowhere it feels, except they must come from somewhere. Martha came up earlier to light the fire in my room, and it's still there, burning away, although it may as well not be for all the good it's doing. A chill has run through me, swamping me with ice and fear. There's no way any of this could be true, is there?

'You found him, didn't you?' Rachel asks me, her voice quieter, more restrained.

'Yes,' I say, unable to stop the image of Matthew lying on the beach filling my mind.

'Was he visibly injured in any way?'

'Not that I could see,' I say slowly.

They haven't revealed the cause of death yet, but even with my limited medical knowledge it was pretty clear that Matthew almost certainly drowned.

We're both silent for what feels like a long time, neither of us entirely sure we want to continue with this conversation, although possibly for completely different reasons. 'You knew Matthew, right?' I ask, trying to get the conversation back on track.

'Yes, of course. He was such a beautiful little boy.'

'Your daughter is the same age?'

'Yes. Sadie and I loved spending time with Matthew. With all of them, really. Emma is such a sweetheart, and JJ was so good with the little ones. We were all very close, before it all got so ugly.'

'He was very trusting, wasn't he?' I say, thinking of Matthew snuggling against me in the Lowes' cinema room. 'He'd do anything for his mum,' I add.

'He was definitely a mama's boy,' Rachel agrees, echoing Adam's words to me, days before. 'But then again, a lot of them are at that age. They're only just beginning to test their boundaries.'

'But he was well-behaved and affectionate. That's what I thought, anyway. If Vanessa asked him to do something, he'd do it.'

'You mean hide somewhere for several days?'

'Well, yeah,' I say.

Once again, there's a contemplative silence at the other end of the phone, and it's still so quiet in my room that the sound of Rachel drawing a deep breath reverberates down the line, right into my chest. 'It's so hard to believe, yet it's exactly what I'm starting to think might be true.'

## Five Months Ago

Rachel can't sleep. Next to her, Tom slumbers soundly, unaware of her insomnia, apparently unconcerned and unperturbed by the revelation of who owns the house he now sleeps in. But Rachel can't get it out of her mind, can't stop wondering why Vanessa and Justin haven't mentioned it to her during their year of friendship.

Was it really of no importance to either of them?

She can believe this of Justin. Although they are close now, Rachel knows he is too busy, too stressed, to worry or wonder whether or not Rachel and Tom were aware that he is their landlord. But Vanessa has been to this house so many times, has had so many chats in the living room, at the kitchen table, in the garden, outside the front door. How can it not have occurred to her to mention it?

Frustrated, Rachel sits up in bed, reaching blindly for her phone in the dark. She tells herself she is reaching for it, rather than her book, because she doesn't want to wake Tom beside her, but she goes immediately to Instagram and Vanessa's feed. There, she clicks on Vanessa's profile photo and pages through the last twenty-four hours' worth of stories. For the most part, it's more kitchen updates, but then, right at the very end, there is a post that punches Rachel right in the chest.

It is a text post, which, from Vanessa, is unusual enough to be a surprise. But it's the content that has her sitting even straighter in bed, heart banging at her chest as she stares down at the words emblazoned across the instantly recognizable multicoloured background.

I'm not normally one to write about things that stress me out here – but I'm having issues with a friend that are really throwing me through a loop, guys. I hate being so on edge over a friendship, especially one I value so highly, but I'm really beginning to feel like I can't trust this person. Has anyone else ever gone through this kind of thing as an adult? Such a familiar feeling from growing up, but I never thought I'd be betrayed by a friend as a 'grown-up', lol. Let me know how you guys deal with this kind of thing. I could really do with some help and advice!

It's about her, of course. Rachel sees this immediately. And, knowing how involved Vanessa's followers are with her life, she feels sure that most of them will be able to guess Vanessa is referring to her. Rachel is easily the most visible person on Vanessa's feed, other than her family, and Rachel's own following has grown exponentially since she started regularly being tagged by and included in Vanessa's posts. But Vanessa has never shared anything as personal – as vulnerable – as this before. She hasn't shared any of her troubles with Justin over the past few weeks, and there has never been any mention of the stress she's dealt with from JJ's misbehaviour at school. But here she is, reaching out into her virtual snow globe of friends, and shaking it up. Rachel knows this is tactical. Just like not complaining about Justin online is tactical too. Because everything Vanessa does online is about shaping and sharpening her image so that it is buffed to perfection. Rachel thinks back to that windswept day last month, the cloud low and grey overhead, as Vanessa poured out her heart to her on the beach about Justin's infidelities. If you looked at her Instagram from the same time period, you would have no idea she was experiencing such doubt, anger and heartache over her husband. But those moments are not photogenic, do not fit into the frame of her otherwise perfectly primed life. So, why is she sharing about Rachel – however obliquely – and why now?

Suddenly feeling hot – too hot – Rachel slips from bed and hurries downstairs. The cottage has started to retain the heat of the summer, and although they have left windows open it is beating with night-time warmth. They have only two fans, which they have left on in the kids' rooms, forgoing the comforting white-noise whirr and cooling breeze for themselves. Rachel opens the front door and steps out into the small garden. She can hear the smashing waves of the sea, feel a faint breeze reaching towards her from the beach. Grabbing keys, and slipping on some Birkenstocks, she quietly closes the door behind her and crosses the street to the pebble beach, aware of how she must look in her gingham nightie. Walking towards the water, she starts to feel better. She needs space and air to think rationally – she has always loved the cottage, but tonight it felt cramped rather than comforting, claustrophobic rather than cosy. It's not just the warmth, of course. She simply can't get Vanessa and Justin out of her head.

She wonders if this was the point all along – to have

them so deeply embedded in her life and her head that she cannot extricate herself from them. She looks at the phone in her hand, thinking about Vanessa's Instagram post. It feels like a bomb about to go off, but why does she care so much? She has already decided to distance herself from Vanessa – finding out she is their landlord is the final nail in the coffin. So, what does it matter if Vanessa is trying to get the last word in? Trying to bend and twist the story so that she comes off as the good guy. All Rachel wants is to find herself and her family a new home, and to start afresh. So, what if Vanessa takes some of Rachel's new followers with her? It's hardly the end of the world.

But all this rational thought doesn't make Rachel feel any better. She starts to think of Vanessa at home in her shiny, reflective box of a house, everything in its place, not a vase or a candlestick out of line, and it makes her angry. She thinks of her children and her husband asleep under the roof of a house that Vanessa owns – has owned all along – and feels sick. Has their whole life here been a lie? She looks out at the rolling black sea. The moon is waxing and almost full in the sky above her, making the pebbles in the dark glisten in its silvery light, the waves almost iridescent. It's too beautiful to leave, and Rachel resents that she has to uproot her family, take them away from this view and the place they have begun to think of as home.

What if she had never met Vanessa? What if she had never tapped her shoulder but instead had kept her at a safe, Instagram-profile remove, someone she followed and watched through social media, rather than someone who controlled and contorted her every move? Who else would she have met? Which other mothers standing at the nursery gates might have become her friends? How else could she have been involved in the town and the community? She takes a deep, lung-filling breath of air. It seems saltier at night, as though she is able to experience more of the sea air, more of its intense purity without the distractions of the day.

Unthinking, she shucks off her shoes, leaving them lying on the shingle, her keys and phone in one, as she wades into the water, the cold waves gently lapping first her feet, then her ankles, her shins, knees, thighs, and finally her bum and waist. Here, she immerses herself.

When she breaks the surface again, gasping for air, she feels strong and whole and ready for a fight.

# 42

'She thinks Matthew's death was an accident,' I tell Vanessa. It's later in the day, and rain is battering at the windows of my room. 'She thinks you staged the kidnapping, for sympathy or followers, or a combination of the two, and that Matthew died somehow as a result.'

I can hear the wind at the window, howling down the chimney, but despite all that noise, I can still hear Vanessa's sharp intake of breath. 'Oh, my God, Callie, that's great. That's amazing.'

'Really?' I say. It's not the response I was expecting.

'Yes – don't you see?' she says breathlessly. 'That must be what she did. She was telling you exactly what she did, exactly what happened!'

'But why would she do that?' I ask, after a pause. I'm finding it hard to figure out Vanessa's game plan here, struggling to understand her motivation. She is fixated on Rachel – has been for months, it seems – and in turn, Rachel is fixated on her. And here I am, somehow in the middle of it.

'Because she's trying to frame *me*, Callie,' Vanessa says,

'You?' I say.

'Yes – don't you see? She's trying to get back at me for blaming her for the fire in the summer. And Matthew . . . Matthew would trust her. I make sure never to talk badly about anyone else in front of the kids, so he wouldn't know how I felt about Rachel. And it's not that long since we were all friends – he was very close with her daughter Sadie. So, he would recognize her, remember her, trust her. It makes sense, Callie, it really does. It's all starting to fit together. And she knows the area around those beach huts where he was being kept. She helped Justin do up the Getaway so she'd be familiar with which ones were always empty.'

It sounds unbelievable to me, preposterous. But then again, everything about my time here has been fairly unbelievable. 'You really think that she could hurt a child like that? Take him away from his home and family?'

'She's not a normal person, Callie. You have to remember that. We're not talking about someone who thinks as we do. She thinks I deserve this. She was punishing me. Is punishing me.'

'I don't –'

'Callie, look, no offence but you don't know her like I do, okay? You weren't here when it was at its worst. I honestly was afraid for my life. It felt like she was capable of anything. And then the fire happened, but I called her out on it, so now she blames me for having to move and start again.' It's a far-fetched theory. But is it any more far-fetched than me – a recently bereaved woman, sent mad by the loss of her own child – kidnapping and killing a little boy she's only just met? And the police certainly seem happy enough to believe that theory. 'I just keep thinking, if only I'd done something more back then, we wouldn't be going through all this now,' she continues. Vanessa is sobbing, her words coming in hard-to-grasp gasps. 'I complained to the police over and over again, but there wasn't anything they could do, and when she moved away, I was so relieved. I just assumed it was all over. Finally. But it wasn't over for her. I should've done more, looked into her background, hired an investigator, I don't know . . . I had no idea how much worse it could all get. I never, ever thought it would come to this –'

Vanessa is interrupted by her own crying, finally breaking down completely, her sobs and staccato breaths travelling down the line to me in broken waves. It takes me a few seconds to realize that someone's talking in the background – the radio? The TV? – but then the other voice gets louder, and someone else is on the phone, shouting: 'What are you doing? Vanessa, who are you talking to? This is unreal, every time I look at you, you're on the fucking phone again. What is wrong with you? Is it a reporter now? Or are you updating your beloved followers again? Can't you give us just one moment of peace?'

The line goes dead and once more I'm dropped into the icy, isolated silence of a winter storm that is now raging outside my window.

## 43

It was Justin, of course. Even with the unfamiliar ragged edge in his voice, I knew immediately it was him. I sit on my bed, staring into the flames of the fire. Every time the wind blows down the chimney, the fire fades, stutters, then comes back to life. I watch this happen for what feels like hours, but is probably only minutes.

Justin.

I could hear his anger, feel his frustration.

I think of his ingratiating smile, his poise.

A model husband, a perfect father.

The death of a child – especially in such traumatic circumstances – can break even the most stable of parents. Can smash you apart, leaving behind something or someone completely unrecognizable. A jagged reflection in a ruined mirror.

And Justin's reflection was too perfect to begin with. It takes a particular type of person to construct a life so perfect it would be the envy of anyone and everyone. And when that image is ruined beyond repair what happens to the person behind the image? The careful architect whose dream house has come crashing down around him?

Mum squints at me, digs her hand into the bag of Minstrels she's brought up with her. I've just told her about Vanessa's call, her husband's irate interruption. 'Couldn't you argue all that about Vanessa herself?' she asks. 'From everything you've told me, and everything I've seen online, she's created a very carefully curated image of herself. And Justin hardly figures in any of that, apart from as a kind of conjugal accessory.'

'Conjugal accessory?' I parrot back. It's the first thing that's made me smile in days.

'What do they call them? Instagram husbands? He sounds a little long-suffering, in my opinion. Vanessa is the one who seems more concerned with how they appear to the world.'

'That's true, I guess. But you haven't met either of them. Justin is lovely – they both are – but there is something so . . . controlled about him. Like he's, I don't know, presenting himself to you, rather than just *being*. Does that make sense?'

'I've met a few people like that in my time. So, Vanessa doesn't seem like that to you?'

'No. I know she probably comes across that way online, on Instagram, but really she just seems so herself in person. Comfortable.'

Mum digs around in her Minstrels packet. Her sweet tooth is legendary in our family. Thea and I were never allowed sweets growing up, yet there was always a KitKat or a Crunchie hidden in Mum's handbag, and a drawer in her desk at work stocked full of chocolate. 'You don't really know these people, though, sweetheart,' she says, through a mouthful. 'You've only met Vanessa a handful of times, after all.'

'And Justin even fewer,' I point out.

Mum shakes her head at me, looking very tired. 'I don't

think any of this theorizing is helpful, Callie. All we need to do is keep our heads down, let the police do their job, and protect you wherever possible. They'll find out what happened to that poor child soon enough.'

As if she has called the moment into being, her phone rings, Bernadette's name lighting up the screen.

'Bernadette?' she says sharply. She's just down the corridor, in her own room, so why is she calling? Her eyes are still on me as she listens to Bernadette. Then she picks up the TV remote, turning to the armoire in the corner of the room where the flatscreen is hidden.

The news is on, and as Matthew's face fills the screen my stomach swoops and clenches in a panic, fear at what may come next swamping my every sense.

## Five Months Ago

Rachel has been in Margate all day, sweltering and sweaty, touring houses with several different estate agents; FaceTiming with Tom stuck in his office on campus when she finally found one she fell in love with; conferring with him during multiple calls over whether to put in an offer without him having seen it, or to wait until the weekend when the house might have gone.

So, although she's been on her phone all day, she hasn't been paying much attention to the notifications, other than those from Tom and the estate agents, and hasn't even opened Instagram since having a quick scroll with her morning tea. She's just stopped to have an iced coffee in a small café when she finally does so, and finds that she has, in fact, blown up. The bomb Vanessa detonated late last Friday night has finally gone off, and Rachel is the shrapnel.

Her breath catches in her throat as she reads the comments – almost all of which she is tagged in – left underneath a post from Vanessa earlier in the day. At first, she's confused. The photo is pretty and innocuous enough – a vase of peonies caught in some early-morning summer sunlight. But the caption confuses her:

*Been sent these beautiful peonies by that 'friend' I mentioned,*
*and now I'll never be able to look at these sensational flowers in*
*the same way again. So many of you recommended cutting this*
*toxic person out of my life when I reached out last week, and I took*
*that recommendation to heart. It's not in my nature to ignore or*
*'ice-out' friends, but when someone betrays you so fundamentally,*
*sometimes it's what you have to do. But what to do when they*
*keep trying to reach out to you? This bunch of flowers was waiting*
*on the porch when I woke up this morning, but once I saw who*
*they were from, instead of feeling comforted, I felt violated.*
*Because this isn't the first peace offering they've sent, and despite*
*my telling them there was nothing left to be mended, they're still*
*sending me little things to remind me of what they did. All I want*
*is to be left alone to lick my wounds, but instead I have to deal*
*with drawing my boundaries, and pushing back. I know it's silly to*
*complain about being sent flowers – who doesn't love flowers? –*
*but when they're sent from someone you don't trust, they may as*
*well be mulch.*

Rachel stares down at the photo for a long time. She hasn't sent Vanessa flowers, hasn't even sent her a text or a WhatsApp in at least a week. It has to be said she had been contemplating reaching out to the other woman. Since her moonlit swim three nights ago, she has had time to think and digest, to contemplate and ruminate, and although she wants nothing more to do with the Lowes, she had thought she should at least smooth things over before Tom and she move to Margate. For the sake of the kids at least. But that was before this. Whatever *this* is. Still staring at her phone, the screen slowly darkening, turning black, Rachel starts to wonder if she's got this all wrong. Is there a chance Vanessa is referring to someone else?

Why would she claim Rachel had sent her conciliatory flowers when she hasn't? And what, exactly, is Rachel supposed to be so conciliatory about?

Maybe this is just a misunderstanding. Taking a long, cold sip of iced coffee, Rachel resolves to do the right thing, the adult thing, and call Vanessa.

'Rachel,' Vanessa says, on picking up, her voice smooth, unruffled.

'Vanessa, hi,' Rachel says, and she is surprised by how nervous she is: her heart pounding, the phone slippery in her now sweating hands. 'Look, I know we haven't talked in a while, but I saw your Instagram post, and I wanted to clear the air. I don't know if you think I sent you those flowers, but I didn't, and quite honestly I'm not sure what you think I've done to you, but I'm sorry if you think I've betrayed you in some way.'

There is silence at the other end, and Rachel gulps air. 'Vanessa, are you there?'

'I think it's better if you don't contact me any more, Rachel.'

'Ness, I'm just trying to figure out what you think I've done to you. You're implying all over Instagram that I've . . . betrayed you in some way. I have a right to know what the fuck you're talking about.'

'You know what I'm talking about, *Rach*,' Vanessa replies, through what sounds like gritted teeth. 'You know what you've done.'

'I really don't . . . Is this about Justin? You know that nothing happened between us. You know I wouldn't ever do that to you. Or Tom.'

'All I know is that you saw him last Friday, when he told me he was stuck in the office all evening.'

'Yeah, we bumped into each other in Sainsbury's, but that's all.'

Vanessa lets out a short, sharp laugh that isn't really a laugh at all. 'Yeah, and the rest. He didn't get home until almost midnight. Were you in Sainsbury's until midnight, Rach?'

'No. I have no idea where he went after I saw him. I've barely seen or spoken to Justin in weeks.'

There is another silence, and even on the phone, in another town, in the overwhelming warmth of the high July sun, Rachel feels its coolness, its sharpness. She feels Vanessa's assessment, her calculations, her judgement, and her chosen punishment.

'I just can't believe you'd do this to me, Rachel. After I confided in you. I trusted you.' Her voice is very calm. That's what strikes Rachel most: the calm, the assurance, the directness. In some ways, it is more threatening than anger and resentment, vitriol and tears.

'Vanessa, please –'

But Vanessa is gone and, sitting outside that little café in the summer heat, Rachel is left to wonder what happens next.

# 44

It's a press briefing. The camera is trained on DCI Varma, who is flanked by several other officials. Justin and Vanessa are at the far right of the long table they're all sitting at. Despite the harsh words I overheard just an hour or two earlier, the couple are gripping hands, leaning into one another. Vanessa's shoulders begin to shake as soon as Varma starts speaking. But we're not here to hear Varma who, after brief introductions, relinquishes the microphone to the older woman sitting to her right, Abigail Bishop, the Kent county medical examiner.

I watch as, on screen, she clears her throat and looks down at her notes. 'Three-year-old Matthew Lowe died as a result of drowning. He was found to have very high levels of the antihistamine promethazine hydrochloride, which we believe was being used to keep him drowsy and sedated, as well as paracetamol, and dextromethorphan hydrobromide. There were no outward signs of a struggle or injury, and although he was undernourished and dehydrated at the time of death, it is my belief that Matthew's captor was looking after him and intended to keep him alive. Matthew's dehydration, and his general tiredness brought about by the high levels of antihistamine will undoubtedly have contributed to his disorientation and exhaustion, both of which may have led to him wandering into the sea by accident, and ultimately to his drowning and death.'

She stops speaking abruptly and looks up at the gathered press. Her eyes avoid the cameras that are beadily watching her, but before she can continue a reporter shouts, 'Can you tell us anything about the antihistamine used?'

Abigail Bishop clears her throat again – a nervous tic? 'It's impossible to be absolutely certain at the moment, but the combination of promethazine, paracetamol and dextromethorphan are the active ingredients found in Night Nurse.'

'An over-the-counter medicine, then?' the reporter asks, pushing his luck.

'Yes. A very commonly used and purchased medication. One that many people all across the country have at home, albeit not in such large quantities as would have been needed to keep Matthew sedated.'

Bishop turns stiffly to Varma, who takes over. 'As you know, we found the location where we believe Matthew was being held a few days ago. We collected several useful pieces of evidence and are currently awaiting results from the forensics lab in Ashford. We are now asking anyone who was driving in the area at the time of Matthew's abduction – which we believe to be sometime between one and five in the morning – to come forward. We're particularly looking for anyone who may have seen a white Ford Fiesta driving in the area. Any information you may have could prove imperative in the next stage of our investigation, and in bringing Matthew's abductor to justice.'

Vanessa and Justin don't speak. Varma wraps up the briefing, refusing any more questions, and the camera lingers on the couple for a few seconds. Vanessa's shoulders are stiff and shaking, Justin's arm around her, as she huddles, her hair covering her face. He appears to whisper something into her ear, soothing sounds maybe, and then, just as the camera is about to cut back to the newsroom, Vanessa's face tilts upwards and she stares directly into the camera, with round, pleading eyes. The shaking in her shoulders stops, and her face is clear, her makeup perfect. Brown eyes framed by black mascara and metallic bronze shadow, without a smudge or tear stain in sight. Without a hair out of place.

# 45

'They're looking for my rental car,' I say, my voice shaking with nerves and tension. 'That's my rental car Varma was describing. A white Ford Fiesta. That can't be a coincidence, right?'

Bernadette exchanges a glance with Mum. 'I was worried that might be the case,' she says.

'Is that normal? To call out a particular car like that? Couldn't it skew people's memories or something? Anyone who saw a small white car that night is bound to call in now,' Mum says.

'That's just the risk they take, asking for help from the public in cases like this. It's a little unusual because obviously they already have the car in question – normally they use this kind of tactic when they're trying to track a car down. But presumably they're hoping to be able to place you at the scene,' Bernadette says.

I nod, taking it in slowly. This was exactly what I assumed they were doing, but it still shoots a wave of nausea through me to hear Bernadette confirm my theory. 'They won't be able to, will they, Callie?' Mum says.

'No, of course not.'

'That's fine, then,' she says.

'But what if someone calls in to say they saw it? But they just saw some other random white car?' I ask.

'Well, hopefully that won't happen,' Bernadette says. 'And in any case, if they haven't found you yet on CCTV, it's unlikely to be usable in a case against you, regardless of whether or not a member of the public claims to have seen you.'

## Five Months Ago

Their offer on the house is accepted.

Accepted.

All Rachel feels when she takes the call from the estate agent later that day is an overwhelming rush of relief. She's at home with the kids and Tom, the sounds of their summer evening all around them, heat permeating the cottage, the smell of the sea wafting through the open back door and into the kitchen. But Rachel has had an anvil sitting on her chest for the past few weeks, and now, with this call, that weight is lifted off and she can finally breathe easily again.

She looks around her at the four walls of the kitchen – a place that has felt so much like home – and in her mind she is already packed and gone, Vanessa, Justin and the whole weird, unruly affair in their rear-view mirror.

'There's a long way to go yet,' Tom reminds her, as he sits down at the kitchen table. 'And it could all go wrong or, at the very least, take a very long time to get into the house.'

'I know, I know,' Rachel says. She's making a vinaigrette for their steak salad, and she is whisking the mustard and vinegar together with happy force. 'But the estate agent said we were in a good position. No chain on our side, mortgage agreed, and the sellers are motivated.'

'Yeah, because someone died there.'

'The owner died in a hospice, Tom, They did not die *there*. Besides, I'd rather live in a haunted house than one owned by the Lowes,' she says, with a shiver.

'Strong words from a woman who won't touch an ouija board.'

'Exactly. That's how bad this is.' She reaches for her glass of white wine. She hasn't told Tom about the Instagram post yet. She wants to, but she dreads the lack of seriousness he'll approach it with. To him, none of this is really that bad. He's not on Instagram, doesn't pay attention to any kind of social media, and has no idea of how far-reaching it is, how much a part of people's daily lives it has become. He knows she checks her account too much, he's aware Vanessa has a lot of followers – is something of a star – but it's all frivolity to him, an added extra to someone else's day, like watching TV or reading a book (except of less value, of course). He won't understand how much damage Vanessa can do with her insidious little posts about Rachel, will probably, in fact, laugh it all off.

But she is being accused of having an affair with Justin, and Tom has to know that it isn't true. So, she takes out her phone and opens up Instagram yet again. She turned her notifications for the app off earlier in the day when it all got too much. So, it's only now she sees that, in her absence, things have got much worse. Vanessa has been on Stories, and instead of subtly implying the ways in which Rachel has betrayed her, she's come right out and said that Rachel made moves on her husband. She hasn't gone as far as to say there's been an affair. No, that would look too bad for Vanessa – who would dare cheat on her, after all? But there she is, tearful and resplendent in her grief and anger, her auburn hair quivering as she talks to the camera about accepting Rachel and her whole family into her life, only to be so betrayed by her.

Rachel, standing in the kitchen Vanessa owns, feels the beat of her heart pick up as she sees all the notifications waiting for her, all the DMs to be seen and read, all the comments she has been tagged in. She watches all of Vanessa's Stories from the last twenty-four hours, so she knows the other woman has been careful never to mention her name, or to tag her in anything, but her followers have figured out who she's referring to, and have taken up the battle. Just as Vanessa had known they would. Just as she'd intended and orchestrated.

'What's up?' Tom says. He has been looking at his own phone, and only just noticed how still Rachel has become. She wants to hold out her phone to him in explanation, but he won't get it, so she begins to tell him what's going on, what Vanessa is doing to her.

Tom sits at the table with her phone in his hands, shrugs, sighs. Rachel tries not to be disappointed by his reaction – it's exactly as she expected, after all – but she can't help it. She wants understanding, support, anger, protection. 'Oh, this will all blow over soon, won't it?' he says.

'But what should I do in the meantime?'

'Delete the app,' Tom says, as simple as that.

'Delete the app.'

'Yeah. We're moving soon anyway. We haven't seen either Vanessa or Justin in weeks, so there doesn't have to be any awkwardness. So, *delete the app*, get some space, ignore all this . . . ridiculousness, and just wait it out until we're in Margate.'

Rachel doesn't say anything, and this gets Tom's attention. He lifts his face to look at her and says sharply, 'Oh, come on, Rach, just delete the fucking app. It's not that big a deal, is it? It's basically the same as playground bullies, right? And what do we say about bullies?' He voices the last bit as though he were talking to their children, and Rachel responds in kind, saying in a sing-song voice, 'Ignore them.'

'Exactly. Just ignore her. All *this* does is give Vanessa the oxygen she needs to continue overinflating her ego. So, stop feeding it.'

Rachel knows he's right. But the thought of allowing Vanessa to continue this virtual vendetta against her without her eyes on it has the hairs on the back of her neck standing on end. It makes her feel itchy with the need to check Instagram, to know exactly what is going on. But wouldn't it be easier simply to ignore it, as Tom says? To delete the app and pretend none of it was even happening? To go about her life as if she had never met Vanessa Lowe?

She takes the phone back from Tom, who has been holding it out towards her as though it were a gauntlet, and holds firmly down on the home screen, watching all her apps dance and jiggle before pressing the little cross next to Instagram.

'And it's over,' Tom says, with a smile.

But it's not over. Rachel knows that. It's simply out of sight.

For now.

## thelowedown

**887K** followers

**Vanessa Lowe**

Wife * Mother * Lover

Liked by **RibbonsRhymesandGoodTimes** and **others**

**thelowedown** I hate having to post something like this. It feels so wrong to bring such negativity into a space that I have specially cultivated to be so positive and affirming – for me, but also for you. And yet. I've been suffering the worst abuse recently. It's truly never-ending. I've always had to deal with the occasional negative Nancy, but that's par for the course when you live online – this is different. I feel truly frightened, and even though I've checked the accounts and reported them to Instagram, they just keep on coming. And I think I know who's behind it – the same person I let into my life with open arms, only to have her betray me by going after my husband. Have you not done enough damage? At this point, all I want is to be left alone. I could leave Instagram, of course, take a break – that's probably what I should do, but I refuse to be bullied and pushed around like this. So, I'm staying. Let's see how far you'll go, how low you'll stoop. Me, I always walk the high road.

5 months ago

# 46

No one comes forward to say they saw my rental car in the area. Or, at least, I have to assume no one comes forward, because Varma doesn't get back in touch with me, and because then, two days later, on the day before Christmas Eve, the exact day I was meant to be checking out of the Getaway and going home for Christmas with my family in London, Vanessa Lowe is arrested for the kidnap and killing of her younger son.

## 47

The contents of the beach hut were covered in her fingerprints. The blanket Matthew had been sleeping under featured Vanessa's hair and fibres from one of her scarves. The iPad screen came away with not only Matthew's fingerprints, but Vanessa's too. And no one else's.

There was a bin bag in the corner, full of empty food packaging, and several depleted bottles of Night Nurse, all of it with Vanessa's fingerprints. There might be more, but the police aren't telling the press, and the press aren't telling us. I spend the morning of the twenty-third staring in disbelief at the TV news and Mum's iPad, going from one to the other, like opponents in a tennis match, when the news stops covering her story, or another programme starts up. Vanessa's Instagram is annoyingly and uncharacteristically void of updates, of course. I know they will have taken her phone from her, yet I can't help checking her profile, looking for the telltale sign that she has created another Story. There are still comments being made on her last post, though, supporters and followers expressing their disbelief at her arrest, shouting their belief in her innocence. A lot of them mention Rachel. She is tagged in a few, even, and I have to wonder what she thinks of all this. She suspected Vanessa before even the police did, and yet, here on Vanessa's Instagram page, these women are accusing her of exactly what Vanessa has been arrested for.

Mum is busy packing her bag. Vanessa has been arrested, I am in the clear, and we can all go home now. Except.

'Come on, Cal,' she says now, clicking her fingers in my direction. 'If we get going soon, we can drop your rental car back at Gatwick and get the train home in time for a late lunch.'

Varma has already been in touch to tell me I'm welcome to pick up the car whenever is convenient for me. She had offered me her apologies, which was something at least, but she sounded stretched, exhausted, and I had to wonder what the past few hours and days had been like for her.

'Why don't you and Bernadette go ahead and get the train back to London together?' I say, my head still buried in Vanessa's Instagram feed. 'It'll be much easier for you both that way.'

'I'm happy to join you in the car, darling,' Mum says, stopping her packing. I look up and see her staring at me, that worried look back on her face, a stillness to her posture that tells me she's almost scared to say the wrong thing.

I smile at her. 'I'll be fine on my own. I made it here alone, after all.'

I can see her thinking, *But look what happened then*, but she doesn't say it. 'Really, Mum,' I say. 'I'll be fine.'

She nods, a little curtly, and goes back to her packing. But she's moving more slowly than before and I can tell she's worried, that she would rather insist on joining me on my journey back to London. But she doesn't.

So, I walk with her and Bernadette to Whitstable station, waving them off before I head to the police station to pick up the rental car. But once I get into it, the space feeling at once familiar and immediately foreign, I drive not to London but to Margate.

## Four Months Ago

'Guys . . . I can't believe this, I can't believe what I'm see-ing.' Vanessa takes a deep, semi-tearful breath and switches the view of the camera on her phone so that her followers can see what she's looking at: the burnt-out remains of her kitchen renovation.

'All that work, all that love, and care, and attention . . . all that *money*, guys!' Here she gives a bitter laugh. 'Luckily, we're insured, of course. But I just can't believe it. This is a nightmare. My beautiful kitchen. Ruined. Before anyone asks, which I'm sure a lot of you will because you're all so thoughtful and caring, I'm fine, we're all totally fine. No one was here luckily, but obviously that was so the perpet-rator could get away with no one seeing them . . . because we all know who did this, of course. It was no accident, as they say.'

Vanessa's phone camera is still tracking over the debris of the kitchen, taking in the blackened cabinets, the smoke-damaged walls, the ash and dust. She switches the camera again: she's back on screen. Her eyes are a little bleary, from tears, and maybe even a little smoke. 'Rachel, if you're watching, all I can say is, please stop. This is too much. I can't take any more. I can't believe you'd put me and my family in danger like this. And you can expect a visit from the police at any moment.'

'Dear Lord,' Tom says, when the video finishes, and the police officer's phone turns dark once again. 'She really thinks Rachel did this? Tried to burn her house down?'

Rachel shifts in her chair, trying to get more comfortable. She's had a long day and sweat seems to cling to every inch of her body. She's opened the back door and a slight breeze flows through the room from their courtyard, but it's not enough. This is the first she's seen of this video, of this new accusation. It is, in fact, the first time she's even looked at Vanessa's Instagram since deleting the app last month at Tom's behest. She had thought it would be better: out of sight, out of mind. But with Rachel looking elsewhere, Vanessa has continued with her attacks and accusations, and now Rachel has been caught off guard. Would it have been better to know this might be coming? But who could have predicted it? She reaches for her glass of water, the ice cubes tripping against one another as she takes an enormous swig. She wishes she could pour it all over her chest and face, like an exhausted athlete.

The red-headed police officer – DC Perry – nods back at Tom, confirming that Vanessa has, indeed, pointed the finger of blame at Rachel.

Rachel takes a deep breath and Perry's gaze snaps to her. 'Well. It wasn't me,' she says, and lets out a laugh. 'I've been in London all day. Only just got back actually.'

Tom nods in confirmation, and Perry says, 'And you can verify this, Mr Donovan?'

'Ah, no –'

'Tom wasn't with me, but both my children were, and I was with my mum and sister too.'

Perry nods. 'That's great, Mrs Donovan, thank you, although we will need names and contact numbers for your mum and sister. Just to confirm what you've said.'

Rachel is exhausted. She wants a shower, she wants a bed in an air-conditioned room, she wants a freezing cold glass of white wine, she wants these men out of her kitchen, she wants Vanessa Lowe out of her life, and she absolutely doesn't want to cook dinner tonight. Fish and chips. Marcus will be delighted.

'Can I just ask how you're acquainted with Mrs Lowe, please, Mrs Donovan?'

Rachel lets out another deep sigh. 'We were friends. And she was my boss, I guess.'

'Was?' Perry asks, at the exact same time his until-now-silent partner says, 'You guess?'

Rachel's gaze flicks between the two of them. Perry's partner is roughly the same age as him, with tawny hair and a nice, healthy-looking tan. The kind of natural tan people get from working outside rather than sunbathing. It's a bit unfortunate for Perry, with his lobster-red cheeks, to be sitting next to him. She can't remember the other officer's name, though. It feels like an age since they knocked on the door and introduced themselves, although it can only have been fifteen minutes ago.

'We were working together on her shop – The Lowe Down – on the high street, and I helped Justin design their Getaway cabin, out by the Sportsman pub.'

'So, you were her employee?' Perry clarifies.

'Yes ... I mean, technically, yes, she was paying my

salary. I was on the payroll for The Lowe Down, but Justin paid me separately as a freelancer.'

'Mrs Lowe claims she fired you, Mrs Donovan, and that you've been trying to . . . get back at her ever since,' Perry says.

'Yes,' Rachel says, pausing for another sip of cold water. 'I'm aware that's the story she's been peddling.'

'Story?'

Rachel nods. 'She's been trying to discredit me all summer. She also claims I was trying to sleep with her husband.' Here she glances at Tom, but they've had this discussion already, been through it all, and he doesn't look perturbed in the slightest. 'And that I've been leaving her "gifts". And now this. I'm an arsonist, apparently.'

'Yes, she did mention something about poo on her doorstep and cupcakes with broken glass?' the tawny-haired guy says.

Rachel closes her eyes for a second and laughs. 'Really? I didn't know about that. I actually unfollowed her, deleted the whole app, as it was getting a bit much. I mean, it's ridiculous, right? It's all completely insane. But really? You know what? I don't actually care about Vanessa Lowe. I certainly don't care enough to harass and abuse her online or put her and her family in any kind of danger –'

Tom's hot hand on her forearm stops Rachel in her tracks and makes her realize she's been talking too quickly, going too far, too fast. 'Rachel, love, ssh,' he says, trying to calm her, but only making her more rigidly angry, self-righteous. What does he know about any of this? He doesn't even have a Facebook account. 'You've got an alibi, love, remember? These gentlemen here will just talk to your mum and sister, and this will all be sorted before you know it.'

'Alibi?' Rachel croaks, her throat dry. The word sounds . . . well, it sounds ridiculous. The idea that she'd even *need* one. That anyone would ask her for one. It's a word for books and TV shows, not real life. What will her mum think? What's she going to say when these police officers call her and ask where she and her daughters were between the hours of so-and-so and so-and-so? Augustina Brown has spent her whole life trying to keep the police away from her children, and now here they are, in Rachel's small kitchen in a seaside town, and it's all Vanessa Lowe's doing.

Rachel takes another deep breath, remembering her yogic ocean breath, thinking of the sea, just a few steps from her door, that she swims in every morning. But her blood is hot with rage, with indignation.

Fucking Vanessa.

Does she really think Rachel is just going to lie down and take this?

# 48

It takes me a while to get my bearings in Margate, and I have to drive around, reacquainting myself with the town, picking out places I recognize from my last visit to find Rachel's house. Because I don't have her address, of course.

Eventually I head back to the café where I first met her and retrace our route, picking out her house on the street because its door is painted a beautiful coral. I find a parking spot after a period of searching, but as I'm walking up to the front door, I realize Rachel is getting out of her own car, which also happens to be a white Ford Fiesta. I stare at it for a second, remembering Varma's call for witnesses of a white Ford on the night of Matthew's abduction. I'd assumed they'd been trying to place my rental car near the scene, but what if I'd got it wrong? What if this was the car they'd been looking for?

What if we'd all got it wrong?

Rachel is wrangling with something in the boot, emitting grunts and sighs as she eventually manages to wrestle it out, and close the lid one-handed.

'Rachel,' I say, coming towards her and she stops, leans against the back of her car and peers at me through thick, tortoiseshell-framed glasses. She blinks for a second, unable to place me, then says, 'Callie, right?'

'Right. Sorry to approach you out of the blue like this. I should've called first.'

'It's fine,' she says, looking down at the turkey she's been struggling with. 'I've just been to pick this beast up and was a little distracted, that's all. Do you want to come in?' She jerks her head towards her house, and I follow her up the steps to the coral door.

She offers me a choice between tea and coffee this time, no cosy Cointreau hot chocolate, and I go for the latter, which she makes in a stovetop Moka.

As she passes me the coffee, I say, 'I was about to say I can't believe the news about Vanessa, but I guess you do. You were saying you thought she had something to do with it from the beginning.'

Rachel takes a seat at the table, and nods. 'It's not as if I'm happy to be proved right, but I can't say I'm surprised. I'm just glad justice might actually be served. For Matthew. And the other kids.'

'The other kids?' I ask.

'JJ and Emma.' She sips her coffee. 'I . . . I have a feeling she might have been very hard on them. There was always something about JJ. I could never quite put my finger on it, but then, when everything happened with the fire and Matthew's disappearance, I realized what it was.'

'What?' I ask, because Rachel has paused for another sip of coffee.

She swallows, wipes her mouth, and says, 'He was scared of her. I'm sure of it now.'

'You think she was abusive?' I say, thinking back to my visits to the Lowe family home. JJ had been recalcitrant, yes. He'd been a little moody and monosyllabic, but I'd seen nothing to indicate anything other than a boy bordering on teenage, bored by his younger siblings, and maybe just a little resentful of the limelight they seemed to hog. But he'd been there, hadn't he? He'd been hanging out with his brother and sister – and mother, for that matter – when he didn't have to. He could've been at a friend's house or upstairs in his bedroom. Just the fact that he was willing to spend time with his family on a chilly December evening indicated warm feelings. In my view, at least.

But Rachel knew the family better, had seen more than I had.

'There was this time,' she's saying now, staring into her coffee cup, 'it was ages ago, but JJ had got into a fight at school, had scratched this other boy on his face. But a week or so later Justin told me he'd taken him swimming and JJ had had bruises all up and down his arms. Justin had assumed it was the other boy, that JJ had got them in the fight, but I don't know. Vanessa was always very concerned about how the family made her look. She would've hated the fact that JJ had got in a fight. Not because of the violence, or because he hurt someone when he shouldn't have, but because it was *embarrassing*. Because it wasn't the way her children were supposed to behave.'

I'm quiet for a while, taking it all in. Looking at Rachel, I can see she's struggling with this, that it's likely something that has preyed on her mind for a long time. But I still feel compelled to defend Vanessa.

'That's quite a leap to make, though, isn't it?' I say. 'Like you say, he'd been in a fight. And if Justin thought it was the other boy . . .'

Rachel takes a deep breath, sighs it out heavily. 'I'm not sure Justin had any idea what was going on in his own house. You know Vanessa accused me of having an affair with him?'

I nod, even though, from my Instagram searching, I'd heard that Rachel had merely come on to Justin, not that there had ever been an actual affair. 'It wasn't true, of course,' Rachel is saying. 'We were friends, Justin and I. There was a time when we were closer than I was with Vanessa, but it was never anything romantic. I do wonder, though . . .'

'What?'

'If he might have been sleeping with someone else. He had done before, so that's why Vanessa was suspicious in the first place.'

'He had?' I ask, trying to work out if I find this shocking or not. I think back to the first time I met Justin, when Vanessa invited me round for dinner. It's not that long ago, but it feels like a lifetime. He had been so welcoming, so ingratiating, so in sync with his wife. They'd not only looked perfect together but seemed to mirror one another. Complementary. Had the man I met – the perfect host, the perfect husband – been cheating on his wife the whole time?

'A woman from his office, apparently,' Rachel says. 'A girl, really. Well, no, that's not fair. She was in her twenties. Young.'

'When was this?'

'A couple of years ago. When Vanessa was pregnant with Matthew.'

'Jesus. Are you sure?'

Rachel sighs again. 'I don't know. That's what she told me. I did ask him about it, and he denied it, but . . .'

'He would.'

'Exactly. Honestly, though, I don't know. There were times when I was sure Vanessa was lying about things, making them up ... I never really knew why. For sympathy? Attention? And that's what I thought it was when she told me about the affair. But then I thought about Justin and how often he's away from home, how easy it would be for him to be having an affair, and it seemed plausible.'

'But what does that have to do with Matthew?' I ask. 'I'm just trying to wrap my head around why – and how – she could possibly do this.'

'I don't know why, I don't know how. But I do know Vanessa needs to be in control. And when she feels she's not in control, she lashes out.'

## thelowedown

**900K** followers

**Vanessa Lowe**

Wife * Mother * Lover

Liked by **WildWildWe** and **others**

**thelowedown** In the midst of everything that's been happening, I missed a major milestone: you lovely, amazing, charming, SUPPORTIVE people got me to 900K. NINE HUNDRED THOUSAND!! Sorry, I just had to write the number out there so that I could try and properly wrap my head around it. I can't believe nine hundred thousand of you are interested in what I have to say, let alone kind enough to offer such words of love and wisdom in support, and supportive enough to buy the products I promote so that I can keep doing what I do. And I honestly can't believe that this is what I get to do with my life. Obviously, the fire has been a big wake-up call for me, and while I could have let it get me down and shut me up, I simply won't let it. I will not be bullied off the internet, and I'm not going to give up my platform for anyone or anything. Next stop: ONE MILLION 🎉 🎊 🥂

4 months ago

# 49

It's dark by the time I get home, although it has only just gone four o'clock. As I walk the streets from the station to my parents' house, I watch as glowing rooms flicker on and off as residents turn on lights, and draw curtains against the coming night. I have always loved this walk, these streets. It is about as picturesque as London gets, and on nights like this, in deep midwinter, it feels like stepping back into the past, history a cloak that the velvet night wears well.

But my phone dings as I walk, pulling me back into the twenty-first century. It's a message from Rachel. She's sent me the Instagram profile of the woman Vanessa claimed Justin had cheated on her with and a message:

> *I'm not sure what Charlotte could tell you at this point, but you seemed like you wanted to know more so could be worth getting in touch. I've thought about doing it myself a few times, but I just want to stay out of that family's drama as much as possible. Happy Christmas, Callie, I'm sorry it's been such a hard few days for you. Rxxx*

Stay out of their drama? I push open the ancient black gate to my parents' house and trudge up the steps to the door. Since when? Rachel was so concerned with the Lowes' family drama that she even turned up to a search party she clearly wasn't welcome at. How is that staying out of things? I have to dig around in my bag for a few minutes to find the right set of keys, but eventually I let myself into the house. Mum texted a while ago to say she and Dad were going to a Christmas party in the neighbourhood that happens every year. She had wanted to make sure I'd be okay, at home alone, but it's pure relief that greets me, with the silence of the empty house.

There's a small sound of welcome as I shut the door, though, and Biscuits, our elderly family cat trots down the stairs to greet me. I spend some time fussing over him, then head into the kitchen. I pull out my phone again while I'm waiting for the kettle to boil, and click the link Rachel sent. Charlotte Vaughn hasn't posted anything since the beginning of December, when she visited an Alpine-themed roof terrace in the centre of London, and shared a photo of her and some friends cheersing with spiked hot chocolate. I scroll aimlessly through her feed for a while, making my tea, then sit down at the worn old kitchen table with it. Biscuits jumps up to join me, head-butting my arm to let me know he'd like the earlier fussing to continue now. I stroke him idly, scratching behind his ears, as I know he likes, while sipping my tea and zooming in on Charlotte's photos every now and again. One in particular interests me. It's a dark shot, inside a Soho bar that fashions itself as a speakeasy. Charlotte has taken a photo of the cocktails on her table, and there's a caption that reads: *Nothing better than a few illicit AWDs.*

But Charlotte's after-work drinks aren't what interest me: a man's hand is visible in the photo, resting on the table, claiming ownership of one of the cocktail glasses. And on the little finger nearest the camera's lens is a ring I recognize as Justin Lowe's. It's impossible to be sure, even when zooming in, as I've only seen it in person a few times, but there's something about the whole set-up that makes me wonder. It was posted in August, which, according to Rachel's account and Vanessa's Instagram feed, was the height of their feud. Was all this fighting just misguided fury on Vanessa's part? Was it possible she had targeted Rachel for supposedly hitting on her husband, when in fact Justin was still seeing his mistress in London? The thought depresses me, but it reminds me of Rachel's comment about Vanessa being unable to handle not being in control.

She couldn't control Justin so she took her frustration out on Rachel.

Was it possible she'd later taken out her frustration on Matthew?

Or is this all a massive misdirect from Rachel?

Why *is* she sending me Charlotte's profile? Why is she telling me to get in touch with her, getting involved when she claims to want nothing to do with the Lowes? I can't help but feel the strings of manipulation being pulled. But, then, there had been times during my stay at the Getaway when I'd felt the same about Vanessa. She had manipulated me into getting in touch with Rachel in the first place, and now here I was, being told to contact Justin's possible mistress by Rachel.

When would it end? And why did I care? I could easily opt out of all of this. I was no longer fielding calls from Varma, no longer a person of interest to the police. It was Christmas, I was at home with my family, safe and warm, and nothing could touch me here.

Why was I even entertaining the idea of getting in

touch with this stranger? Maybe because I wasn't so sure of Vanessa's guilt. She could be manipulative and controlling but did that mean she had killed her son? Misgivings over Vanessa's guilt or innocence aren't the real reason I feel so invested, though. I know that. I'd known it all along, really. For me, this was about Ada. Because when Rachel spoke about Vanessa's hatred of feeling such a loss of control, I didn't have to imagine how that felt: I knew. Having no control over a situation that is so life and death is a dizzying, disorienting, disenfranchising experience. It's like being divorced from your body and watching as it walks towards an oncoming freight train, unable to stop the crash. And that is how I have felt since those five days in June when Ada was born, Ada lived and Ada died. In a constant loop of emotional paralysis, unable to control anything, unable to change anything, unable to do anything. Until Whitstable. Until Vanessa. Until Matthew. Here – here I could do something. I could change something. I could make something better, or at least, make something make a bit more sense, rather than sitting in the senselessness of death, the unknowing chaos of being alive.

Charlotte's feed is still up on my phone, and I almost head back to my home screen when I press the Send Message button instead. If she doesn't message back, fine, but I have to honour my own curiosity. I want to see this through. She messages back within seconds, though, tells me she recognizes me from some of the news footage, and then, when I send her my number, she calls me almost instantly.

'Hi, Callie?' she says, almost breathless when I pick up.

'Yeah. Hi, Charlotte. Sorry to message you out of nowhere like that,' I say.

'Don't worry about it. I've been desperate to talk to someone about all this. You're friends with Justin, did you say?'

I nod, as if the little white lie I told in my original message could be made any less of a lie if I just don't speak up. But then I remember she can't see me nodding, and so, through a crack in my voice, I say, 'Yes, I've known him a while.'

'And have you spoken to him recently? I've been calling and calling, but nothing. I can't imagine what he's going through.'

I try to think of the last time I saw Justin. Was it when he dropped me off at the Mermaid Inn? And then I remember those overheard shouts when I spoke to Vanessa on the phone a few days ago. The violence of his voice. The anger. But I can't tell Charlotte about that. So, I take a deep breath, and dive further into my lie. 'No, but he texted me and asked me to get in contact with you. But he forgot to send me your number, and I think he's turned his phone off now.'

'Reporters probably,' Charlotte says. 'I bet they've been calling night and day.'

'Most likely. He wanted me to check you were okay, that no one had been in contact with you.'

'No. Thank God. That's the last thing anyone needs, isn't it? Me muddying the waters.'

'Right . . .'

'You know,' Charlotte says, and I hear what sounds like her inhaling on a cigarette and wonder where she is, 'he kept me away from his family, of course, never really spoke about them with me. But I did start following Vanessa from a fake account. I know I shouldn't have, but it was just too tempting. And he was gorgeous, wasn't he? Matthew. Justin's told me all sorts of things about her, and I know first-hand how deranged she can be, but I really did think she loved Matthew at least.'

'Deranged?' I say.

'Yeah. You know she followed me home from work one day and threatened me with a knife? If I hadn't let Justin convince me not to call the police or press charges, this might not have happened.'

'Sorry, Charlotte. I didn't know about that,' I say.

'Oh. Shit. Oh, well, I guess Justin wanted to keep it under wraps. But it does mean I'm not exactly surprised by all of this. But, like I say, I never would have thought she'd hurt Matthew.'

'No,' I say quietly, 'me neither.' And then, 'She threatened you with a knife?'

'Yeah, God, it was mad. It feels like something that happened to someone else when I think about it now, you know? Maybe because I've never really talked about it. Justin calmed her down, and talked her out of it, but I remember just standing there thinking, What the fuck is happening? How did I get into this mess?'

'But you're still with Justin?' I say, and although I'm trying to sound calm and casual, I can't help the note of accusation, of judgement, that leaks out of my voice. 'Sorry, I didn't mean to sound so . . . What I meant was, it didn't make you think twice about being with him? That's a lot of baggage to deal with.'

'We're not together any more,' she says, her voice

clipped. 'He's tried to leave her so many times. At least, that's what he always told me. I bet he's regretting not doing it now.'

I blink into the cosy gloom of the kitchen and, without thinking, stretch my fingers out to feel the warmth of Biscuits's fur, the gentle, reassuring up and down of his tiny breaths as he sleeps beside me.

'Right,' I say, my voice thin. 'Why did he stay, do you think?'

I hear her exhale smoke, and imagine it disappearing into the cold night air. I can hear traffic sounds in the background, and can see her out on a balcony somewhere, looking over her patch of London, thinking about her older, married boyfriend and his mad, murderous wife. What a cliché.

'I don't think he had a choice. She'd never let him leave, not alive anyway.'

Her words make my stomach lurch and my hand jerk, knocking over my mug of tea and disturbing the cat in the process. Biscuits gives an annoyed yowl, jumping down from our bench and sending me a reproachful look before heading out through the cat flap.

Suddenly I want nothing to do with any of this. None of it will bring Matthew back, or justify his death, or help make sense of it.

And none of this will bring back my own baby or help make sense of that loss.

My hands are trembling still, and my shoulders have started to shake before I even realize I'm crying. I put the phone on the table, hanging up on Charlotte without saying goodbye, not even feeling sorry for it, and then it's just me. I sit in the cold kitchen of my parents' house and cry for a life I can never get back, a person I'll never know, the self I was before, the daughter who might have been, and the baby I was only allowed to hold in my arms moments before she died.

## Three Months Ago

They move in the middle of September. It is, their estate agent tells them, one of the fastest house purchases she's ever witnessed, and Rachel takes this as a good sign. As confirmation of the right decision made, of all stars pointing to Margate and their new life there, away from the Lowes and away from Vanessa.

She had been dreading bumping into Vanessa either at nursery or the school gates in those few weeks before they moved, but she doesn't see the other woman, except in profile through the window of her Range Rover, or hovering behind the till at The Lowe Down as Rachel rushes past. Not that the nursery gates have been exactly welcoming, even without Vanessa there. Since making friends with Vanessa, Rachel hadn't had much interaction with the other mums and, in all honesty, she'd sometimes wondered if they even liked Vanessa – they certainly didn't seem to have the warm and fuzzies for her in person. But online was a different story, apparently. Because they may not be *friends* with Vanessa, but they are *followers*, and follow her they have: right down the rabbit hole that has led to Vanessa accusing Rachel of arson. Rachel is annoyed with herself for how run-out-of-town she feels but, really, she wants nothing more than to be away from

Vanessa, away from this picturesque town, and this whole sorry mess, and never have to worry about bumping into Vanessa again.

But when she enrols Sadie at her new nursery in Margate, she still can't help but think about the day when she first met Vanessa. She thinks about the coffees bought, the ice creams eaten, the scooter donated, and all the ways in which Vanessa made her feel welcome, and wanted. It is strange – so strange – to think that that was only last year. So much has happened, so much has changed, yet here Rachel and Sadie are, doing the first day at nursery again.

This time Rachel doesn't tap anyone on the shoulder, or attempt to make friends. She smiles, of course, to other parents picking up their children, but she hangs back a little. She'll let this happen more organically this time. She'll make friends, she knows she will – she always has. She'll just do better at picking them this time.

It's actually embarrassing for her when, a little over a week later, one of the other mums, who happens to be standing next to her as they wait, turns to her and says, 'I know you from somewhere, don't I?'

Rachel tells her she doesn't think they've met before, but the other woman insists until, finally, she clicks her fingers and says, 'You're Vanessa Lowe's friend, aren't you? Didn't she accuse you of burning her house down?'

Rachel is about to excuse herself, embarrassed, when the woman continues, with a roll of her eyes: 'God, that was so outrageous. As if you'd burn her kitchen down. I stopped following her after that. It was all a bit embarrassing and needy, wasn't it?'

Rachel manages to croak out her agreement, and the other woman laughs, holding out a hand to introduce herself. 'I'm Penny, by the way. My little girl is Lia.'

'Oh,' Rachel says, this time sounding more like herself. 'Sadie's mentioned Lia. I think they've been getting on –'

'Like a house on fire?' Penny interrupts, with another laugh and a sidelong look. 'Sorry, couldn't resist.'

Rachel laughs with her this time, and she has a momentary flash of something – guilt, maybe? Or, no, perhaps it's just the relief of actually laughing. Of laughing at the ridiculousness of all that has happened to her in the past year, of laughing at Vanessa, which seems to defang her somehow, revealing her for what she really is: a needy narcissist with a compliant following, ready to lap it all up. Except this woman, Penny, who also seems to have seen through her. 'I assume you're not following her any more either?' Penny continues.

'No. Actually, I've taken a break from Instagram for a while,' Rachel says, which is mostly true.

Penny nods. 'Right. I noticed you'd been a little quiet on there recently.' And then, a blush blooming on her cheeks, 'Oh, God, this is so embarrassing. I should've mentioned I followed you too. Didn't want to sound like a complete creep.'

Rachel laughs, shocked. The poetic circularity of this is not lost on her. 'I didn't think anyone still followed me any more, to be honest.'

'Oh, did everyone unfollow you after all that fire business, then?'

The doors to the nursery are opening, and their attention turns to it, watching for their daughters. 'There was a bit of a mass exodus, yeah,' Rachel says, scouring the tops of tiny heads for a sighting of Sadie.

'Well, don't worry about that. Who needs Vanessa's acolytes anyway?'

'That's exactly how I feel too,' Rachel says, with a warm smile at Penny.

The children arrive, and they talk over their daughters' heads for a while. A play date is mooted, but they part company there, going in separate directions, Sadie tugging at her mum's hand telling her all about her day. She asks for ice cream, even though the day is blustery and cool, much colder than is usual for September, but Rachel shakes her head. 'We've got ice cream for pudding tonight, love. Let's wait till then, share with Dad and Marcus.'

Sadie nods, her need sated, and the two continue their short walk back to their new home.

# 50

I'm deeply asleep when my phone vibrates on the chest of drawers beside me. I have no idea how long it's been ringing when I finally answer it, and say, my voice thick with barely remembered dreams, 'Yes?'

'Callie? Callie? Is that you? It's Vanessa.'

Vanessa.

I sit straight up in bed, suddenly awake, adrenaline coursing through me, as if shot by an epinephrine pen.

'Vanessa? What are you doing? How are you calling me?'

'Merry Christmas to you too,' she says.

'Aren't you . . . in prison?'

'I've been released on bail. It's so close to Christmas that the courts are closed and my arraignment won't be until the twenty-seventh.'

'Oh,' I say, trying to wrap my head around all this. Vanessa is calling me. Vanessa, who may have killed her own son but who has apparently been allowed to go home for Christmas because the courts aren't open. 'Where are you calling from? Are you at home?'

'Yes, but I don't want to stay here. That's what I'm calling about. Justin has taken the kids to his mum's in Edinburgh for Christmas and I really want to join them, but I need some help.'

'Justin's in Edinburgh?' I say, my voice thick again.

'Yes, with JJ and Emma. But I can't bear spending

Christmas without them. It's . . . Oh, it's horrible here. The house feels like a tomb, and there are reporters and camera crews outside and all through the town. I need to get away.'

'Vanessa, I don't think . . . I don't think you can do that, can you? You can't just leave. Hasn't your solicitor explained this to you?'

'Yes, but it's Christmas, Callie. I need to be with my kids.'

I blink into space. It's early still, and it's dark outside, the midwinter dawn taking its time. But my eyes have adjusted to the morning gloom and my room is coming into view. Biscuits is asleep at the bottom of the bed, a ginger swirl amid the monochrome tones. Despite the onrush of adrenaline, my brain is slow, lagging behind my body, which is tensed and ready, heartbeat rapid, chest squeezed tight, knees at my chin in a position even I can recognize as defensive. But Vanessa is miles away on the Kent coast, reporters at her door, the sea raging beyond her windows. At home, and plotting her escape.

'You can't go to Edinburgh, Vanessa,' I say slowly. 'They . . .' Here I take a deep breath, close my eyes, brace for impact. 'Surely they've said you can't see JJ and Emma.'

'They're my children, Callie,' Vanessa says, in a low, slow voice. 'Wouldn't you do the same, if it meant spending Christmas with Ada?'

I suck in my breath, winded by Vanessa's words, shocked that she would even mention Ada. I have been so trusting of Vanessa, so on her side, but she doesn't sound like the woman I met a couple of weeks ago.

'I'd do anything, *anything*, to be with them right now,

Callie. I know you understand. Don't you understand what I'm going through, Callie?

'I – I –' I stutter, stupidly.

'Callie, please. I'm begging you. I'm on my knees. I really need your help here. Didn't I help you out? I never once thought you'd hurt my baby.'

'I know,' I say slowly, trying to align my thoughts, trying to think of the best thing to say. 'But you need to talk to your solicitor about this. They'll be able to tell you what you can and can't do better than me.'

'They're my kids, Callie,' Vanessa says immediately, and through gritted teeth, her tone suddenly changes completely. '*Mine*. I don't need a solicitor to tell me when I can see them. I can see them whenever I fucking want.'

'I don't think that's true any more, Vanessa,' I say in an almost-whisper.

Vanessa gives a strangled yell so loud that Biscuits stands up, lamp-like eyes on me, annoyed at the disruption.

'Callie. I'm not asking you for legal advice,' she says, every word emphasized. 'I am asking you to help me see my children at Christmas. Are you still in Whitstable?'

'No,' I say. I'm relieved that I'm in London, away from this woman, away from this responsibility.

She is silent for a while, assessing, and then she laughs, the sound harsh and vibrating. 'Oh, my God. You think I did it. You think I killed my son.'

'No, no,' I say, in a rush, trying to cover myself. Biscuits is cleaning himself and I focus on him, his attentive, rhythmic washing as naturally calming as anything I can think of. 'No,' I say again, this time slower. 'It's just the legal implications I'm worried about, Vanessa.'

'No, you do. You really think I'm guilty. After I defended you when they were questioning you. Come on, Callie,' Vanessa wheedles. 'You know this was Rachel, you know it was. She's taken my baby from me. Please don't let her take the rest of my family from me too. Not at Christmas.'

I take a while to answer, but finally say, 'I'm sorry, Vanessa. But I can't help you with this.'

I can hear her breathing at the other end. It's heavy, laboured, fraught with tension and a kind of controlling menace. But then the line goes dead, and I look at my phone to confirm that she's hung up on me. Not knowing what else to do, I watch Biscuits for a while. I consider putting my phone down, turning it off even, sliding under the duvet and going back to sleep. Biscuits is purring now, and the room is still dark, heavy curtains blocking any light that might be creeping into the sky at this hour. I could hide up here. It's Christmas Eve after all, and I'm at home, being looked after. I can stay in my pyjamas. I can stay in bed, wait for this happy season to be over, and for the end of the year to come.

But I've spent so much of this year waiting, so much of it in stasis, in a kind of suspended animation. First, the wait of pregnancy, the counting down of the months, then weeks and days until she was ready. Then the wait of labour. The moments between contractions, the suspended sense of time, speeding up and slowing down, down, down until suddenly she was there in a rush of raw pain.

And then the wait of NICU. The hush, the hermetically sealed world of babies trying their best to live. The counting down, again, but this time towards an end, rather than a beginning, towards death, rather than life. The numbness and the void when it came – the abyss.

And then the monotony of grief and depression. Post-partum, and post parting. Another abyss: immeasurable, unfathomable, infinite. Making yourself at home there, finding a way through by not finding a way through.

I pick up my phone again, get out of bed and open the curtains. It's not quite light yet, but it's getting there, a low winter morning to usher in the Christmas spirit. I think of Charlotte's words last night: that Vanessa would never let Justin leave, not alive at least. But he has left and Vanessa has nothing but the broken shards of the reputation she'd so carefully forged and managed, created and controlled.

I'm done with waiting, I decide. Especially over something as important as this. I could hear Vanessa's desperation, her urgency. I can't stop thinking about Justin, Emma and JJ fleeing to Scotland, trying to find some safety and security in this strange time. What will Vanessa do when she gets there? Who else will she hurt? I can't wait to find out – I have to do something. So, I pick up my phone and call the only person who might be able to help.

## Nine Days Ago

'What are you doing?' Tom says, from over the top of the Saturday edition of the *Guardian*. 'God, you're scrolling Instagram, aren't you? I'd know that look of concentration and thumb twitch anywhere. I thought you'd deleted it.'

'I did,' Rachel says, reaching for the cafetière and pouring herself another cup of coffee. It is a lazy winter morning, the dining table still littered with breakfast leftovers, bits of American-style pancakes stuck to plates by the glossy remnants of very expensive maple syrup. Through the archway to the front room, Rachel can see Sadie on the foam play mat, Marcus on the sofa, his face slack with attention as he watches TV. The house feels like a home now, every inch painted and changed according to her taste and designs. There are photos, prints, and pictures everywhere, and wherever she could hang wallpaper, she has done so, the prints big and boisterous, the colours clashing and complementary.

She has never felt happier or more at home.

'But you couldn't stay away,' Tom says now, somewhat archly.

'I didn't want to.' Rachel smiles at his expression, which manages to convey self-righteous disapproval and indulgence. She glances back at the children and says, in a lower voice, coming clean, 'I put up a new post the other day. The first in four months.'

Tom shakes his head a little. 'I don't get it, Rach. It was so horrible for you, all that fire stuff, everything Vanessa implied and her little followers bullying you.'

'I know, but I just . . . I like it, okay? I know it's not perfect, but what's so wrong with looking at nice photos? In terms of vices, it could be a lot worse.'

'I don't know about that. It did bring the police to our door, after all.'

'That was all sorted out in the end. Anyway, I don't want to let Vanessa take this away from me. I was on there before I met her, and I enjoyed it before I started following her . . . Instagram isn't the Vanessa Lowe show, you know.'

'Just as long as you're not following her,' Tom says. 'You don't need that toxicity in your life, Rach. *We* don't. You've been so much happier since we moved to Margate. Don't let Vanessa bring us down again. Not here.'

A few months ago, Rachel might have bristled, but she knows he's right, and that his words come from a place of love and protection. Besides, she'd never give Vanessa the satisfaction of a follow. But she still keeps tabs on her, still checks her account a few times a week, just to make sure. She was caught off guard by those police officers in August, had no idea what plans Vanessa had burning away when they knocked on her and Tom's door in Whitstable. She isn't going to be caught out like that again. She was surprised, at first, that Vanessa hadn't blocked her, but then, when she thought about it, she realized it was classic Vanessa. Of course she'd want to leave the door open for

Rachel to follow her. She wants as many eyes on her as possible. She just isn't showing the full picture.

'Oh, my God,' Rachel says now, sitting up in her chair. She has navigated to Vanessa's profile, expecting to see another of her expertly styled and photographed flat-lays: muted tones, sharp winter light, everything just so, minimal and perfect.

Instead she sees Vanessa's Instagram Story, uploaded less than forty-five minutes ago.

'What?' Tom says, frowning at her.

'Matthew's missing,' Rachel says, on a gasp.

'Matthew who?'

'Matthew Lowe, Tom. Vanessa's son.'

'Jesus,' Tom says, putting down his paper and taking off his glasses to rub his eyes. 'So, you do follow her?'

'No, I don't, and that's hardly the point right now, is it?'

Rachel turns up the volume on her phone so she can hear Vanessa talking to the camera in her Story. Her face is a patchwork of red and white: pale skin, red eyes and no makeup. Her lips are trembling as she speaks, and tears and snot run together, snail tracks on her usually perfect face. Despite herself, Rachel has the urge to grab a tissue, hold the other woman's chin in her hand, and wipe it all away. And Vanessa is holding her phone at such an angle that Rachel is powerfully reminded – of all things – of the iconic scene in *The Blair Witch Project*, the one that had got her and her friends, young and naïve as they were, to believe that the movie could be real.

'What's she saying?' Tom asks. 'I can't hear.'

Rachel flicks her gaze back to the children, making sure their attention is still on other things, and turns up the volume. Tom has stood up, is leaning over her shoulder watching Vanessa with her.

'I woke up this morning and Matthew was gone,' Vanessa is saying, her voice wavering and breathy. 'I went to check on him, as I always do as soon as I'm up, and there was nothing but an empty space in his bed. Of course I went downstairs immediately, thinking, Oh, it's fine, he'll be downstairs playing on his own, but he wasn't there, and that's when I started to panic. I want you to know that we've called the police. Justin is out checking the garden and the beach but, oh, God, I am so, so scared. Justin keeps telling me that it's going to be all right, that he'll be hiding somewhere or have run off, but where would he run to? He's a baby still. I just can't help imagining the worst, and I know all you mamas out there will understand. So, I need your help, please. Start spreading the word. Especially if you're local. I am absolutely terrified that someone has taken my little boy, and – oh, God, what if we never see him again?'

Here, Vanessa starts sobbing, shoulders heaving, her whole body in motion. Eventually, it abates enough for her to speak again. She takes a gulping breath and continues: 'I know you all know where – who – my thoughts went to as soon as I realized he was gone. I feel like I'm going mad – I mean, who could possibly do this to such a darling little boy? How could you want to hurt and punish me so much? But, really, if you're watching please just bring him home. Give me my little boy back.'

She doesn't say 'Rachel' but she might as well have done, and Rachel stares, dumbfounded, at the phone in her hand.

'Oh, my God,' she says eventually, unable to form a thought or a sentence more complex than that.

'Jesus fucking Christ,' Tom says at the same time, backing away from the table, hands pulling at the peaks of his fair hair. He looks as Rachel feels: as if she has just witnessed a ten-ton truck mow down a street full of people.

She feels sick. Or not sick exactly, more like her stomach has been ripped from her body. 'Oh, God,' she moans.

And then Sadie and Marcus are standing at the top of the flight of three steps that leads to the living room, 'What's wrong, Mum?' Marcus asks, his face a picture of worry and confusion.

'Nothing, love, nothing's wrong,' Rachel says quickly, as Tom rushes over to the children, kneeling on the bottom step so he is more their height.

'Nothing's wrong, guys. Don't you worry, we were just being a bit silly.'

'We heard someone crying,' Marcus says.

'It was on my phone,' Rachel says, which is true, of course, but barely begins to cover it. As if nothing that happens on her phone is real. As if there aren't people at the other end.

Rachel stays in the house all day, paranoid. As if by leaving it she might be admitting guilt or, worse, set upon by pointing fingers, like some scene from a long-ago witch trial. Tom takes the kids out. They go to the beach and the playground, despite the cold weather, and later warm up with cheese toasties and raspberry doughnuts from one of the town's many cafés. They've been back a little while when the front doorbell rings. Rachel is in the kitchen.

She'd been planning on making a slow-cooked *ragù* on Sunday, but decided to do it today instead, the care, attention and concentration it takes calming and soothing her. But as soon as the bell rings all the tension rushes back, and her muscles stiffen and tighten, pulling together in anxiety.

Tom has already answered the door, and she hears voices in the hallway. She already knows who it is by the time he leads them back to the kitchen and says, in a soft voice, 'Rach, it's the police. They've come to talk about Matthew.'

Rachel carefully puts the lid back on her beautiful grey-blue Le Creuset – a housewarming present from her mum and sister – and turns to face them while wiping her hands on her apron.

It's the woman who steps forward first. She's short and compact, a similar height to Rachel, with a mane of black hair, and thick black-framed glasses. She smiles as she says, 'Rachel Donovan? I'm DCI Varma. I need to ask you a few questions.'

Rachel glances at Tom, who is hovering in the background. 'Yes, of course. Do you want to sit down?' She motions towards the dining table, and the detective nods, indicating to her colleague that he should sit as well. As they're taking their seats, Rachel asks, 'Can I get you anything? Tea, water?'

But Varma shakes her head, apparently answering for both of them, so Rachel is left with nothing to do but take a seat at the table with them to answer their questions. She has a glass of red wine on the go, opened to use in the *ragù*, and looks at it longingly but leaves it where it stands and joins them. Answering police questions with a glass of wine isn't the best look.

'So, we're just following up a line of enquiry in our investigation into the disappearance of Matthew Lowe. You've heard that he's gone missing, is that right? Your husband indicated as much when we arrived,' Varma says.

'Yes. I haven't stopped thinking about it all day.'

'Okay. So, it was brought to our attention by Mrs Lowe that you and she had something of a falling-out recently.'

'Recently? Well, it was in the summer. She . . . she accused me of having an affair with her husband, then started this sort of vendetta against me on Instagram.'

'Right,' Varma says, staring keenly at Rachel.

'I know she thinks I had something to do with this but, honestly, that's just so ridiculous. I'd never hurt Matthew. I'd never hurt any child.'

'Well, Mrs Lowe seems to think this is more about you wanting to hurt her . . . You understand that we wouldn't normally approach someone with this kind of hearsay, but when it comes to a missing child . . .'

'No, it's fine, I understand. Believe me, I want Matthew found alive and well just as much as anyone.'

'You were quite close? The two families?'

'For a while, yes. And especially Sadie – my daughter – and Matthew. They're the same age, only a couple of months apart.'

Varma nods, still staring. 'Well. Could you tell me where you were last night, Mrs Donovan? Between the hours of midnight and seven a.m.?'

Rachel lets out a short bark of laughter. 'I was here. At home.'

'With your family?'

'Yes, of course with my family.'

Tom, who has melted into the background, gives a cough and moves forward, joins them all at the table, taking a seat. 'We were in all night, watched a couple of episodes of *Russian Doll* after the kids went to bed.'

'Actually, we almost watched the whole season,' Rachel reminds him.

'Yeah, have you seen it? It's addictive. We didn't go to bed until almost midnight.'

'Okay. And you didn't get up at all in the middle of the night, Mrs Donovan?' Varma asks.

'No,' Rachel says. 'No, I didn't.'

'Well, actually,' Tom says, and Rachel looks at him, her heart falling through her like a dead weight, 'didn't Sadie wake up a couple of times?'

'Oh, yeah, you're right, she did,' Rachel says, relief washing over her so that she sags back in her chair. 'She's been having nightmares recently. We think it might be related to the move,' she explains to Varma and the other police officer, who has yet to say a word.

'Okay. So, you did get up?'

'Yes, but only once. Tom got up the first time, I got up the second.'

'And around what times were these?'

'I guess we hadn't been in bed that long when she woke up the first time, so maybe it was about one, one thirty?' Rachel looks to Tom for confirmation. He nods. 'But the second was much later, maybe about four?'

'I think it was more like five,' Tom says.

'Yeah, four or five,' Rachel says.

'Okay,' Varma says again, with a definitive nod.

Rachel wants to ask questions, wants more detail, wants to know who else they are questioning, where they are looking. She wants to point out to Varma that the Lowes own several properties in the Whitstable area: could Matthew be hiding in one?

But she doesn't ask any of her questions. Because she knows they wouldn't answer them, and because she wants them out of her house as soon as possible.

## 51

Varma's voice is steady on the phone as I stand in front of the window of my childhood bedroom and stare into the garden below. A fox is slinking through the grass, back from a dawn scavenge. It stops in the middle of the lawn – the grass is long – and turns its face to the sky, eyes closed, taking a deep sniff. When it opens its eyes, I swear it's staring right up at me. Then it blinks again, trots on, disappearing into the undergrowth at the end of the garden.

'We'll let Justin know, Callie, but she's not getting to Edinburgh, don't worry.'

'I just don't understand how she's even at home,' I say. My breath is misting the window, I'm standing so close, and I draw an X in the condensation with my finger.

'She wouldn't be if it was up to me, but she is.'

'She sounded . . . I don't know how she sounded. Like she was about to have a breakdown.' There is a noise behind me, and I start, only to turn and see that it was just Biscuits, jumping off the bed and padding out of the room. 'She's still obsessed with the idea that it was Rachel Donovan. That she framed her somehow.'

'Framed her?' Varma says, and then, all business again, 'Look, Callie, I know you're worried, but I've spoken to Justin about Vanessa's views on Rachel, and they're . . . clouded to say the least. Vanessa's the unreliable narrator of her own life.'

Varma sounds certain, calm. But instead of reassuring me that she's got it all under control, it makes me panic more. 'Yes, I know,' I say, through gritted teeth. 'I'm beginning to understand that. But you don't understand – she was on the verge of something. Something . . . big. She's not going to sit at home like a good little girl today. She's angry, desperate, reckless, and has nothing to lose. I'm worried she's going to hurt somebody.'

'She's not going to be able to get to Edinburgh, Callie. You needn't worry about that.'

I shake my head. Why isn't she getting this? 'What about Rachel? Her family? What about them?'

'We have –'

'She's not going to sit back and take this. She thinks Rachel kidnapped and killed her son, then set her up. We're not talking about a rational mind here.'

'I'm well aware, Callie,' Varma says, and the way she says it, I know she's annoyed, that she wants to get me off the phone.

'You'll warn her? Rachel?'

'Callie, you have to trust that we're doing everything we can,' Varma says, but as we end the call, I can't help thinking that it's Christmas, that surely – surely – police officers will be distracted and preoccupied by celebrations, by having to work when others don't. A few minutes ago, I'd been glad to be so far away from Vanessa, free of her grip, her strange enchantment. But now I bite at my bottom lip, troubling the skin there, wishing there was something I could do.

## Now

Rachel doesn't notice anything until it's too late. Doesn't hear the sliding door being pushed open, doesn't feel the waft of cold air, doesn't notice the soft pad of Vanessa's feet on the heated tile floors.

Sunlight is streaming through the windows, bathing everything in a Christmas halo of light. The children are laughing, Rachel's mother pretending to tell them off in her sing-song voice, Tom laughing along. And suddenly everything changes and it's already too late.

Vanessa has a knife against Sadie's neck, and the room erupts. Rachel can't tell who is making which sound, but she does know that Sadie, with that blade against her neck, is the only one not making a noise. Tom stands to attention, knocking his chair to the floor with a crash.

Sadie is shaking, trembling, eyes filling with tears, and Marcus, sweet, sweet Marcus, drops to the floor, to his knees, hiding under the kitchen table.

At the head of the table, still sitting in her chair, Augustina's eyes are pinned on Vanessa.

Rachel is standing, but she can't remember how, or when she stood up.

Her legs feel like lead and liquid at the same time.

Tom is saying something, but whatever it is, Rachel

can't hear it, can't hear Vanessa's response, whatever that is.

'Vanessa,' Rachel says at last, finding her voice. The other woman is standing there, with the blade in her hand, supernaturally still. Rachel looks into Vanessa's eyes, and where she thought she'd see mania, she sees nothing of the sort: she sees resolve, steady as a rock, and that scares her even more. It feels as though the world has stopped and been put on fast forward at the same time. Has twenty minutes or two seconds passed since Vanessa came into the room? Rachel can't tell, but at least her voice is working now, coming out clearer, steadier than she expected. But maybe, on some level, she has been expecting something like this all along.

Expecting Vanessa to return to their lives and rip a seam through it, the kind that can't be mended, can't be fixed by moving away.

Rachel's mother has always claimed that anything is fixable, that anything broken can be mended. But Rachel knows, even as she gives her mother the barest of glances, that she wouldn't be able to fix this.

'Vanessa,' she says again. 'Vanessa, please take that knife away from Sadie's neck. I know you don't want to hurt her.' But, looking at her, she knows nothing of the sort. There is that burning clarity in the other woman's gaze. Vanessa's hand is steady, her breath even.

She looks sure of herself, more certain than Rachel has ever seen her. Not just more sure of herself. More herself.

It is as if Rachel has never truly seen her before, and now here she is: the truth of Vanessa finally revealed, holding a knife against Rachel's squirming daughter's skin. She's had her suspicions, of course, that at the core of Vanessa lay something like this. But Rachel had no idea how sharp it would be, how it would glint in the sun, reflecting and refracting, too terrible to look at directly.

'Sadie,' Rachel whispers, desperately. 'Stop moving, baby. Please.'

Sadie whines, a high-pitched baby whine, animal and yearning.

Vanessa doesn't even flinch, makes no move to indicate she's heard a peep from the terrified child in her arms.

'Listen to Mummy, Sadie,' Tom says. 'Stop wriggling about, okay? If you stay still, the nice lady will let you go, won't she, Vanessa? This is all just a joke, a misunderstanding.' Tom spreads his hands in front of him, looking intently at Vanessa, trying to communicate a message she'll never bother to decipher. Or, perhaps, never be able to.

'Nice lady,' Vanessa says, the first words she has uttered since slipping into the kitchen unnoticed. 'Nice lady. Yes, I suppose I am a nice lady.' The words have the ring of mania to them, yet she sounds as she looks: completely steady, utterly sure of herself.

But, then, Vanessa Lowe has always been utterly sure of herself. It's everyone else who has been left so completely, so dangerously in the dark. There is a short, desperate silence as Rachel, Tom and Augustina take in these worrying words, and then, 'This is ridiculous,' Augustina says suddenly, from her end of the table. Vanessa's head whips towards her, as if she's just noticed her there, as if she hadn't even considered her. 'You are behaving like a wild animal. Like a small child. Behave like the grown woman you are.'

Vanessa laughs, and it is a laugh Rachel has never heard from her before. Normally, her laugh is warm, rolling. It envelops and draws you in. But this laugh comes from somewhere deeper, low and threatening. Repels you. Not a laugh really, but a warning.

'Mum, don't,' Rachel says desperately, as she realizes her mother is about to continue trying to reason with someone who cannot be reasoned with.

'Augustina, maybe you could take Marcus upstairs, and Vanessa, Rachel, and I could have a nice little chat down here,' Tom says instead, his eyes not leaving Vanessa's face as he speaks.

His mother-in-law looks at him as if he is an idiot, knowing full well, just as Rachel does, that Vanessa isn't about to let anyone leave this room.

'No one's going anywhere,' Vanessa says smoothly, her left arm still strapped across Sadie's slim torso, cleaving her to the kitchen chair. Sadie is finally still. She has taken heed of her mother and father's beseeching requests, but her fear is transmitted through her big brown eyes, which are now so wide that they seem to take up her whole face. 'You took my baby from me, Rachel, so now I'm taking yours. You ruined my life. So, now I'm ruining yours.'

Her arm tightens across Sadie's chest, and the little girl, unable to fully control herself, yelps. Rachel's heart lurches inside her chest, as if it could reach across the room and grab her, save her.

'Vanessa, you know I didn't harm a hair on Matthew's head. You know that, I know you do. Wherever all this is coming from, you know I didn't kill your son,' Rachel says slowly, trying – and failing – to control her breathing. Her voice comes out ragged and raw, sandpaper being dragged over the teeth of a deadly buzz saw.

'Yes, you did. You wanted to make me look crazy, to make people think I'd kidnapped him.'

'You don't exactly need any help making yourself look crazy, do you?' Tom mutters.

Vanessa's eyes narrow at him, and Rachel gives him a look that, after ten years together, he knows means *Shut the fuck up*. He gives her one back that says, *Well, I'm not wrong, am I?*

'Vanessa,' Rachel says, her voice shaking now more than she would have liked it to. She isn't concerned with betraying her fear to Vanessa. In some ways, she thinks reducing herself in front of the other woman might be the quickest way to defuse the situation. Vanessa has always liked being completely in control. 'What is it that you want, really? Whatever you want, I'll give it to you. I'll go to the police right now, and tell them I was with you and you couldn't possibly have kidnapped Matthew. I'll be your alibi.'

Both Tom and Augustina stiffen at this suggestion, their twin breathing ragged with fear. 'Rachel,' Augustina says warningly, her voice low, but Rachel holds her hand up.

'Oh, and give yourself a nice little alibi in the process too? No, I don't think so, Rachel. Besides, it's really not necessary, thank you,' Vanessa says, her eyes pinned on Rachel. 'I already have an alibi. I don't need you. I just need you to know that you're not going to win this.'

'Win this? Win what?'

'This,' she hisses, her teeth suddenly bared, her beautiful face stretched into a terrifying grimace.

Rachel's gasp is sharp with sudden understanding. Vanessa, she realizes, doesn't think like her, doesn't think like anyone, really.

And if Rachel is to get her family out of this alive, she's going to have to learn to think like her.

To win.

'How long did it take you to plan all this?' Vanessa asks, her eyes still square on Rachel's, her hand still resolutely holding that knife up to Sadie's neck.

'Plan what?' Tom asks, turning to Rachel.

'She thinks I kidnapped Matthew and framed her for it.'

A look of sheer consternation crosses Tom's face. 'Vanessa, you can't possibly believe that. This isn't . . . This isn't how normal people behave. That's just not what normal people do.'

Her gaze flicks to him, sharp and brilliant in the sunshine, and then back to Rachel just as quickly. And Rachel understands then that she's never known what Vanessa is thinking or feeling, that she has only ever simulated whatever she wanted Rachel – or whoever else was around at the time – to think or feel about her. But here she is, finally showing them the real Vanessa. The mask hasn't just slipped; it's been torn off.

'Vanessa,' Rachel says slowly, holding up her hands, submitting to the alpha in the room. 'If you do this . . . if you hurt Sadie, all you'll be doing is convincing everyone, and I mean everyone, that you really did hurt your son. No one will ever believe you when you say you were set up, that you're innocent. You said you had an alibi for the night Matthew went missing. Why don't you just tell the police about it? They'd have to drop the charges, and then you can go back to trying to convince everyone it was me who took Matthew.'

Rachel catches Tom's eye just for a second, hoping he knows what she's doing, trusts her to know what she's doing. Augustina is still carefully watching Vanessa and Sadie. Rachel doesn't have to worry about her.

'Oh, you'd like that, wouldn't you?' Vanessa spits. 'Make me look like a fool.'

'How would that make you look like a fool? If it proves you're innocent, what does it matter?' Rachel's voice is shaking, vibrating at her highest pitch, just like the rest of her body is.

Vanessa again bares her teeth at Rachel, and she instantly thinks of a wild animal protecting her young. Only Vanessa isn't protecting anyone but herself, and the young she has in her grip is Rachel's, not her own. 'I'm not falling for that,' she says, as though she's talking to someone particularly stupid.

'Right. That's it. I've had enough. Vanessa, if you don't release my daughter now, I'm going to call the police,' Tom declares.

Rachel whips around to stare at Tom, eyes wide. How can he possibly think he can just declare this situation over and walk out alive? Vanessa is operating in a world without rules, without logic: Tom and Rachel have to descend to her level to get them all out of this. As if proving Rachel right, Vanessa angles the knife ever so slightly closer to Sadie's skin in response to Tom's threat. Rachel and Augustina let out a duet of yelps. 'Don't be stupid,

Tom. The police can't help you now. You may have been able to convince them you had nothing to do with the fire, but you're not going to get away with this,' Vanessa says.

'We didn't have anything to do with the fire, though, Vanessa,' Tom says, exasperation leaking from his every word, but Rachel can hear he's on the verge: there are tears and fear – very real fear – behind his veneer of frustration.

'Yes, it was you who was framing Rachel,' Augustina says.

Rachel shoots a desperate glance at her mother, willing her to stay quiet. She doesn't understand how neither Tom nor Augustina have figured out that Vanessa very clearly has the upper hand here – and that hand is holding a knife against her daughter's throat.

Vanessa's hold on the knife tightens even as Rachel is watching her now, and she feels all the bones in her body stiffen, her blood rise through her. Looking into her daughter's eyes, seeing the fear, she also sees something else: a little girl looking right back at her. A little girl who has never known her mother do anything but the best for her. Sadie's look isn't one of desperation: she knows her mum will get her out of this.

Rachel's breathing deepens, evens. She thinks of the extra reserves of energy and lung capacity she calls on when she's swimming in the sea and has gone out further than she thought. She can make it back to shore now.

She always has done before.

Her phone is in her hand. She can't call the police. That would be too obvious.

She can't be obvious about this at all. Any shift in her

stance, her demeanour, her confidence will alert Vanessa. She has successfully submitted to her, convinced her that she – Vanessa – is in control.

She's the one with the knife in her hand.

But a phone.

A phone can do so much more than make a call. Vanessa should know that really.

Rachel's thumb glides over the screen effortlessly, even while she is still staring at Vanessa, holding the other woman's gaze.

'You know I didn't set that fire, Vanessa,' Rachel says, picking up her mum's line, as she opens Instagram and starts a Live session. 'I wasn't even in Whitstable that day. How could I have set fire to your kitchen?'

'You wanted what I had. You wanted my life, didn't you? Wanted to *be* me. First it was Justin, and when you realized he'd never leave me, you wanted to take my home, so when that didn't work, you took Matthew.'

Rachel shakes her head. Is it possible that, even as Vanessa stands there, lies pouring out of her, her hand moments from taking Sadie's life, that Rachel feels sympathy for her? She had thought she hated the woman. But to live so solidly inside a delusion like this: what kind of life was that?

'No, Vanessa,' she says softly. 'I didn't do any of that. I didn't want any part of your life. And even if I did, please don't take it out on Sadie. Think of Matthew, of how much he loved Sadie, how much you loved him.'

Rachel is staring into Vanessa's eyes, trying to see any change in the other woman's face and mind as she mentions Matthew. Vanessa's face is a closed book, though – you wouldn't think she was holding a knife, threatening a child's life. Until, that is, they hear the distant sound of sirens getting louder, nearer. The telltale whine, a warning and a lifeline.

Vanessa's eyes flare, her face a picture of thwarted effort.

'Vanessa, please,' Rachel says, her voice still soft, but stronger now she knows help is on the way, so nearly with them. She has to tread carefully, though. That woman's arm is still stiff around Sadie's torso, the other hand gripping the knife, like a fatal talisman.

Vanessa doesn't take to being thwarted, Rachel knows, but she has to hope the other woman knows when she's beaten.

But she's not beaten yet, and Rachel's voice, preparing to offer another entreaty, gets lodged in her throat as Vanessa's grip tightens and beads of blood begin to bloom red on Sadie's throat as Rachel's words turn into a wild animal scream.

## *Eight Weeks Later*

Callie leans back in her chair, signalling that she's finished reading the draft of Rachel's article on her iPad. 'It's good, Rachel. Really good. It's clear, precise – your memory is amazing, the detail is ... But there's emotion and depth too. I'm assuming you've still got to write the conclusion, right? How the police arrived and all that?'

Rachel nods, leaning forward to top up Callie's coffee cup from the cafetière. It's another glorious day – almost as bright and brilliant as that sharp Christmas Day when everything in Rachel's article happened. But it's early March now, and winter seems to be waning. When Rachel walked Sadie to nursery earlier, she swore she could smell spring. The change in the air that marks the slipping of the seasons. Rachel's a city girl, yet she's always been able to tell when the weather's about to change, when rain's about to fall.

'I can't believe it was Instagram that got her in the end,' Callie says now, smiling a little grimly at Rachel, and bringing her back to the moment. 'There's something so poetic about it.'

Rachel nods, agreeing, although it's hard to find anything approximating poetry in any of this. Callie is taking a term off from her studies – or a semester, as she referred to it in her message to Rachel. She's come back to Kent, to the sea, to find or at least search for something to soothe her. But she's also been writing about her experience at Christmas: about Matthew, the Lowes, and the strange way she got caught up in all of it. She wrote a brilliant article for Maven that Rachel saw and enjoyed, and that got her thinking about writing something of her own. She had thought, in the immediate aftermath of 'the event', as it is now referred to in her household, that she would never want to think about or consider Vanessa Lowe again, or feel the need to relive seeing someone hold her little daughter against her will like that.

But she has needed to. She's needed to make sense of it – not to make peace with it exactly, but to come to a conclusion.

Vanessa is a difficult woman to come to a conclusion about. She still finds it hard to believe what Vanessa did, who she ended up being. 'Who was it who called the police in the end, do you know?' Callie is asking her.

Rachel shakes her head, 'There were dozens of callers, they said. I've had a couple of women reach out to say it was them. It's very weird to feel like you owe your life to a stranger on the internet.'

'I bet,' Callie says.

What had saved them in the end was Instagram Live. Well, a combination of Instagram Live, Rachel's quick thinking, and her followers who rang the police on seeing Vanessa Lowe holding a knife against the neck of a three-year-old girl on Christmas morning. Rachel wants to meet the women who saved her and her family. She is thinking of getting them all together in a round-table discussion for her article. Although she already knows she will be a mess when she eventually meets them, the strangers on the internet who saved her daughter's life.

'Have you heard from Justin?' Callie asks.

Rachel nods. 'He called on Boxing Day. He'd seen it on TV.'

'How did he seem?'

Rachel takes a moment to answer. How did Justin seem? He had seemed lost, overwhelmed, a man unmoored. But there'd been something else: the grit of resilience maybe, the determination to survive all this. 'He mostly just wanted to check we were all right. Safe. And to say sorry.'

'Hardly his fault,' Callie says, taking a sip of coffee.

'Well,' Rachel says.

'You think he knew what she was capable of?'

'I think he had his suspicions. I know I did. And I hadn't been married to her for over a decade. He sounded guilty. Rueful.'

'I suppose that's understandable. I felt completely taken in by her. Fooled. And I'd only known her two weeks. It didn't feel good.'

'No,' Rachel agrees, 'it didn't.'

'Those poor kids, though. I can't believe what they've been through. When I think about JJ now . . . He just seemed like a normal surly kid at the time, but now, knowing everything, it seems so obvious. He was scared of her.'

Rachel has thought this before, voiced it to Callie even, but the other woman seems to have forgotten about her warnings so she simply says, 'Yes. He was.'

'He'll have a hell of a time at the trial.'

Rachel groans and nods. Vanessa has been charged

with a litany of crimes, so many it is almost impossible to keep track and keep count. But Rachel and Callie have been called as witnesses. She can't imagine it, not yet. Being in the courtroom. Seeing Vanessa in the dock. Seeing Vanessa. Vanessa has continued vehemently to deny her involvement in the kidnapping and death of her son. Rachel had thought – or rather hoped, for the sake of JJ, Justin and Emma – Vanessa might plead guilty, admit her wrongdoing, accept her sentence, and let the rest of them move on with their lives. But Vanessa will have her moment in the dock, one last dose of the limelight, and the thought of it makes Rachel see red. Vanessa has already given several interviews from prison. Rachel isn't sure how – there must be protocols in place to stop this happening, but certain newspapers appear to have their ways. In them, she has continued to accuse Rachel of her own crimes. When that hasn't worked, she has told reporters about her own childhood abuse, whether to excuse her crimes or elicit sympathy, Rachel can't tell, but she has her doubts about these claims. She never met Vanessa's mum, has no idea what their relationship was like, never heard Vanessa speak about her childhood. She knows only one thing: Vanessa lies. And not only that, but when cornered, Vanessa will reveal her claws, take a swipe at anyone who comes near her. She was never going to claim responsibility for any of this, she doesn't have it in her, so Rachel sees it all as one last, desperate attempt by Vanessa to reclaim her narrative, to write it the way *she* sees it.

Rachel shudders, and tries to push the other woman from her mind while she and Callie finish their coffee in heavy but companionable silence.

'Well, shall we go?' Rachel says softly, eventually.

Callie nods, but Rachel can already see the tears forming in her eyes.

They're going to visit Matthew's grave. Rachel had gone to the funeral, but Callie hadn't felt able to, and this will be the first time she's been. Even now, these few months later, in the beautiful, daring light of an early spring day she didn't feel able to go alone. So, she reached out to Rachel – the woman Vanessa had convinced her to conspire against with her – and asked if she would accompany her. Rachel said yes.

Rachel drives them to Whitstable Cemetery, the day so bright that they are compelled to put on sunglasses. It's quiet when they get there, the solemn, reverent quiet of cemeteries deepened by the lack of other mourners. As they walk the paths – Rachel remembers the way – they lift their chins when they hear the call of a robin.

Rachel turns to Callie and smiles a little. They are thinking of the same things: of death and rebirth, winter and spring, of the sheer, obstinate bravery that it sometimes takes to survive, to step out of the hibernation of winter and face the renewal of spring.

# JJ

Six Months Ago

# I

It's a violently hot summer's day. There hasn't been a summer like this for years, decades, even. Whitstable is burning in the heat of the day, the whole country gasping for air, heading straight for the coast at every chance they get.

It's Sports Day. On the hottest day of the year, during the hottest summer on record.

Vanessa is filming the whole thing. It's not her usual content, but her Instagram Lives have been doing well recently, and she's already got more than a thousand people watching. It helps that Justin is here. For once. He's playing in the Dads versus Sons five-a-side football match that JJ has been dreading all week. Vanessa isn't worried about this competition, though: she can't lose with her son playing on one team, and her husband on the other.

The 500-metre dash is a different prospect.

JJ is on the under-15s county athletics team as well as the cricket under-12s. He can't be shown up by losing out to a bunch of normal kids. Vanessa is watching her son from the sidelines. He's standing apart from everyone, head down in concentration, toeing at the ground. There's already sweat pricking at his hairline. JJ's head jerks up and he sees his mother staring pointedly at him, lifting her chin. He knows what she's saying; Don't lose. Don't embarrass me. Don't make me look stupid.

He watches as, in the pushchair next to his mother, Matthew gabbles something and Vanessa crouches next to him. She directs the camera of her phone at the small child, and he gurgles and blabs happily, used to this kind of attention. JJ watches as Vanessa coos to his little brother. Matthew shouldn't be out in this heat, not really. Even JJ knows that. But Vanessa can't bear not to have him right next to her at all times, to show Matthew off while showing JJ up.

He's still watching his mother and brother when his sports teacher claps her hands, pulls all the competitors together, tells them it's about to start. JJ looks back at his mother. She's drawn herself away from Matthew at last, is staring at JJ instead.

He realizes he should feel something in this moment. Nerves, excitement. But he doesn't. All he wants is to get it over and done with. He doesn't even really care if he wins or not, although it would be better if he did. It's always better not to disappoint Vanessa.

He's starting to understand that this isn't normal either. He can feel the fun and joy, support and love radiating off the other parents – not all of them, of course, but most. He's heard the shouts of *Do your best! Give 'em hell!* and *Come on, son!* There don't seem to be any caveats if their best isn't good enough.

As he gets into place he can still feel his mother's eyes on him. He squints, searches for his dad. He's there, waving, a big smile plastered on his face. JJ feels something then, a surge of something, but he's not quite sure what. Sometimes he hates his dad almost as much as he hates his mum. Hates him for pretending, just like Mum does, but in a different way. They're all liars. All hiding something.

He's ready for his teacher to tell them to go. He thinks he might even win, but then he thinks how annoyed Vanessa will be if he doesn't, and that little surge of something flows through him again. He straightens his back, squares his shoulders.

Across the playground, Vanessa watches as JJ finally gets into position, finally starts looking like a winner.

He doesn't win, though, and although JJ has been talking to someone, a friend, he can feel when his mother starts walking towards him, and he turns to stare at her as she saunters across the playground. Anyone watching would see JJ staring directly at his mother, standing stock-still, and think it looked like a challenge.

But just before Vanessa reaches him, JJ turns and walks away from her.

# 2

JJ can still feel the sting of his mother's hand on his face as he walks down to the beach. The tide is out and it's so hot it's otherworldly. He feels as though he could be on another planet, far from here – light years away – where nothing could ever touch him. It's partly the quiet. He'd thought it would be busy, people coming to the beach to refresh after school and work, but it's so hot still, even at five o'clock, that everyone is hiding inside. He imagines them all, behind closed blinds and curtains, cowering from the towering sun, the images from their television screens flickering across their darkened rooms.

He could've retreated to his bedroom. Could've retreated to a video game, where problems exist just to be solved, but instead it's him alone on this big wide empty beach. He reaches up to touch his face where she hit him. He doesn't regret it. By losing the race, he beat his mother. This was the first time he'd ever lost on purpose. The first time he'd taken the decision to defy her openly, rather than just disappoint her, which is what he always seems to do anyway. He's still in his trainers, stupid on the beach, so he leans down to untie them and pulls off his socks. The sand burns his feet. It's the first time he can remember that happening here, and he runs, full pelt, his trainers and socks in his hands, down, down, down to where the sea has retreated, and doesn't stop until his feet feel the relief of the cool, damp sand.

# 3

Upstairs, in the music room, JJ throws his trumpet onto the floor. He is grade eight in piano, but his mother insisted he play another instrument too. The irony is that he quite enjoys the trumpet. But it's not even ten o'clock in the morning, in the middle of the summer holidays. Why should he have to be fucking practising it now?

JJ prefers the days when his mother seems to forget he exists. On those days, he can slip outside, spend the whole day away from the house that is too perfect to live in. Or he can spend it in his room, playing *FIFA* and *Call of Duty*, and when he's feeling particularly listless, *Animal Crossing*. Her attention is like a laser – sharp, focused – and when it's directed in one place for too long, it burns.

She stands in the doorway now, quietly seething. He can feel her hard, insistent anger even from across the room. Vanessa's moods can change the energy of a room, a house, could have changed the direction of the *Titanic*, yet he seems to be the only person who truly understands this. His father has made a life out of ignoring his wife's moods, which could direct tides just as the moon controls the sea. Standing in the doorway now, JJ wonders what Vanessa will do.

The trumpet lies between them on the floor. It was a childish move, JJ knows. He wishes he could do something to hurt her, something that would really affect her, but nothing seems to. She will be angry, he will feel the repercussions of that anger, and then it will be gone. She'll be back to being Vanessa Lowe again.

'I just came up to say congratulations,' Vanessa says to her elder son, leaning against the doorframe.

'What?' JJ says, childish surprise leaking from him in that one word.

'You got into Tonbridge. Isn't that fantastic news?'

'What?' JJ says again. The music room is a mirror image of his father's study at the other end of the hall and is surrounded on two sides by windows. On a morning like today, it's so hot he can already feel the sweat dripping down his back. The room crowds in on him as his mother talks, and he swallows, desperate for a drink, suddenly not sure if he's even breathing.

'Don't keep saying "What?" like that, darling. It makes you sound stupid. And obviously you're not, because look how clever you are, getting into a school like Tonbridge.'

JJ wonders who this performance is for. Usually, Vanessa saves this kind of BAFTA-winning turn for an audience, like her precious band of Instagram followers, but it's just the two of them, him and his mother, grinning at him. There is something canine about her, he thinks: a fox in a henhouse. 'But I don't want to go to Tonbridge,' JJ says uselessly. 'I don't want to go to boarding school.'

He'll be away from her, though. That violent laser beam will be focused elsewhere, for whole terms at a time. He'll be free of her magnetic moods, her tyrannical tides. He begins to feel something lift, a weight he's been carrying for so long. He can't let her know, though, can't let her see that this might end up being something he wants. She believes she's locking him up at boarding school, throwing away the key, but really she's setting him free.

'You'll do whatever I tell you to do,' Vanessa says. She's still smiling as she points to the trumpet lying on the floor. 'Now pick that up and start practising. You should treat your lovely things with more respect.'

As she closes the door behind her, he hears the lock click into place. She's locked him into this burning room on this burning day.

# 4

JJ has figured out a way to watch his mother without her realizing. It means he can check where she is, what she's doing and, hopefully, stay as far away from her as possible. It's pretty genius, and better yet, it uses her favourite things against her: Instagram and oversharing. Or, at least, oversharing the bits of her life she wants the rest of the world to see. He can follow her every move on Instagram if he wants: from home to the shop to the rental houses they're doing up to Matthew's nursery. JJ can't believe she geo-tags the nursery. Does she have no idea how dangerous that is? But, no, she wants other mums to know that her son goes to one of the most expensive daycare options in Kent. She's even geo-tagged their own house. It's all a horror movie waiting to happen.

So, JJ decides to bring the horror movie to her.

It starts small. He sets up a fake Instagram account, finds photos from Flickr and other free stock-photo archives, and populates his fake page with the kind of banal photos everyone of his mother's age seems to put up on Instagram. From this account, he starts to leave comments on his mother's posts. She doesn't notice at first – so JJ ups the ante, starts tagging her in them, and soon Vanessa is drawing her followers' attention to the horrible comments that are being left under so many of her most recent posts. She takes screenshots of them and shares them in her Stories, and then she shares all the messages of support she gets from her legion of loyal fans, and then she shares the DMs JJ has sent her in response. It's a never-ending cycle and at first the thrill of it fizzes and pops in JJ's veins. The secret of it fills him with a sense of power, and he feels like a helium balloon about to take off up, up, up into the skies above them. He is untouchable for a while. Anything she says is like water off a duck's back – and this new insouciance, his seemingly impermeable new shield against her, sends Vanessa mad.

This is how JJ spends his summer.

Taunting and torturing his mother in the same way she's been taunting and torturing him for years.

He doesn't like what she gets from it, though. No matter how many cruel and hurtful comments he leaves on her posts, her followers leave many, many more of love and support, which seem to fuel Vanessa. At one point nearing the end of that long, hot summer he realizes she's enjoying it. She has started to blame Rachel Donovan, which is an unfortunate consequence of his actions as JJ likes Rachel, but at least it means Vanessa doesn't suspect him.

And then something strange happens.

His mother uploads a photo of a bunch of flowers. They're nice flowers – the kind she likes, but in the comments she is claiming to have been sent them by a 'friend' who has apparently betrayed her. Only JJ knows his mother bought those flowers.

This pattern continues for a couple of weeks. A box of freshly made cupcakes with broken glass as decoration, a bottle of wine she claims she doesn't dare drink lest it's poisoned.

JJ watches all this with a mixture of amusement, bafflement and growing fear. His mother is going to greater lengths than he's known before, and he's not even sure what the end game is. More followers? More sympathy? More love?

When they eat dinner on those long summer nights – almost always out on the back patio, the sky still a faint blue, the sun sinking – she rattles off lists of impenetrable facts and figures: her growth statistics, her level of engagement, something about an algorithm she appears to be beating.

'I mean, it's amazing,' she says one night, twirling the stem of her white wine glass in her long, strong fingers. 'This is kind of the best thing that could ever happen to me.'

'What is?' Justin asks, and JJ sees genuine confusion on his father's face. Matthew has long gone to bed, and Emma is practically asleep at the table. His parents seem to have forgotten he is there.

'This – this stalker, this abuser, whatever you want to call it. Rachel's vendetta. I mean, my follower count is through the roof, and she's losing them like crazy. My inbox is full – absolutely *full* – of collaboration offers, sponsorship deals, free stuff, interview requests.'

Justin blinks at his wife. Her face is inscrutable in the setting sun. She has always had a sphinx-like quality but it's never been more obvious than now. 'So, you're getting more followers?' he asks, trying to work his way through the thicket of whatever his wife is saying to him.

'So many more,' Vanessa says.

'So, what is this then? All just an elaborate PR stunt?' Justin asks, and JJ is surprised by how astute his father's question is. Does he have at least a little sense of who his wife is?

'No, of course not,' Vanessa says smoothly. She is looking at her husband, feigning hurt, but JJ sees through it. 'I'm being harassed, Justin.' She says this very slowly, blinking at him, as if to punctuate her sentence.

'You're being . . .' Justin searches for the right word '. . . pranked. Punked. You're not being harassed, Vanessa.'

Vanessa squints at her husband at the other end of the table. JJ can see his mother's knuckles whiten against the stem of her glass, which she is gripping very, very tightly.

*Oh, no*, JJ thinks. *What are you going to do now?*

What Vanessa does next is set fire to their kitchen and accuse Rachel Donovan of doing it.

## 5

JJ doesn't know how she starts the fire exactly, but he knows that she is the one to do it.

He's just got back from a walk along the beach – he's made plans to meet a friend, and has come back to pick up a football from the garage. The day is hot, as it has been all summer. They've all gradually acclimatized to it – the kind of summer other countries take for granted, but in England is labelled an unprecedented heatwave. The sun is hot so early in the day that JJ finds it impossible to sleep late: he's waking early, getting out of the house while the weather is still bearable, and spending the afternoons at friends' houses, or hiding out in the screening room, watching several movies in a row. He tries to be away from Vanessa as much as possible, while keeping an eye on her through her ubiquitous Instagram posts and incessant Story uploads. He has barely seen her all week, except at long, painful dinners, so the sight of her auburn hair jolts him when he notices it.

She's doing something in the kitchen that he can't quite figure out. She looks furtive, weird, as he watches through the newly installed Crittall windows, but he doesn't want to draw attention to himself, so he shrugs, and wanders back onto the promenade, suddenly very keen to find his friend and play some football under the high summer sun. He doesn't figure out what she was doing until he gets back later in the afternoon, and police are sitting around the dining table, and the half-done kitchen is singed and burnt, ruined, covered with ash and building dust.

'JJ, thank God,' Vanessa says, standing up at the table at the sight of her elder son. JJ raises his eyebrows at the performance but says nothing.

'Hello, son, d'you want to come and take a seat at the table with us? What's your name, then?'

JJ turns his attention to the officer talking to him. Violently red hair paired with a scattering of freckles and an unfortunate level of sunburn across his cheeks. He sits on the same side of the table as his mother. He would have preferred a chair with a clear view of her, but those are all taken. 'What's happened?' he asks, looking around.

'There's been an accident, JJ,' Vanessa says soothingly, placing an arm along the back of her son's chair. She doesn't touch him, but JJ can feel the heat of her skin against his back and he recoils from it, leaning forward with his elbows against the table instead.

'The kitchen's burnt down,' JJ says bluntly, to the police officers sitting opposite him.

'That's right, JJ, yes,' the redhead says encouragingly. 'You're all very lucky no one was inside at the time, and your mum got back in time to call the fire brigade so they could stop it spreading further.'

'Yes, very lucky,' his mother demurs next to him.

JJ turns to her, daring her to look at him, but she's staring coyly at the table. He takes a deep breath and says, 'Where's my dad? Where're Matthew and Emma?'

'They're all safe, JJ, don't worry,' the other officer tells him.

'Well, where are they?'

'Dad's on his way back from work, love, Matthew's upstairs, and Emma's still at Dottie's house,' his mum says. 'We're very lucky we were all out at the time, aren't we?' She directs this at the officers. She is merely repeating what the redhead has just said, but they nevertheless nod at her as if she had come up with this breakthrough in the investigation. JJ realizes that she's already worked her magic. With a lot of men, all it seems to take is her mere presence. He bristles at the way the two officers are staring adoringly at her. And then he watches her smiling warmly, conspiratorially at them, as if they were all sharing something rather wonderful. JJ sighs heavily and seems to catch the attention of the redhead once more.

'So, JJ, can I just ask where you were?'

But Vanessa jumps in before he can answer. 'Oh, JJ had cricket practice, didn't you, love? He's on the county team, the under-twelves.'

And it's then that JJ discovers his mother has no idea where he was. Whether he was in the house or not. And that she may or may not have checked. All he can do is nod mutely at her, feel the heat rising on his neck and face, as his body fills with the shame of this knowledge: that she does not care.

And he wants to tell the officers she's lying, that she's always – in some way, at some level – lying. But he can't bring himself to admit to them that she doesn't care, that he's nothing but an afterthought to her, a piece of debris to be cleared up and swept away, just like the rest of her destroyed kitchen.

# 6

In a way, the timing of the fire couldn't have been better for JJ. He needed to wrap up his pursuit of Vanessa before he was packed off to boarding school, and the fire coming near the end of the summer holidays represents a suitable crescendo. Vanessa's done the work for him, of course, but there's no way to top it so he abandons his online alter ego, and leaves his mother to it. Rachel had an alibi apparently, but that doesn't stop Vanessa proclaiming her as the perpetrator at home to Justin, at nursery pick-up in front of all the other mums, and of course – most loudly of all – on her Instagram account. For a while, all she can talk about is taking out a restraining order on Rachel, but apparently there isn't enough evidence of her so-called harassment of Vanessa. Or, at least, nothing to prove the harassment is at the hands of Rachel.

Then, suddenly, Rachel and her family are gone from Whitstable.

JJ is confused – Rachel isn't guilty – but he can at least sympathize. He can't wait to get away from his mother, to start boarding school, and what is that if not his own kind of retreat?

Vanessa makes a huge deal out of JJ's matriculation to Tonbridge. She throws a big party, ostensibly for him, but it's far too grown-up and Instagrammable for a twelve-year-old boy. It turns, subtly, slowly but very noticeably, to him at least, into an end-of-summer party. The weather has changed – not completely turned yet, but the air is cooler, the days shorter, the endless summer finally drawing to an end. The kitchen renovation has been finished in record time after the fire, and Vanessa uses the party as an excuse to show it off. Adults he barely knows keep congratulating JJ on getting into Tonbridge, telling him how excited he must be to be going to boarding school.

*So grown-up*, they all seem to say, chucking him under the chin, ruffling his hair, lightly punching his shoulder.

One or two more perceptive adults ask if he's worried, scared, anxious, anticipating homesickness. He answers them as truthfully as he can: 'I'll miss Emma and Matthew,' he says, over and over and over again. 'And the sea,' he adds occasionally. Because it really is special, his salty, otherworldly backyard playground.

He drifts through the evening, weaving between the groups of taller, older guests, but the night is overtaken completely with the arrival of Uncle Adam.

It's a bit of a commotion at first: Adam wasn't aware a party was going on, hasn't been invited, and the sight of his battered Transit van pulling up the driveway doesn't go unnoticed or unremarked upon. JJ distinctly overhears someone say, 'What are the builders doing at this hour?'

But it's not the builders, it's Vanessa's ex-stepbrother, and JJ searches the house for her, finding her on the front doorstep, jaw pulsing, hands comically on hips, biceps flexed. Vanessa is a controller, a curator; any flaw in any of her well-laid plans is met with hostility and anger so strong it can suck the air from a room and she is not happy about this unexpected arrival.

'Hey, Ness,' Adam greets her. His tone is bright, friendly, warm, but JJ can detect nerves there too. He is passing the keys of his van from hand to hand, and he hasn't yet approached his once-sister, who towers over him from her vantage point on the porch.

And then: 'Hey, Jaje!'

Adam is the only person to shorten JJ's already shortened name to 'Jaje'. Even Matthew, who used to call him the same, now calls him JJ.

Vanessa turns stiffly, immediately sees her son standing behind her in the open doorway. 'Go away,' she says to him, making a movement with her arm as though she is waving away an unwanted persistent insect. It is a cutting, deadly movement, and with a giant, well-worn sigh, JJ heeds it. Waving feebly at his uncle, he retreats upstairs and into the guest room. There, he can hear everything happening on the front steps from the open doors of the Juliet balcony.

'What are you doing here?' Vanessa demands, through bared teeth.

JJ leans forward and he can just about see his uncle, who is looking uncomfortable, embarrassed.

'It's not good, Ness,' is all he says in reply.

'It's never good with you, Adam,' she retorts tartly. Adam sighs, seems to admit that this is very much the case. 'Let me guess,' Vanessa continues. 'You're broke.'

'Not completely, but yeah. Getting there,' Adam says.

There is silence from Vanessa and JJ wishes he could see his mother's face.

Suddenly, Justin's voice can be heard echoing down the hallway, 'Adam!' he calls. 'My man! What are you doing here? I thought we'd lost you to Falmouth for ever?'

The two men embrace, slapping backs, smiling at one another as Vanessa looks on. JJ watches as the three adults go into the house. He knows Vanessa will be annoyed by Adam's arrival, the interruption to her perfectly staged party, but for now, at least, the show must go on.

# 7

Justin picks JJ up for the holidays. The school breaks early for Christmas and with the weather so mild – so unwintry – it barely feels like Christmas at all.

JJ opens the door of his dad's car with the heaviness in his chest, arms and legs that he hasn't felt since half-term. He is happy to see his dad. At least, he thinks he's happy to see him. But Dad always means Mum, and he's not looking forward to three weeks at home with her.

'Hi,' he says to his dad now, as he slides into the car and sits down.

'Hi, son!' Justin says, too brightly. JJ squints at him, furrows his forehead, wonders if his dad has ever called him 'son' before.

'Everything in the boot?' Justin asks, and JJ nods as Justin presses the ignition button and the car starts.

'Double celebration when we get home, eh?' Justin says, one eye on his son as he steers the car down the long driveway at the school.

'What?' JJ says.

'Well, we missed your birthday, so we'll have to celebrate that *and* Christmas.'

'It's not Christmas yet,' JJ points out. And, besides, he's already celebrated his birthday. It was his best yet. He's made friends easily, thanks in large part to his involvement in so much sport and music. Something he has his mother to thank for, although he'd never admit it to her face.

The night before his birthday he and almost every boy in his dorm had snuck down to the cricket pavilion to celebrate with a bottle of vodka someone had miraculously got, and a cake with a single lit candle, which had felt just as miraculous to JJ. It was the type of thing you read about in books by Enid Blyton – except the vodka, maybe – and he'd assumed this kind of high jinks would have been relegated to the past, but it wasn't, and it had been, well, perfect. He doesn't tell his dad this, won't tell his mum.

Maybe he'll tell Emma, but she's so young still she probably won't understand.

The school isn't all that far from home. But JJ feels like he's returning to another planet, travelling a vast distance from happiness to the pit in his belly that never goes away, from freedom to fear.

The house is decorated for a celebration when they get back, but not for Christmas. Vanessa has filled the dining room with those huge metallic Mylar balloons, spelling out WELCOME HOME over the table.

JJ looks at them, his face a blank screen.

'Welcome home, JJ!' Vanessa squeals. She goes over to her son, squeezes him against her, almost obscuring him completely.

Matthew has joined his mother and brother now, is hugging JJ's legs, waggling between them like a small dog, desperate to join in. JJ pulls away from Vanessa and leans down to scoop up his little brother. 'Hey, hey, little Matty-man,' JJ says into his younger brother's face. He is the only person who calls Matthew that, and the glow that emanates from the three-year-old as his older brother showers him with attention is incandescent.

# 8

JJ wakes to a sound he's never heard before. Or, rather, it's a sound he recognizes all too well, but it's coming from the wrong place. It's too far away, not right in his ear as it normally is. He lies rigid in his bed, willing himself to accept that it was all in his dream – all in his head – so that he can go back to sleep.

But he can still hear it. That sibilant hiss, the malevolent whisper.

He reaches for his phone to check the time. Three thirty in the morning. His room is a black box, no light anywhere except from the blue light of his phone. Outside, on the other side of his blackout blinds, he knows there is also nothing but darkness.

He wants to stay in bed, but he also wants to be sure. Getting out of bed, he is careful to miss the creaky floorboards, to open his bedroom door so it produces no sound. The landing is dark too, but the door to his sister's bedroom next to his is open a sliver. Creeping towards it, the sound gets louder; only taking a step towards it, he realizes it's not what he was expecting to hear.

He leans, as still as a statue, against the door frame, placing his ear right where it's ajar. It takes him only a second to grasp that the sound that woke him was his sister crying. He pushes the door open and the sobbing stops with a sharp, desperate inhalation of breath. He carefully closes the door behind him and whispers Emma's name as he walks as quietly as possible towards where she's huddling in her bed.

'JJ?' she gasps back.

'It's me,' he says, crouching in front of her bed. 'What's wrong?'

But Emma is silent. She doesn't want to tell. She can't tell.

'Was it Mum?' JJ asks. 'Was she in here with you?'

Emma stays silent, but she nods. Yes.

'Was this the first time?' JJ asks, although he thinks he knows the answer, as Emma shakes her head. 'When did she first come in here? At night, I mean.'

Emma makes a movement that JJ thinks is a shrug. It's hard to tell as she's lying as still as possible. 'Was it before I left for school?' JJ asks quietly.

There are a couple of beats of silence while Emma thinks, but eventually she shakes her head again. 'Was it before Halloween?' JJ asks, trying to think of dates and occasions Emma might remember.

This time she nods. 'It was after you left,' she says, and it's so quiet, JJ has to lean towards his sister to hear her properly.

JJ grips the edge of the bed. He didn't think. Stupid, stupid, stupid. He didn't think what his leaving would mean for Emma or Matthew. He was only thinking about himself. Just like her. He feels sick. He wants to throw up, but he doesn't want to scare Emma. 'How many times?' he asks, after catching his breath.

Emma shakes her head. 'I don't know.'

'It's not every night?' JJ says.

'No,' Emma says.

'Okay. That's good,' JJ says. It's something at least. It's not every night. Yet.

'JJ, why does she do it?' Emma whispers to him and JJ feels the lead in his limbs, in his chest, weighing him down like an anchor, securing him in place even though it means he'll end up drowning.

'I don't know, Emma. She's . . . she –'

'She hates me,' Emma says, tears leaking from her eyes again, tracking down her cheeks, joining the tearstains that already blotch her face.

'No,' JJ says firmly. 'No. She hates herself.'

She does, even though it seems, most of the time, that the only person she really loves is herself. He's asked himself the same question so many times though: why? Why is she the way she is? Why does she creep into his bedroom at night, and whisper words full of hate and venom into his ear?

It had started when he turned eight. He had thought it might just be him, that Emma, so much more beloved to their mother than JJ, might be safe, but clearly he was wrong. How long does Matthew have before their mother turns on him too?

JJ stays with his sister until her crying stops, her breathing stops hitching with sobs, evens and deepens. Until she sleeps. It's still dark when he finally steals out of her bedroom and back into his own, but it's almost five o'clock. Morning.

He lies awake in bed. He's opened his blinds, wants to see the world wake up, the light at the edge of the horizon get closer. Wants to be reminded that even here, at the edge of everything, there's always something more. Something else. Somewhere different.

He has to do something. He wants to go back to school in January, to get away from here and from her, but he can't leave Matthew and Emma unguarded and alone. Not again.

He doesn't want to stay but he has to.

But there's no way Vanessa would ever let him. It would be a failure for one thing: for him to leave Tonbridge after just one term would look bad. For him. But, more importantly, for her.

He has to figure a way around it.

# 9

It's late afternoon, light draining, the day waning, when JJ notices it. The door to the beach hut is ajar – barely noticeable, really, but there's a light wind coming off the water, and the door creaks as it flounders to and fro. They have their own beach hut, of course, but that would be too dangerous. Vanessa might remember she needs something from it, or she might decide on a midwinter swim and the need for a reviving cup of tea afterwards. In which case, his whole plan would be screwed.

But this abandoned, unlocked beach hut could be the answer to his desperate prayers.

He looks around him, making sure the beach is as abandoned as he thinks it is, before opening the door and stepping inside. It's an old one. Downtrodden and smelling of mildew. JJ wonders who it belongs to. These beach huts are some of the most coveted in the country, but they tend to be passed down from generation to generation, stay in families for years. If he had to guess, he'd say this belonged to someone old, without grandchildren. There's something distinctly stale and unloved about it, something overlooked. Which is perfect for what he needs.

JJ's watched enough TV and seen enough movies to know he has to be careful not to touch anything. He's already wearing gloves, but he's smart, careful, resourceful, and knows that even with gloves he should leave as light a touch in here as possible. He knows he can do this. Looking around, he sees a camp bed he can set up, a hurricane lamp, a torch, a great big pile of blankets.

He'll need some stuff from home if it's going to work, though.

He'll need a padlock, but he knows exactly where to look for one of those. He'll find one of his mum's old iPads too, maybe some books. Another blanket wouldn't go amiss, some pillows too. He has to make it as comfortable as he can for what he needs, and even then, looking around, he's worried it's too small. It'll have to do, though.

He'd already thought about the boathouse, but it's too close to the house, too obvious. Any of the rental cabins or holiday homes would be perfect, but Vanessa would be sure to notice a set of keys going missing, and he doesn't want to run the risk of guests turning up. It's almost Christmas after all.

It's a crazy idea, but it has to work. He doesn't have any other options. He has to stop Vanessa doing any more harm.

It's funny, but she's the one who gave him the idea in the end. All that stuff with her friend Rachel at the end of summer – none of it was true, of course: JJ had seen right through it. Mum had set the fire herself. She'd sent herself those flowers and cupcakes. Of course, he'd left those comments on her Instagram – he'd set up multiple accounts to do it. It had only spurred her on, though, turned her into some sort of Instagram martyr. He hadn't meant it to go as far as it did, hadn't imagined she'd set that fire and blame Rachel for it. It had scared him, how far she was willing to go for . . . for what? A few more followers? The never-ending adoring attention? A sense of self-righteousness? He has no idea what drives his mother on, but he knows he has to stop her.

And it's going to take a lot more than a few anonymous online messages.

## 10

JJ knows it's not the perfect plan, but Matthew will never be in any real danger. He's so young, he'll barely know what's going on, JJ reckons, and he won't remember it anyway, will he?

He'll be fine.

JJ is standing in the small, draughty beach hut, looking at his handiwork. It's been surprisingly easy to creep out here every day, which bodes well. Vanessa is in a phase of largely ignoring him, too distracted by the woman staying in one of their beachfront cabins – her new pet – and Uncle Adam, who's been coming around a lot lately. She keeps JJ's little brother within arm's reach at all times, of course, but JJ still thinks he'll be able to get Matthew away from her when the time comes.

And the beach hut is perfect now. He's created a cosy nest for Matthew: a tent of blankets and a tarpaulin to protect him from the winter wind that has a tendency to whip through the old wooden boards of the hut. It looks so good that JJ is tempted to take a photo of his work but, of course, he doesn't. He knows Matthew will love it. They haven't made a fort together since the summer, so this will feel like an extra treat for Matthew.

JJ's also been raiding the first-aid kit. Vanessa's something of a hypochondriac, keeps it well stocked at all times. It's full to the brim of child-locked Calpol, and even stronger Night Nurse, which should prove helpful in getting Matthew to sleep and to keep him drowsy during the day when he might otherwise start to get antsy and too loud, attracting unwanted attention.

JJ doesn't feel great about this part of the plan, about having to drug his little brother to keep him quiet and malleable, but it's necessary. It's to keep him safe. Him and Emma and JJ. He has to look out for them all now, has to do what he can to make sure their mother is kept as far away from them as possible.

Standing in that cold, blustery beach hut, JJ thinks about all the times he has lain in bed, waiting for his mother's midnight visits, all the times she has wrapped an arm around his shoulders only to squeeze so hard at his biceps it leaves a bruise, all the times she's locked him in his bedroom, or the music room, the screening room, or the boathouse. All the times he's been sure his dad has overheard how she talks to JJ when she thinks no one is listening. All the times he's seen him glance at the purple, green, yellow bruise on his eldest son's arm and said and done nothing. All the times he's heard them fighting, the tight, whispered words, like a frayed length of rope stretched so far it's about to snap. He's been waiting for the announcement of a divorce to save him.

But Vanessa would never let that happen.

And when it comes to his wife, Justin has no fight in him.

But even if it did happen, even if they did miraculously divorce, JJ is smart enough to know it might not save them anyway: they could – and probably would – end up living with Vanessa, alone, with not even the slightly negligent, often absent eye of their father to watch over them.

JJ starts to take an inventory of everything already in the beach hut, and everything he needs to retrieve to be ready for Matthew's arrival. He still needs to get a cool box from the garage to keep food, juice and milk cold. He's already sourced some old picnic plates, cups and cutlery – they're on the otherwise empty shelves now. He sits down with his back against the wall and runs through meal plans for Matthew: he can keep a box of cereal here, with milk in the cool box for breakfast. He'll get stuff to make sandwiches for his lunch, and it shouldn't be too hard to bring Matthew some leftovers of whatever dinner they've eaten that night.

He has to hope that no one will notice him slipping in and out of the house, but he's counting on his parents being too distracted by Matthew's disappearance to pay much or any attention to him. He wonders if he should tell Emma his plan, so that she doesn't get too upset about Matthew going missing. He doesn't want to scare her more than he has to, but he's worried she might let something slip. It's hard to tell how she'd react to his plan: she's young enough to want to turn to an adult with her problems, but he can tell she's already scared of Vanessa. That she's had enough midnight visits to know Vanessa is no longer the safe harbour she'd thought she was.

JJ gets up, brushes dirt and dust from his trousers. If he thinks too much about his mother, everything goes black: blank with his anger, his hatred, his fear.

He feels better whenever he's in this dank little hut, feels better when he's away from her, when he's planning, and prepping, and ticking things off a list. He's running out of time, though. He needs Matthew to go missing before Christmas, before the family skiing trip over New Year's Eve. Tomorrow, he thinks. He'll do it tomorrow night.

That gives him the rest of today and all day tomorrow to get everything ready for Matthew.

JJ lies awake until three thirty in the morning. He listens carefully for Vanessa's night-time visit to Emma's room, listens for her return to her own bedroom, then waits for as long as possible, so that he can be sure she's gone to sleep. He feels bad about letting her get to Emma – it feels like he's sacrificed his sister – but he tells himself it will all be over soon. Vanessa will be out of their lives for good, and they'll all three be safe.

Matthew is easy to wake up. All it takes is a little shake of his tiny shoulder, and his green eyes are open, staring at JJ in sleepy wonder.

'Hey, Matty-man,' JJ whispers. 'Ready to go on an adventure?'

Matthew's eyes widen – he's already in a state of near-hysterical excitement – and JJ has to press a finger to his mouth, telling the little boy that this is a quiet adventure, that they can't make *any noise at all.*

JJ's got a rucksack on his back, packed with some of Matthew's favourite toys, and his old blue duffel coat. He's already ransacked the piles and piles of old clothing Vanessa has in the boathouse – clothes that are perfect still, but have already been worn and featured in a #spon-con post so can't be seen again. All this is already safely stored in the beach hut, waiting for them.

Downstairs, JJ silently helps Matthew get his yellow

wellies on, and does up the fake horn toggles of his duffel. They leave by the back door, creeping down the
garden path, to the gate that leads onto the beach. JJ does
a funny walk for Matthew, exaggerating his movements
so that he looks like a robber from a cartoon. Matthew
giggles, unable to mask his laugh completely, but JJ thinks
they're safe now anyway: the crashing waves hide the
crunch of their footsteps, the rustle of their clothes.
When they're far enough away from the house, JJ clicks
on his torch. Matthew is holding his other hand, swinging their linked arms back and forth in only slightly
repressed joy.

'Where we going?' the little boy asks.

'We're having a sleepover,' JJ says, looking down at
him. Matthew's eyes are still so wide and round with surprise and excitement, JJ wonders if they'll ever shrink
back to their normal size. 'I've built us a fort, but it's a
secret, so you can't tell anyone about it, and we need to
stay really, really quiet, okay?'

Matthew nods, his auburn curls a burnished beacon in
the moonlit night. He looks around, at the path they're
taking along the beach.

'Not far now, I promise. Okay, Matty-man?'

Matthew nods again. In his yellow boots and blue duffel coat he looks like Paddington Bear, waddling down the
promenade hand in hand with his beloved big brother. JJ
swallows the vast lump that has lodged itself in his throat.

He's doing the right thing.

Matthew will be safe the entire time.

In fact, JJ tells himself, he'll probably be safer in the

rickety old beach hut with the wind sweeping through it than he is at home with their mother.

They get to the beach hut quickly enough, although it probably feels like a long time for sleepy Matthew and his tired little legs. JJ unlocks the padlock he found in the shed, and picks Matthew up to carry him into the small hut. There's no light to switch on, but JJ shows Matthew the hurricane lamp set up by his camp bed, and turns on a string of old, battery-powered fairy lights that he found in the garage. He's strung them up, like bunting, all around the shelves of the cabin, and they give the hut a low, cosy glow. Matthew sighs in delight as he looks at them while JJ pulls off his wellies for him.

From his rucksack, JJ takes out a Thermos flask and, joining Matthew on the bed, says, 'Shall we have some cocoa?'

Matthew nods furiously, but JJ can see the sleepiness in his eyes, feel the heaviness of his body as Matthew leans against him. JJ settles in next to him, hands him a cup of cocoa and pulls out his battered copy of *Peter Pan*.

The little boy is asleep long before JJ finishes the first chapter, but JJ stays until just before dawn, when he tucks Matthew in, creeps out of the hut, locking the padlocked door behind him, and runs all the way home.

# 12

JJ wakes with a headache. He's barely slept, and every inch of him feels heavy and exhausted, as if he could sink down into the springs of his mattress, never to resurface. The house is awake, though. It shakes with sound and anxiety, fear and recrimination. He can hear Vanessa shouting at Justin, although he can't decipher the words.

At first he thinks: Business as usual. But then he remembers. Remembers why he is so tired. Remembers that instead of lying in his bed, Matthew is missing, and currently curled up on a camp bed in an abandoned beach hut several hundred metres away. Lying there, JJ is rigid with fear and disbelief at what he has done, and then, in that very moment, his father bursts into the room.

'JJ,' he gasps, breathing heavily, 'are you awake? Is Matthew in here? Have you seen him?'

JJ sits up in bed, wiping something away from his eyes. 'What?' he says.

'JJ!' Justin says sharply. 'Have you seen your brother?'

'What are you talking about? I just woke up. Of course I haven't seen him. Where is he?'

'We don't know. We can't find him.'

JJ is scrubbing at his face with his hands, sitting on the edge of his bed. 'What do you mean, you can't find him?' he says thickly.

'He's not in his bed, mate. Matthew's missing. He's not anywhere. We've checked everywhere.'

JJ looks at his dad blearily, as if he doesn't understand what he's saying and Justin sighs. 'Okay, it's going to be okay. Just get dressed as quick as you can, and help me look for him, yeah? We'll find him. Your mother's on the phone to the police.'

JJ is reaching for a pair of jeans abandoned on the floor when he freezes, looks at his dad standing in the doorway. 'What? She's calling the police?'

Justin nods rapidly, and JJ is reminded suddenly, fiercely, of his baby brother. What has he done?

'Why's she calling the police? He'll just be hiding in the boathouse or down on the beach, or something.' He says this as nonchalantly as possible, but his heart skids beneath his breastbone, a stone skipping on the surface of otherwise still, glassy water.

Justin shakes his head tightly at his son, tears threatening to fall from his eyes. Between the two of them, Justin is the crier rather than Vanessa, although Vanessa knows and understands the power of tears, and isn't above using them against anybody. But JJ knows when his dad cries that it's at something real – even when he's tearing up over something fictional on a TV show or even at an advert, it's because of a truth that lives within him, not a lie to get what he wants. 'It's just a precaution,' Justin says, of the call to the police. 'We want all the help we can get in finding him. He'll be fine. We'll find him.'

He doesn't look as if he believes any of this. He looks as if they're being called to pick up the pieces.

# 13

Much later, JJ finds Emma curled up in the corner of the huge L-shaped sofa in the living room. She has built herself a kind of fort of pillows and blankets, looks swamped by them. There are strangers and near-strangers all over the house. They've been searching for Matthew all day, and now police officers in their intimidating all-black uniforms are searching the house for other clues.

JJ's heart hasn't stopped banging in his chest all day and he hasn't found time to sneak away and check up on his little brother. He can't stop thinking about Matthew curled up in the beach hut, how scared he must be, how confused. He'll be starving too. Bored, terrified, alone. JJ's realized he hasn't really thought this through. He'd thought he had, thought he'd been meticulous, careful and smart. But he can only be as meticulous, careful and smart as his thirteen-year-old experience allows, and it hasn't been enough. The realization has him in a cold sweat and, much like Matthew, he hasn't eaten all day and feels sick every time anyone even mentions food. He's been gnawing at the inside of his cheek, and at the skin around his right thumb all day. Vanessa hates both habits and has tried to train them out of him, but she's been distracted enough not to notice.

He can't believe what he's done, can't believe so many police are swarming their home, can't believe that any of this is going to work out how he's planned. But it has to. Matthew is depending on him. Emma, scared and unknowing, is depending on him.

He sits next to his sister, sees how pale she is. He reaches for one of her hands, hidden underneath a soft wool blanket, and holds it tight. Neither of them says a word.

## 14

JJ doesn't dare leave the house until much, much later. He slips away as he did with Matthew the previous night, out of the back door, down the garden path, then onto the promenade. He holds his breath, not letting himself breathe easily until he's several paces away from the house, and half running down the moonlit beach towards his brother.

Matthew has filled the potty in the corner, and soaked though his pyjamas. He's starving, and mewling, and has obviously been crying, confused and alone, for most of the day. He is happy as soon as JJ appears, though, and JJ feels an almighty tug of guilt: that he is the reason Matthew is so upset, and yet Matthew is still so innocent, so forgiving, that he sees him as his saviour.

JJ reminds himself sternly that he is his saviour. Matthew's, Emma's and his own. He'll save them all. He's not the monster here. He just has to act like one to get them away from the real monster in their midst. He soothes Matthew, coos and cuddles, gently tugging the ruined pyjamas from his brother's body and changing him into a clean, almost identical set. He empties the potty outside, rinses it and places it back in the corner. He pulls Matthew's dinner from his rucksack, no longer warm, but it'll have to do, and then the *pièce de résistance*: more cocoa.

Matthew smiles through all this. He is no longer as

giddy as he was last night. He is clearly lost, unsure as to what is going on, why he is here, where JJ has been for so long. JJ pulls more food from his rucksack – several sandwiches that he made in the dark of the kitchen – telling Matthew that these are for his breakfast and lunch tomorrow.

Matthew swallows the mouthful he's eating. 'And I'll be back as soon as I can,' JJ promises, getting a nod from his little brother.

'Why can't you stay?' Matthew asks, through another mouthful of food.

JJ pauses. Why hasn't he thought of a reason for why Matthew has to hide here? Why didn't he think his brother might ask questions?

'We're playing a game, right?' he says, waiting for a sign of Matthew's agreement. 'It's like hide-and-seek.'

Matthew nods again, his eyes wide in the low light of the dusty beach hut. 'And I'm hiding?' he whispers.

'Yup. You're hiding. But this is an extra special version of it, so we're on the same team, and I'm hiding you, trying to keep it a secret from Mummy and Daddy and Emma.'

'And they're the seekers?' Matthew asks.

'That's right, Matty-man. They're the ones we're hiding from. And we're doing really well, because they have absolutely no idea where you are at the moment. Isn't that great?'

Matthew's grin stretches to fill his small face. 'We're winning?' he asks.

'We're winning, yeah. Definitely.'

'Why isn't Emma on our team?' Matthew asks, his forehead creasing in confusion.

JJ swallows, takes a breath. He feels bad aligning their sister with their parents, but it's best for now, he knows. Matthew won't understand that, though, so he has to think of something else, and he remembers Emma sitting silently on the sofa earlier in the afternoon.

'Well, she is kind of on our team, but she's not feeling very well, so she's taking a break from the game,' he explains.

'Okay,' Matthew says, happy with this answer.

'But she's on our team,' JJ says. 'She's definitely on our team.'

## 15

JJ stays as long as he can in the beach hut. The Night Nurse-laced cocoa has once again done its work and sent Matthew off into what he hopes is a dreamless sleep. But he wants to be there when his brother wakes up, to reassure him that nothing's wrong, that he'll be back as soon as possible. To make sure he eats his breakfast sandwich, and drinks his box of juice.

So, dawn is breaking when he walks back into the house, and his mother is sitting at the kitchen island, waiting for her Nespresso to be ready, staring at JJ as he walks into the room through the back door.

'Where have you been?' she demands. Her voice is gravelly with the morning, but still as sharp, caustic, as it is whenever she addresses him these days.

'Looking for Matthew,' JJ replies, just as shortly.

'Looking for Matthew,' Vanessa repeats mockingly.

JJ doesn't say anything, instead gulping down orange juice straight from the carton in the fridge, defying his mother's look of rebuke, staring her down the whole time.

She looks terrible, he thinks, her face a patchwork of red and white, no makeup, no sleep, no coffee yet either. He knows better than to think all this worry is for Matthew. For his welfare. She wants him back, of course, but not for the reasons most mothers would. Not for that knee-deep love, that anchoring weight. She doesn't experience those feelings, doesn't reach for her children out of love for them: she sees them instead as accessories. As beautiful additions to bolster others' view of her, like another kitchen extension, or the house in Italy she keeps bringing up with Justin.

He feels something stir in her, some change in the air around her, a magnetic charge, and he knows he's gone too far – although how far he's gone, she has no idea – and it's this knowledge that makes him smirk at her, sending her over the edge. She reaches for him, yanking him towards her, her surprisingly strong fingers making marks and indents on his upper arms.

Baring her teeth, she opens her mouth to say something, but they both hear it at the same time: Justin's tread on the stairs, more laboured than usual, but distinctive, nonetheless.

Instead of releasing JJ, though, she pulls him even closer, wrapping her arms around him, so that she looks like she's giving her elder son a hug as her husband enters the kitchen and stops dead.

'Everything all right in here?' he asks.

'No,' Vanessa says, letting go of JJ at last, but not before showily smoothing his ruffled hair off his forehead. 'Everything is not all right. We miss Matthew.'

JJ turns away from his mother, cannot bear to look at her, and meets his dad's wary gaze. He looks very solid standing there in the early-morning winter light, staring at his son and wife. Solid and stuck.

JJ is suddenly filled with the certainty that he's doing

the right thing, despite how dangerous it is, despite how worried he is about Matthew hidden in that beach hut.

Justin is too stuck to save them.

And Vanessa will never let any of them go. At least, not willingly.

# 16

Vanessa's mum arrives later that day, and everything gets a little bit harder for JJ. Usually Vanessa is on edge when her mother is around, constantly watching the older woman's reactions, as if waiting for something to happen. But not this time. This time, Vanessa's panic, her crisis, blots out her usual anxiety and JJ's grandmother seems almost winded, diminished by it. Normally she dominates her daughter, makes demands, criticizes and belittles, but now, with her younger son missing, Vanessa demands all the oxygen in the room, and even her mother seems to have realized there's no use fighting it. Nevertheless, with Nanny Janet watching over him and Emma, it's much harder to sneak away to see Matthew. Towards the end of the day, when Janet has tired of childcare, and is on the phone to friends, discussing everything that has happened in great detail, with a great big gin and tonic – which she instructed JJ how to make – JJ gets a chance to leave the house. Emma has gone to town with Justin and Vanessa to help with the search there. JJ thought about going with them and breaking away from the search to see Matthew in the beach hut, but decided it was too dangerous. Anyone could see him wandering off, follow him, and find Matthew.

Matthew has to be 'found' eventually, of course, but not yet. He has to make sure people have started to suspect Vanessa.

So, he feigned a stomach-ache, which Justin put down to worry over his little brother, and with Janet settled in the living room with her G and T, he leaves by the back door again. When he gets to the hut, Matthew is asleep. JJ has to give him stronger doses of Night Nurse than he'd intended, because he's so worried Matthew will make a noise and alert someone nearby to his presence in the hut. He feels bad about it, and worries about running out of the stuff too soon, but there's nothing he can do about that. He has to keep Matthew hidden for a little while longer.

He goes through his routine of emptying the potty and sorting out the food while Matthew sleeps on, but he can't help noticing how ripe it is in the beach hut now. Matthew's only been here two nights, but already the beach hut is a foetid hovel, and JJ internally berates himself for not packing baby wipes or even hand sanitizer. His movements wake Matthew eventually, and when the little boy calls out to him, he's reminded of Matthew's baby years.

Emma as a baby had been colicky and a crier. There is a big enough age difference that JJ can vividly remember following the nightly shouts and cries in Emma's nursery, where Vanessa stood over the crib yelling at her tiny daughter. There had been times when JJ hadn't known what his mother would do next, what she was capable of. Sometimes he had been frightened for his sister's life. After one particular ordeal – Vanessa standing in the middle of the living room, dressing-gown slipping from her shoulders, baby almost slipping from her arms, face red from screaming, hair matted and greasy – Justin had taken

JJ aside, tucking him up in bed, and explaining that Mummy wasn't very well. That it was quite normal for mums to find it difficult at times, that things would settle down soon. But JJ knew there was something wrong with Vanessa and that whatever was wrong with her had been there long before Emma arrived.

When Matthew was born, JJ had been worried about history repeating itself, about what Vanessa might do to baby Matthew, about the ways in which she might take out her frustration – her complete loss of control – on him, and Emma, and the baby. But Matthew had been as sweet and charming as he is now from the very beginning. His first word had been 'wuv', as in 'love', closely followed by 'Jaje', for JJ. JJ still glows a little to think of it, the knowledge that the golden child had chosen him to love more than anyone else. Vanessa had hated it, of course: the first time she ever left a bruise on his arm was when she was pulling him, viciously, away from cooing over baby Matthew. JJ rubs at his arm now, thinking of it, and looks at Matthew. His eyes are open, and he's following every move JJ makes, but he's still curled up in a near-foetal position, sucking his thumb, tucked up under a layer of blankets.

Vanessa has never hurt Matthew as far as JJ knows. But what he does know is that one day she will. He'd thought – hoped even – that it might just be him. That she'd picked him out to punish and bully, but her night-time visits to Emma proved his hopes fruitless. Matthew might prove the exception, of course – he is by far and away her favourite – but there's no telling what might happen as Matthew grows older, becomes less cute, less babyish, and less biddable. And, besides, it's not enough for Matthew to be safe from Vanessa: JJ has to save them all.

JJ doesn't leave until he gets a text from a friend at his old school saying he'd just got back from helping his mum at the search for Matthew – and where was he? JJ replies, telling him he's not well, but stuffing his phone back into his trouser pocket, he realizes that if Alex is back from the search, his parents and Emma might be too.

Matthew is quiet and listless, but he has eaten and had some juice, and takes the medicine JJ proffers without a word. Shutting up the beach hut and locking the padlock once again, JJ's startled by a sound. Looking around, he sees he's as alone as always. A magpie clattering around on the roof of a nearby hut surprised him. 'Hello, Mr Magpie,' he whispers into the wind, then sets off for home, confidence renewed. But, in the creeping gloaming, a shadow appears on the path ahead of him.

He knows the shape and stance so well, even through the winter gloom, and begins to prepare his excuses before he realizes it's not Vanessa standing on the promenade outside their house, waiting for him, but Janet.

Her face is creased as he approaches and she barks, 'Where have you been?' reminding him so much of Vanessa's discovery of him that first morning that it sends a shiver down his spine.

'I was feeling better, so I decided to join the search,' he says, as casually as possible, not stopping to greet her, but passing her and walking up the path to the back door.

'You should have let me know, Justin. Your little brother *is* missing after all.'

His grandmother Janet is the only person – aside from

all his teachers at Tonbridge – who calls him Justin rather than JJ. He has overheard her say that she thinks it's the height of narcissism to name your child after yourself, and JJ can't help agreeing with her.

'I didn't want to disturb you, Nanny,' he says now. 'You sounded like you were having a good chat.'

'God, please don't call me "Nanny", child. It makes us sound like characters in a Henry James story.'

'Who?'

'Never mind. Get inside and make "Nanny" another lovely G and T, please. Are you hungry yet? I could make you some cheese on toast or something, I suppose.' She adds this last part idly, as though it's only just come to her attention that she's supposed to be caring for a child.

'Won't Mum and Dad be home soon?' JJ asks.

'No, they've been waylaid at the police station for a bit. Someone's giving Emma a lift home.'

'Let's wait till Emma gets back and then we can order pizza,' JJ suggests.

Janet doesn't respond, as though she's offended by JJ's rejection of her insincere offer of cheese on toast, and JJ takes the opportunity to ask, 'Have they searched the beach huts yet? I was just down there, and it didn't look like they have.'

'They've searched the ones they can get access to, I believe, but most of them are locked and the owners away, so they need to get permission first.'

Inside his chest, JJ's heart stretches and pulls. What if they get hold of the owner of the beach hut and it's searched by the police? His hand shakes a little as he pours gin into his grandmother's glass, the clear liquid splashing against the ice cubes. But he wants Matthew to be found, doesn't it? He can't stay in the hut for ever, so maybe it would be good for him to be found by the police. And sooner rather than later. That way, Matthew will get to come home, and Vanessa will hopefully be taken away in handcuffs.

## 17

It's getting close to Christmas now, and it still hasn't got really cold yet, but JJ shivers as he trudges down the promenade towards the beach hut. It's all going wrong. It's been days since Matthew went missing, and he still hasn't been found. He thought for sure he would be, once the police finally got the permission they needed to search the beach huts, but it turns out JJ picked his abandoned hut a little too well, and the owners failed to come forward to let it be searched.

His shoulders hunched against the wind, he tries to think of a way out of all this. Could he claim to have found Matthew himself? He's been pretending to go out and look for him every day as a reason to leave the house and see his little brother, but would that look too suspicious? It would confuse Matthew as well. He's told him already that when he's eventually found, he can't mention JJ. It's a risky strategy, of course, but Matthew will do anything to keep JJ out of trouble: he trusts his older brother completely, trusts that if JJ tells him it's important not to let anyone know that it was JJ who hid him he won't tell anyone.

JJ has a plan, but as he stands in front of the hut, fingers tense and stiff from the cold air and nerves as he unlocks the padlock, he wonders if it's the right plan. He needs Matthew to come home, to be found, but what if, by leaving the hut unlocked overnight, as he plans to do, someone finds Matthew and takes him? Or worse?

It has to be done, though.

He has to get him home.

# 18

'So, you understand the plan right, Matty-man?' JJ asks for the third time. He's getting ready to leave the beach hut for the last time, and he's nervous.

Matthew nods slowly, staring into JJ's eyes with what JJ knows to be complete trust. It doesn't make him feel good, though. It makes him feel guilty, and manipulative, and like a terrible big brother. And, to be honest, much too much like his mother. He squirms a little at the thought, until he reasons that Vanessa hasn't felt an ounce of guilt about anything, not a day in her life. So, he can't be too much like her. As Matthew nods, he starts to repeat the plan back to JJ. 'I have to leave in the morning, when it's daytime, and walk along the beach back to our house.'

'That's right, Matty-man. And can we just go to the door again, and you show me which way is home? So I know you know?'

Matthew nods again, and follows JJ to the beach hut's rickety old door, where they both stand with it partially open, bracing themselves and it against the wind. 'Which way is it then, little man?' JJ whispers to his brother.

Matthew points, and JJ breathes in relief. Matthew isn't confused about which way is home. He'll be fine.

'And then, when you get home? What do you say?'

'I say Mummy took me and hid me, and wouldn't let me come home.'

This is where it could all go wrong. The lie. Matthew isn't used to lying, doesn't understand it. There have already been tears as JJ explained the plan to him. Matthew doesn't understand why he has to say Mummy was the one to hide him – and JJ can hardly give him the real reason – so he's had to spin some other reason, one to do with the 'game' they've been playing, but it doesn't make sense, and he knows it.

Matthew knows he can't mention JJ, though. That the only way they can 'win' this big fun game of hide-and-seek is if no one knows it was JJ who was hiding Matthew all along.

JJ crouches down now, gives his little brother a big hug. Tells him he's done brilliantly, that he's so proud of him, that they're so close to winning. And he means all of it: they are so close to winning. To beating Vanessa, to making the whole world see just who and what she really is.

When JJ shuts the door of the beach hut behind him, he leaves the padlock undone and crooked, hanging off the handle. Walking away from the hut, he lets the key slip through his gloved fingers, falling onto the sand. He shivers a little: it's turned cold now, and it's a steel-grey evening, hard and menacing. Beyond him, down across the beach, the horizon is hidden. If he looked up, he'd see the fog coming in, but JJ is consumed by his mission, and by the thought that it is nearly over. That Matthew will soon be home, and his mother will soon be gone from their lives for ever.

## 19

JJ can't breathe. His heart is five sizes too big, bursting out of his chest, pushing down on his lungs. He runs to the bathroom, locks himself in and stares wildly around the room, as if seeing it for the first time.

What has he done

What has he done

What has he done

He beats his head against the door, bracing himself against it

He wants to die

To be as dead as Matthew

Matthew

Dead

The words keep repeating in his head, as rhythmic as his forehead banging against the door

Matthew

Dead

Matthew

Dead

He wants to claw his eyes out, to pull his brain out of his skull through his own eye sockets

Matthew

Dead

Matthew

Dead

He hears soft words suddenly, his sister's voice. She's calling his name through the door, and even through her hushed nine-year-old whisper, he can hear the alarm at her older brother annihilating his forehead against the bathroom door.

'Let me in, JJ, please,' she's saying, the hush and sweep of her small voice so at odds with how he feels and what is happening.

He opens the door, though. Because, if nothing else, he is still his sister's big brother, and her voice still tugs at something deep inside him, even with what he's done, even with Matthew gone

Matthew

Gone

Matthew

Gone

Matthew.

Dead.

My fault.

All my fault.

# 20

The five days between when Matthew is found and his mother is arrested are the worst of JJ's life. He is aware, somewhere inside him, that these terrible days will continue until the day he dies, that there will never be a moment when he doesn't think of Matthew, when he doesn't close his eyes and see his baby brother's face.

But the red-raw expanse of those five days will never be repeated. His brother is dead, his mother still free to torture him and his sister. He hears her cry, sees her tears, doesn't believe them. He hears her words of grief, sees her performance of loss, doesn't believe them. He feels her stares, hears her words of abuse, is terrified of them. He wishes, not for the first time, that there was a lock on his door from the inside. He thinks about running away – he has friends from Tonbridge who live far enough away that it would feel safe – but it's almost Christmas and his brother is dead.

He watches and reads the news, stares at DCI Varma every time she visits the house, tries to communicate silently to her just who his mother really is. Luckily – although there is no luck involved with any of this – Vanessa doesn't suspect JJ's involvement at all.

She does seem to realize she's being set up, but she thinks it's all Rachel Donovan's fault. She is a rod of lightning, of white-hot rage, shouting the other woman's name whenever she gets the chance, her face a smear of righteous anger whenever DCI Varma is in the house, screaming at the inspector to arrest her former employee *right fucking now*. Varma is cool and alert whenever she speaks to Vanessa, though. She will not be drawn into the grieving mother's madness. When speaking to JJ or Emma – or even Justin – she is warm and as transparent as possible, always sure to tell them when she doesn't know something for certain, rather than trying to project an air of impenetrable knowledge, which JJ thinks a lesser police officer might attempt to do in this situation.

One evening – he is barely aware of which day it is, doesn't sleep much any more – he overhears Varma talking to his father by the door as she leaves.

'Have you spoken to her at all? Rachel Donovan, I mean,' Justin asks.

'Yes, we've interviewed her several times.'

'She didn't have anything to do with it, of course,' Justin says. 'We were all reasonably close at one point, and honestly, from what I know of her, this is just completely . . . well, completely impossible.'

'Yes, we're fairly certain Rachel Donovan had nothing to do with your son's abduction and death, Mr Lowe,' DCI Varma says, but there's something in her voice that tells JJ that 'fairly certain' means 'absolutely certain'.

'Yes. I assumed you would have figured out that much by now. I just think maybe . . . maybe she needs to be made aware of how, ah, fixated my wife is on her guilt? For her safety, I mean. Her and her family.'

'Do you have reason to believe your wife might in some way attack Mrs Donovan or another member of her family?'

JJ is sitting on the landing, some way above his father in the hallway, but he swears he can hear Justin swallow before he says, 'Maybe not "attack" but "antagonize" perhaps.'

'Online, you mean?' Varma asks.

'Online, maybe. But the Donovans still live close enough, don't they?'

'They're in Margate,' Varma says.

'Exactly.'

There's a pause before Varma says, her voice even lower now, 'Mr Lowe, have you thought about taking your children somewhere else while all this is happening? It must be incredibly traumatic for them, and they're still very young. I was just thinking in terms of the press coverage and media attention, not to mention –'

'My wife?'

'Do you have any other family who could help out? Other than Mr Fuller and Mrs Lowe's mother?'

JJ wants to hear his dad's answer, is intrigued to realize that Varma seems to have found the rotten core at the heart of Vanessa's family. Justin gives a strangled, embarrassed cough, and says, 'My mother's in Edinburgh. I'm planning on taking Emma and JJ there as soon as possible.'

'That might not be a bad idea,' Varma says, after another long pause. 'Although we'll probably want to interview them before they leave.'

JJ tenses, muscles knitting in concentration, blood beating at his skull. Interview? The police have spoken to him and Emma already, of course, but they have been softly spoken, soothing moments, and only slightly probing. 'Interview' sounds spikier, though, more official, with much more opportunity for JJ to flounder and slip up. He wonders how he will ever be able to hide this from everyone. It's too momentous, too much. He feels as though he's vibrating with so much pain and guilt, at such a high frequency, that someone else must be able to hear it, must be able to tell.

There have already been a few times when he thinks Varma has noticed. She's too good at her job, too empathetic, too observant. How will he ever be able to stop her seeing right through him?

## 21

The interview doesn't happen where or how JJ imagined it would: in a cold box of a room with a steel table, and a two-way mirror in front of him, an image he quickly realizes he has drawn entirely from TV and films. Instead he is in a small but comfortable room with a large old sofa, two bean bags, a play mat for smaller children, boxes of toys and children's books. DCI Varma is there, but she is not doing the talking or asking the questions. Or, at least, not the one doing most of the talking. That task is left to a softly spoken Irish man – JJ thinks he's Irish at any rate – in a navy-and-white gingham shirt, undone at the top, no tie, woollen blazer, and thick-framed glasses almost identical to DCI Varma's. He seems like a primary-school teacher.

He is actually a child psychologist, who specializes in victims of crime and trauma. He is called Paul, and he sits on the low coffee-table in front of JJ, who sits on the sagging sofa.

'JJ, I want to ask you a few questions about your mammy and your daddy, and your brother and sister. Is that okay?'

*Mammy*, JJ thinks. He means Mummy, of course – JJ thinks it sounds better Paul's way, but still the word makes him cringe. He has never called Vanessa 'Mummy' in his life. He realizes he hasn't said anything, and that Paul and Varma are staring at him intently, so he nods.

'Okay, JJ, that's brilliant. You're doing really well.'

JJ nods again, takes a deep breath, even though he doesn't think he's doing brilliantly, and that Paul's words are a bit premature.

'What are your mammy and daddy like, JJ?' Paul asks.

'What are they like?' JJ croaks. This isn't the question he was expecting. He thought they would ask all about where he was when Matthew was taken, what he's been doing while Matthew's been missing, who's been in and out of the house. He's prepared answers to all these questions, but he hasn't prepared for this one. What are his parents *like*?

Vanessa isn't *like* anything. She's a natural disaster waiting to happen, the calm, deadly centre at the eye of a storm. But how can he possibly say that to these lovely, normal people?

'Okay, how about this,' Paul says, shifting about on the table, making himself comfortable, 'do they fight at all, your mammy and daddy?'

JJ wishes he'd stop calling them 'mammy and daddy', but answers nevertheless. 'Yes,' he says hoarsely.

'A lot?' Paul asks.

JJ nods. 'Yes. A lot.'

'How often is a lot, JJ?' Varma asks quietly, from her corner of the room.

JJ shrugs, looks around the room, as if thinking.

'Is it every day?' Paul prompts.

'Not every day,' JJ says slowly. 'Dad isn't always home every day. And . . . I've been at boarding school this term so I don't know. But normally most days.'

Both Varma and Paul nod, Paul encouragingly, Varma

as though confirming a suspicion. They are very different people, JJ thinks, looking between them, but they're both trying to help him. So, he takes a deep breath and says, 'Mum . . .' but he doesn't seem able to continue as Varma stiffens with her bright alertness, and Paul leans towards him, trying to soften the situation, provide a cushion for JJ to land on after he takes this giant leap.

This is what he's here for, though, isn't it? This will make it all worth it.

Yet he's never said any of it out loud before, and now he's not sure he can. It's too huge: a vast ocean he has to swim across before getting to dry land, to safety.

He's a strong swimmer, though.

He always has been.

So, he takes another deep breath and dives right in.

## 22

JJ can't remember starting to cry, doesn't know when he started to shake. He knows his heart was pounding at his chest the whole time, beating out a violent tattoo full of fear.

Varma and Paul can smell the fear coming off him, taste the tears. They can feel the guilt and shame too, which JJ is full of. But shame and guilt are the twin strands of DNA that appear in the abused, so they're not surprised. He has shown them the bruises on his arms – fresh from two nights ago when Vanessa squeezed him so tightly, pressed her fingers in so deeply that JJ thought she might melt right through his skin and start digging into bone. He's told them about all the times she has locked him in rooms – the music room, his bedroom, the boathouse – and they have shared a look that says, *We've got her.*

And now, finally, they're asking about her movements during the time Matthew was in the beach hut.

'She doesn't sleep much,' JJ says. He's explained about her night-time visits – how they started with him and graduated to Emma while he was away at school. They've asked him difficult questions – about whether or not and where she has touched him, but he shook his head, said, 'No, she just sits next to us and whispers horrible things into our ears. I always pretend I'm asleep.'

'Did she come into your room at night while Matthew was missing, JJ?' Varma asks.

'No,' he says. 'No, but I could hear her. I . . . I don't sleep much either.'

Paul nods his understanding as Varma asks, 'And was she going into Emma's room at all?'

'No, she wasn't. She was leaving the house.'

'Leaving the house, JJ? You're sure?' Varma asks. She's moved out of her corner throughout this, come closer to the boy breaking his heart open all over the sagging sofa.

'Yes,' JJ almost-whispers. 'My room is above the kitchen. I can hear the back door open. And I saw her leave a few times. I went to look out of my window, to see what she was doing.'

'And what was she doing?'

'Walking down to the beach.'

'Could you tell if she had anything with her, JJ?' Varma asks.

'Yeah, she always had a rucksack or a bag with her.'

'And you were sure it was her, JJ? Even though it was dark?' Varma asks.

'Yes. It was her. Dad's taller.'

'And what about the night Matthew went missing? Did you hear anything then?'

JJ is quiet for a long time. He doesn't – he can't – look at either of the adults in the room. They are so desperate to help him, to hear him out. He is crying again, or still, he can't tell, and he finally starts to speak just as everything in the room blurs beyond his tears.

'I heard something. But I thought . . . I thought it was Mum going into Emma's room. And I really didn't want her to come into mine, so I didn't do anything and I didn't say anything. It was only when they said Matthew was gone in the morning that I remembered I'd heard the back door opening and closing in the night. I'm sorry, I'm so sorry, it's my fault. I should've done something, I should've said something –'

But Paul stops him, comes and sits next to him on the sagging sofa, puts an arm around him. JJ wonders briefly if this is allowed – both Varma and Paul have been so careful not to touch or physically comfort him up to this point. But he can't accept this offered comfort, can't look at either of them, so he presses his hands over his eyes and leans forward, doubling over his own lap.

'None of this is your fault, JJ,' he hears Paul say, but all this does is make him shake all the harder, letting out a muffled howl as he stares into Matthew's clear, green gaze, eyes that meet his every time he closes his own.

## 23

JJ supposes he should feel something when they arrest his mother, but he feels nothing. Or maybe not nothing: relief, which is a kind of nothingness.

By the time Varma and the uniformed police officers come for her, Vanessa has dropped her mask. She is a towering wall of rage and righteousness. She screams and shouts, elbows in the face one of the officers attempting to handcuff her, calls Varma all sorts of vicious, hateful, racist names, finally revealing her true self.

JJ watches all this from the stairs. He's told Emma to stay in her room: she doesn't need to see any of this. But he does.

He is surprised by his dad's surprise at his wife's behaviour. How deep did Justin's delusion go? He is pleased with how unsurprised Varma appears. He feels sure she'll see this through to the very end. He trusts her, and that trust warms his blood, zips through him strong and sure.

It's been a long time since JJ trusted an adult.

# 24

They take the sleeper up to Edinburgh, where Grandma Rosalind meets them at the station, bundling them into a black cab, checking the crowds warily, as if expecting photographers and reporters to have followed them all the way from Kent, then London and, finally, Edinburgh. Everyone is quiet in the cab. Both Grandma and his dad stare out of their own windows, lips pursed in the exact same way. Emma is drowsy and almost asleep next to him, leaning her weight against his shoulder.

Grandma Rosie, as she has always insisted they call her, isn't the type to shout. When she's angry she goes into herself, her thin frame getting somehow miraculously thinner, and then she takes herself off for a bracing walk, coming back better and brighter, the cobwebs blown away, as she always says.

So, he's surprised to hear the eruption that happens almost as soon as they get to the house. Grandma has sent him and Emma straight upstairs for showers and to change their clothes, crumpled and rumpled and smelly as they are. But Justin followed her as she walked down into the kitchen, and these old walls can't smother his grandmother's words. JJ stays stock-still on the landing for a while, listening to his grandmother shouting at her only son. Eventually, Emma comes out of the shower, sees him standing exactly where she left him and asks what's going on.

JJ can't answer, though. Everything's so messed up.

He doesn't know what's going on.

Matthew should be here. He keeps expecting to turn around and see his brother's small form appear silently from somewhere. He was always creeping up on JJ, surprising him with his burst of bubbling laughter when JJ finally spotted him.

His chest is tight. Too tight. He presses both hands against it, but he can't breathe. There's a great weight pressing against his lungs and he can't breathe.

He can't breathe.

Emma is staring at him, still in her towel, hair dripping down her bare back. Her eyes are huge as she stares at JJ. Her mouth is moving but he can't hear anything she says, and then suddenly she's tearing down the stairs, screaming for her dad and grandma.

Justin is kneeling in front of JJ before he even realizes what's happening.

But Rosalind pushes her son aside, crouches in front of her grandson despite her knees, presses her own hands on top of his, which are still pressing down on his chest.

'JJ,' she says, her voice smooth and soft and sweet, ice cream falling lovingly out of a Mr Whippy machine. 'JJ, look at me. Look into Granny's eyes.'

Her eyes are her son's eyes. Her grandson's eyes. Matthew's eyes.

JJ swallows, looks into them.

'JJ, we're going to count to ten, and you're going to try to breathe in time with me. Okay, darling?'

JJ thinks he nods in response, but can't be sure. He is locked into his grandmother's eyes, keeping hold of them, and he stays deadly still, listening to her voice as she counts to ten. He's surprised when he starts to hear his own breaths in time with her counting: one, two, three, four, five, six, seven, eight, nine, ten, again and again and again.

# 25

Christmas Day dawns hard, sharp and bright. The sun seems to follow JJ throughout his grandmother's house, glittering across every surface, a miracle of light in the darkness of winter. It seems to hit his eyes just so, making him squint in the glare, forcing him to close them. He doesn't want to celebrate – he has nothing to celebrate, and neither do the rest of the family, although Rosalind still insists on their gathering around the Christmas tree and watching her grandchildren unwrap the presents she bought for them months ago. Both JJ and Justin wonder what she has done with Matthew's.

Emma manages to feign some delight – or maybe she's not pretending. JJ isn't sure how she's dealing with everything, whether she understands quite what's going on: that their brother is never coming back, and their mother has been arrested for killing him. Opening his own presents, JJ looks at his dad. Justin is listless on the sofa, staring at his son with unseeing, sunken eyes. JJ has never seen him so worn, so gaunt, so broken down. His phone is balanced on the sofa arm next to him, and he's startled out of his black hole as it starts to vibrate insistently.

'Oh, Christ,' he mutters, at the name on the screen. 'Janet,' he adds, by way of explanation, looking at his mother, who flattens her mouth into a hard line.

It takes him a little longer than it should, but Justin

438

eventually answers the phone, heading out into the hall-way to address his mother-in-law.

JJ can't hear his other grandmother's words, just his father's.

'Janet, I really don't think – What? No, no, I haven't. I've been avoiding – No, right, okay, okay, I'm turning it on now. Are you and Bob okay?'

Justin comes back into the living room, turns on the TV, paging through the channels until he eventually finds BBC News, where they watch as JJ's mother is led out of a handsome Margate townhouse in handcuffs.

'Dear Lord,' Rosalind says, standing up from her seat. 'Is that Vanessa?'

'Yes,' Justin croaks, staring at the television screen, try-ing and failing to take any of this in. 'Christ,' he says softly, realization dawning. 'Is she at Rachel Donovan's?'

JJ doesn't know what to do with himself. He doesn't know what to do with everything he's feeling – it needs some-where to go, some way to be released, but he's terrified of himself, terrified of what damage he could do.

Watching Vanessa being led out of that house, he is terrified of her. This isn't a new fear – he's been terrified of her for ever – but he's terrified in a more frightening way now. Because he's worried he's more like her than he knew.

He might finally be safe now – they might all be safe now – but he has done something so much worse than her, something no one will ever forgive him for, some-thing he will never forgive himself for. Matthew.

# 26

It's gone two a.m. and JJ is still awake. He cannot bear sleep now. Whenever he closes his eyes, all he sees is Matthew's face and now, tonight, he has the image of his mother attacking Rachel and her family in his head too. He feels sick that what he did – what he has done – led to even more people being hurt. They stayed watching the news earlier, so he knows Rachel and her children are okay, but they were all silent, deadly silent, as they watched Sadie being led to a waiting ambulance.

So, here he stands, in his grandmother's cold kitchen, watching the dark, dark garden beyond the French windows. He doesn't know how long he's been standing there when he hears something, someone behind him. If he wasn't so tired, so dazed, he'd turn to see who it is, but instead he stays, transfixed by the night. He thinks he can hear someone saying his name, calling to him, but he still doesn't make a move. His body feels weighted down, pinned to the floor, yet it also thrums with pain, guilt, exhaustion. With grief.

Someone says his name again, and JJ realizes it's his dad standing in the kitchen behind him. He feels so heavy he can barely make a move, but he twitches his head slightly and then he can see him in the window's reflection. Does his dad look scared? He has seen him look scared a lot recently, but now is it possible he looks scared of JJ?

'JJ?' Justin says again, and this time JJ hears him. He still can't move, but somehow he finds his voice.

'Dad,' JJ croaks, his voice breaking into a million pieces in the empty cold air of the room, and suddenly he is shaking, shivering as his dad moves quickly towards him and JJ collapses into his arms.

# Epilogue

It's not even seven o'clock on Boxing Day morning and Justin has already made several life-altering decisions. Decisions he and his family will have to live with for the rest of their lives. Decisions that will ricochet and echo down through the lives of his children – most particularly his son's – and no doubt haunt him until the end of his days. Wherever he ends up, wherever he finds himself, Justin is certain that when the time comes and it is all over, it is this morning, these moments, he will be thinking about.

But he is certain he's made the right decision.

Justin thinks about everything DCI Varma and the Irish therapist reported back to him after JJ's interview. He knows it's all true. He's worried he's known it for a long time: that Vanessa's most recent heinous, horrifying actions have only fully exposed everything he'd suspected was happening in his own home. But it was easy to ignore it, to bury it, to believe the perfect picture Vanessa painted, just like everyone else did. But he remembers now a story Vanessa told him about her childhood. It was years ago, when they first started dating, when Justin was tumbling headlong in love with her, was trying to figure her out, piece it all together. She had been just as beautiful then, almost as glamorous, but there was something gritty too: a scrappiness that Justin had loved but which Vanessa had gradually, carefully, filed away. Even now, he can remember the conversation vividly, feel the sensation of Vanessa's hair on his chest, see the sharp, crystalline sunshine of winter pouring through the windows of his Clerkenwell flat. She'd been trying to explain her mother to him. Vanessa hadn't spoken to her in months, something that Justin found strange but to Vanessa was totally normal: her mother was difficult, only ever ravenously demanding attention or coldly withholding it, depending on her mood and when Vanessa had last disappointed her. Vanessa told him then of how, when she came home from primary school, her mother would lock her into the garden shed for hours. She was never told what she had done wrong – if anything – and Vanessa, as a little girl, simply came to expect and accept this part of her daily routine. It was only when they moved to Cornwall to live with Harry, Adam's father, that Vanessa realized there was anything wrong with the way she spent her afternoons. She was older by this point, but when she came home from school to find her mother drunk and bleary-eyed, she didn't bat an eyelid at being dragged out of the house by the older woman and locked into one of the outhouses. But it was March, and freezing still, and when Adam came home from football practice, it didn't take him long to find her. The fight that ensued between her mother and her stepfather apparently lasted days, and had Vanessa wondering if this new home was about to become her old home. Justin can't remember when or why he forgot about this story. Had it ever floated up inside his memory when he left his mother-in-law in charge of their children? If it had, he had rapidly pushed it down, once again choosing an easy solution to a difficult reality. And then, later, Vanessa had continued the cycle her mother had started, and Justin, well, Justin had let her.

He feels the loss of Matthew as something visceral, something huge and weighty, sitting on his chest. A weight he will now never live without. He still can't quite believe everything JJ confessed to.

And yet, it makes a kind of twisted sense. Not just JJ's tragically flawed logic in trying to save himself and his siblings, but the fact that Vanessa's warped treatment of her elder son would leave him believing his only option was to set her up for the kidnapping of her younger one.

Justin will never tell anyone the truth of it.

He will never repeat the words his son uttered in the otherworldly quiet of the night. He will not tell his mother, he will not go to the police, he will never confide in a friend, or trust this truth to a future lover. He and his son will take it to their graves. His wife will go to prison, and he will do his best – the actual best, the real best – to give his children the home they deserve. One of safety and certainty.

They will mourn Matthew.

He will get JJ the mental-health help he needs.

He will get himself the mental-health help he needs.

He will watch his wife grow old behind bars.

He will move on from Vanessa.

His children will grow up.

They will mourn Matthew.

And he will never, ever breathe a word.

# Acknowledgements

First thanks go to my agent, Emily – I started writing this book before the pandemic, AKA in another life, a lifetime ago, and during that time I parted ways with my previous agent. What ensued were eighteen months or so where I thought I may never publish again, let alone publish *this* book, but signing with Emily signalled a sea change and I couldn't be more grateful. Many thanks also to my editor Grace, and the team at MJ, including the amazing cover designers and my excellent copy-editor, Hazel.

Thank you to my sister, Ruthie, as well as Katie, Corinne and Jess, all of whom read very early versions of this book and continue to be not only very enthusiastic supporters, but also always up for reading basically whatever I write. Thank you also to Sophie – not least for the Whitstable trip!

Many thanks always to Betty, Shaks, Fi and Smem as well as to Alicia, Isabel, Alice, Zoe and James.

And thanks to Caroline – my long-distance, book birthday twin.

Last but not least, thank you to my parents – the best of the best.

And finally, I have to thank Instagram, I suppose, where I have spent many hours scrolling – it's a fun place to spend time but I wouldn't want to live there.

# He just wanted a decent book to read ...

Not too much to ask, is it? It was in 1935 when Allen Lane, Managing Director of Bodley Head Publishers, stood on a platform at Exeter railway station looking for something good to read on his journey back to London. His choice was limited to popular magazines and poor-quality paperbacks – the same choice faced every day by the vast majority of readers, few of whom could afford hardbacks. Lane's disappointment and subsequent anger at the range of books generally available led him to found a company – and change the world.

*'We believed in the existence in this country of a vast reading public for intelligent books at a low price, and staked everything on it'*
**Sir Allen Lane, 1902–1970, founder of Penguin Books**

The quality paperback had arrived – and not just in bookshops. Lane was adamant that his Penguins should appear in chain stores and tobacconists, and should cost no more than a packet of cigarettes.

Reading habits (and cigarette prices) have changed since 1935, but Penguin still believes in publishing the best books for everybody to enjoy. We still believe that good design costs no more than bad design, and we still believe that quality books published passionately and responsibly make the world a better place.

So wherever you see the little bird – whether it's on a piece of prize-winning literary fiction or a celebrity autobiography, political tour de force or historical masterpiece, a serial-killer thriller, reference book, world classic or a piece of pure escapism – you can bet that it represents the very best that the genre has to offer.

## Whatever you like to read – trust Penguin.